QUEEN OF BLOOD AND VENGEANCE

Secrets of the Faerie Crown, Book 4

EMBERLY ASH

ISBN: 978-1-964408-11-8 (ebook)

978-1-964408-12-5 (paperback)

Cover Art: Selkkie Designs

Beta Analysis: Made Me Blush Books

Map Design: A. Andrews

❀ Created with Vellum

For the girls that are healing
The road is long and dark and twisted
But so long as we have books, we'll never walk alone

CONTENT WARNINGS

Secrets of the Faerie Crown is a fantasy romance series with elements of dark romance. While it is not a true dark romance, the themes are heavy and may be triggering for some readers.

Content warnings include: blood play, child abuse, references to rape, murder, death of a loved one, explicit sexual content, battle and war sequences, and graphic depictions of death, violence, and torture.

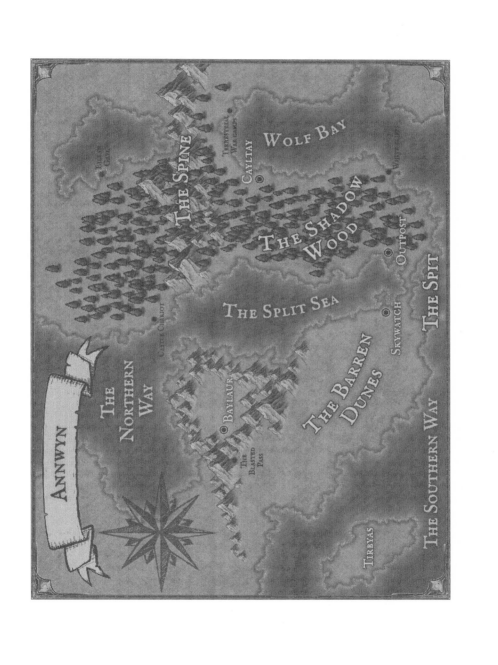

THE VOID AND ETHEREAL
PROPHECIES

Then comes a queen in the age of uncertainty, when shadows cast doubt upon the realm. Born under a double moon and marked by a radiant star, a faerie queen shall rise to command the depths of the voids of darkness.

Twice blessed, the realm of shift and mist, when comes the awaited queen who shall possess ethereal might. With a touch, she will feel the heartbeat of her subjects and she will unlock the secrets they guard within.

Together they must stand, to defeat what once thought dead. Together they must give, if any shall to the end.

I

VEYKA

There is sleep, and then there is *sleep*.

The kind where nothing can touch you, where the world falls away and you are totally consumed by the darkness. Not the darkness of despair or loss, but of comfort. Sweet oblivion.

I'd always loved sleep.

Even in the water gardens, I used it as an escape. I would drift off to the sound of water crashing into a still pool and try not to see the parallels to my own life, to my mother's endless attempts to force something to grow inside of me which simply was not there. I practiced with my blades, battled invisible enemies, so that when I lay my young head on the pillow, exhaustion would blot out the nightmares.

After my brother's murder, I slept endlessly. Hours that blurred into days interspersed with drinking and fucking and begging the Ancestors to take the pain away. Then one day it was gone, replaced by a numbness that felt like salvation. But that was wrong.

Salvation came months later, in the male who was first my enemy, then my lover, and then something more. Not something —everything.

That was when I discovered what it truly meant to rest.

For the first time in my life, I slept without fear. Without some fraction of my consciousness trained on the world around me. Even when I'd longed for my own death in the wake of my brother's, there had been the specter of revenge to keep me anchored. But in Arran's arms, even those pieces of myself ceased to matter. With my head pressed to his chest, the Talisman inked there warm against my skin, his heart beating in time with mine—then, and only then, did I finally, truly, sleep.

I gave myself up to a darkness blacker than the void I'd come to love. I let my body and mind unmoor, with no fear of being lost forever to the in between.

It was not that he was my mate, though I was so often lulled to sleep by the humming growl of his beast. Nor was it the fact that he was every inch the Brutal Prince who'd given himself to me and to Annwyn at the Offering nearly a year before.

We had chosen this.

For my entire life, choices had been stolen from me. But loving Arran Earthborn was a choice I'd made again and again. I would never regret it. Even though it would end.

That, too, would be my choice.

My sacrifice. For my kingdom, my friends, and my love.

I was no longer a princess without choices. I was a queen, and I would make my final choice count.

2

ARRAN

The entire world shifted beneath our feet.

I grabbed for Veyka instinctively, but she held her ground even as the stones of the bridge shook. My fingers closed around her arm, feeling the jolt of pain where I touched her freshly inked Talisman as sharply as if it were my own. But I did not let her go— could not. Not with the castle behind us shaking on its foundations, the lake splashing up over the parapets.

"Can you feel it too?" Veyka shouted.

Of course I can feel it, my beast growled through the bond. But the concern ebbing through our connection was not for me. Veyka's eyes were still fixed on Gwen, through the portal rift Veyka had opened. The shining white spiral edges wobbled and pulsed, but it was impossible to tell if it was the quaking ground or the nature of this new extension of Veyka's power.

Gwen dropped into a crouch, one hand splayed for balance on the goldstone floor. She could feel it in Baylaur.

The entire continent was shaking.

Then, just as suddenly as it had started, the world around us stilled. It took several heartbeats to realize it, with the waves still gnawing at the stone around us, our bodies still trying to compensate for the movement that was no longer there.

Veyka's arm slipped from my hold. Gwen rose cautiously to stand.

The ground remained steady for a full minute, but our reality was no more stable.

We did not have time to contemplate what could have possibly caused the entire continent of Annwyn to shake as if unmoored from the earth itself.

Gwen said again, a slight tremor at the edge of her voice—"Baylaur has fallen."

Even as my heart struggled to comprehend the words, my mind understood. The strategist within me began to calculate the meaning, this new shifting of weight within the war. Was there time to muster the terrestrial forces from Wolf Bay? If the city was truly lost, then it was time to regroup and save our soldiers for a battlefield of our choosing.

The thoughts echoed through my mind simultaneously, crashing together and forming new, more nuanced plans. Until all of them coalesced into one single, coherent realization.

The war had begun.

A moment was all I could give to my mate, frozen at my side, gripping her weapons hard enough that her knuckles matched her moon-white hair. It was not enough.

Veyka's face contorted with disbelief, her pale brows knitted tight together, her lips parted in a silent cry of protest. I needed to grab her to me, to reassure her that this was not her fault, to marvel at this new, magnificent feat of power. But I could do none of that.

That was not what she needed from me now.

I turned back to Gwen. "Are there survivors?"

Gwen's eyes darted between me and Veyka, then back the way she'd come in her dark lioness form moments earlier. I listened to the screams in the distance only enough to calculate their proximity. There was no space for sympathy or sadness in battle.

Gwen's gaze was steady as it connected with mine, a lieutenant reporting to her general. A dance we'd done dozens of times. "In the old palace," she said. "We were able to barricade a small contingent of females there."

They'd figured out that the succubus only came for males. *Thank the Ancestors.* But that information did not feel like a blessing, not now. It only spoke to the depth of the destruction that they'd been able to deduce as much.

"Males?"

Her head jerked to the side. "Some. We separated them into rooms in groups of two and three, to try and contain those taken by the darkness. But it all broke down two nights ago."

And in those two nights, Gwen had not seen a moment of rest. I could see it in the thick lines around her amber eyes. We'd fought longer than that before, but she'd never been in command. The female that stared back at me through the shining spiral rift was not the one we'd left behind in Baylaur months before.

"What about the city?" Veyka rasped.

She did not—or could not—disguise the agony in her words.

Gwen did not flinch as she met Veyka's gaze. "Gone."

The edges of the spiral flashed a blinding white, but did not falter. Veyka remained still, weapons raised, her only movement the blinking of her eyes as she fought back tears. She may be young, inexperienced with war. But she realized that there was no time for those personal indulgences now.

Later, I would hold her. We would grieve for our city, our people.

But tonight, we would fight.

"Can you go for help?" I asked, my ears honing in on the sounds of revelry leaking from the hall of Eilean Gayl behind us. Even well gone to drink, the terrestrials within would constitute a considerable fighting force. One that had already faced the succubus.

Veyka shook her head. "Not while holding this open."

I took a step closer to the rift. It *was* a rift, I felt certain. Not a mere window but a passageway through the void. A new depth of Veyka's power; one that could change this war.

But all of that would be explored later. Now, she had to hold the rift open.

"I'll go." Every second was precious, but I did not shift. Not before issuing a final command to the two headstrong, desperate females. "Wait here. The terrestrials will need a guide to reach the survivors." And then to Veyka, "Do not go through that rift."

Not a command but an entreaty. I was begging her to remember the promise we'd made, never to be parted again. If Veyka went through the rift, if it sealed behind her, I would be powerless to help her.

I could feel the maelstrom of Veyka's emotions through the bond. But it was Gwen who answered. "If they come, she will close it."

I waited for the argument.

But Veyka jerked her chin down. Agreement.

I held her gaze for a heartbeat more, then I shifted.

ૐ 3 ૐ
VEYKA

Wait.

I'd never been a patient female. But what Arran asked was nearly impossible. It could not have been more than a few minutes, but each one felt like a century as Gwen and I stood on opposite sides of a continent but separated by mere feet. Both of us listening to the screams of our people.

A clash of metal echoed through the corridor beyond Gwen. She tracked it, head tilting to the side as her eyes scanned what I could not see. The rift I'd opened was like looking through a doorway. I could see directly behind Gwen, but the peripherals were mostly obscured.

Voices—unrecognizable, but discernably male. More metal, an entire cascade of it. The heavy clunk of furniture crashing down. Screams.

Then silence.

Gwen's shoulders twitched, but she did not flinch. Two days, she'd said. Two days she'd spent fighting. The sounds of death must mean nothing to her now. If she let them shake her, I doubted she'd still be standing.

And I couldn't fight. If I ran to the aide of those voices, the rift would close behind me. Would I be able to be open it again? It had taken me months to learn how to control the void, to move through it with purpose and to eventually bring others with me. But I did not have months to hone this new power. The passageway was open now. I could not risk closing it.

I could already feel the tension building within my body. The cost of my magic had already been paid with Arthur's death, but that did not make wielding it easy. Maybe one day, I would open rifts like this with the same ease I now moved through the void. But now, when it was most important, it took nearly all of my concentration to simply hold the way open.

I could not fight with my blades, not yet. But I could arm Gwen with information. "They are called the succubus."

Her golden eyes snapped to mine, widening as she incorporated the information.

The Great War, my void power and its role in the return of the succubus—those were nuances for another time.

Behind me, the music slipping from Eilean Gayl ceased. Arran had command of the great hall.

If Gwen could hear the change, she did not show it. "What else?"

Excalibur's swirled blade glinted in the white light emanating from the spiraled edges of the rift. "Amorite is the only way to kill them."

That earned a response. Gwen's golden eyes widened slightly, her gaze dropping from my face to the weapon in my hand. We'd known it was special, even before we realized why. But now, Excalibur and its brothers could be the difference between surviving the succubus or succumbing to the darkness.

Another crash from behind Gwen. Closer, now. But her stance held firm.

"We've been using fire," she said.

"It will hold them back but only for a time." And it was a weapon that only the elementals had at their disposal. There were dozens of fire-wielders in the elemental court, Cyara's family among them.

My heart twisted but I refused to let myself ask. The strain of holding the rift was growing, a low ache settling in my limbs. If I lost control of my emotions it might collapse in on itself entirely.

"I am well aware," Gwen said.

Of course, she was. Two days since the goldstone palace descended into chaos. But that said nothing of how long it had been under attack.

Guilt clawed its way up my throat.

I should have been there to defend my court. I should have opened the rift sooner, or taken myself through the void, if only to tell them about the amorite. Help could have come sooner. More might have lived.

I wanted to press my eyes closed, to try to quell that internal battle warring to life inside my soul. But I did not have that luxury. As I blinked into Gwen's gaze, I knew she understood.

The conversation turned silent. Not like Arran and I, speaking into one another's minds through the golden connection of our mating bond. Gwen and I exchanged sorrows that needed no words to be understood.

Then Arran was back—and not alone.

"Veyka..." Cyara breathed, her voice laced with shock, thick with the emotions she so rarely lost control over.

"Is that the goldstone palace?" Lyrena whispered, her voice utterly humorless. No doubt Arran had given them some explanation, but hearing and seeing were unequivocally different prospects. Even I could not quite believe what my power had done. What I was still doing.

"Form the lines," Arran ordered from my periphery. "Lyrena at the front." Because of her fire. "Those with amorite blades on the perimeter. No matter what happens, hold your formation."

Osheen barked orders, arranging the terrestrials.

Three neat columns formed behind Arran. Beyond them, Barkke organized a dozen or so more. One group to retrieve the survivors in the goldstone palace, another to guard the rift should the succubus try to overtake us and attack Eilean Gayl. It took less than two minutes. Brutally efficient.

The Brutal Prince.

He lifted his battle axe, cut a sharp nod to the assembled troop and turned with unmistakable purpose glinting in his black eyes. I could see exactly who he was, then—who he'd been for the past three centuries. Arran Earthborn, the terror of armies on this continent and many others. There was no mercy in the line of his jaw, no hesitation in the set of his eyes. The fear in my gut eased fractionally. I could trust Arran above all others to do what must be done.

But he did not step through the rift to lead his troop into battle.

He turned to me.

He did not need to speak, aloud or through the bond, for me to read the question on his face.

No, I was not all right. But that wasn't really what he was asking —he already knew that answer. He could surely feel the despair in my soul.

So I answered the question I could. "I don't know how much longer I can hold the rift."

The shining white edges of the rift cast shadows across his face. "As long as you can," Arran ordered. "But don't push yourself to collapse."

I opened my mouth to argue.

He took a step closer to me. "When this is over, we'll need you standing. If you cannot hold the rift open, you'll have to come for us one by one. We will barricade ourselves in the old palace until you come." And they'd be safe. Every single one of the males assembled wore a sparkling amorite stud through his ear. Only a third bore amorite weapons. It was not enough. There would be losses.

The hand that did not hold his axe brushed against mine. The briefest, subtlest touch. All that he had time to offer, and all that I could stand without breaking. "Annwyn needs its queen."

And I need you, his beast growled softly.

My fingers closed around his.

Arran's mouth crashed down upon mine, teeth and lips grabbing desperately for anything I could give. I took as much as I gave, drawing his tongue into my mouth for a too-brief second before we were separated again.

We ripped apart as suddenly as we'd come together, and Arran did not spare any more words or touches. He was through the rift, then Lyrena, then the lines of terrestrials behind them. They walked through the rift I'd opened to Baylaur as if it were nothing more than a door. I felt the impact of each body passing through, like the tightening of a belt notch by notch. The power inside of me squeezed tighter, tighter, tighter. It threatened to burst, but I summoned a lifetime of control.

I would not let the rift close.

Arran had once declared that he was the greatest power Annwyn had ever seen. But he was wrong.

I was.

4

ARRAN

The entire palace reeked of decay. Black bile coated the once shining goldstone floors. It adorned the walls in a ghoulish duet, mingling with the coppery tang of fae blood. How had Gwen borne it in her lioness form, with her senses even more heightened? I did not dare ask. She barked orders at my side, but I recognized a soldier a second from shattering. Even the mighty Guinevere could not hold her composure forever.

"End of the corridor, opposite corner of the courtyard, down the flight of stairs," she said, each word closely clipped.

I kept my tone equally brusque. "How many dead?"

"In the palace? Hundreds. I don't have a count on the city. The messages stopped coming a week ago."

No emotion clotted the blood pounding through me, fueling my muscles and my mind. In this place of violence and bloodshed, I was immune. It was what made me such an effective commander—and had earned me my title of Brutal Prince.

We reached the end of the corridor. Deserted. We made the turn and the courtyard came into view. The wave of shock was palpable as it rolled through the column of soldiers behind me. The courtyard was not just painted in black bile and blood. It had been submerged in it.

Bodies were everywhere, three or four thick in places. Some were clearly fae. But so many were nothing but a ghastly remnant. Elemental males who had been taken by the succubus long enough that their skin had melted away in places, dark bone visible. Half charred, where the elementals had fought with fire.

Yet the grotesque transformation of fae to succubus was nothing to the carnage those monsters had wrought. Females. Children. Dismembered, eyes gouged out, shredded by black fingers worn away to blacker bony nubs.

One of the terrestrials behind me vomited.

"Ancestors help us," Lyrena breathed from over my shoulder.

"The Ancestors deserted Baylaur weeks ago," Gwen said from my other side.

She wasn't wrong.

I tallied the dead—succubus and fae—storing away the ratios for future battle scenarios. But the numbers told a story, and begged a terrifying question. "How have you survived this long?"

From the periphery of my vision, I watched Gwen work her jaw. "Fire slows them. So does beheading. They cannot heal. If you chop them up into small enough pieces, then eventually you can incapacitate them."

A scream echoed behind us—from one of the offshoot corridors, rather than where Veyka waited at the rift. But the reminder was effective. Our time was dwindling.

"The suite is at the bottom of those stairs," Gwen said as she strode the length of the courtyard. She did not try to sidestep the gore. "There's one connecting hallway."

Two weaknesses to guard. Two possible egresses.

I dispatched three amorite-armed terrestrials to each and led the rest down the stairs into the bowels of the goldstone palace. The walls were thicker here, masking the wails of death. On another day the foot-thick goldstone walls might have felt protective. But all I could feel was their inward press, tighter and tighter.

This is what the war would come to—limited amorite weapons deployed strategically. Others left helplessly without it to face the succubus in any way they could, fire or flay. With little more than prayers to the Ancestors who'd left us in this mess.

There was the door, just ahead. Thick, encrusted with diamonds and aquamarines in a jagged pattern of sharp points. Like ice.

Memory flashed through me. These had been Roksana's quarters. Once, Veyka and I had dined here, eating rich cream-drenched pasta and rolls of spiced, stuffed meat. Another life. Another male.

No time for reflection.

Gwen pounded out a pattern on the door. Three swift strikes with the ball of her fist, followed by two rhythmic slaps with the flat of her hand. A code that promised safety.

For several long heartbeats, there was no response. The door was too thick to hear anything from the other side. Gwen had mentioned children. Male children as well as female, presumably. How long, how old, before a succubus could slip into the mind of an unsuspecting male? When did they become vulnerable?

Lyrena inhaled sharply, but before I could glance to the side to see if her face mirrored the horror I kept staunched within me, the door began to move.

A face I recognized appeared on the other side.

Elora stood in the center of her mother's repurposed apartments with the graceful menace I'd come to expect from the female Arthur had appointed to lead the elemental fighting forces. Behind her, two dozen palace guards stood between us and the survivors of the elemental court. Ancestors, was that all that remained of the elemental army?

Before I could ask, we were ushered in, the thick door closing protectively behind us.

Elora and her guards—all female—eyed the terrestrials, especially the males, with heavy gazes. They did not shift their protective array an inch.

"All of the males here are protected. They cannot turn to succubus—be taken by the darkness," I corrected. Darkness, nightwalkers, succubus. We'd been away so long, had learned much, but missed more. Fuck. We'd need a month to sort it all out, once we got back to the safety of Eilean Gayl. A month we did not have.

Elora's force dispersed, taking up positions near the doors, the balcony, and otherwise strategically throughout the apartments. As they did, the plight of the surviving elementals became even more clear.

At least they were alive.

Little more could be said about their state. The scent of unwashed bodies, overused facilities... and fear. That was the sharpest tang in the air. It hung there, permeating every female, child, piece of furniture, even the walls of the goldstone palace itself.

The healer who had once tended Veyka's broken bones after she'd come crashing through the void presided over what looked to be a makeshift infirmary through the adjacent archway. A half-dozen children huddled close to their mothers, an abandoned game of ball and hoop in the middle of the balcony. The most vulnerable among us where always the ones with hope. The adults? There was precious little in their eyes. Not after all these weeks of constant attack.

Like the rest of the goldstone palace, there were no doors to separate the balcony from the interior of the apartments. But this one faced out into the valley, rather than into one of the inner palace courtyards which would have made them vulnerable to the succubus swarming the goldstone palace. Elora and Gwen had selected their refuge well.

A white-winged female came to stand beside Elora, arms crossed over her chest and thick braid neat despite the conditions. I would have recognized her even without the streaks of copper nestled amongst the gray of her braid. Cyara's mother wore a face nearly identical to her daughter's.

"Have you come to liberate the city or rescue us?" the elemental female said sharply. Sharp, because she knew we could only do one.

"We are getting you out," I said, then louder— "Take only what you can carry, and only then if it will not slow you. Speed is our greatest ally in escaping the succubus."

The maternal female's eyes widened slightly, but she did not argue. She exchanged a look with Gwen, then Elora. An alliance had been forged in mine and Veyka's absence. These three were the de facto leaders of the elemental court... what remained of it. They'd kept everyone here alive. I would not argue with them now.

Cyara's mother broke away, going to the healer and then to another knot of upright females. The courtiers began to stand, to ready themselves. She had her talents, it appeared. And I had mine.

I turned to Elora. "The elemental forces?"

"Decimated," she said without preamble. "Females only in service. Two dozen here. Another two dozen were guarding the doors of the remaining males, along the southern level facing the Effren Valley above the library. But since the nightwalkers—the succubus," she corrected. "Since the succubus broke out of the dungeons, I have not been able to get an accurate count."

Fuck. "What about the troops stationed in the mountains?"

Elora straightened. "I sent them away when the outbreak started. We thought the spreading of the darkness might be related to Baylaur specifically."

They might still be alive. It was possible the succubus' attack on Baylaur was specific. Related to Veyka, maybe. The way they'd tracked her at Castle Chariot was burned into my nightmares, sleeping and waking.

Gwen said something to Elora, making plans for our escape. But the firelight—a single hearth lit in the center of the adjacent wall— caught my eye. Or rather, the glint of the fire off of the jeweled pattern encrusted on the wall did.

"Amorite." I raised my voice above the growing din. "Any you have. Dig it out of the walls if you have to. We need every gem."

Elora frowned. "Amorite? What—"

The entire apartment fell silent. The scent of fear rose again, filling the space, waking my beast from where he slumbered in my chest.

Someone was pounding on the door.

Some*thing*.

And not in a pattern.

⚜

We opened the door to chaos.

Kay stood on the other side, his pick-axe ready on his shoulder, its blade as wickedly curved as one of his tusks when he took his boarish beast form.

He wasted no time. "Three of them, middle of the stairs."

Soldiers were used to attacking the enemy, not escorting refugees. But Elora's squad had been protecting the elemental survivors for weeks. I sent three more terrestrials wielding precious amorite blades to join the fight on the stairs.

By the time we reached the place where the corridor branched off, more succubus had joined the fight. Attracted to the sounds of steel and their next meal.

A glance was all I needed to know that the terrestrials were losing. Even with their amorite blades. The truth had been there in the courtyard. Dozens of elementals brought down by only a handful of succubus.

But they held them off. And for now, that was all they needed to do.

Lyrena led the charge around the corner, toward where the three amorite-armed terrestrials I'd posted there minutes before were now scouting ahead. A stream of survivors, interspersed with the terrestrials I'd brought and Elora's guards, followed at a steady clip. But then they stopped. Just as quickly, they began to move the other way. Faster. They were tripping over each other now.

Fuck, what is happening—

The heat of flames burst overhead. There was only one reason for Lyrena to summon a wall of flame. The succubus had cut off our escape from that direction, too.

Fuck.

The stairs might be our best option. I reached the foot of the staircase in less than a second. In time to hear the scream of death.

Kay shifted, but too late.

The succubus ripped out a chunk of his stomach, his entrails spilling across the goldstone tiles. The monster did not even react to his sharp ivory tusk as it speared through its arm while Kay's boar writhed in agony.

The terrestrial at his side—Vera, his niece—swiped up his amorite dagger in one hand. But she did not waste the time trying to free him from where the boar had become entangled with the succubus. She used the distraction to drive the amorite blade deep into the center of the succubus' chest.

It fell. But another came.

Another flash of heat and Lyrena was at my shoulder, Gwen a step behind at hers.

"We need another way out," I said, even though it was painfully obvious. In the heat of battle, the obvious could get lost too easily.

"These apartments once belonged to a member of the Royal Council. There must be a concealed door somewhere along this corridor," Lyrena said, her eyes already searching. She braved the first step of the stairwell, a foot closer to the succubus, to get a better view over the heads of the panicked elementals.

"The secret passageways." Gwen's voice dropped several octaves, flattened out. It was more than emotionless—those words were barely alive.

But even if Lyrena noticed, she did not soften the reproach in her eyes as they cut to Gwen. "Haven't you been using them?"

"I haven't had time to clear them," Gwen ground out. "I may well have been leading survivors straight into an ambush."

I cut off my own reaction. Lyrena was right—Gwen had made a mistake. A potentially deadly one. In all the time I'd known her, I'd never seen Guinevere falter. But as she turned away, there were unmistakable tears gleaming in her amber eyes.

"There," Lyrena yelled. "Behind the drapery."

I saw what she meant immediately. Layers of blue and white

gossamer hung on a rail that framed the entrance to Roksana's old apartments. With the shuffling and press of bodies, what looked like no more than golden filigree detailing revealed more.

"Do you know the way?" I asked Lyrena.

"Yes."

"Good. Then lead us."

Hand held high, flames swirling at her fingertips in a beacon, Lyrena parted the crowd and wrenched open the partially concealed entrance. It was a narrow opening. Even going through one at a time, the adults would have to angle their bodies to pass through. But as soon as it opened, the desperate elementals began surging for escape.

Two lines of terrestrial soldiers fell back to cover our retreat. Before I ducked into the tunnel, I grabbed for Gwen. "Watch the rear."

A dark lioness snarled back at me.

5

ARRAN

We were taking too long.

The golden thread of the mating bond in my chest was still there, connecting me to Veyka. But it was taut. She was pulling on the other end—because she needed me, or because we'd stretched it to the limit, physically on opposite ends of the continent, even with the rift open between us?

Either way, the compulsion started in my chest and spread through my veins with every heartbeat, an incessant demand. *Veyka. Veyka. Veyka.*

"How much farther?" I demanded over the heads of the elemental courtiers. We'd been slowed to a walk by the tight quarters of the passageways, and each second might have lasted a decade.

"A few more minutes," Lyrena called back.

My growl of frustration reverberated against the goldstone, sending a flicker through the torchlight.

The torches set in the goldstone walls flared to life as we snaked through the narrow passages, lit by Lyrena or one of the elemental survivors. Cyara's mother was only a few steps ahead of me, her white feathered wings tucked in tight to avoid scraping against the walls. I knew better than to touch one—I'd spent enough time around Cyara.

"Lady—"

"Just Minerva," she said sharply, wing-tips contracting tighter still above her head. But I could see the wary look she shot me over her shoulder. She gestured to the ragged survivors around her. "They are doing the best they can, Majesty. We have lived in constant fear for weeks."

She'd mistaken my growl of frustration, thinking it aimed at the survivors.

No, for them I felt only pity.

But the Brutal Prince was not known for such emotion. I was no hero, nor savior. I had never wanted to be.

Yet I still asked, "What about the males? Are there still some who have not turned?"

I watched the silhouette of her throat bob in the torchlight. She was married. Or at least, she had been when we'd left Baylaur.

"If there are," Minerva said, "They are in the rooms above the library."

"How far from here?" I asked.

Lyrena answered. "By the passageways, a short detour."

Now or later. Now or maybe never.

A tremor quaked through my muscles—not my own. *Hold on, Princess.*

"We don't have time—"

"I will go, Your Majesty." Elora spoke from behind me.

I opened my mouth to argue—we needed Elora's expertise on the battlefield. But the grim set of her eyes stilled my tongue. This was the battlefield. And Elora was ready to do her duty.

"Take two of my terrestrials with you," I said instead. "And an amorite blade."

Elora nodded sharply. A loud yell, and she was able to move past the elementals separating us and Lyrena, listening attentively to the latter's directions for navigating through the concealed passageways. By the time she arrived back at my side, I had Vera and another terrestrial ready to join her.

But she paused, exhaling slowly. I braced myself for her words.

"The Dowager is there as well."

Igraine. How had I forgotten her? It was a failure as a mate and a commander.

The urge to go to her flooded my senses. After everything we'd learned at the Battle of Avalon, after what she and Gorlois had put Veyka through... my beast roared inside of me, demanding vengeance.

"Is she restrained?" The beast growled through my mouth.

"Yes."

For Veyka, I wanted to shift. To follow the directions I'd heard Lyrena give to Elora, to tear through any succubus that dared to cross my path. My jaws would rip their heads from their bodies, one by one, until I reached the Dowager. Then I would kill her. More brutally than any succubus could hope to do. I would make it hurt. I would punish her in kind for every brutality she'd heaped upon my mate.

But another tremble was taking hold of me, an ache settling into my bones. Veyka.

For Veyka, I said, "Leave her." And for myself, I added, "For now."

Veyka would never forgive herself if another member of her court fell to the succubus at the expense of her own revenge. To save the males closeted away in their cells, yes. But for Igraine? Never.

Watching Elora's contingent split away was nearly painful. But we were almost back to the rift. I could feel the change in the bond.

The tunnel curved and then there was a burst of light. Lyrena pried open the doorway out of the passage, sending a wall of fire to repulse any succubus on the other side. But the corridor beyond was blessedly empty. A small mercy among the losses we'd already sustained.

An audible gasp rolled through the crowd of elementals as they spilled out into the hallway. For half a breath, I saw the rift as they must have. A rip in the very fabric of the world, opening into a dark and unknown void. And at the center, the glowing edges of the rift illuminating her face and skin so that her entire body seemed to be glowing, was the High Queen of Annwyn.

I shoved the courtiers aside, none too gently, to get to her. Without a thought, I stepped through the rift, earning another cry from the crowd behind. The Queen they'd never seen exhibit any type of magic now stood in control of a power that barely existed in legend. Terror shone in their eyes. One female lifted her hand, sending a spiral of water through the rift from one side to the other. It passed through unchanged, but still they held back.

It was a mother who took the first step. A female who could not be more than sixty years old, with a golden-haired girl on her hip and an older boy's hand clutched in hers. She was more plainly dressed than most of the survivors. Even disheveled as they all were, the differences were apparent. She wore no jewels, her gown was simply made, her children dressed in pale brown. Servants, I realized.

The most desperate among us even before the invasion of the succubus.

But perhaps those with the most determination to live.

The young mother held her children close and stepped through the rift.

She stumbled slightly as her feet went from the smooth gold-stone tiles to the rough-hewn stones of the bridge to Eilean Gayl. But she was upright in a moment. There was my own mother, a hand on the female's shoulder, ushering her forward.

After that, it was a flood.

The Lady of Eilean Gayl had things well in hand. Even if she had not, I doubted that I could have been any help. Not with Veyka standing there in such obvious distress.

It hadn't been an illusion. She was glowing. White light emanated not just from the rift itself, but from every inch of her exposed skin.

Her eyes glowed as well. Not the vivid ring of blue desire that circled her pupils when she looked at me. This blue was bright as the center of a flame and it encompassed everything—the pupil, the iris, the whites of her eyes. She might have been a goddess from some other realm entirely.

But it was my mate's voice that said clearly, softly— "Hurry."

Veyka's entire body trembled with the effort of holding the rift open. This new dimension of her power should have been explored systematically, with careful observation and testing to explore the nuances and limits.

All magic had a cost. The Ancestors demanded it.

But the Ancestors could not have my mate. Not now, not ever.

"Faster!" I yelled into the goldstone palace.

A second later, Minerva stepped through, the healer behind her, each of them shepherding an injured elemental under their arm.

Cyara waited only long enough for her mother to hand off her charge before flinging herself forward. They embraced, faces tucked in tight, their shaking wings the only indication of the sobs that overcame both females.

"Father?" Cyara managed to ask, her face wet and turquoise eyes round.

Minerva's pause answered the question before the sideways jerk of her chin.

I did not see Cyara's reaction. One of Veyka's knees buckled.

My arm went around her waist, bracing her body with mine. Lyrena was at my side in an instant, then Gwen.

"She can't keep holding the rift," I shouted. "Where is Elora?"

Lyrena lifted her sword. "We'll go after them—"

"No, we don't have time." I eased my face down to Veyka's, though she gave no sign of noticing. "Close the rift. We can come back."

Neither Lyrena nor Gwen dared to argue. They fell back to make whatever preparations they'd been trained to. I tightened my hold on Veyka's waist. The skin of her stomach, where her gown was open, was cold to the touch. Usually, it was just her hands and face, but now... it was as if the lifeforce was being drained from her body.

All magic has a price, my beast rumbled softly, more gently than was possible.

Veyka did not respond. Could she even hear me, as deep as she'd dove into her power?

"Arran." When she titled her head, still facing the rift she'd opened but so her eyes could connect with mine, I saw every dimension of her magnificent, resilient soul shining out at me.

I knew, then. She would hold the rift until every soul was liberated from Baylaur. She did not need me to argue with her—she needed my help.

"Veyka," my beast growled. Then me, "You can do this, Princess." I let the corner of my mouth lift in time with my voice. Somewhere between teasing and challenging, where Veyka and I had thrived since the moment we first met in the scrubby forested hills of Baylaur.

Her chest lifted and fell against mine, the slightest hint of a scoff.

"Do you remember when you told me you were powerless? Look at you now, Veyka. You are no longer the Queen of Secrets. You are Queen of the Void. Queen of this realm, and every realm, should you desire it." I watched her as I spoke, the words pouring out of me easier with every syllable. A crash sounded from the direction of the rift, and I was aware of another wave of elementals crashing through it, heard Elora's voice in the background. But every sense was tuned to Veyka—the scent of her exhaustion, the tangible crackle of her magic against my skin. She glowed brighter with every heartbeat as I went on:

"The entire world is at your fingertips. Worlds that I cannot even imagine, beyond what the rest of us can see and hear and dream. Immortal? No, not next to you. You are not the elemental queen, or the void queen. You are an Ancestors-damned goddess. And after this, everyone in Annwyn will know it."

"They're all through!" someone yelled from the distance.

I lifted one hand, cupping Veyka's face where the Talisman showed as dark cuts into the light that emanated from her pores. "You can let go now, Veyka."

She went rigid against me, flashing with light in time with the rift. The spiral contracted violently in on itself until it was nothing more than a pinprick of light. And then complete darkness.

The price has already been paid, Veyka's voice caressed my mind.

What in the Ancestors-damned hell did that mean?

She collapsed against me.

I went to my knees, holding her upright. She wasn't unconscious, but she wasn't in full control of her body either. Where seconds before she'd been trembling, now she was eerily still. I found myself pressing a finger to her throat to check that she was still breathing, her heart still pumping. When I'd reassured myself of that much, I just let myself hold her. I heard my mother issuing orders, shepherding the elemental males into the great hall to have their ears pierced with amorite immediately. I shielded Veyka with my body, the stone parapet at her back, so that none of the courtiers, elemental or terrestrial, could get to her.

But I felt them come, their presence steady as they assembled around us. Cyara, Lyrena, Guinevere... the Knights of the Round Table. Another few minutes, and with Parys sorted by my mother, we'd be complete for the first time in months.

They stood arrayed around us, unflinching sentinels until Veyka regained herself.

Her voice was raspy when she finally lifted her head and spoke. "Where is Parys?"

Gwen did not speak. Nor did Lyrena. Or Cyara.

It could not be. Gwen would have told me—should have told me, the moment she had me alone. Surely it had been clever Parys who had deduced the plan for separating the males, who had helped keep the survivors—

Veyka straightened in my arms.

"Guinevere." The High Queen of Annwyn's voice did not shake.

But Gwen's did. "He is gone, Your Majesty."

❧ 6 ❧

VEYKA

There was such silence in my head.

Blessed, beautiful silence. I was not kneeling on the rough flag-stones of Eilean Gayl's ancient bridge. Nor was I surrounded by the ragged remnants of my court, my Knights of the Round Table. I did not disappear into the void or try to escape to a realm beyond description or imagination.

I did not exist at all.

How could I?

He is gone, Your Majesty.

Silence reigned. I did not hear those words. I felt them.

The threads of my being snagged and severed. The twisted, intricate knots of love and friendship that held me together suddenly frayed—one critical, crucial, beautiful string severed forever.

I needed that second of silence to stretch out forever. A thousand years. Longer. Even that would not be enough to mourn him. But what I needed was no longer a consideration. I sucked in a breath that could not become a sob.

Then the world came crashing in once more.

Elayne's voice, giving sharp, precise orders to terrestrials, organizing accommodations for the elemental survivors. Crying—there was so much crying. Children who'd lived through hell and now were a continent away from everything they'd ever known clung to mothers whose elemental facades had long since shattered. I heard Maisri's dulcet tones, singing a soft terrestrial lullaby to a squalling babe.

Lyrena recounted the details of the rescue to a sniffling Cyara. My handmaiden had lost her father tonight. Or weeks ago. Ancestors, there was so much I did not know. The weight of it pressed in on me, heavier with every word and whimper.

Beneath it all, the low rumble of Arran's beast vibrated, a constant reminder, an eternal threat.

I needed to speak. They all awaited my reactions, my orders. But when I opened my mouth, no words came out. Just silence.

Arran's arms tightened around me. No words came into my mind through that bond between us, but I knew he understood me just the same.

"Tell us," Arran commanded, his voice grave.

I couldn't bring myself to look up at Gwen. I let myself stare past Arran's shoulder, to the scarred rocks that formed the walls on either side of the bridge. If I looked at anyone, I would break. My own grief was too heavy all on its own.

Gwen sucked in a measured inhale, but she could not hide the trembling of her voice. "Merlin and Igraine conspired with the Shadows. In attempting to ascertain the depth of their treachery, Merlin escaped. I went after her. Igraine captured Parys." Her voice broke. "I was too late."

Too late. He is gone. Too late. He is gone.

The chorus created a sickening cacophony inside my head.

Cyara choked back a sob. Lyrena dug her heel into the ground, grinding it against the stones. Beyond, the sounds of terrestrials following orders had begun to drown out the cries of the elementals. There was so much noise in this night.

Arran's arms tightened around me as he waited for more words of explanation. So tight, the curls of my new black Talisman began to burn. But Gwen did not speak again. I waited for the anger to rise inside of me, expected the words of rage to dance on my tongue, demanding more from her. But there was no room for anger amidst the sadness that had settled into every corner of my body.

What else could she possibly say? Parys was gone.

Gwen could blame herself.

I could and would and did blame myself.

But there was one word that stood out to me from the explanation that she'd given. One name. *Igraine*.

"Does she live?"

No one asked who I meant.

"She is imprisoned in Baylaur," Arran answered.

Not even the promise of being able to punish the Dowager myself cut through my grief. What little energy my body had retained deserted me. I sagged against Arran.

I felt the alarm that tremored through him. He stood, sweeping me into his arms in one motion.

Arran's orders were brisk and direct. "The Lord and Lady of Eilean Gayl will see to the refugees and the wounded. Cyara, go to your mother. Lyrena, rest and replenish yourself. Your fire saved us; we may need it again sooner than we realize. We will reconvene at sundown."

The steady steps and gentle rustle of wings told me that Lyrena and Cyara had departed. But the faint feline sense of being watched lingered.

"What is your command, Your Majesty?" Gwen asked quietly.

I wanted to tell him to be gentle with her, that I could sense her a second away from shattering. How often had I been in such a state, myself? But even the energy it took to lift my eyes in her direction was too much.

"Do whatever you need to make yourself whole, Guinevere. I need a general, not a broken warrior," Arran said. So terribly brutal, those words. He'd said nearly the same thing to me when he first came to Baylaur, calling me useless.

But he was right.

Arran did not linger. As he carried me back toward the castle, I could feel their presence. My Knights of the Round Table lingered still, waiting to see me to safety.

I had friends—a family. They were each grieving, reeling from the revelations of the last hour. But they did not turn away. They did not falter. They wanted to take care of me.

Just this once, I let them.

❧ 7 ❧

GUINEVERE

She climbed the familiar spiral staircases of Eilean Gayl without a downward glance, nor a hand raised to steady herself on the jagged stone wall. There was no regaining the internal balance that had crumbled weeks ago.

Gwen could pinpoint the moment it had happened. It had not been after the devastation of Parys' death. Nor when the succubus, as she now named the darkness, overwhelmed the guards and she'd made the decision to retreat into the abandoned quarters in the oldest section of the goldstone palace, abandoning anyone beyond the apartment doors to their fate.

It was the Ancestors'-damned book. Even as she stomped up yet another flight of punishing stone stairs, her fingers curled for the tome. She'd left it in Baylaur. But even a continent away, the words of *The Travelers* haunted her.

Gwen could recite the entire damn book. When she'd snapped it closed for the tenth time, that was when everything changed. It was when she truly understood her powerlessness. Terrestrial heir, Goldstone Guard, Knight of the Round Table—it all meant nothing. She still did not know why Parys had carried the book right up to the moment of his death. She'd failed her friend, and in doing so her kingdom and Arran and Veyka.

She reached the top floor. No more staircases appeared to extend her retreat. But there was an attic. In her fae form, it was beyond her. So she shifted.

Her lioness disappeared into the darkness with one bound, into the most isolated, forgotten corner of Eilean Gayl that Gwen knew.

She shifted back to her fae form. Wedged herself tight against the bare stone wall. Sleep was a waste of time. Tears were a weakness. But Gwen could not be strong a moment longer.

8

ARRAN

I did not stop to speak, no word of comfort nor royal decree. I carried my mate into the castle just as dawn lit the horizon, gilding the green mountainsides opposite Eilean Gayl in gold. For once, not a single cloud lingered in the sky. A clear and cold day was coming. Veyka may be too stunned by her grief to think and plot, but I was not. As Veyka slept, I met the rising sun, and I planned.

Two dueling priorities danced in my mind. Annwyn and Veyka.

We had to muster the terrestrial army encamped at Wolf Bay and arm them with amorite. Then find what remained of the elemental forces—if anything remained at all. Word must go out to every corner of Annwyn, warning commoners and lordlings alike of the succubus and how to fight them. Information was as powerful a weapon as steel now. I would do everything within my power to protect Annwyn—except sacrifice Veyka.

She was willing to give all, but I was not. There had to be another way to banish the succubus. We had both survived such torment, such torture together and apart. The succubus could not have her. Annwyn could not have her. If that made me every inch the villainous Brutal Prince the realms believed me to be, then so be it. I could bear their hate. But I could not bear a world without Veyka in it.

Maybe this new facet of her power would be of use. It would certainly change the calculus on a battlefield.

Behind me, Veyka shifted, rolling over in her sleep. She was so pale, her skin nearly translucent beneath the streaming morning sunlight. Ancestors, was this the cost demanded for opening that portal?

The price has already been paid, she'd said. Delirium? Or something worse.

Her words had the ring of prophecy. I'd heard enough of them over the last year to recognize. But I'd be damned if another prophecy was allowed to claw at the edges of the frayed happiness that Veyka and I had found together.

She'd kicked away the coverlet, despite the fact that her body had been cold as ice when I laid her in the bed. The raging fire might have something to do with it. Our room was now near sweltering, but still, I did not bank the fire or open the window. I'd shed most of my own clothing. What remained of the sheets tangled around Veyka's body, leaving limbs haphazardly exposed.

My eyes traced the line of her long leg. Even relaxed in sleep, I could see the defined muscles of her thigh and calf. Those muscles had trembled beneath her and then given out completely when the rift she'd opened overpowered her.

If she could learn to sustain rifts like that, we could move units around a battlefield in seconds, rather than minutes. We would never be able to fully supply our armies with amorite weapons, but using the portal rifts I could create specialized amorite-wielding units and move them around at a moment's notice to wherever the fighting was thickest.

As I watched, she shifted in her sleep, rolling away to face the door with one arm draped over the curve of her hip. Her newly inked Talisman extended from her cheek, down her neck, twining all the way around her arm to stop just above her wrist.

An elemental had never been inked with a Talisman. Never.

Unlike mine, hidden on my chest most of the time, Veyka's tattoo would be on display to every elemental and terrestrial she met for the rest of her life. It was the ultimate symbol of unity. Only a terrestrial could have inked the tattoo. She'd proven herself to the citizens of Eilean Gayl by fighting to the death to defend them from the succubus. She was truly the High Queen of Annwyn.

For three hundred years, I had not particularly cared if I lived or died. All that mattered was the next battle, the next war to be won. I did my duty, to prove to the world that I—and by extension, my family—was worthy. When I'd assumed the helm of Terrestrial Heir, I had not really comprehended what that meant. I'd accused Veyka of being selfish.

But maybe Veyka had been right all along. She'd retreated from her role as elemental queen and heir because she had understood the full gravity.

Had I forced her into this? Pushed her to become queen, to fully assume her role, and thereby assured her death to fulfill this one last prophecy? If she'd run after the Tower of Myda, like she'd always planned, we'd have never become mated. She would never have fulfilled the Void Prophecy. Her end would not be fated.

In loving her, I'd doomed her to death.

Fuck. It was my fault. All of it.

But my mate would not pay for my mistakes.

I stepped closer to the bed, close enough that I could see the callouses on her hand. She'd built them over years spent with a blade in her hand. She would be a formidable weapon on any battle-field, even without her void power. With it, she would fly around the enemy, stepping in and out of the void, dispatching the succubus faster than even I could. She would change the ratios of fae to succubus that I had committed to memory in the halls of the goldstone palace.

Her body was no longer glowing, but her pale skin still shone, revealing her for what she was—a beacon of hope in this dark war.

My hands ached for her, but I held them closed and backed toward the window once again. I would not disturb her rest. As my eyes traced her body, reassuring myself of her safety and her strength, I played through battle plan after plan in my mind.

Every scenario I considered had one motivation. If we could defeat the succubus with our armies, then maybe Veyka would not have to sacrifice herself.

Maybe is not an option, my beast growled.

I would find a way to save my mate and Annwyn both. Or I would take her and sail across the ocean to a distant continent. She could take us through the void to another world entirely. But I would never let Veyka die.

Annwyn be damned.

Arran.

Veyka's voice slid through the mating bond, reaching out for me instinctively. My gaze snapped to her face, only to find her blue eyes wide and waiting. Glowing.

"You should still be sleeping."

She stretched an arm overhead, lifting her breasts above the bedsheets. "Do you presume to tell me what to do?" The words were sharp, but her eyes were soft. She pulled sarcasm around her like a familiar cloak, shielding her from the torrent of emotion.

I did not miss the way she forced her lips to curve. But I also did not challenge her. She deserved to cope in whatever ways she could.

"Yes," I said, crossing my arms over my chest. "And if you don't listen, I will pin you to that bed until you exhaust yourself battling me and fall back asleep."

The smile she'd forced began to fade. Without meaning to, I stepped closer to her, reaching out and cupping her face.

"What sort of battle are you suggesting?" she said quietly.

She arched her neck, tilting her chin so that her cheek pressed harder against the curve of my palm. All the while, her hand tugged the bed sheets down past her navel, exposing the rest of her glorious body.

"Not that sort," I ground out, pulling my hand away, forcing myself back again even as my cock tightened. "Rest."

"Stay." *Please.*

Giving up my brooding by the window was easy when it was Veyka doing the asking.

I meant what I'd said. She needed sleep to replenish her strength after that enormous expenditure of power. She would need that strength to face the rest of this day and the war council to come. Our next meeting of the Knights of the Round table would be no less.

But when Veyka reached for me, I was powerless to resist her.

She hooked one arm around the back of my neck, pulling me down hard and fast. One knee landed on the bed beside her hip, the other leg stretching out to mold my body against hers.

Ancestors, she felt so fucking good. She arched her body into mine instantly, as greedy for the feel of me as I was for her. She didn't go straight for my mouth, dragging her teeth over the line of my jaw instead.

She did not want tenderness.

She needed to know she was alive.

I could give her that.

I caught her wrists with my hands, pinning them down to the bed on either side of her head. Veyka's eyes flared. I expected a saucy retort. Instead I got a feral mewl of frustration and fire.

With her hands pinned, I lowered my mouth to ravage her throat. Her skin was still cold; I'd warm it with my tongue. I licked the column of her throat where her lifeforce beat just below the skin, letting my sharpened canines drag just enough to send her hips thrusting up into mine. I caught those too, pausing only long enough to slide free my trousers before bracketing her hips with my knees.

My cock pushed urgently into the thick curls between her legs, but I did not thrust into her. While I held her hands, I let her control the pressure building between us.

Veyka seized that power readily. She circled her hips, each pass nestling my cock closer and closer to her entrance while my mouth moved down from her throat and began to worship her breasts.

With her arms pinned up overhead, the glorious white orbs lifted, her dusky pink nipples stark and firm against her pale flesh. I nuzzled each one, glorying in their heavy, fully weight before I sucked her peaked nipple into my mouth. Veyka groaned as I circled the sensitive bud with my tongue. When I nipped it between my teeth, she came off of the bed entirely.

The air between us heated with every passing second, thickening with the scent of arousal and silent demand. Veyka filled that space with moans, long and animalistic. She was no longer in her head, beyond grief or sadness or thought. Pure feeling, pure need, surged between us.

Surrounded by death, haunted by the promise of her own, Veyka needed to reaffirm that she was still among the living. Even if half her court was missing or dead or taken by the succubus, her oldest friend among them, we were still there. Together. Fighting.

I abandoned her breasts and slid lower, over her soft stomach, the need to taste her pussy on my tongue suddenly overwhelming.

"Arran," she whimpered, thrusting up at me. "Now. I need you now."

My needs could wait.

I surged up her body, burying my cock inside of her with one swift thrust.

Veyka cried out, locking her legs around my hips, and I let out a deep groan to match her.

Her eyes were closed, teeth sunk deep into her lower lip. She gave herself over to the punishing rhythm I set. But I could not tear my eyes away from her. She was so fucking beautiful. Tangles of white hair splayed out across the deep burgundy bedsheets that highlighted the flush rising over her pale skin; her breasts rose and fell with each breath, each thrust, a magnificent display just for me. I couldn't last.

I drove into Veyka again and again, my cock already pulsing. I released her hands, reaching down between us to touch her clit. There was no way I could take my pleasure without giving her release.

But she swatted my hand away, eyes flying open. She arched her hips against mine, and I understood. Her pussy tightened around me, her climax ripping from her in a scream loud enough to shake Eilean Gayl to its ancient foundations.

She took me right over that edge with her. My cock spasmed inside of her, spurting rope after rope of searing hot come against the pulsing walls of her cunt. Veyka's legs held me tight through each one, her hips milking me for every drop of pleasure.

When I collapsed against her, she was ready. Eyes closed again, she buried her face in the curve of my throat. I thought I heard a sob. But if she'd chosen to hide it against my skin, I would not force her to expose herself. I braced myself on one elbow, sinking the rest of my weight down on top of her, hoping she knew—here, she was safe. In my arms, with my body as a shield, no one could get to her. She could be as broken as she needed. I would always be there.

I lingered there on top of her, cock still buried deep inside, our bodies joined as one. My mind wrapped itself around the golden thread of our mating bond, more vibrant and strong than it had ever been, despite the horrors of the last few hours.

But the strength of the bond also gave me clearer access to her mind. As the euphoria of climax ebbed away, it left agony in its wake.

Once, more than a hundred years past, I'd been caught in a storm at sea. The terrestrials in Wolf Bay, largely ignored by Uther Pendragon, had sent me forward to raid the dredges of a once great kingdom across the ocean. It had taken less than five hundred terrestrials to sack the capital city. But on our return, ships heavy with gold and other treasures, we'd been caught in a storm.

Three of the five ships were swallowed by the waves. I stood on the bow, watching as solider after solider died. I was the most powerful fae alive, and there was nothing I could do. I possessed no elemental magic to calm the stormy sea or sky; nor did any of my soldiers. The storm raged from above and below, and there was nothing I could do but watch.

I felt every bit as helpless as I saw the grief and despair and anger crashing together in tumultuous waves within my mate's soul.

I could not change the past any more than I could calm those waves. But I would be the shore that they crashed against. I would be her safe harbor, always.

I rolled to my side, tugging Veyka against me. My legs tangled with hers, one arm cradling her head and the other claiming her waist. She was no longer cold. Still, I pulled her tighter, until not even the cleverest wisp of wind could slip between us.

Sleep, my beast growled. This time, she did not challenge my command.

9

VEYKA

We awoke just as the sun began its descent.

Arran was wrapped around me, holding me as if he could personally chase away every threat that came my way. But Parys was still dead, and Arran could not protect me from that.

We ate in near-silence. Then dressed in it as well. What was there to say?

The only sound was the near constant rumble of Arran's beast at the back of my consciousness. He was on high alert. Perhaps he always would be now that the Second Great War had truly begun.

Voices began to filter in through the door that connected our bedroom to the shared sitting room.

I stared into the mirror above my dressing table. When a servant had brought us our meal, I'd asked them to send word to Cyara that I would tend to myself this evening. I brushed my hair, managed a serviceable plait, and washed my face. Thick lines framed my eyes, their blue duller than usual.

The ache inside of me was different than when Arran lost his memories, but still so cruelly sharp. If Arran was my soul, then Parys was my smile. As I stared at my reflection, I wondered if I would ever feel my lips curve in genuine happiness again. Or would every smile, from now until eternity, be forced?

I did not have eternity, I reminded myself.

My life was the cost of banishing the succubus. I only had to fake the smiles until then. Somehow, that made it easier.

Arran appeared over my shoulder, his gleaming dark hair still wet from his bath, brushed back and tied at the nape of his neck. There hadn't been time for him to shave, and the shadow on his jaw was more beard than stubble now. It suited him, made him even rougher and more brutally handsome.

"Are you ready?" he asked.

No.

A dramatically melancholy sigh slipped from my chest. "I will never be ready for war."

Arran's jaw ticked. "Ironic, for someone who loves bloodshed."

Ancestors, he knew me so well. A few sarcastic comments and he already knew that was the armor I'd wear to protect me from the weight of my mourning.

He held out a hand. I accepted it, pulling myself to stand. "At the time and place of my choosing. Not like this."

"You are not alone." Arran squeezed my hand. "You never will be again."

Oh, Arran.

I would not be alone. But he would.

There were no sarcastic comments to dull the sharpness of that realization as it lodged between my ribs, as devastating as any blade.

I would confide my fear to him eventually. My intentions. He deserved that much. But in that moment, Annwyn had to come before my own selfish desire to live.

So I squeezed his hand back and let him lead me through the doorway to join the rest of our court.

Lyrena paced the length of the room, her Goldstone armor freshly polished, hair plaited with gold, more rings than I'd ever seen on her fingers. Gold, gold, gold. She was practically glowing with it. Armor of a kind, I supposed.

By comparison, Cyara was so pale she looked like she wanted to disappear. She was back in white, the color she'd always worn in the goldstone palace, though the cut of her gown reflected our terrestrial sanctuary. Her skin was nearly as pale as her wings. The only splashes of color were the copper of her hair and the bright red ringing her eyes. She'd been crying.

As Arran and I moved into the room, the outer door swung open and a little tornado burst in.

Osheen was half a step behind his ward, snagging her by the back of her wool dress and tugging her backward. "Maisri," he admonished. "Out with you. A war council is no place for a child."

Maisri squirmed from his grasp in the way that only a child could manage. "But—"

"I summoned her," I said sharply. I heard Arran's dry chuckle behind me. Everyone else was silent.

"Osheen, come forward," I said, stepping up to the rectangular table that had been serving as our meeting place since our arrival at Eilean Gayl. My voice softened. "I thought you'd want Maisri here for this."

All eyes were on me as I lifted my hand and placed Excalibur on the table. For months, I had been unable to touch it, knowing it had been the weapon in my hand that delivered Arran's near-fatal wound.

But I understood now that I could not run from the curse of my Pendragon blood—and that included the sword that had been passed down from parent to child for more than seven thousand years.

Osheen's throat bobbed as he looked first to the sword, then up at me. "Your Majesty?"

"This is not the Round Table. But these are my Knights." I gestured to the others assembled before me and Arran. Then I unsheathed Excalibur. "I should have done this months ago."

I felt Arran step up to my shoulder, and it was he who said, "Kneel."

With careful grace, I lowered Excalibur's swirled amorite blade to Osheen's left shoulder. "Do you swear fealty to Annwyn, to protect the Terrestrial and Elemental Kingdoms of the Fae, and to offer your true and wise counsel when called upon by the High King and Queen?"

His eyes were not on me as he spoke the vow, but on Maisri. "I do."

I lifted the blade over his head to rest on his right shoulder. "Osheen, I dub thee a Knight of the Round Table. For all that has been and all that will ever be. Rise."

The rectangular table was nowhere near as auspicious as the one Guinevere had gifted me. But as Osheen rose, the others stepped forward to encircle it, taking their places as they might have taken their seats.

All except one.

"A table of destiny," Gwen whispered.

She'd stepped in behind Osheen and Maisri. She stood with her back pressed to the door. Her face may well have been hewn from the same stone as the wall on either side of her for all the emotion it showed.

Cyara finished for her. "*Five shall be with you at Mabon. One is not yet known, but the bravest of the five shall be his father. When he comes, you will know that the time for the Grail is near.*" Her voice caught, just for a second. "*The last is the Siege Perilous. It is death to all but the one for which it is made—the best of them all—the one who shall come at the moment of direst need.*"

As she spoke, the fine hairs on the nape of my neck rose. I'd heard too many prophecies in the last year—and suffered their rewards and consequences. Merlin had made this one when Guinevere first gifted me the table.

Merlin—the Shadows, Igraine, killing Parys. The determination that had settled in my chest threatened to crumble.

"After the Tower of Myda, we were five," Lyrena said. She lifted her hand and began ticking off names. "Arran, Parys, Lyrena, Cyara, and Guinevere."

"And me. That makes six," I choked out, forcing down my grief.

I could not force it down forever; I'd learned that lesson well enough. But I could contain it for now.

"You are not a Knight of the Round Table, you are the High Queen of Annwyn," Cyara said, wings twitching.

Panic flooded my veins. Another prophecy. Another price to pay.

Arran's hand landed on the small of my back. I sucked in a breath, centering all of my attention on that steady weight. "What does that make Arran?" I hoped I sounded more flippant than I felt.

"The table was given to *you*, Veyka, as was the prophecy," Cyara countered. "Anyone who sits at it is one of your Knights. Even the king."

"That leaves two unfilled seats. The Siege Perilous and the one not yet known," Lyrena mused.

"And who will be this supposed male's father? Arran? I promise you, I am not with child." Arran stiffened behind me at the mere mention.

Down, boy, I soothed his beast. *I'm sure you will know before any of us when I'm carrying your pup.*

I received a growl in response.

I rolled my eyes, returning Excalibur to its sheath as I spoke. "This prophecy could take hundreds of years to come to fruition."

There was a beat of silence where I thought the topic blessedly dropped.

"What if facing the succubus is not the moment of direst need?" Cyara said quietly.

Then there was actual silence.

Arran's hand slid from the small of my back to my waist. He was not content to rest it there; his fingertips dug into my side through the draped silk layers of the dressing gown I'd donned.

I will always protect you, his beast growled.

I did not have the heart to tell him that I was beyond his protection now.

I leaned forward, planting the palms of both my hands flat on the rectangular table where my Knights had gathered. "Prophecies can be twisted. Merlin may well have left out a line or two for spite alone. Merlin is lost to us. But Igraine is not."

Discussion ended.

And another begun.

"Maisri," Cyara said promptly. "Go find my mother, Minerva. She will have use for your quick hands."

I waited until the door closed behind the child before lifting my gaze to Gwen. "Tell me how it happened."

Not the succubus. My mother.

She understood. In painstaking detail, she recounted her own attempts to dismantle the Shadows while Parys researched in the goldstone palace library. She told us about the arrival of the humans from Eldermist and the protection she'd offered in my name. And finally about the night she and Parys had snuck through the secret passageways in a fatal pursuit.

Arran stiffened behind me at the mention of the passageways, but his beast was silent.

Somehow, Gwen kept her composure as she detailed the coming of the succubus to Baylaur. It had begun in the palace guard barracks. Many had died in that first wave of attack. For nearly two months, while Arran struggled to regain his memory and I tried to secure amorite, Gwen had held together a crumbling city.

When she finished, I had but one thought. "Death is too kind a punishment for the Dowager."

Arran's fingers tightened to the point of bruising.

But before anyone could murmur assent, a sharp knock sounded from the door.

We turned as one to the sound.

"Enter," Arran said.

I blinked at the female who entered. I'd seen with my eyes when Elora stepped through the rift from Baylaur to Eilean Gayl. But I had not seen with my heart.

She was clean, no doubt thanks to the hospitality of Lady Elayne, but a bath could not disguise the fatigue of living through the trauma Gwen had just described. Elora's dark brown skin was duller than usual, and deep purple bruises beneath her eyes spoke to weeks without enough sleep.

"Elora," I said, trying hard to keep my voice steady. "I am glad to see you here. Guinevere has told us of your efforts to protect Baylaur. We are in your debt."

She bowed deeply. "It is nothing more than my duty, Majesties."

Exhaustion was not the only change the months had wrought. A sort of preternatural stillness had settled over her. A calm and self-assurance that had not existed before, in her mother's shadow.

"I want to debrief with you in detail. Report to the Great Hall after breakfast tomorrow. Osheen and Gwen, you will join us," Arran said, clear and concise.

"Of course." Elora nodded. "But that is not my reason for coming. One of my guards reported something strange to me at the evening meal. I thought it best you hear for yourself."

She stepped back towards the open doorway, motioning in someone from the corridor beyond.

I nearly stopped breathing at the sight of her. The female who entered wore little more than rags. What had once been a draped gown was in shreds, the edges darkened with black droplets, as if... as if the succubus had torn and clawed at her. As she stepped through the door, her legs became visible, as did the sharp red gouges that marred them.

She was an adolescent, no more than fifteen or sixteen years old. I opened my mouth to ask where her parents were—and shut it.

If they weren't with her now, it was not by choice. Ancestors.

"Y... Your Majesties," the girl trembled, attempting a bow that sent her stumbling. Lyrena rushed forward, catching her arm to keep her from falling face first onto the flagstones.

"Rise and be welcome," I said. My heart twisted at the sight of her legs quaking beneath her. "What do you have to tell us?"

"Well, it could be nothing." She glanced wildly around the room, her eyes lingering on Osheen and Arran. Terrestrials—she'd probably never left the goldstone palace in her entire life, and now she was in a strange land, surrounded by strangely powerful fae, alone.

I caught Cyara's eye. A tilt of my head, and she understood my meaning, pulling out a chair and helping Lyrena ease the girl into it. Osheen and Arran both stepped back toward the opposite wall, giving her as much space as the room would allow.

"Tell us," Cyara urged with more gentleness than I ever could.

"It could be nothing," the girl said again. "But I was with the injured, and the healer had us near the balcony so we could get fresh air." She paused, taking in a few rapid breaths. "It may have been the herbs she gave me, truly. It could be nothing..."

I sank down to one knee before her. I could think of nothing else to do, other than that I was tall and wide and imposing, even in a dressing gown. I did not know her; not even her name. But I knew about trauma. I understood a child whose entire world was ripped away from them, layer by layer, until nothing but pain remained.

I took her hand.

She still could not bring her gaze to meet mine, instead focusing on where our hands joined on her knee.

"Fires, Your Majesty," she said. "We saw fires in the mountains."

Feeling flooded my chest. For a moment, I longed for the sweet oblivion where I'd dwelled after Arthur's death. Numbness was so much easier than caring.

But I did care. And that feeling that flooded my chest? It was hope.

I turned to look at Elora. "The elemental troops you sent away?"

Elora shook her head. "They know better than to light fires and risk alerting the enemy to their presence. It must be civilians."

That dastardly hope flared brighter.

"Come," Cyara said, replacing my hand with hers. "I will take you back to your lodgings and find you something clean to wear." She led the girl out of the sitting room, closing the door firmly behind them.

My words were a heartbeat behind. "We have to rescue them."

Arran's eyes darkened. "We do not know if that is viable."

"They may have already met up with our troops in the mountains," Elora reasoned. As she spoke, she produced a map, smoothing it out on the rectangular wooden table. It was worn from the heavy use it had seen since the siege of Baylaur, but I recognized the Effren Valley instantly.

"The fires she spotted were here." Elora pointed to the Blasted Pass. "There are other ways in and out of the Effren Valley, but civilians do not know them. Nightwalkers—succubus—do not build fires. They must be escapees from Baylaur."

"But are there males among them? They could have been decimated by the succubus already, since the girl saw them last," Arran reasoned. I hated that he was right.

"We communicated as much as we could with the city, but there is no telling when they fled. They may not realize the danger their males pose," Elora confirmed.

But Elora and Arran were not discussing how to rescue them. They were discussing *whether* to rescue them. "I will not leave my subjects to die alone in the Blasted Pass when we have the resources to save them."

Arran wisely did not reach for me as he said, "There are casualties in every war, Veyka."

My hands went to my waist instinctively; like an idiot, I had not donned my belt and scabbards.

"If we deploy any energy around Baylaur, it would be best used finding what remains of the elemental army," Arran continued. "We need to prepare for war at the time and place of our choosing."

"This *is* my choice."

"The humans in Eldermist will help us." Gwen no longer stood by the wall.

"Humans?" The word slid off of my tongue like the insult it was.

"The envoy you sent arrived in Baylaur. We gave them succor; fae females to guard their village." Gwen pointed to the map. "The rift is here, not far from the Blasted Pass. We could bring the survivors in the mountains through the rift and the humans could shelter them. The last communication that came through, they were still in control of the village."

"How long ago was that?" Arran asked.

"Ten days." Gwen did not meet my eyes.

But Arran did.

My gaze bore right back into his. *You are asking me to trust my subjects into the care of humans?*

The humans were not responsible for Arthur's death. He must have seen the murder in my eyes, because he added—*Not wholly.*

I did not say or think a response to that. The problem with letting myself feel was that those feelings overwhelmed me.

Arran stroked a thumb over the head of his axe as his eyes scanned the map. *There are already fae warriors among them.*

I laughed derisively, not caring what everyone else in the room thought was happening. Some arguments were just for the King and Queen. *The survivors in the mountains are not warriors. They are commoners. The humans could slaughter them in their sleep. You remember how they were when we were in Eldermist.*

I do.

Arran lifted one hand to my cheek, cupping it as if we were alone, without a war council forming around us. He narrowed the world to just the two of us with that single touch. *We have all changed since then. Maybe they have, too.*

I closed my eyes and let myself pretend for a moment that we were not High Queen and King, that we did not have these monumental decisions to make every other minute.

We could bring them here.

Eilean Gayl is already bursting with the survivors from the palace. Eldermist is closer to their home. Arran's warm breath caressed my skin. *So they can return when we take back our city.*

A promise—that we would win this war and restore our kingdom.

I opened my eyes. "Fine. Plan it."

❧ 10 ❧

CYARA

The priestess's sanctum had been converted into an infirmary. She knew she'd find her mother there, keeping herself busy to avoid the debilitating weight of her grief. Cyara had cried her tears through the night and well into the dawn. But by the time the sun finally shined its pale, watery light over Eilean Gayl, her despair had hardened itself into resolve.

She would not lose another loved one to the succubus. And most certainly not her queen.

Every available surface was occupied by a wounded body, and what surfaces could be converted had been drafted into service as well. The priestess's once carefully arranged possessions were shoved onto shelves with all of her books. Eilean Gayl's priestess was flora-gifted, Cyara recalled. It made sense that she'd stepped in to help the healers. Her affinity for enhancing the efficacy of plants made her particularly valuable in crafting teas and tinctures.

Framed in the doorway, it took Cyara a few moments to parse the chaos. Those in the outer reading room were mostly vertical, sitting or standing while their wounds were tended or they awaited care. Which meant that the most critical, including those who had been injured during the rescue of the refugees from the goldstone palace, were likely in the inner bedchamber.

Healers, elemental and terrestrial alike, moved quickly through the room, navigating around the central table where Cyara had once sat and read with Diana. The stacks of books had been replaced by vials of liquid, jars of dried herbs, and various medical implements that Cyara could not begin to identify.

Elemental healers used carefully applied wind to coax flapping skin together, needles made of ice to pierce the flesh and then dissolve at will. Terrestrial healers must have their own approaches, Cyara mused as she paused to examine the assortment on the table.

Some herbs she recognized, their applications both medicinal and flavorful. Others were a dangerous mystery. Movement beyond the table caught her eye, pulling her gaze through the open door from outer room to inner.

Eilean Gayl's terrestrial priestess stood side by side with the head healer from the goldstone palace, bent together over a prone figure Cyara could not see clearly enough to identify. Hovering beside them, her white skin and hair stark against the dark tones of firelight, was Isolde. Soft white healing light emanated from the faerie's extended fingertips, topped with their curved white claws. In another life, Cyara might have marveled at the incredible unity that simple fact illustrated. But the events of the past year had made her nearly impervious to surprise, and she'd been excellent at hiding such feelings even before that.

None of them were the reason she'd come down here, in any case.

Nor was her quarry anywhere amongst the bustle. She ventured a step closer to the bedchamber; spotted her mother holding a compress to a young male's head. But Cyara purposefully avoided catching her attention, instead pressing back into the reading room.

She'd have to search elsewhere.

Perhaps her grief was impacting her more acutely than she'd realized. Her instincts had sent her to the lowest levels of the castle, certain she'd find—

"Diana." The name came out half-strangled with surprise as Cyara narrowly dodged the woman's rounded form. She'd plowed through the door with her characteristic lack of grace—and total disregard for who might be standing on the other side of it. Cyara smoothed her nose before it could wrinkle; despite Cyara's affection for the human, Diana had not learned much from her fae hosts.

Her brother, however, was a quicker study.

Percival sidestepped Cyara and almost managed to cover the look of apprehension that her appearance brought to his face before she noticed it. He covered the small slip with an emphatic sigh directed squarely at his sister.

"There are elementals here who can see to this," Percival grumbled, one hand catching Diana's upper arm to steady her—but too late to prevent water from sloshing down the front of her dress.

Diana glanced down to note the wetness, but dismissed it with a small shake of her head. "They are otherwise occupied," she said. "I can carry water up and down some stairs."

Despite his protestations, Percival also carried a pitcher of water, and he did not argue when she took it from his arms, balancing it dangerously with her own, and left them to venture into the bedchamber.

Percival's arms were already crossed over his chest when Cyara slid her eyes to observe him.

She slid them away just as covertly. "She wants to be helpful."

Percival snorted. "She should be scared."

She took his meaning without any explanation. Diana had been held captive by a terrestrial fae, Gorlois, who'd collaborated with the Dowager Elemental queen, Igraine. Diana had every reason to hate and fear the fae. And yet...

"That she is not is a testament to her healing," Cyara observed, letting her voice soften. "It is natural that she wants to help tend the wounds of others after what she has endured."

Trauma affected everyone differently. Veyka had hardened, anger and rage honing her into a sharp weapon whose spiky exterior had taken months to allow anyone near. Diana had been no less traumatized, but she'd coped with tears and inward retreat. She, too, had taken months to trust that every time a hand lifted, it was not meant to strike her.

What thoughts passed through Percival's head as he watched his sister moving in and out of view, Cyara could not say.

But she was not surprised when he asked, "What do you want?"

He knew that she'd come with purpose. Trauma had taught him lessons, too.

Cyara tilted her head toward the open door, into the relative darkness of the temple beyond. It was littered with a few faithful, beseeching the Ancestors, but most of the refugees from Baylaur were beyond prayer.

Cyara had noted the emptiness in the eyes of those who did linger in the temple when she'd passed through to these rooms. Their conversation would be next to private.

Percival narrowed his eyes, his dark brows pulling together until not even an inch of deep ochre skin separated them. But after one last glance to reassure himself that Diana was well, he led the way out.

"So?" he said abruptly, turning on his heel in the center of the darkened temple.

Cyara did not hesitate. She folded her own arms over her chest and let her wings lift subtly, just enough to add to her physical stature as she said, "Tell me about the Sacred Trinity."

11

GUINEVERE

The meager breakfast she'd eaten an hour before came up violently, burning her throat before it spewed across the reddish dirt. She would have hit the ground herself if not for the gold-laden hand that closed around her upper arm and held fast.

Going through Veyka's void was *nothing* like stepping through the portal rift she'd created to Baylaur. Maybe it was the fact that they'd crossed realms as well as the continent. Or maybe it was always this fucking terrible.

It's no less than I deserve, Gwen thought as she jerked her arm from Lyrena's grasp and pressed the back of her hand to her mouth. When nothing else came up, she lowered it and took stock of their location.

"We passed through this copse of trees on our way out of Elder-mist. Backtrack over that mountain. The village is just on the other side of the pass," Veyka said. The queen appeared unruffled by the swirling black hell they'd just traveled through. Gwen's stomach clenched again. She forced herself to focus on the words instead.

Veyka's description was generous. The copse was a small cluster of four bare-trunked trees, their ragged fronds crackling overhead in the crisp wind. Gwen's eyes traced the route Veyka indicated—

away from the scant protection of the trees to the jagged orange mountain and then beyond, to the village that had long taken up residence in Gwen's imagination.

"It gets easier every time," Lyrena said, slapping her on the shoulder.

Gwen did not disabuse the other female of her assumptions. She could have done with a quieter companion for this task. Osheen, perhaps. But at least Lyrena was competent with the sword strapped to her bejeweled belt.

"You should be there in less than an hour. Another hour to prepare. Then I'll open the rift." Veyka repeated the plan, though Gwen had already fully committed it to memory. "Here," Veyka added, extending her hand.

Gwen palmed the white crystal. Veyka had explained its use. Another fault laid at her feet. If she'd been able to get the truth about the communication crystals out of Igraine, she could have called for help. Baylaur might not have fallen to the succubus.

"Tell us if there is any delay," Veyka said. She stepped back, well clear of them, even though Gwen suspected it was not necessary. In the months of her absence, the queen's control over her new power had grown.

"Are you certain the crystals will work from so far away?" Gwen asked, still staring at the faceted white pillar. It was easier than looking at the queen.

"Make sure we don't have a reason to find out." Veyka winked at Lyrena, and then she was gone.

For a second, Gwen yearned for her presence. She recognized Veyka's irreverence for what it was—a shield to keep her real feelings at bay. Or at least, to allow her to function while those feelings took their toll privately on her soul. But when Veyka was there, with her wicked grins and sarcasm, it was a little bit easier to forget the darkness bleeding into her own soul.

The crystal would work. Igraine had kept one in her possession; presumably to communicate with Gorlois in the human realm. Gwen was still processing all of the details that had been shared with her. So much information, given so fast, started to lose all meaning.

She pocketed the crystal and pointed her boots in the direction of the jagged pass. But before she could take her first step, a blur of gold flashed by her. Lyrena—starting up the mountain at a run. She paused only long enough to throw a wide grin over the gleaming shoulder of Goldstone armor.

Lyrena and her fucking golden grins.

Gwen shifted. Let the golden knight try to keep up with her dark lioness.

⚜

She should have stayed in her lioness form all the way to Eldermist. Not two minutes after she shifted back into her fae body—to drink from the canteen and force down a few bites of nourishment—Lyrena began badgering her.

"Tell me about the humans who came to Baylaur," Lyrena said around a mouthful of dried oatcake.

Gwen ground her teeth. "You were with the king and queen in Eldermist."

She could practically hear Lyrena rolling her eyes. They were almost to the pass. The path they'd followed dwindled away beneath their feet, disintegrating into the sand. This high up, there was no shrubbery or even scrawny trees. The wind ripped away everything. If the humans used this pass in and out of Eldermist, any evidence of it was thoroughly wiped away. Good for isolation and protecting the village, bad for two outsiders finding their way.

Lyrena lengthened her stride, closing the small gap between them. "Yes, but I was not in Baylaur after."

"You heard my report," Gwen said sharply. One more drink of water and she would shift back—

"You have gotten grumpier."

Gwen stilled. She forced herself to stopper the canteen, then to return it to its place on her belt. She checked her weapons by rote, each move mechanical. Even her words. "Watching your friends die has that effect."

Lyrena laughed.

How in the Ancestors-damned hell could she laugh? Even acerbically.

Gwen's throat burned with anger, until Lyrena added, "You are not the only one who has lost loved ones."

No, she was not.

Veyka chose sarcasm. Lyrena chose humor.

Wounds all healed differently. Gwen could not help but admire that they'd managed it at all.

Before Lyrena had departed Baylaur with the king and queen, they'd forged a tentative truce. They were both Goldstone Guards, formidable warriors, Knights of the Round Table. Foremost, they both were intent upon Veyka's protection.

But these months had changed everything. Whatever pull she'd felt toward the beautiful golden knight, Gwen refused to entertain it under that harsh desert sun. There was a war to be fought. Many would die—too many already had.

But Lyrena spoke the truth. She'd suffered her own losses. That did not mean that Gwen was ready to confront those, either. "I don't want to talk about Arthur."

"Good. Neither do I," Lyrena said, shouldering past her and starting down the other side of the pass.

They walked in silence for several minutes. Despite the fact that Gwen had offered no answers, Lyrena did not press. She kept walking resolutely on towards Eldermist, with little idea what she was walking into, because her queen commanded it.

Maybe it was admiration for that steadfast loyalty that had Gwen opening her mouth when all she wanted—really, truly—was to curl up inside of herself.

Gwen cleared her throat. "The humans were desperate. I sent female warriors to guard them—some of the best we had." She paused, bitterness temporarily clogging her throat. "If those females had been in Baylaur, the city might not have fallen."

Lyrena's steps hitched, but only slightly. It could have been merely unsteady sand turning beneath her foot.

"You had no way of knowing that the succubus could infect fae. We all thought it was a human scourge," the golden knight said. "Arran spoke of your competence as a commander in battle."

Gwen felt her own features hardening, her instincts for self-protection so deeply ingrained she did not even need to consciously summon them.

"Yes. But in battle, I always had someone above me giving orders. It is different when you are the one responsible for every decision." It was a truth she'd realized in those long, endless days trying to defend Baylaur. With the city falling down around her, Gwen had realized another truth as well.

She would have been a terrible queen.

Someday, she hoped she would find the courage to tell Veyka. To admit that the right female sat on the throne.

"What if the humans refuse to help us?" For the first time, Lyrena sounded worried.

Gwen realized why a moment later—the first curls of smoke had appeared over the horizon. They were almost in Eldermist, and not a minute too soon. From the tracking path of the sun overhead, they'd already lost some of their second hour to the trek.

Gwen picked up her pace. "Then we will have to convince them."

"At the end of a blade?" As she spoke, Lyrena drew the sword from across her back and slid it into a slot at her belt instead.

"If necessary," Gwen said grimly.

If Sylva was still in Eldermist, she knew the old woman would convince the humans in time. But they did not have much time to squabble. When Veyka opened the rift, they must be ready.

Gwen stopped herself from reaching for her own sword. They should arrive peacefully, with weapons to hand but not *in* hand. She did pull out the communication crystal. Even as it burned in her hand, an ever-present reproach, she forced herself to keep it ready.

If things went amiss, she would not waste a single moment in getting word to Veyka and Arran.

But even Gwen was not prepared for the sand itself to come to life.

She swung the crystal up, the incantation already on her lips.

But a blade came down on her wrist so hard she couldn't keep her fist closed. The crystal fell into the sand; a booted foot kicked it beyond her reach.

Lyrena fared better. Her sword was in hand, her back pressed firmly into Gwen's, giving her cover. They were too close for her to pull her sword, but she was just as good with a dagger. She could shift if she needed to.

The thoughts raced through her mind at the same time that it tried to make sense of what her eyes saw.

They emerged from the sand itself. Thick sprays cascaded off of their dun-colored cloaks, only to be caught in the wind and swirl around where Gwen and Lyrena stood back-to-back, creating a funnel of red that clogged their eyes and lungs.

Through the miasma floated a disembodied voice. "I suppose your words will have to be enough to convince us."

Ancestors. How long had they been followed? They'd walked into a trap, clearly. But even two or three humans were easily handled. But not when she couldn't even see them—not when she was supposed to be convincing them to give refuge and succor.

"Drop your blades," the voice commanded.

Gwen gripped hers harder.

But as the sand settled, realization rose in its place.

They were surrounded.

12

CYARA

Taking him back to Veyka's quarters was a risk, but it was also where she had the least chance of being disturbed. Unlike the communal sitting room or the bedchamber Cyara shared with Lyrena on the other side of the suite, no one dared to enter the royal bedroom. Cyara saw to all of the queen's needs herself, including changing the sheets and cleaning the room. Back in Baylaur, she'd shared the duties with her sisters. Since Gawayn and Roksana's massacre, she'd seen to it on her own.

The memory of Carly and Charis' deaths bolstered her determination. Carly. Charis. Parys. Her father. She would not lose another beloved friend or family member. She would not lose Veyka.

Percival stood only a few feet into the room, waiting as Cyara closed the door behind them, staring around the bedchamber but rooted to the spot. He'd never been invited in here, Cyara knew. At least he wasn't pissing on Veyka's bed or something equally ridiculous. To say there was no love lost between the man and the queen was a gross miscarriage of truth.

"Sit at the table." Cyara softened her order by walking to the tea station set up to one side of the uncomfortable wooden throne Veyka avoided at all costs. "I will make us something to drink."

From the corner of her vision, she watched Percival move wood-enly to the small round table positioned in the corner of the room. He took the seat that Arran had occupied mere hours before.

A flick of her fingers and a flame rose beneath the kettle. She turned her back so he could not see as she retrieved the bottle she'd slipped into her pocket while perusing the priestess's collection. He was none the wiser as she tipped a palmful of leaves into her mortar, crushing them along with the rest of the fragrant blend. She set it to steep.

"Have you and Diana made any plans for where you will go?" Cyara asked with feigned casualness, her hip resting against the straight wooden throne.

Percival's eyes narrowed. "I was not aware we were at liberty to do so."

True enough. But she wasn't intent on an argument about those particulars. "If you could, where would you go? Back to Avalon?"

She did not have him at her mercy yet; he was perfectly free to lie to her. But she'd asked these same questions of Diana in passing. And while they technically shared their witch blood, Diana contained none of her brother's predilection to prevaricate.

"A return to Avalon is not possible." Percival left the second half of his sentence unspoken—*they will not have us.*

An internal clock refined by thousands of pots of brewed told her that the tea was ready. She poured them each a cup. "The human realm, then?"

Percival accepted his and drank without hesitation.

Bile rose up in the back of Cyara's throat, but she did not lift the tea to her own lips to stifle it.

"Somewhere deserted. Far away from any beings that might be infected by the succubus." Percival set down his teacup. "Human or fae."

It was a clever plan. Percival *was* clever, for all that his good judgement had been impeded by his desire to protect his sister.

He realized quicker than Cyara estimated.

"You are not drinking." His eyes darted to her untouched cup. Then back to her face, one hand falling to his stomach, where the first pangs of pain were surely making their presence known. "What did you give me?"

"Hellroot. In small doses, it merely causes indigestion. However, the amount in your tea will be fatal within the hour," Cyara said calmly. She lifted another vial. "If I do not administer the antidote."

Percival's eyes flashed with anger, but he did not try to get up or get away. "What happened to chains? Were they not sufficient to have me at your mercy?"

She tucked the vial of antidote away in the heavy folds of the gown she'd crafted herself. It was not as comfortable and airy as the ones she'd worn in Baylaur, but it was infinitely better suited to the snow that had begun falling outside of Eilean Gayl.

"This might take more than three questions," Cyara admitted. "I need to know about the Sacred Trinity, and I do not have time for half-truths or bartering."

Percival made a sound halfway between a growl and a sigh. "Then you'd better be quick about it."

"Will you tell me the legend of the Sacred Trinity, as you learned it in Avalon?" Cyara asked. Her voice did not shake.

Neither did Percival's as he answered, without hesitation, without fighting the compulsion in his blood— "Yes."

He picked up the teacup again, swirling the dregs around and around. For someone whose stomach was roiling with poison, he took several breaths before he began to speak. When he did, it was with the monotone syllables of recitation:

"The Sacred Trinity was forged in Avalon so long ago that not even the priestesses know the original creators. Tens of thousands of years. Long before your Great War. It took great power to forge the sacred objects—the power of all combined. Faerie, witch, and human. The sword will only present itself to the worthy wielder. No other will be able to pull it from the stone. The bearer of the scabbards shall be protected from injury. Not a drop of their blood may be spilled while they wear them. The chalice gives life. Drink from it once, and you are healed of any ailment. Sip from it forever, and you shall never die. It is said when they are united, the bearer will be master of death."

Cyara did not interrupt him, though a thousand questions sprang to her mind.

She compartmentalized her anger as she began to ask them. "That part about power combined—faerie, witch, and human—why have you never mentioned it before? You were there when I was scouring the priestess' collection of journals for any information about the Sacred Trinity."

She expected an irreverent shrug. Instead, Percival frowned. "You did not have all three items. I did not think it was worth divulging extra information that could be of used to barter for Diana's life later."

Honesty. He'd answered her honestly. Cyara swallowed down a lump of emotion. "Did you mean what you said before? That you believe there is a connection between the 'master of death' and Veyka's void power?" It was the question that had haunted Cyara's every breath since they'd found that last stone in the ring of mono-liths—the one that declared Veyka must die to banish the succubus forever.

Percival nodded. Whatever anger he felt about her ruse with the poison, there was none of it in his eyes now. The dark brown orbs were intent, emphatic, in a way Cyara had rarely seen except when he defended his sister. "It cannot be a coincidence that she already bears two of the sacred objects. And she even spoke of the third, the chalice. About one in Baylaur."

Cyara recalled the conversation. The chalice where Veyka and Arran's blood was joined during the Offering.

It cannot be that easy... The chalice was in Baylaur. True, the gold-stone palace was overrun with succubus. But with her void power, Veyka could be in and out in a heartbeat. Even if it necessitated a search, surely it was worth the chance at saving her life...

Another thought dawned in her mind.

"Why do you know so much about the Sacred Trinity? We have never even heard about it in Annwyn, yet you can recite the tale word for word."

This time, Percival did sigh. It was so heavy, so full of regret and pain and anguish that for a moment, Cyara regretted the poison. He and Diana were caught in this war as well, against their will. And nearly powerless to defend themselves.

Powerless, except for the witch blood in their veins.

"There was a time in my life when I sought out any connection to my witch heritage," Percival admitted. He still stared intently at the tea—the tea that would kill him soon. But his words remained unrushed. "Even the brief mention of a witch's power combining with that of the humans and the fae was enough to hold my interest."

Cyara handed him the vial.

Only after he had swallowed it down did she ask another question. One he could answer or ignore of his own free will. "How did you and Diana come to Avalon?"

His chest moved in a soundless, joyless chuckle. "Annwyn may have cast out the witches, but in the human realm many still worship them. Every year a sacrifice is made. Men compete for the privilege, to be the one to cross the strait and present himself on Tirbyas."

Cyara envisioned the map she'd studied of Annwyn in her youth. "Tirbyas. The Isle of the Dead?"

Percival nodded, now inspecting the empty vial rather than his teacup. "It has the same name in the human realm as it does in Annwyn."

She did not want to ask; but she'd begun this. "What sort of sacrifice?"

Percival lifted his eyes to hers. "The sort that bears children born without fathers."

"I see." By habit, trained by years of comforting herself, she almost lifted the poisoned tea to her lips. She stood and dashed it into the fire. "You are twins, then?" she asked.

Percival rose, dumping the remains of his cup as well. "Born of subsequent years. Children born of such couplings are rare. Twice in as many years... it was a special circumstance. Or so the priestesses thought. Our mother did not give many details when she deposited us as babies on the lakeshore." His voice hollowed out as he spoke. "Witches do not make good mothers."

"I imagine not," Cyara said softly. If she'd thought for a second he'd accept her comfort, she would have reached for him. But she had no right to even offer it, not when mere moments before she'd poisoned him. Something he was taking uncharacteristically in stride.

For several minutes, there was only the sound of the crackling fire and the soft rustle of her wings.

Percival and Diana's origin was interesting and heartbreaking. But as far as Cyara could tell, it had no bearing on the current struggle with the succubus, nor on the quest for the Sacred Trinity.

Finally, Percival stepped away. He retreated for the door and Cyara made no move to stop him. But when the door opened, yet did not close again, she lifted her eyes to find him staring at her.

"You could have just asked," he said. "You wouldn't have even needed the poison."

Then he broke her gaze and left.

Cyara dropped to her knees before the fire. She had no tears left to cry, but she pressed her face into her palms nonetheless.

She did not move when she heard the door open—the one that connected Veyka and Arran's bedchamber to the main sitting room. The one that had been ajar when she first led Percival into the room.

"You heard everything," she said between her fingers.

"Yes," Osheen said, coming to stand beside her. His boots were black leather. "It might not be the right chalice. And even if Veyka bears all three, it might not be enough. It is a guess, and a tenuous one at that. This could change nothing."

"Or everything," she said softly.

Osheen did not argue. She let her hands fall away. One of the legs of his trousers was torn at the edge. The loose fabric had been dragged through mud that had dried to a thick brown slash.

"Was it worth it?"

Cyara bit her lip. She knew precisely what he meant.

The cost to her soul, to do such things—to poison someone who had done her no harm? Her answer was unequivocal. With careful movements learned from a lifetime of counterbalancing her heavy wings, she rose to stand. She looked directly into Osheen's eyes as she answered. "If she lives, then yes."

Face to face, they were much closer than she'd realized. Mere inches separated them. If she were to light a fire with her fingertips, it would surely incinerate the charged air between them.

Osheen's gaze slid from her eyes, down the column of copper plait that hung over her shoulder. "You stopped braiding pearls into your hair."

"I try not to look too long in mirrors these days." She swallowed. "I am afraid of who might look back at me."

"War changes everyone. Those that survive it."

Osheen lifted his hand as if he would touch the end of her braid. When his eyes came back to her face, she knew that touch would be just the beginning.

She wanted to let him. More than anything in that desperate moment, Cyara wanted to tilt her cheek into his palm, to let the caress she'd imagined a hundred times in her dreams finally become reality.

But war changed everyone, as he'd said. And she had already been changed irrevocably by her part in it. How that fit with another being, Cyara was not sure. She did not know if she would ever be ready to find out.

She stepped back. "I must go."

There were a thousand excuses she could have offered. Tending to Veyka's belongings. Assisting Lady Elayne, who was busy rearranging the castle to provide long-term accommodations to the elemental refugees. The Ancestors knew she ought to look in on her mother, who despite her endless strength was still grieving.

But Cyara gave none of them. None were sufficient to ease the ache or longing. So instead she walked out without another word.

❦ 13 ❦

VEYKA

I longed to linger in the void, to reach for one of those realms that I'd begun to sense just beyond. Beyond what, I could not exactly say. Only that they felt as real to me as the cutlery on the table at a meal. All I had to do was reach out and I could touch them. But exploring those other realms was a dream for another time. Maybe no time.

Instead, I landed beside my husband where he stood barking orders in Eilean Gayl's outer bailey. With Osheen and Elora's help, he'd assembled a combined force of terrestrial and elemental warriors. For now, they were divided into two units, each commanded by their own lieutenant. I knew it rankled him; he'd spent three hundred years learning how to balance powers to create the strongest possible fighting force, and splitting the elementals and terrestrials apart went against every instinct he had.

My Talisman swallowed up the weak sunlight. I was the only elemental who'd ever borne one. We were still a kingdom divided.

"Are they in place?" Arran asked without looking at me.

"Yes," I confirmed. "I am going to scout the survivors' camp now. Will you be ready when I return?"

I felt Arran's tension at the same time that the low rumble

reverberated in my chest. His chest, actually. But we might as well have been one.

Do not engage, his beast growled.

They are my subjects. That did not mean they were harmless. They could not be to have survived this long. But I would not allow myself to fear them.

Do not make me chain you to my side.

There were no chains in evidence, but the clench of his fist was enough for me to imagine. *You'd enjoy that, wouldn't you? Having me completely at your mercy?*

The growl in my mind turned absolutely feral.

I clenched my thighs together, lest the dozens of warriors assembled scent the need building between my legs. Having Arran back, body *and* mind, had unleashed something within me. That physical need had always been a constant demand; now, it was like breathing. I wanted him fucking me morning, noon, and night. And a few times in between.

Fuck.

I'd meant to distract him from worrying and instead I'd managed to work myself up into a burning ball of need.

Fuck.

I grabbed him to me, reveling in the gasps of surprise from the terrestrials. The elementals were naturally better at covering their reactions. The residents of Eilean Gayl ought to have expected it by now. Arran had fucked me right in front of them at the head of the Great Hall in the aftermath of the succubus attack.

But their reactions were secondary once I had Arran's tongue in my mouth. Ancestors, he tasted amazing. The deep earthy flavor of him mingled with the tang of wine he'd sipped at his last meal, melding into an intoxicating mix I could not stop myself from devouring.

I took and took with no thought of comfort or reassurance. I caught his tongue between my teeth, scoring a deep line down the side of it so I could taste the coppery tang of his blood in my mouth. He caught my lower lip, getting in a bite of his own. Then our blood mingled together. I could taste the magic, the combined power of us. If I let this go on a moment longer, I'd mount him right here—

I shoved myself back, several feet between us that felt like nothing. It would take continents to separate me from my mate.

"An hour," I said, making a show of licking our blood off my lips.

Arran growled and I disappeared with a laugh.

Another step through the void that felt like nothing and I was in the mountains perched high above the Effren Valley.

The young female's report indicated I should begin my search near the Blasted Pass. The survivors were heading away from Baylaur, and therefore so was I.

But I could not stop myself. I had to look.

From the distance, everything appeared normal. A few pillars of smoke rose from Baylaur itself, but that was not unusual for a city of its size. The goldstone palace gleamed, its tall spires swirling up towards the sky completely unmarred. There was no way of knowing that the inside was coated with black. The most startling difference was seeing it in the bright sunlight, rather than under the silvery-white light of the moon.

I'd only ever snuck this far from the palace under the cover of night. When we left to search for Avalon, we'd gone through the rift to the human realm well before reaching this side of the mountains.

The urge to go down into the city itself pushed in on my mind. I could go see for myself. Search for any survivors. An hour was more than enough time to find the camps in the mountains, using the void rather than traveling on foot. If I could save a few—

I might end up dooming many.

Every moment the survivors in the mountains were left alone became more perilous. They needed amorite and information. They needed their queen.

I forced myself to turn my back on my city.

It took me less than fifteen minutes to find them.

Which was fortunate, because I knew upon sight that it would take all of my remaining time to convince them to come with me.

The smell of fear was so strong it was a wonder that the succubus had not found them by that alone. If the succubus could smell at all. We knew they came for males while they slept, but we did not know what attracted them to one male over another. Or what attracted them to me in particular.

This had to be done fast. The thought had lingered in my mind —had my presence in Eilean Gayl drawn the succubus to those insurgent males who'd refused the amorite? Were their deaths on my hands as well?

I pushed back that thought.

The weight of my kingdom was already on my shoulders. Any more and I might break.

I gave myself exactly five minutes to make my observations and formulate a plan—one that would fit within the larger one Gwen and Arran had already crafted.

In an hour, I must open the rift from here to Eilean Gayl and bring the troops through. It was too dangerous to attempt to move a group of any size without amorite-armed warriors on hand. One succubus would be all it took to kill dozens of civilians. The crystal in my pocket had not warmed, which must mean that Gwen and Lyrena were making progress with the humans in Eldermist, preparing to receive the refugees.

I identified the patrols—two figures on each edge of the roughly rectangular camp, patrolling in an overlapping pattern. There were only a few fires. Communal meeting places that had probably sprung up naturally. This was roughly the location that the young female elemental had described; which meant they weren't moving around, at least not anymore. This camp was relatively stable. Small mercies.

But for all of that, the movements of the civilians were erratic. Very few emerged from their makeshift tents and those that did ran from place to place. And I would have recognized the scent that clung to the air, even in my dreams. The succubus had been here, and now they were fuel for those fires.

At least they'd figured something out.

I sucked in a breath—not too deep, or I'd gag—and started down into the camp on foot. A queen coming to her subjects. I hoped they'd have me.

❧ 14 ❧

GUINEVERE

"Drop your blades."

A half dozen human women formed an even circle around them. Three on either side of the meager path into Eldermist; they'd closed ranks once Lyrena and Guinevere were directly between them. A half dozen humans against two of the most formidable warriors in Annwyn. If Gwen had still possessed the ability to laugh, even her composure would have cracked at the absurdity of the implied threat.

Lyrena let loose, her back shaking with mirth where it was pressed against Gwen's. "No, thank you," she said with mock politeness.

The same woman who'd given the initial command ground her teeth. "That was not a request."

"And we do not answer to you." Lyrena lifted her sword in challenge, silently daring them to try to come and take it from her.

This was a different side to the golden knight. The bright smile had always been there, but the sharpness was new.

Gwen was not the only one who had changed these last months.

But they did not have time for trading barbs.

"Stop antagonizing them," Gwen said over her shoulder, too quietly for the humans to hear.

"You are not my commander," Lyrena bit back, her voice equally low. "And I will when they lower their weapons."

Gwen ignored both of those responses, addressing the humans instead. Particularly the one who appeared to be their leader—a tall woman with red-gold hair and a sour face. "We are Goldstone Guards, Knights of the Round Table, sent by Their Majesties Arran Earthborn and Veyka Pendragon, High King and Queen of Annwyn."

Gwen could sense the ripple of reaction around them. Arran and Veyka had stopped in Eldermist in their quest for Avalon. Gwen herself had sent fae guards to help the village, in Veyka's name. But they did not know what had happened here in the intervening weeks since Baylaur had fallen. Those promises might mean nothing now.

"Are you infected?" This from a dark-haired woman on Lyrena's other side.

"You know as well as we do that the succubus only takes males," Lyrena scoffed.

"It has a name," their leader breathed.

Lyrena's head snapped in her direction. "Even the evilest things do."

Gwen empathized with the women, their eyes darting between one another. She'd felt much the same when Veyka opened the portal rift from Baylaur to Eilean Gayl. So much information, so fast, could be nothing but disorienting. Especially when they were already living under conditions of stress. This would be the moment to disarm them. She could feel Lyrena tensing, her assessments the same. But physically overpowering the humans was not the goal. They needed their cooperation.

"We seek council with Sylva and the Council of Elders for the village of Eldermist," Gwen said, hoping the old woman was still alive.

. . .

Silence echoed around them, off the mountains and down into the valley below.

"Most of the Council of Elders are dead. Taken by the succubus, as you call them. And put down by the guards your queen sent," the leader finally said. She struggled to control the emotion in her voice; Gwen did not have to be an elemental to realize it. And where once she would have remained impartial, her heart twisted.

"But the village stands. Your children and families are safe." Gwen did not let herself intone it as a question.

"What remains of it after the earthquake," came the hollow answer. "Our womenfolk survive. At least, those that did not refuse to be separated from their husbands and sons."

Gwen felt Lyrena tense against her. Elemental though she was, her laughing façade always in place, even she was not immune to tragedy. Gwen wished that was a comfort. Instead, it made her wary. She could not trust herself anymore. She needed Lyrena to be steady.

"We are peaceful envoys," Lyrena said before she could. Something like relief eased the tension in Gwen's stomach.

A silent conversation passed between the women around them. Gwen could not help but be impressed by their steadfastness in the face of two clearly superior warriors. But whatever they communicated with looks and shrugs, it was their leader who spoke for them all.

"It remains to be seen if Sylva will vouch for you. Until then, surrender your weapons or you'll go no further."

At her words, four of the women stepped forward, two to each of them.

Lyrena lifted her sword into an attacking position, her voice silky and lethal. "Try me."

She'd been to Eldermist before, Gwen remembered from Arran and Veyka's recounting of their journey upon leaving Baylaur. The humans had threatened Veyka then, and Lyrena had not forgotten it.

The red-haired woman shrugged with feigned nonchalance that

belied the growing tension in the air. "If you are as peaceful as you say…"

"Give them the sword, Lyrena," Gwen said. They were both lethal without weapons. A wave of her hand and Lyrena could set all six women's clothes on fire. The weapons were symbols of authority —and symbols of goodwill when surrendered.

But Lyrena tightened against her. She did not turn her head when she spoke, her words so quiet that Gwen almost missed them and the humans certainly did.

"It was a gift from Arthur."

Gwen's heart did that terrible clenching thing that it had started after Parys' death. If she did not get it under control, tears would be next. And there could not have been a worse place to fall apart.

But the tears did not come. Her eyes did not burn. Lyrena— imperturbable, smiling Lyrena—was tense with anxiety. It unlocked something inside of her; a strength and steadiness she had thought completely gone.

"You will get it back," Gwen promised. With the hand that did not hold her own weapon, she reached back. Lyrena jolted at the touch, but Gwen did not pull back. She curled her fingers around Lyrena's. "I will get it back for you."

A silent heartbeat passed. Then Lyrena's fingers answered hers, and she held out her sword to the humans.

⚜

Even disarmed, the humans held their formation as they escorted Gwen and Lyrena down into the village. Gwen scanned the buildings they passed, taking in as much information as she could. Information was always useful, either in battle or bargaining. She knew Lyrena did the same at her side. Their hands were no longer linked, but she could sense the taut energy emanating from the golden knight.

The glowering patrol leader took them to what appeared to be the village square. It was mostly as Veyka had described it, though two of the buildings were half tumbled down. An effect of the earthquake they'd felt across the entire continent? There were not enough people to match the buildings. Gwen counted less than twenty as they worked their way into the center of the village, and most of those were hidden behind cracked windows.

The village was still under the humans' control, but they had not survived unscathed.

Someone must have seen their approach and run ahead. The door of the largest building—a half-collapsed guild hall of some kind—flew open and three humans spilled out, a familiar face in the lead.

"Sylva." Gwen bowed her head.

The elderly woman returned the gesture of respect. "Lady Guinevere."

"This is the Council of Elders?" Lyrena asked, disbelief crowding the syllables.

Sylva nodded. "What remains of us, yes."

Lyrena had seen them before, Gwen remembered. Before.

Sylva, another woman with graying hair, and a middle-aged male watched by a fae guard that Gwen recognized as one of the contingent she'd sent to the village, though she could not recall her name. How many had there been before? How many males had the fae female cut down because they were taken by the succubus?

Lyrena swallowed beside her. "What happened—"

"We don't have time for that." Nor could Gwen stand to hear another story of death and darkness. Most of their two hours was already gone. "Baylaur has fallen to the succubus. We are here as royal envoys on behalf of High Queen Veyka Pendragon and High King Arran Earthborn. The Queen and King are involved in rescue operations for the last of the survivors from Baylaur. They seek your permission to bring the refugees here."

"Here," the woman at Sylva's side managed, her mouth gaping. An elder, but not nearly as composed as Sylva. "Fae refugees in Eldermist."

The man, his thick hair unkempt and bruises of exhaustion beneath his eyes, was unequivocal. "Absolutely not."

"Without their guards, we would not be alive," Sylva reminded him. She did not voice support one way or another; simply pointed out a fact. She was practiced at this game of managing her co-councilors. Gwen remembered her steadiness from her time in Baylaur.

"And if there are males among them, we will become nothing more than a meal," the other woman said, regaining her voice.

Lyrena found hers as well. "None of the males will fall to the succubus. We will provide all of them with amorite."

"You cannot buy our allegiance. We are past caring for such things." It started with a sneer, but the councilman's words ended in a desolation that Gwen recognized in her soul.

Her voice was gentler than it should have been, dealing with humans. There was no accounting for it. She still blamed them for their part in Arthur's death. *Didn't she?* She'd agreed to help Sylva when she came as a supplicant to Baylaur. But on Veyka's orders.

"Amorite is the only thing that will stop the succubus from invading a male's body and mind," Gwen explained. "The High King and Queen will give you enough to pierce the flesh of every man and male child in your village."

"You will save us," Sylva breathed. She, better than either of her two companions, understood what those words meant coming from Gwen.

Gwen swallowed. "In exchange for sheltering the refugees."

"And if we refuse?" the man barked.

Lyrena responded before Gwen could, her grin back in place. "The Queen will pull back her guards. She will need them to protect the survivors from Baylaur, wherever she can find to lodge them."

Gwen had not been surprised to hear Veyka's order back in Eilean Gayl, nor was she surprised to hear Lyrena wield it with such evident vindictiveness. The wounds between their realms would take more than a few months of tentative cooperation to heal.

Without an explanation, the three humans stepped back toward their ruined guildhall. Gwen could not tell if the damage was from the earthquake or some other dire event. There were tree branches twisted up with the ruins. They did not go back inside, merely lowered their voices. Gwen knew that if she strained hard enough, she would still be able to make out their words. But the echoes in her own head were too difficult to silence.

They did not take long to decide.

"The Council of Elders gives our agreement. Eldermist is open to you," Sylva said, the two council members flanking her on either side.

Lyrena's smile widened. "Good. Because the queen is about to open a rift in the middle of your village." Then she held out her hand. "We'll need our weapons."

⁂

What few humans there were retreated with screams when the portal rift opened.

It was a terrifying sight. At first, it looked like a star had dropped from the heavens into the center of the village square. Except that it was daytime, and if it that was a star, it was about to explode.

The edges pushed outward, their rippling white edges expanding inch by inch to reveal a world beyond. Annwyn. Gwen knew it was coming, understood that this was an expansion of the queen's void power, but still it took her breath away. The queen that had left Baylaur was scared of her power, denied its very nature. But this... Veyka had embraced the darkness and the light and shaped them into something wholly new and utterly terrifying.

The three councilmembers stood with their backs pressed against the wrecked front façade of their guildhall. There had been no time for planning or organizing. No sooner had Gwen and Lyrena received their weapons had the rift appeared. No time for explanations. Not even for a few hasty words using the communication crystal that the woman guard had finally returned.

After what felt like a lifetime but she knew to only be seconds, the glowing edges of the portal rift stopped expanding. They revealed a mountainous landscape, not unlike the one surrounding Eldermist. Though where the human realm managed to grow trees and a bit of long grass, the mountains of Baylaur were barren and orange-gold.

But the landscape was not what elicited gasps from the Council of Elders. It was Veyka Pendragon, standing at the center of the rift, her white hair lifting off her shoulders with the force of her magic, her blue eyes shining with an unearthly glow. And at her side, dark as she was light, was her mate and consort Arran Earthborn.

She'd done exactly what they'd planned—found the elemental survivors, convinced them to follow her, and then brought Arran and his warriors to their encampment to escort them to safety.

For a moment, Veyka's feet seemed to lift off the ground. She looked like she was floating, suspended in the space between worlds.

Then in the next, her booted foot hit the ground and she stepped through to Eldermist. She turned back to the rift, her eyes still glowing and intent. Arran stepped through behind her, and behind him a river of refugees.

Guilt clawed up Gwen's throat, its talons sinking deeper into her soul with every fae who passed through into Eldermist. Every survivor represented dozens of dead. And every single one of those dead left their blood on her hands. She'd sent soldiers into the city of Baylaur. But it hadn't been enough. And when the goldstone palace itself descended into gruesome black chaos, she'd done nothing to help those trapped in the city below.

These survivors—families, orphans, males and females—they were alive *despite* her. Not because of her.

Yet no one looked at her with blame.

Lyrena rushed forward, helping those who limped or carried heavy burdens. Veyka held the rift open. Arran ushered them through, more a High King than a Brutal Prince. Behind her, Sylva had managed to come forward and begin issuing orders. To whom, Gwen could not see. Humans, presumably, though where she'd conjured them from Gwen could not have said.

No one noticed Gwen at all.

She counted every body that passed through the portal rift. Two hundred and seventy females. Eighty-four males. One hundred and ninety-nine children. All that remained of a city of thousands.

Gwen was going to be sick.

But she did not get the chance.

The last of the refugees passed through. Veyka closed the portal. Arran went to her side immediately, slipping an arm around her waist and pressing a fierce kiss to her head. The queen leaned into him for a few seconds, then straightened and walked to meet the Council of Elders under her own steam, her mate at her side.

"We meet again, Your Majesties," Sylva said, bowing low. Her two companions bowed as well, though likely more from fear than respect.

Veyka did not stand on ceremony. "Thank you for giving refuge to our civilians," she said, her sigh heavy and her tone genuine.

"We did not have much choice," the councilman bit back. Stupid and afraid, then.

Veyka did not take the bait. She planted one hand on each hip and addressed the man directly. "You could have died. Once, I would have rather given myself to the succubus than accept the help of a human. Let alone ask for it." She bowed her head to each of the remaining council members. "You have our thanks."

There were murmured platitudes that Veyka met with a nod.

Arran took his queen's arm. "Lyrena and Guinevere will remain behind in Eldermist to see the refugees settled. We cannot linger." He was already turning to where the rift had been.

"Call on the communication crystals when you're ready to come back to Eilean Gayl," Veyka said to Gwen. Lyrena was with the refugees, her familiar Goldstones uniform no doubt giving some solace to the ragged bunch.

Veyka had almost caught up with Arran. Once she reached him, they'd disappear into the void. This was her only chance.

"I am not going back."

The humans could not hear Arran's beast growl. Neither could Gwen, not really. But she could feel the pulse of magic rolling off him. Several people nearby paused, casting wary glances their way, some ancient sense alerting them to the danger that wave of power represented.

Gwen stood her ground, even as Arran snarled, "Your place is at the queen's side. You made a vow when you became a Goldstone Guard."

Her hand fell to the belt at her waist, a wide swath of leather plated with goldstone. It was one of the few pieces of the uniform that Gwen had opted to wear. While Lyrena wore every single ostentatious piece available, none was technically required. Armor was not what made her worthy or marked her as Veyka's personal guard. It was her deeds.

Gwen angled her chin with every bit of imperious command she'd learned, both from her father and from Arran himself. "I do not wish to break my vow. But I know myself and how I can best serve my queen."

The sharp pitch of Veyka's elbow into Arran's side cut off whatever angry words rose to his lips. He turned those murderous black eyes on Veyka. As usual, the queen was unmoved.

"Make your arguments," Veyka said, staring at Gwen intently.

"The humans are an untapped resource."

"They are not effective against the succubus," Arran cut in. A human woman coming out of the door of a darkened shop flew back inside at the sound of his harsh voice.

Gwen gritted her teeth. That woman would tell her friends about the brutal barbs the fae royals exchanged freely in the village square. It would make it even harder to rally the humans. But Gwen pressed on, though her voice was lower.

"Not scattered and divided as they are. But if there are enough of them, it becomes a matter of numbers." She'd seen in Baylaur just how many fae it took to bring down a single succubus. It would take at least twice as many humans. But that morbid calculation did not change her stance.

Arran made those same calculations. Of course; he was the one who'd taught her the importance of understanding the deadliness of the enemy.

"You'd sacrifice the humans as chattel for your own revenge."

Once, maybe, Gwen could admit to herself. But not now.

"I would work to unite them in common purpose. To share what we know as an act of goodwill and to teach them how to defend themselves as best they can," she explained, struggling to keep her voice calm. The composure that she'd spent over a hundred years honing, to prepare herself to rule Annwyn, had deserted her during the siege of Baylaur. This plan had come to her in the night after their escape, alone in the darkest, tallest tower of Eilean Gayl.

Veyka's hands tightened and then relaxed around the hilts of her daggers, belted in their scabbards at her waist.

"The succubus will come for them either way. At least if they are trained and organized into an army, the humans might manage to take a few succubus with them," she said.

Something like relief rose up in Gwen's chest. Arran stepped between the two females, intent upon squashing it.

"Leave someone else to do this," he commanded. "We need you."

Gwen heard the words he did not say. *I need you.*

To defeat the succubus. To protect Veyka. To stop the queen from sacrificing herself to save Annwyn. But Gwen could not do any of those things; not as well as she could do this. She knew it would feel like a betrayal to the male who had trained her, whose side she'd served at for more than a hundred years.

She held his gaze as she spoke. "I already have the trust of their leader, Sylva."

Murder flashed in Arran's dark eyes. Then he was gone— shifting into his massive beast, bounding off between the squat buildings. Gwen tracked his flight by the sound of startled human screams.

Veyka's eyes went distant. Just like Gwen could not hear Arran's growl, she could not hear the words that passed silently between the queen and her mate. But she knew an argument was raging, and she knew it was about her.

She also knew the moment it ended.

Veyka's hands dropped away from her daggers, flexed and then relaxed at her sides.

"You have our permission," Veyka said. "But you will keep the communication crystal to hand. We will not lose contact this time."

Reasonable. "I will not let you down again." *Ancestors, let it be true*, Gwen prayed.

Veyka's bright blue eyes sharpened, and then she was moving into the space Arran had vacated, closer to Gwen than was reasonable or comfortable. "If that was what I meant, I'd have said it."

Never, not once, had Gwen felt intimidated by Veyka Pendragon. But the power that swirled in her eyes, that poured out of her without even trying... it took all of Gwen's fortitude to hold her ground. Not to step back, to put space between them.

Veyka trapped Gwen's gaze with her own. "This is an act of penance." A statement of truth, not a question. "You blame yourself for Parys' death."

Gwen could barely breathe.

Was the death blow coming now?

Part of her had been expecting it since the moment she'd told her of Parys' death. It was her fault. The queen deserved vengeance. If relegating her to stay with the humans was not enough, if she judged the only fair recompense to be Gwen's life, then she would not argue. She would accept her punishment.

"It was my fault," Gwen said, every sound painful as it scraped out of her throat by way of her heart.

"That is a lie," Veyka snarled. "I know, because I have told them to myself a thousand times. More, maybe. Arthur was murdered to put me on the throne. Arran nearly died because of my hubris. The succubus gained entry to my kingdom, ravaged innocents, because of my power."

Veyka was not keeping her voice low. Everyone—human and fae—within two blocks must have heard every word. But the queen was incandescent as she stormed on.

"But they are all fucking lies, Guinevere. Igraine did this. And Gorlois. And the succubus themselves. They are evil, all of them. And their greatest crime of all is that they convinced us we were to blame. If we believe that lie, we are paralyzed. We are unable to fight. We are powerless."

Veyka's chest rose and fell rapidly, unshed tears of emotion glistening in her eyes. There was no mistaking them at this distance. Gwen exhaled a painfully shaky breath. Veyka could not help but feel it on her skin.

All at once, she seemed to realize how close she'd gotten. She took several steps back until she was nearly on the other side of the square. Gwen watched as Veyka's eyes tracked around the perimeter, noting their observers. But she did not lower her voice when she spoke again.

"The choice is yours, Gwen," Veyka said, her breaths still heavy. "But I will never be powerless again."

🪲 15 🪲

ARRAN

Our war council had outgrown the quarters at Eilean Gayl. The Great Hall might have accommodated us, but the fear in the humans' eyes when Veyka had opened the rift in Eldermist was enough to convince us none of them would be willing to come through it. Even with the concessions we made—no weapons, convening in their realm—only the elderly female Sylva deigned to join us.

We were up on the hill above the village, where we'd first come through the rift after leaving Baylaur all of those months ago. I could not see them at this distance, even with the benefit of my sharpened fae eyesight, but I could feel the human eyes upon us.

Gwen had given them fae warriors for protection. Their Council of Elders had agreed to give refuge to the civilians from Baylaur. Maybe they would see this as an act of good faith; maybe they would be willing to fight—and die—alongside us.

Veyka brought everyone through in groups of two. I did not question why she did not open a portal rift. Even after a full night of sleep, there were lines around her eyes. She was not just jumping between realms, but across the continent as well. I noted the wonder in the eyes of those who'd never experienced it before—

Barkke, Elora, my father. Others, like Percival, Cyara, and Osheen, landed on their feet, their teeth gritted against the wave of nausea. As Gwen, Lyrena, and Sylva climbed the hill from the village, Veyka stepped in front of the massive standing stone.

I saw the monolith now for what it was—an ancient marker left by the Ancestors. The carvings were not identical, but there could be no mistaking the placement. It marked a rift—and the rifts led to other realms. To the succubus. It was a warning, just like the ring of them on Accolon's island.

It framed Veyka—a makeshift throne, a symbol of her interminable power. I stepped into my place at her side.

My father and Barkke talked quietly. Elora's eyes darted around, one hand on the hilt of her blade. Cyara stood at the edge of the hill, gazing down at the village.

"What happened to the buildings?" Cyara asked softly.

"The earthquake brought down nearly a quarter of the village," Sylva said as she gained the hill. Despite her age, she was a step ahead of Gwen and Lyrena. This terrain was her home, and she climbed it like she knew every rock and ditch.

"And they still welcomed the refugees from Baylaur," Gwen inserted, coming to stand beside the woman.

"We are most grateful," Veyka said with a regal tip of her head. She'd donned a circlet I had never seen her wear before. Made of unadorned, pounded gold, it circled her forehead and disappeared into her moon-white hair at her temples. It provided a sharp contrast to the ornate diamonds and sapphires that studded the shells of her ears.

"For it to be felt here as well..." Cyara trailed off, massaging her wrists as she continued to stare out. "That cannot be insignificant."

"Maybe. But we have enough trouble of our own. We cannot afford to go chasing any more," Veyka quipped.

Cyara exchanged a glance with Percival, who stood silent at her side.

My beast rumbled instinctively at the history of threat. *Why is Percival here?*

I could feel Veyka's frustration through the bond, a slightly muted companion to my own. *Cyara insisted.*

To what end?

Veyka did not answer that thought. Her arm nudged mine. The group had gone silent. Unlike the royal council meetings Veyka had once presided over in the goldstone palace, there was no ceremony to war.

But I had fought and led many. I'd never wasted time on platitudes. War was a time for facts.

"We do not know when or where the succubus will strike next." The warriors among the group straightened. The planners tilted their heads. I had their full attention. "We do not know how they organize themselves, if they do at all. We do know that the only way to kill them or prevent possession is with amorite."

"Are they sentient?" my father asked.

"No. They are mindless monsters," Elora growled. The already frigid temperature dropped several degrees, but no ice appeared at her fingertips.

I mentally reached out for my mate. We'd discussed this—every word I was about to say—at length. But particularly whether to share the succubus' attraction to her. I worried that if word spread, there were those who might try to blame her. She'd argued no one could do that any more effectively than she'd already done herself. And knowledge was one of the few advantages we had.

I shifted my attention to Elora. "They are not entirely without intent. They are drawn to Veyka."

There was nothing I could do to deflect the attention as every being on that hilltop turned their eyes on my mate. Their queen, but more. A female who'd walked hand in hand with torment, yet could still love. A warrior who'd trained herself, when no one else was willing to. A prophecy come to life.

Veyka rolled her shoulders and winked. "Lucky me, eh?"

It was difficult to read the faces of our companions. The elementals kept their faces neutral—even Cyara, Veyka's hand-maiden and closest confidant. Gwen's was blank as well; though I suspected that had more to do with her own inner turmoil than anything else. Sylva, the human woman, wore an expression of outright pity. Barkke hooted softly through his beard-covered lips.

"Whether it is because they can sense the strength of her power or the nature of her ability to move between realms, they assess her as a threat and will try to get to her over others." I knew they must have a thousand questions, but we did not have time for them.

"It could be an interesting tool to utilize in battle," Osheen said with a heavy sigh. Beside him, Cyara's turquoise eyes had blown wide. The winged handmaiden looked up at her new fellow Knight as if he'd sprung a second head.

Veyka's laugh sliced through the air, sharp and acerbic. "We can discuss whether or not to use me as bait later," she said. The smile she gave me was absolutely feline, completely at odds with the gravity of our discussion. "Go on, Brutal Prince."

"We have two main objectives—ready the armies we have and secure allies," I said. Veyka slid her hand up my spine. She was trying to distract herself.

On any other day, she would have succeeded in distracting me as well. But the success of our efforts directly impacted whether my mate would live to see another summer. Even she could not distract me.

"Gwen has already agreed to remain here in the human realm. With the assistance of Sylva and the Eldermist Council of Elders, they will rally what human fighting forces they can. Elora, take a selection of your remaining soldiers and remain here as well. You'll use the village as a base to go through the rift and search for the remains of the Elemental Army in the mountains." No surprise flickered in Gwen or the elderly human woman's eyes as I spoke; they'd already had time to take counsel and knew what to expect.

Lying in bed that morning, still warm from lovemaking and basking in the glow of a successful rescue, Veyka and I had planned and plotted. Argued, fucked, and finally agreed.

Elora nodded her assent, but not without question. "It would be faster with the Queen's help," she said, dividing her gaze between Veyka and me.

"Undoubtedly," Veyka said with a broad wink. "But unfortunately, I will have the pleasure of meeting my subjects in Wolf Bay."

No gasps of surprise at that edict, either. Wolf Bay had been the target of our conversations since we'd secured the amorite. Which, thankfully, was still coming in regular shipments from Castle Chariot.

"Ancestors help them when you get there," Barkke said with a grin, his emerald eyes twinkling with mirth.

Veyka licked her lips. "You're coming too."

I interceded before I needed to rip out Barkke's throat for the way he was looking at my mate. "Barkke and Lyrena will accompany me and Veyka to Cayltay. We will prepare the troops camped in Wolf Bay and begin our search for the Ethereal Queen."

Veyka planted her hands on her hips as she continued. "Isolde will travel with us. If the succubus are drawn to me, then the fighting will follow me as well. We will need her healing magic." The faerie was back in Eilean Gayl, assisting the healers, but she'd already given her assent.

I looked to my father next. "The Lord of Eilean Gayl will rally and ready troops north of the Spine."

My father was not a warrior. In the centuries since his marriage to my mother, what little prowess he'd honed in his youth had dulled farther still. But he was as effective a leader as any I'd ever met. Males and females alike took to him instantly. Not inspired by fear, like my own troops, but by true affection. If anyone could rouse the grumpy, taciturn lords and ladies entrenched in the frigid north of Annwyn, it was him.

But we had not expected arguments from any of those we'd doled out quests too thus far. And the next one was not mine to give.

Veyka stepped toward her handmaiden, palms up, entreaty on her face. It took a different kind of strength than what I'd used to command, to ask. It was a different female who stood before me than even a few months ago.

"Cyara, you will accompany Osheen and Maisri to the Faeries of the Fen," Veyka said. Although it was phrased as a command, the question was evident in every tensed muscle of her body.

The only emotion Cyara showed was the drawing of her wings together behind her back. "I would not be parted from you, Majesty."

Veyka reached her, hands out. Cyara did not spurn the offer. She placed her smaller ones into Veyka's, gripping them tightly until there was not a single one among us assembled who could not see the shining white of her knuckles.

"Nor I, you," Veyka admitted, her voice as even as Cyara's had been. "But the Faeries possess unique and ancient magic. We cannot afford to ignore them, and there is no one I trust more than you."

Their gazes collided. One stormy blue, tumultuous as the soul beneath. The other clear and constant turquoise. I had to look away from the force of what passed between them.

I knew no one shared the soul-bond that Veyka and I did; but in that moment, I could have sworn that a silent conversation passed between them.

"As you wish," Cyara said softly.

Veyka returned to my side, and this time it was my hand that went to her back.

"What of my sister?" Percival cut in on the emotionally fraught moment. Typical.

"You shall remain in the custody of the Lady of Eilean Gayl," Veyka said sharply, all softness drained from her eyes. Replaced by barely contained distaste.

Percival lifted his chin. "Until?"

"Until I give an order otherwise." Veyka turned away from him —not even assessing him as sufficient to deserve her regard. What-ever her feelings towards the humans in general, Percival had more than earned her ire. She'd given him one of her precious daggers, and he'd driven it into her Goldstone's back while delivering us to Gorlois.

The fact that she no longer required him shackled to the wall was still a surprise to me.

"What about Avalon?" Lyrena asked before the group could begin to disperse.

"Avalon is neutral," Veyka countered, hands back on her wide hips.

"They saved Arran," Lyrena argued back.

"Debatable."

It was not a moot point; I'd brought it up to Veyka as well. But we could not be sure of the Lady of the Lake's allegiance. She may be Veyka's half-sister, but she'd kept secrets. "An ally that could not be depended upon was no ally at all," I said, imbuing my voice with a finality that Lyrena must have recognized. She did not argue further.

Veyka rolled her shoulders and reached unconsciously for her belt. The scabbards were there, but the daggers were not. One of the conditions to get the humans to the discussion—no weapons. As if every one of us was not dangerous enough, merely existing. Veyka hooked her thumbs around the empty scabbards, scraping her thumbnail over the jewels. Now that it was done, the parting came. That would be the hardest.

She opened her mouth—to say something sassy or profound, I could not have guessed—but drew up short.

"What about the Sacred Trinity?" Cyara asked.

Veyka froze.

But she was not the one who drew everyone's attention. Nor was Cyara. It was Gwen—on her knees, golden eyes blown wide, warm brown skin turned completely ashen. "What do you know of the Sacred Trinity?"

16

ARRAN

I'd never seen her like this. Gwen was stoic. She was composed.

In the wake of the fall of Baylaur, she was frazzled. When she asked to remain in Eldermist, she was coming apart at the seams.

But this... a feral beast raged in her eyes. Not the calculated feline she became when she shifted, but something much wilder.

She did not try to stand. From her knees, she looked from person to person, head whipping rapidly around the loose circle we'd formed, searching each face.

"What do you know of the Sacred Trinity?" she asked again, her voice cracking. Tears shone in her golden eyes.

Ancestors. What happened to her?

Veyka's voice was soft and sad in my mind—*Parys.*

Her hand curled into mine. I could feel her agony filling the bond, stretching across the golden thread between us. The same agony that shone out through Gwen's eyes.

"Percival," Veyka said. This time, there was no malice in it.

Despite her distaste for him, the half-witch had been the one to recognize Excalibur and the scabbards for what they were—to tell us of the Sacred Trinity in the first place during that harrowing journey across the human realm in search of Avalon.

"The Sacred Trinity consists of three ancient magical items, forged in Avalon long ago. They are said to make the wielder the master of death," Percival said tonelessly.

Gwen stared at him, her face inscrutable but for the pain etched on it. What else was there—confusion, relief, fear, hope—it was impossible for me to parse. Veyka's hand tightened in mine; maybe she saw more than I did. Her grip went tighter still when Gwen began to speak.

"Not all travelers are welcome. Some invade the body, others the mind. For this reason was the sacred trinity created. What once was one then became three. The sword. The scabbards. The chalice. Only united can they banish the darkness. Three kingdoms created them. Only when wielded as one can they serve the purpose for which they were made."

My heart understood before my mind did, surging with something so white hot, so powerful, I rocked back a step.

Beside me, Veyka's skin was white enough to match her hair. "Is that a prophecy?"

Gwen shook her head. "A book. *The Travelers.* Parys was carrying it with him when..." her voice broke, but she steadied herself. "When Igraine murdered him. I read it front to back, again and again, trying to understand why he though it so important to hold on to with his dying breath."

"Three kingdoms," Percival said quietly. "Human, fae, and witch. A representative from each came together to forge the Sacred Trinity. That is what the legends in Avalon say as well."

"What does it mean?" Gwen asked, her voice only slightly less desperate. Lyrena was at her side now, easing her fellow Goldstone up to stand.

"It means that if the Sacred Trinity is united, it can be used to banish the darkness," Cyara said, louder than I'd ever heard her speak. "The Sacred Trinity can defeat the succubus."

Veyka would live.

My mind sprang to action immediately, reorganizing the plans we'd made. Everything was different now. I'd vowed to her that we'd never be parted again. I'd vowed to myself that I would find a way to save her, even at the cost of this blasted kingdom. But here it was, for the first time since we'd reached that final standing stone atop Accolon's island.

This feeling burning in my chest was hope.

"Veyka already has the scabbards and the sword," Cyara explained. "We believe the chalice to be the one that was used at the Joining."

"Merlin took it with her," Gwen said, disappointment lining her words.

Her revelation barely dented the growing hope within me. Merlin could be hunted. With Veyka's void power, we could search the entire continent. We'd have to send someone in our stead to Wolf Bay. Or divide our time.

Veyka—

"No."

The word reverberated across the hilltop, through our mating bond, between the very fabric of the realms.

Veyka.

Cyara stepped toward her queen, wings quivering. "You were only too keen to expend resources on the Sacred Trinity before. Why not now?" *When it is your life we stand to save.*

"Merlin is gone," Veyka replied, unflinching. "She stole the chalice, and with it any chance of uniting the Sacred Trinity."

The copper-haired harpy was not intimidated. "That is little more information than we have on the Ethereal Queen and yet you will not stop searching for her."

There were no thoughts in my head. *Veyka.*

Veyka gnashed her teeth. "You speak out of turn."

Cruel, to the most steadfast friend she had. But Cyara was undaunted. "You were the one who granted your Knights the right to speak our minds."

I could feel the void calling to Veyka, sense her desire to throw herself into it and escape. But her booted feet remained firmly planted in the human realm. "The two are not the same. Finding the Ethereal Queen and joining her power to mine is the only way to banish the succubus."

"That we knew of," Cyara countered. "But now we have another way."

"Another *possibility*." She said the word as if it burned her. "It is too late to waste resources on vague hopes. You all have your quests. I expect you to fulfill them to the best of your abilities."

She turned on her heel and walked away—not toward the village, but in the opposite direction. Toward the mountains. But she did not disappear into the void. I could follow her.

Down the hill, up the next. Increasing in speed. She broke into a run, sucking in the bitter cold air and then exhaling it in angry, ragged puffs. The voices of our friends and allies died away to nothing as we climbed deeper into the mountains. I could feel her exhaustion through the bond—but nothing else.

She was trying to block me out. Or maybe she was so fraught that she was beyond all feeling.

I could not take it a second longer.

"Veyka."

I expected her to ignore me. *Ancestors*, she was fast.

"We agreed," she said without turning, driving step after step into the side of the mountain, climbing ever upward as she pushed the words out. "We talked through all of our assets and our needs and we made a plan. A cool-headed, comprehensive plan of attack. You are the battle commander. You are the one who told me the importance of—"

"Veyka." She was fast, but I was faster.

"—making decisions from a place of reason rather than emotion—"

I grabbed her arm, pulling her down. She dodged me as I tried for the other, wrenching the one I held. But I was stronger and bigger and more desperate, even than her.

I grabbed her by both forearms, shaking her hard. "Veyka!"

She stopped fighting, but she refused to look at me.

"Tell me why," I demanded.

"I already did," she seethed through clenched teeth.

I did not dare release her arms. She'd run again in an instant. So I lowered my face to hers instead, using my jaw to force hers up, only pulling back far enough that I could look straight into her eyes. "You can hide from them, but not from me. Your soul is mine, and you cannot hide a single slice of yourself from me. Tell me the truth."

Veyka caught her lower lip between her teeth.

"You have been obsessed with unraveling Arthur's secrets. Why stop now?"

She tried to look away, but I pressed my forehead to hers.

"Tell me, Princess," I breathed.

I felt the crack within her as the wall of ice she'd thrown up shattered.

"There is no time, Arran!" she cried, jerking away. I held her tight, but I let her rage. "He gifted me the scabbards. He left me the sword. Did he know that Igraine would try to kill him? Did he know about the Sacred Trinity all along? Or was it all fate, the fucking Ancestors playing with him the same way they've played with me? I could spend a lifetime unraveling Arthur's secrets. But I don't have a lifetime."

Her lower lip shook. That's why she'd bitten into it before. Her entire body shook as she spoke. "All that matters now is saving Annwyn. My life is forfeit. The Sacred Trinity, whatever Arthur planned, it does not signify."

"No."

She closed her eyes, a single tear sliding down her cheek. "Arran."

"I will not lose you." I wasn't holding her in place anymore. She was in my arms, trying to fuse her body to mine. I wrapped one arm around her shoulder, the other around her waist.

She was mine. Annwyn could not have her.

I let myself breathe in her plum and primrose scent, savor the silk of her hair against my jaw, before I drew back again. It was too far, too much distance, but I needed her looking into my eyes as I said it.

"Hear this vow, Veyka. To all of Annwyn, you can be queen and warrior, even savior. But before all of that, you are my mate. We will find another way or I will let this realm tear itself to pieces."

Her throat bobbed. Another tear slipped down to join the first.

"Arran," she breathed, halfway to a sob.

I did not let her break away. I pulled her even tighter, ready to fuse our bodies the way we'd already fused our souls. "Do you believe me?"

Her eyes gave one answer. But her mouth formed another. "Yes."

I held her there for seconds that turned to minutes, needing to share breath with her, to feel the life and love that flowed through her veins.

After an eternity, I pressed my forehead against hers. "What do you want, Princess?"

She exhaled softly, her voice so quiet that the winter wind almost stole her words. "I want to live."

17

VEYKA

Arran did not answer me with words. What words could he give me that would possibly mean more than his vow?

He let his body tell me. His lips, his hands, his cock.

His mouth started on mine, his tongue plunging deep into my mouth with all the confidence of a male who knew my truth. I was his. Unconditionally.

His hands roamed my body, claiming every inch he touched with enough force to leave bruises. This would not be a gentle fucking. He lifted his mouth from mine to snarl, as if he'd heard the thoughts in my head. Maybe he had.

"When you look at yourself in the mirror, you will remember this," he growled. "Every bruise, every mark—you are *mine*." His teeth dragged along my collarbone, the sharp tips of his canines piercing my flesh and filling the air around us with the coppery tang of my blood.

His cock pressed against my belly, his trousers doing nothing to disguise the rigid outline as he rocked his hips against me. He lifted one hand from my body long enough to rip the fabric away, freeing himself against my bare midsection. He was already unbearably hot.

"Are you going to spill yourself all over my stomach?" I teased, my voice and pussy quivering in time.

"A beautiful fucking sight," he said as he alternated bites and sucks on my shoulder. "That soft belly of yours, wobbling as you touch yourself, as I rain down my seed on you so that every male in this Ancestors'-damned kingdom knows you belong to me."

Ancestors. I was going to come just from his words alone.

"Not yet," he commanded, the wall between thoughts and words obliterated by the strength of the golden bond between us. "First you're going to mark me."

Arran dropped to his knees. I didn't have a second to think. He'd hiked my skirt up, grabbed my leg and slung it over his shoulder, and drove his mouth into my pussy. He plunged his tongue between my folds with the same intensity he had my mouth, and just as much teeth.

He sucked my clit between his lips, then nipped at it with his canines. The sharp prick of pain mingled with pleasure as he drove his tongue deep inside of me, past my pussy lips and into my cunt itself. One hand held my leg in place, the other kneaded the soft flesh of my ass. I'd have marks there too. Fuck, I was going to be one big, sexually charged bruise by the time he was finished with me.

"Moan for me, Veyka," Arran demanded, his voice muffled between my legs. "Let me hear that beautiful voice of yours while you ride my face. Let all of them hear you."

There was no one here but us. But I understood what he did not say.

He was trying to remind me of what I had to live for.

I needed no reminding. I felt it with every breath—the love I bore for my friends, who I'd kept so carefully at a distance but had managed to worm their way into my heart anyway. My subjects, whose faces were written with awe and fear and adoration as I'd lead them through the mountains to safety.

And Arran.

A thousand years spent in his arms, even that would not be enough. Not when he was my world. He was everything.

He nipped at my clit again and I did exactly as he said. I tangled my fingers in his hair, pulling hard enough to tear, and threw back my head to the gray sky.

"I'm coming," I moaned.

"Louder."

"I'm coming. Ancestors, Arran, yes. I'm going to come all over your face, fuck. I need—"

I didn't get to say it. He rammed two fingers inside of me, curled the tips, and I came in a flood of juice that covered his hand, his face, and splashed down onto the frosted ground. But he didn't stop there. He sucked hard on my clit while his fingers went deeper, again, fingertips over that sensitive spot inside of me that I'd never been able to reach on my own, until another waterfall spilled from me, coating us both in my pleasure.

Arran lapped up every drop, licking the inside of my thighs, his fingers, the trembling lips of my pussy. "Good girl," he murmured against my folds as he slicked his tongue along my slit one last time.

My thick thighs were powerful, but even they could not hold me after climaxes like that.

He rose, my skirt fisted in one hand and my glistening pussy bare to the cold. But he wasn't gone for long, his body covering mine, his strong arms keeping me upright.

Pressed against my bare belly again, his cock was even hotter than before. I was desperate for him.

I closed my fingers around him, glorying in the thickness as I stroked from base to tip. He thrust into my hand, rewarding me with a moan of his own. His crown was already wet with the first droplets of seed. I smoothed it over his head, then lifted my thumb and sucked it into my mouth, savoring the salt-tinged sweetness on my tongue.

But before I could guide him inside, he shoved my hand away.

The hand that had kneaded my ass rose.

His fingers closed around my throat. "You will live, Veyka."

Even now, I wanted to argue. I opened my mouth. His grip tightened.

"You will live, because I say so. Because I will not let you go." The beast spoke now. The wolf. The primal part of Arran that had earned him the name Brutal Prince.

He squeezed tighter. I tried to suck in a breath, but he cut it off.

Arran was in control. He would not let me go.

Black clawed at the edges of my vision. Tears squeezed out from the corners of my eyes.

"You will live," he said again. He held me too tight, there were no words I could say. My lips formed the word. *Yes.*

Arran slammed me down onto his cock.

The second he was fully sheathed inside of me, he released my throat. "Breathe."

I sucked in a desperate breath as Arran exploded within me. My inhale became a scream as his seed flooded my pussy, searing hot against my core. I came with him, clung to him as I rode out the waves of my orgasm.

Tears flowed freely down my face as I buried my face in his throat. "I love you," I heard myself say. Sob. "I love you. I love you. I love you."

He lowered us to our knees before either of us lost the ability to stand. I knew he had no capacity to speak, but I felt the beast's deep rumble in my soul. *You are mine.*

❧

Usually, I was content to stay wrapped in Arran's arms forever. But the human realm was fucking cold.

No one expected us to return to that hilltop. Not that I would have felt any shame in going back, Arran's scent coating my skin, a potent reminder of the vows he'd made. But I knew most of them well enough. They would not waste time waiting around for a decision.

I did not have an answer for them, anyway.

Arran wanted to go after the Sacred Trinity. I knew it was a fantasy.

We were co-rulers. We had to reach some sort of accord. But it was not going to happen today. Waiting another day would not change the reality. But I had felt the pain in Arran as he made that vow to me. I could give him a day to come to terms with the loss of that fickle hope that Gwen and Cyara had offered.

I wished I could give him more.

We were supposed to have a thousand years.

No. I would not flinch from my fate now.

I did not pull away when Arran tucked me in at his side.

We found what remained of our war council drinking hot tea in Sylva's house. I opened a portal rift with half a thought. The growing power inside of me might have scared me once. But now, I allowed myself to revel in it. If mere weeks or months remained to me, then I deserved to enjoy them in any way I could.

I brought us to the edge of the lake. I'd have preferred to go directly to our quarters, but the residents of Eilean Gayl, old and new, needed to see us. High King and Queen of Annwyn. United, strong, competent, with our loyal Knights arrayed around us.

But as the terrestrial mountains took shape around us, so did something else. The turrets of Eilean Gayl were crowded; so was the bridge. A disturbance at the far end of the lake drew all eyes.

A massive orb made of water moved steadily across the lake. As it approached the castle, what appeared to be shimmers were revealed to be undulating ripples of water, moving in a steady motion to create the sphere.

I was dimly aware of Barkke drifting closer, taking up a place at Arran's side.

"What is that?" he asked aloud, echoing the thoughts in a thousand fae heads.

I knew. I'd seen theatrics like this before; twice, in point of fact.

"It's Merlin."

❧ 18 ❦

VEYKA

Arran, Barkke, and Elora tied her to a chair.

She offered no resistance, allowing them to bind her hands, feet, and neck. She could not even turn her head without the rope burning into her pale gold skin.

And she still had the nerve to look calm and composed. Her perfect black hair fell straight, nearly to her waist, not a tangle in sight. Her slanted dark brown eyes were unmarred by bruises or wrinkles. I wondered what the cost of her powerful water magic was; clearly it was not physical. Not like the exhaustion that Lyrena's fire brought or the ache in Cyara's wrists.

Merlin stared at me with clear, unruffled grace.

Maybe her cost was madness. She'd have to be insane to stare at me without fear.

Either way, I'd make sure her death was slow and painful.

Barkke and Elora retreated to the other side of the door. Eilean Gayl did not have proper dungeons, so we'd put her high in a tower room. One window, which Arran covered with vines a foot thick, and one door, guarded by both elemental and terrestrial warriors.

I drew a dagger from my waist.

"How difficult would you like to make this, Merlin?" I asked, lifting my blade to the torchlight.

"I do not intend to make it difficult at all, Majesty. You want to know about the Sacred Trinity."

Arran stilled beside me. The head of his axe was still in his hand. He always drew it in the same motion. He hooked his thumb and forefinger around where the head met the shaft, and slid it up with one quick flick of his wrist until he had the shaft perfectly positioned in his grasp.

But his fingers were still curved around the metal head.

Merlin divided her attention between us, nodding with what we were supposed to see as respect.

"I cannot bow, obviously. But you do not need to torture me. I will answer your questions."

Anger surged through me. Rage I had not allowed myself to feel in the aftermath of hearing about Parys' death. I had not fetched Igraine from Baylaur myself, merely held open the portal rift while Arran and Lyrena did it. I'd let her linger in Baylaur long enough. Now that Merlin was here, I could not delay facing the truth and all of its ramifications. I mourned, but I did not let it overtake me. I could not. I did not have the luxury of hiding as I had done in the months after Arthur's death.

But confronted with Merlin's perfect calm, I snapped. I lunged for her, my second dagger already in my hand. "That is where you are wrong. You murdered Parys—"

"I did not murder anyone," Merlin quipped. She did not flinch away—not that she really could, given how tightly she was restrained—but her eyes were clear. As if she was ready to die. "Unlike Your Majesties, some of us are able to accomplish our tasks through nonviolent means." She was practically begging me to kill her.

I swung, aiming for her thigh. A deep wound there would be painful, would gush blood, but would not impede her ability to talk.

Arran's hand closed around my wrist.

How dare you, I raged, but I was met with a stern growl.

"You collaborated with the Dowager," Arran said. He did not release my arm, keeping me a full two feet away from drawing blood.

"Briefly," Merlin admitted freely. Wisely, her eyes focused on me, rather than Arran. If I went through the void, even he would not be able to stop me. "I had nothing to do with your brother's death, and I was long gone before Igraine killed your friend."

"You knew about Igraine's involvement in Arthur's death," Arran said, his grip on me loosening fractionally.

"You are guilty," I snarled. I shook free of my mate. A breath, that was all that stood between me and gutting the traitorous priestess.

But it was not my mate's hand that held me now. It was his hope. I could feel it, small and white and glowing, deep in his dark soul.

Merlin exhaled. "Of not intervening? I suppose so. But I knew the Void Prophecy as well as your mother. Better, in fact. Because I knew what that coming darkness meant."

I staggered back a step. I could not help it. Not even a lifetime of elemental composure could keep me in place.

"You knew about the succubus," I breathed.

Merlin actually smiled. "Why do you think the Ancestors diminished the power of the priestesses? Too many of the witches were taken by the succubus; they had to be destroyed and their sacred object taken. They entrusted the grail to the priestesses. Nimue and Accolon felt that was sufficient power."

The witches and the priestesses had both been eliminated after the Great War, in their own ways. I knew that, had seen the evidence. Only two witches had been left in Annwyn—one in the Tower of Myda, and one in the mountains of the Spine. I'd met them both and killed the first. The priestesses were not killed off, but their power reduced so that they were never more than one priestess and one acolyte at any given time. I'd punished Merlin in Baylaur for violating that law.

But we'd never known the true purpose behind those actions

taken by our Ancestors. The explanation that Merlin offered was sobering in how perfectly it made sense. Witches' minds could become unmoored from the present, making even the females vulnerable to the succubus. I'd seen as much in the Tower of Myda, guarded myself against it when I confronted the witch in the Spine, and leveraged it when Cyara used Diana to search for Accolon's truth.

Percival had said that three joined together to make the Sacred Trinity—fae, witch, and human. Gwen corroborated it with Parys' findings. And now, Merlin echoed them and added more.

It could not be. The answer could not have been sitting there in Baylaur all along. What did that mean? Arthur had died for no reason? All of the citizens of Baylaur, my subjects, dead because I had not realized? Not believed?

I rocked back another step.

"The priestess here had no knowledge of the succubus," I said.

Merlin shrugged. "It has been seven thousand years. Much knowledge has been lost." "But the grail was passed into my keeping, and with it the knowledge of its importance."

I could feel Arran through the bond. While my insides screamed, his brooded. A dark, coalescing storm cloud. And at its center, that kernel of hope that he was so carefully nourishing.

"Why didn't Accolon and Nimue use the Sacred Trinity to banish the succubus the first time?" Arran demanded, battle axe fully in his grip now. "Why carve those stones and lead us to believe that only Veyka's sacrifice—"

He could not finish.

Merlin lifted her dark brows, exaggerating the slant of her eyes. I lifted my dagger in threat.

"They never united the three. The scabbards were entrusted to the humans, and the humans never offered them nor revealed their location during the Great War," she said, one eye on my weapons, the other on Arran.

Outwardly, he was unchanged. But inside, I felt the clouds drop away until only that white ember remained. "The legend of the Sacred Trinity is true."

"Yes," Merlin said.

Another step back. Far enough that I could press my eyes closed as I tried to stem the swirl of feelings inside of me. "Where is it?"

"The grail is hidden."

Arran's snarl filled the small room, careening off of the curved walls, crashing against the wooden ceiling, echoing through our bones. He was a second from shifting. I could feel it in the air, that strange charge of energy that always filled the space before his beast took over. The wolf would rip out her throat.

He threw himself at her, the fatal blade of his axe pressed against her throat. He'd cut through rope and skin in a second, and she'd be headless. Truly dead. "Chalice, grail, call it whatever you like. But where have you hidden it?"

Arran was going to kill her. And I was inclined to let him.

Except for that glowing white ember inside of him. The one he'd been keeping alive, even as I let my own die inside of me.

I wrapped myself along the strong golden thread that connected us, slid my soul deeper until it was fully entwined with his. I caressed that precious hope he'd nourished—desperately, unflinchingly.

She cannot tell us if she is dead, I purred to his beast.

Slowly, so wretchedly slowly, I felt the beast recede and Arran's conscious mind take hold once more. His hand was in mine. He stepped back, lowered his axe.

Merlin released a slow, measured exhale. "It is no small thing to be master of death. It is not something that I can simply bestow upon you."

I hooked one thumb around a scabbard, the weight of the mighty sword sheathed down my back suddenly heavy. "Arthur bestowed the scabbards and sword."

"No. You pulled the Excalibur from the stone. Arthur was only able to give you the scabbards because they are an heirloom of your house. The human that forged the scabbards for the Sacred Trinity eons ago was a Pendragon."

I actually laughed. "You cannot mean that I am human?"

And yet, it would explain so much. Why I had never manifested elemental powers, why the scabbards had come into my possession. Why I was fated to be the one to banish the succubus.

"A distant ancestor was," Merlin said with a shrug. "Tens of thousands of years have passed since the forging of the Sacred Trinity. Human and fae were not always as estranged as they are now. Is it so difficult to believe your mighty line might have a human or two mixed in somewhere?"

No, it wasn't.

Once, maybe. But after everything I'd lived through in the past months, I knew better than anyone that history recorded only what its authors deemed most important. Elementals prized lineage over everything else. If there had been a human named Pendragon somewhere in my ancestry, the elementals would certainly have erased them long ago.

"It does not matter," I said slowly, to myself and to the thoughts tumbling through my head. Because it didn't matter. I *was* fated to banish the succubus. I'd already accepted that. But maybe, just maybe, the cost would not have to be my life. "Where is the grail?"

Merlin spared no glance for Arran. She stared into my eyes as she said, with that irritating ring of prophecy, "You must find it for yourself."

I understood. "Finding the grail is some sort of test."

She nodded. "A quest."

I'd thought from the moment Arran dragged her in here that she was ready to die. That assessment had been correct. She'd die before she told me the location of the grail. Guarding it was her destiny, just as banishing the succubus was mine. I was ready to die for my fate; why shouldn't I expect her to be as well?

But Arran's thoughts had taken a more practical turn. "Does that mean she must find it herself?"

Merlin smiled. "I did not say that."

"Fucking priestess," I swore, spinning away. I paced to the door and then back again. On my second turn, Arran intercepted me.

"This is more than fickle hope, Veyka," he said, taking both of my hands in his. "This is real."

It hurt to hope. It hurt so much.

But I didn't stop him when he went to the door and wrenched it open. Elora and Barkke appeared immediately. The expressions on their faces said all—they had heard every word of the interrogation.

Somehow, I managed to keep my throat from closing as I gave the order. "Summon Cyara and Osheen. We have an amendment to their quest."

19

ARRAN

I planned my timing carefully. If Veyka chose to descend to the Great Hall for supper, Lyrena would be at her side. But on that evening, Veyka and I had dined privately with my mother and father. Which meant that in the hours between eating and sleeping, the golden knight would slip down to the kitchens to drink and carouse.

While Veyka coaxed more stories of my childhood out of my mother, I made an excuse about finalizing the division of amorite weapons with Osheen. If Veyka suspected the lie, she did not show it. The golden thread of our mating bond remained steady but silent.

But rather than making my way down into the armory, where Osheen was diligently at work, I climbed the spiral staircase to our apartments. I found Cyara exactly where I expected, doing what I expected—in the chamber she shared with Lyrena off of the communal sitting room, preparing for the journey ahead.

She sat on the floor, legs folded gracefully underneath her, and white-feathered wings tucked in tight to avoid upsetting any of the already-packed parcels stacked behind her. Across the carpet was a large spread of items, some of which I recognized—a bowl of tea, a fine-toothed comb—and others which remained a mystery, such as two small metal instruments with sharp hooks at one end.

She started to stand, but I waved her down as I closed the door behind me.

"Your Majesty."

"Arran is fine."

The corners of her lips turned in a small smile. It had taken her months to finally call Veyka by her given name rather than her title. While she'd been at our side for months, I was not surprised that she still reverted to formality. I could count the number of times we'd shared a private conversation on one hand. She was Veyka's closest friend, and I had no desire to insert myself into that. My mate deserved the simple comfort of a friend.

"Your preparations are thorough," I said as I scanned the contents laid out before her again. My own travel pack contained only the basic necessities—clothing, weapons, emergency rations, and a bar of soap.

As I considered the spread, Cyara picked up a neatly cut square of linen, measured a spoonful of tea leaves into the center, and then twisted the ends into an efficient little knot. A twinge of regret lodged itself in my side. For the first time, Veyka was sending her handmaiden away. My mate would not have these small comforts, all a far cry from the luxury she was entitled to as queen.

I vowed to myself to go back over and reassess what I carried in my own travel pack.

Cyara continued her ministrations without looking up at me. Patience and silence were her weapons, but she was no less a warrior. *Good.* I was counting upon it.

There was no need to clear my throat or get her attention. I knew she was already aware of every breath I took.

"It is Veyka's wish that you secure the alliance of the Faeries of the Fen before you begin your search for the Grail," I said plainly.

Her fingers paused over the neatly stacked rows of tea satchels she'd created. "I am aware."

"Your discontent with that command was obvious."

Next she unrolled a rectangle of leather tied with twine, revealing lengths of glittering jewels, the type that elementals often wore woven into their plaits. She carefully began to disentangle them, arranging each in a vertical line beside the next.

"Are you here as her enforcer?" she asked, her voice carefully neutral, and only after she had rewrapped the roll.

"Veyka does not need me to enforce her edicts. She is plenty ruthless all on her own."

Her wings fluttered over her shoulders, though her voice remained level. "On that we are agreed."

She'd moved on to grooming items. Slender bars of soap, a vial of pale violet liquid, washcloths made of supple, soft fabric. Of all the elementals I'd met, Cyara was the best at hiding her emotions and reactions. Which was truly a distinction, given that the skill was drilled into them from birth.

But I'd spent months observing her love for Veyka. I'd watched it grow as Veyka leaned into it, giving pieces of herself and receiving bits of her handmaiden in return. I knew enough to take the chance.

"I suspect that is not the only matter on which we are of one mind," I said.

Cyara's careful, continuous movements did not pause this time. But she communicated that she understood with the shift in her tone. "You have my attention."

Now or never.

Veyka might never forgive me. But I could live with that.

"A war will be fought. No matter how or what you find, no matter what alliances we do or do not secure. There will be battle, and the succubus will slaughter human and fae alike in numbers that even Veyka cannot yet comprehend. When and if we find the Ethereal Queen, many will die."

Cyara began stacking all of the small packages she'd arranged in the center of a larger swath of fabric. "I have come to the same conclusions."

"But Veyka will not be among them."

She folded the edges of the fabric and wrapped it with sturdy twine. "No, she will not."

"Go to the human realm. Take Percival and Diana if you must. Meet with the Faeries of the Fen if it is helpful. But allies are not your concern. Your quest is for the Grail."

She cinched the final knot into place and lifted her turquoise eyes to mine. I saw everything I needed there, but she still said the words— "You have my promise."

I was not good at emotion. Feelings only made making difficult decisions harder. Only with Veyka did I allow myself to be vulnerable. But I tried to let the emotions shine through my eyes in that moment—to let Cyara know just what that vow meant to me. And I saw them reflected back in hers.

I nodded sharply and turned for the door. There was nothing else to say.

"Arran."

I froze with my hand on the door handle. Soft rustling told me that Cyara had risen. When I turned, she held out the package she'd been so carefully preparing. "Here."

"What is this?"

"For Veyka."

Understanding shifted into place. The shadowvein tea that Veyka took each morning. The strands of jewels—I'd never seen Cyara wear them, but Veyka almost always did. All of her careful preparations were not for her own sake, but for her queen's. I accepted the package as an even deeper understanding took root.

Cyara would keep her promise. Or perish in the pursuit.

20

VEYKA

One last task remained.

Excalibur strapped to my back, heavy fur mantle over my shoulders, I climbed with my travel pack down the curtain wall of Eilean Gayl to the small strip of bare ground that encircled the castle before giving way to the lapping waves of the lake. Lyrena was already there, flanked by several terrestrial guards.

Hands and legs bound, her fine features contracted into an ugly snarl, stood my mother.

Lyrena did not hesitate to drag her forward for my inspection.

"Remove your hands or I will drown you where you stand," the Dowager hissed, her voice as serpentine as any snake shifter in the terrestrial kingdom. Once, that voice had haunted my nightmares. But no longer. She could not lay claim to a single piece of me, not even in my dreams.

Lyrena's laugh rent the air, harsh and sharp as I'd ever heard it. Instead of pulling her hands back, she gripped the Dowager's upper arms harder, harder, harder—until wisps of smoke curled into the air between them. Another fierce laugh, and Lyrena released her charge, stepping away to reveal the charred fabric and angry red skin where her fire had burned right through the Dowager's sleeves.

This moment was not just for me, I realized. Lyrena had loved Arthur. Gwen had befriended Parys. All of Annwyn had been subjected to the Dowager's cruel whims in a thousand ways, large and small. For Annwyn, and for the friends that had become family, I would not flinch.

I stepped out of the shadows of Eilean Gayl's round tower.

"You are no longer in a position to give orders," I said.

The Dowager only deigned a glance in my direction. She'd detected Arran, coming around the foot of the tower, rope in hand. She judged him to be the bigger threat. But what she made of the small wooden dinghy he tugged through the water, I did not know. I'd never wanted ethereal powers, least of all in that moment. I'd suffered the malignant darkness of the Dowager's mind. I would rather bring my own dagger to my throat than venture inside of it.

Arran reached her, taking her bound hands to force her into the small boat. Her pale brows arched in disdain even as her feet moved. "Water? A poor prison for an elemental. You've spent too long with the terrestrials, daughter."

Even as she stepped onto the boat and Arran pushed them away from shore, she did not reach for her power. She did not believe she needed to.

Her lips curved. "Did the death of your foolish friend teach you nothing?"

Anger and grief danced through my veins. But all around them rolled a current of certainty. This time, I would write the ending.

A swirling wind carried voices down from the battlements, where elementals and terrestrials both gathered to watch. It was not every day that one could bear witness to regicide. I'd anticipated the audience. Encouraged it, even, through well placed conversations. I may be High Queen of all of Annwyn, but I'd been an elemental first. I knew how to manipulate perception. I wanted stories of Igraine's death written into legend. Not to immortalize her, though that was inevitable. I wanted every living being in Annwyn to understand that I would not flinch from my duty to protect them—even if it meant slaughtering my own mother.

Arran's oar cut through the water with brutally efficient strokes. A few breaths, and the boat reached the single pillar sunk into the water several yards from the castle. When I'd first spotted it from our bedroom window, Arran told me that it had once been part of the island itself, used as a whipping post. But the millennia had eroded away the land until all that remained was the narrow strip of grass and mud beneath my feet.

I'd decided to put that post to a new purpose.

Arran said something to the Dowager—something that made her flinch. In another life, I would have wanted to know what my devious mate had thought of to gain the upper hand, even if only for a moment. But I did not reach down the golden thread of our bond, nor seek out his beast's comforting rumble.

Whatever it was, I was grateful that it kept her from resisting as Arran adjusted the chains at her wrists and ankles to bind her to the post. When he pushed away, sending the small boat clear, the Dowager's face was once again impassive.

Arran shifted, swimming back through the water in his beast form even faster than he'd paddled. I did not ask what motivated his shift.

A wave of her hand and Lyrena set the boat and its oars aflame.

Igraine was alone.

For several heartbeats, nothing happened. I counted each one, wondering academically whether I would reach ten, or twenty, or thirty. It did not matter. The outcome would be the same.

I made it to six before the smooth surface of the water broke.

Whether it was the same fuath who had feasted on the fauna-gifted terrestrial at my welcome feast or one of its kin hardly mattered. The claws that rose from the black water were unforgiving, clamping down on the Dowager's wrist and severing it from her body in one jolting motion.

"How dare you?" Igraine screeched.

She'd played along with my game, waiting to see what I intended. But even though that hand would regrow, she'd had enough. She reached for her power, her remaining hand clenching and releasing as she called to the water surrounding her.

And found that it did not answer.

"A fitting end." I'd thought long and hard about how I would punish my mother before realizing there was nothing I could do to repay her for the pain she'd wrought. But a powerful water wielder, surrounded by her weapon of choice, unable to call upon it... there was poetry to it that I'd only ever found when killing.

The Dowager's ice blue eyes narrowed, her mouth forming a word even as her ironclad will protested against it. "How?"

A small smile turned the corners of my mouth. "Legends and prophecies are not always what they seem. You ought to know that better than anyone." As I spoke, I heard their too-loud footsteps behind me. Despite living among us for months, the two half-humans had not mastered the fae silence.

Half-human. But also, half-witch.

I tossed a wink over my shoulder. Percival rolled his eyes. Diana squeaked. Typical.

I turned my irreverent gaze back to Igraine. "Witches are not as extinct as you taught me to believe."

An old witch spell had bound her power. Sealed with the right combination of ingredients in her morning wine, it would not inhibit her magic forever. But it was enough, and long enough.

She began to thrash against her restraints, turning to the strength of her physical body to save her where her magic had failed. But the movements only attracted the lake's occupants. Another massive claw emerged from the water, snapping at her remaining hand. She twisted away, just avoiding it.

Igraine did not beg for her life. She did not look to me at all. As always, she was much too preoccupied with herself to notice as the smile on my face deepened.

A better female could not have watched.

But I was more than the monster she'd made me.

Given all possible ends, I'd chosen this one for my mother, the

Dowager High Queen of Annwyn. And I watched until there was not a single shred left of her to piece back together or heal.

I did not flinch when a massive, fanged fish leapt from the water, taking a deep bite from her breast before splashing back beneath the surface. Not a tremor as leeches the size of my thumb began to crawl up her body, leaving a trail of greenish slime that mingled with the rich red of her blood.

I watched as a great tentacled creature rose from the depths of the lake, wrapping its arms around her legs and sucking so hard that holes opened up in her pale flesh.

I saw the moment the shining hatred in her blue eyes went out.

I'd expected revenge to taste different. Better, maybe. For freedom to flood my pores. But my mother had taught me many things. As I finally turned my back on her, I understood one final lesson. Freedom is not something that can be given. Only taken. And I'd taken mine from her months ago.

Arran shifted back into his fae form. Lyrena stepped to my side. I took their hands, my mate and my friend, and stepped into the void.

✣ 21 ✣

EVANDER

There was nothing but the swirling blue and turquoise around them. The light that shimmered overhead, casting the world around him in sharp relief, was made for this place alone. Tiny motes of life, so small that he could not see what they were, shimmered in suspended animation. She would know. She knew every creature that lived in her kingdom, no matter how small or seemingly insignificant. If he asked, she'd go on for hours about the life she could feel just in this one corner of her world.

Their world, he reminded himself. He no longer belonged to that land of harsh red sand and elemental politicking. Here, he could be exactly what he wanted to be. What he *was*. Warrior. Protector. Consort. Husband.

He was all that and more. It was the most beautiful thing about this world she'd shown him—the ever-undulating ripples. He would never be stuck, never held to a single identity. This world moved. It changed with every wave, never the same from one moment to the next. For over a hundred years, he had tried to mold himself into what others wanted him to be. Only to discover this place—this female. To finally understand that he contained infinitely more than he'd ever been taught. He could be more than he'd ever imagined.

Here, in the depths of the sea.

But the world above would not leave them alone. And it was the worlds beyond, between, that had brought them together. Those same worlds made their demands now.

Evander turned in the water, dragging in a breath. The severweed wrapped around his torso allowed him to breathe indefinitely, giving his elemental lungs the ability to harvest what his body needed from the salty sea water rather than the air. Still, it had taken months for him to not notice the difference. Water was heavier, thicker, took more energy to breathe in and out. Less breaths were required, making the practical difference negligible. Maybe in another hundred years, breathing water would be as normal as breathing air.

It would take at least that long for him fully realize that the female swimming ahead of him was his.

She angled her body with the current, the soft blue-green of her skin catching the rays of sunlight that filtered down through the water. It reflected off of the amorite piercing in her navel and lingered in the sea glass bracelets and necklaces that adorned her wrists and throat. Evander picked up his pace to catch up. He could not protect her from this far away. But his wife was damned fast. Muscular though they were, his legs were no match for that tail of hers. His arm had regrown, but it was still not as strong as it had been before. *Damn Arran Earthborn.*

Three more lashes of her tail and she'd be at the surface. Evander had learned to measure her gait and how to match his. He clenched his jaw, kicked harder, faster, summoned every bit of speed and strength that his elemental fae heritage entitled him to—

She still broke through the water a half-second ahead of him.

She tossed back her head, spraying water across the crystalline surface of the Split Sea as she shook away the extra weight from her hair. Ancestors, she was just as beautiful above the surface as below. Her blue-black hair was already beginning to curl around her shoulders, free now of the water and speed that pulled it straight.

He knew if he reached out his leg, he'd find two of them in

place of the tail that had been there moments before. The gift of her kind, halfway between elemental and terrestrial. She could shift between tail and legs at will, changing the parts of herself that adapted to land or sea as easily as blinking.

Evander, meanwhile, had to cut away the severweed before he could take a breath of air.

As he dragged in that first breath, tucking away the severweed for future use, he tried to catch her hand. Only to find one of those legs he'd been imagining moments ago lifting out of the water, the graceful curve appearing just long enough to cause his abdomen to tighten in appreciation—and to splash him in the face with seawater.

Evander blinked through the droplets.

"A rather ignoble entrance for a queen," he said, catching her ankle in his grip.

He knew they had an audience. He did not care.

His wife grinned, her eyes flaring with a ring of desire when he lifted that ankle to his mouth and pressed a kiss to the insole of her foot.

"At least there was no earthquake this time," she said, twisting her leg away.

He let her go. The glow in her eyes ebbed away, and he knew she did not need to touch his face to know what he was thinking.

The earthquake was a portent—and not a good one. Only harm would come to them above the surface of the Split Sea. Evander was certain of that. But he could no more hold his wife back than he could stop the lapping of the waves on the shore.

Beneath the waves, she slipped her hand into his. But it was her gaze that held his attention. He followed it away from the open sea behind them to where the shore rose up, a swath of black sand that was both barrier and bridge between land and sea.

On it stood two males, both of whom Evander recognized.

The temperature dropped several degrees, a cold wind swirling into the space between them and the party waiting on the shore.

Below the surface of the water, Evander's cold elemental wind was muted. But here he was powerful. Here, he could protect her.

As if she could not protect herself.

"Stop it. Gooseflesh is unbecoming for a queen," she said, sending a little wave of water his way to enforce her point. She did not need to lift her foot to command the water.

Evander sighed heavily. "Mya—"

"What is the danger? If they have ill intentions, I will know it. If they try to hurt me, you will end them. Quite safe." She nodded sharply to punctuate her point.

"Nothing about this is safe," he growled. Though it was harder to sound menacing while treading water.

Of course, Mya made it look easy. He'd never tasted her blood, but he would not be surprised to find it laced with salt water.

"Nor is retreating back to the sea," she responded. "We've already discussed this. At length. I have made my decision." She did not wait for him to acquiesce—simply began kicking toward the beach.

It was perhaps the only part of his new life that Evander questioned. How had he managed to go from one domineering queen to another?

But the smile that Mya shot over her shoulder answered that question. The one he'd been foolish to even entertain.

The Queen of the Aquarian Fae may be a force unto herself, but she could not have been more different from her elemental counterpart, Veyka Pendragon. The counterpart who did not even know that she existed. Both the elementals and terrestrials had forgotten their water-dwelling sisters and brothers.

But the succubus was coming for them all.

22

VEYKA

I still hated camping.

But there was a certain romanticism to sleeping in Arran's arms beneath the night sky. It was bitterly cold in the terrestrial kingdom, though according to my mate this was a relatively mild winter. I burrowed into his side, letting his skin heat my own, careful not to move too much or the cock pressed against my stomach would become a demand I could not ignore.

I tried to gather as much of his heat into me as I could. I'd tended towards cold my entire life. Jumping between realms and expending ungodly amounts of power had not shifted that reality. Arran was forever warming my hands between his own. But tonight I did not want him awake. Not for this.

Despite the need to move surging through my veins, I forced myself to lay still as I counted off the time in my mind. When he'd been still for five full minutes, I finally eased myself out of his grip. Dressing in the tent without waking him would be impossible. I slid my feet into my boots, grabbed my clothing, and forced myself out into the night.

Ancestors' fucking hell, it was cold. The wall of night air slammed into me, sucking away the breath from my lungs and clawing at my extremities. For a second, I considered taking myself through the void to the Effren Valley just so I could get some Ancestors'-damned warmth. But it was night there was well, and still winter. There would not be any snow on the ground, but it would hardly be a reprieve.

And if I went back to Baylaur, I'd never be able to leave. Not knowing that the succubus held my city.

I tugged on my wool tunic—Arran's wool tunic, actually—my leather leggings, the knitted gloves Cyara had packed for me, then the heavy fur-lined cloak. Every movement was painfully slow in service of being silent. Now that I was outside, I risked waking Lyrena or Barkke.

Technically, Lyrena was awake. She was on watch.

But she'd seen me slip away before and I knew she would not raise a hue and cry now.

My eyes found her at the edge of the clearing, expecting her to meet my gaze and give me that knowing grin of hers. But she wasn't looking at me at all. Her head was tipped back, golden braid dangling behind her—

I almost forgot to stifle my gasp.

It was almost worth it.

The sky was wide awake.

I watched in awe as the colors danced. Bright green faded away to reveal the shining stars beneath, only to be replaced a second later by waves of purple and pink. I'd never seen a painter at work, but I could easily imagine how they might capture this, dragging two paintbrushes in tandem across the sky in a sinuous wave that felt almost sexual.

Not quite sexual. Primal. The bright lights in the sky spoke to something that lived deep inside of my soul. An understanding that I was more keenly aware of than perhaps anyone else living—the infinite smallness of the world in which I stood. This realm was but one of many. And even though I'd been into the void more times than I could count, had seen the spinning fabric of the world with my own eyes and sensed the endless realms, it was in that moment that I truly felt humbled. *This* was magic.

Arran had spoken of the lights that danced across the sky north of the Spine, but I had not comprehended what he meant. This was beyond description.

As I watched, the ethereal green lines fractured, multiplying until there were a half dozen trails of green. The colors merged and danced upward, green giving way to turquoise then violet and finally a vibrant rose that dissolved into the stars themselves.

I could have watched it for hours. What would it feel like to be surrounded by those colors? I'd never tried to walk upon a cloud, but suddenly the idea of dancing among that brilliant midnight rainbow felt as essential as my next breath.

My life was too measured now to miss it.

I could not forget my reason for sneaking away from Arran. But I could delay it for a few minutes.

I threw myself into the void and emerged among the stars.

23

CYARA

"Can you make animals out of fire like Lyrena?" Maisri asked, throwing a hand out in the direction of the fire that burned steadily at the center of their small camp.

Percival did not look up from the leather strip he was carefully wrapping around the hilt of a new dagger. "No."

Maisri bounced on her toes and flung her arm in the opposite direction. "What about that tree. Right there. Can you make it— do something?"

Percival sighed. "No."

She shoved her hand under his nose, between his face and his task, a tiny snowdrop flower tripling in size within her palm in the space of a breath.

"Flowers?"

Percival's throat bobbed. "No."

Maisri flung the snowdrop over her shoulder, landing it squarely in the flames of the campfire with impressive aim, considering the weight of the sigh and the intensity of her whining. "What *can* you do?" she demanded.

Percival lifted a hand to his temple, the blade abandoned at his side. "We—"

"I thought you were part witch!" the child cried. She threw herself down onto the log that Osheen had dragged up for makeshift seating, not caring or not noticing that the force of her seat had thrown Percival's tools to the ground. "Witches can do *terrible* things! Dangerous things! That's why the Ancestors locked them away after the Great War—"

"Maisri." Osheen's voice brought her up short. Cyara suppressed a smile at the roughness of it. He sounded like he might have been ordering around a soldier rather than a daisy fae child. "I thought you were managing the laundry."

"Yes," she said slowly, her head rotating to where her guardian had appeared at the edge of the clearing.

"Then why is Diana down there at the creek, and you are up here warming that log with your bottom?"

Maisri shot to her feet as if the aforementioned bottom burned.

Osheen was halfway to the fireside. Just enough time for Maisri to arch her dark brows in Percival's direction. "Later. Think of something. *Anything.*" Then she scampered down the hill, leaving a trail of tiny snowdrops sprouting up through the permafrost in her wake.

Percival stared after her, his hand scrubbing away the mop of tangled black hair that had fallen forward over his brow.

"I traveled with you for weeks. I thought she'd have given up by now," he said, not directing his words at either Cyara or Osheen specifically.

"Children are more tenacious than adults," Cyara said, rising from her seat on the other side of the fire. She'd finished grinding the spices for their evening meal.

"And twice as irritating," Osheen added, dropping a heavily feathered bird beside the fire.

Cyara lifted a brow in his direction. She'd have given anything for a court of mischievous children rather than conniving elementals. "That is a matter of opinion."

Osheen shrugged. "Well, now you know mine."

"And mine," Percival said faintly. "I'm going to collect fire-wood." And then over his shoulder— "Don't tell her where I've gone."

"No promises," Osheen said under his breath as he dropped down to the ground along with the bird. He hadn't bothered with a field dressing; that told Cyara he hadn't had to go far from camp in order to catch it. Good to know that the surrounding land was plentiful. And birds were always the easiest to catch.

"At least he's more helpful this time," Cyara observed as Percival disappeared beyond the tree line.

There was a marked difference between the sullen man from their first journey through the human realm and the one accompanying them now. He was still plenty prickly; but without Veyka to needle him constantly, he was at least polite. Veyka had not taken them far—just through a rift of her own making, from the edge of Eilean Gayl's lake to its less auspicious counterpart in the human realm.

They would make the remainder of the journey the slow way—on foot.

For now, at least. Cyara buried that thought deep before even a trace of it could show upon her face.

"And she's only cried once." Osheen nodded to where Diana kneeled at the edge of the creek, wringing out fabric. He turned back to his task—preparing the bird to be cooked—without looking at Cyara. "Why are they here at all?"

She was not surprised by the question, nor that it had taken him multiple days of travel to ask it. Like her, Osheen watched first and asked later. He was observant, but not as used to the day-to-day subterfuge that life in the elemental court demanded. That would be one of her few advantages when the time came.

"Percival studied the Sacred Trinity during his time at Avalon. He is our best hope of finding the grail. And where he goes, Diana goes," Cyara said. With a flick of her wrist, already aching, she banked the flames down to the coals required for cooking.

"Our first priority is to secure the alliance of the Faeries of the

Fen," Osheen said, working easily in tandem with her. "I'd think those two would be more of a hindrance than a help."

"Percival has been there before," Cyara reminded him. "Besides, all we really need is Maisri."

Osheen paused to quirk a brow.

Cyara bit back her sharp laugh, letting out a softer version in its place. For all his watchfulness, Osheen had missed one of the most important details from their time with the Faeries of the Fen. His paternal concerns clouding his observations, most likely. Cyara could admit freely that where her heart was involved, she struggled to be an objective observer.

But she was not even pretending to be objective anymore.

She had one goal on this journey—and it was not to secure allies.

Cyara's voice was smooth and unruffled as her eyes drifted down the hill to where Maisri was busy making Diana laugh. "She made fast friends with the faerie children. Irritating though they might be, children *are* more tenacious than adults. If anyone is going to wear down the parents, it will be the children. That is universal— human, fae, faerie. Children are our hope for a better future. Perhaps even a future where they do not have to hide in caves."

Osheen followed her gaze. As they watched, Maisri grew comically large snowdrops up from the ground, big enough for them to drape the wet laundry over to dry.

Maisri would convince the faeries. Cyara entertained no doubts. The daisy fae was irresistible.

"Will you question them about the Sacred Trinity?"

She darted a glance at Osheen from beneath her lashes, under the guise of returning to the fire, where she tied a three-footed spit into place over the coals. She surreptitiously searched his face for any sign that he suspected her intentions. He was better at dissembling than most terrestrials; but what he'd implied...

But his face remained focused on his task. A single wrinkle indented between his dark brown brows; the tip of his tongue slipped out from between his lips. Her gaze lingered too long there on those lips. The ones whose shape she'd already memorized. Imagined. Dreamed of.

Ancestors. He still awaited an answer.

She rocked back on her heels. "I will not pass over any opportunity to find the grail." Careful. She had to be so careful.

Powerful flora-gifted terrestrial that he was, Osheen could not contain the harpy. But Cyara needed Percival's help as well, and he was a liability. She could not trust her harpy not to harm him or Diana.

But Osheen did not push her further. He hung the trussed-up bird from the tripod she'd created and walked down to the creek to wash his hands. Leaving Cyara alone.

Alone was better, she told herself. If Osheen crossed that bridge between them, it would make what she had to do even harder.

❦ 24 ❦

GUINEVERE

She'd stared at the map for so long, the shorelines and mountains had become indistinguishable from one another. The words blurred together, the tiny characters fracturing and then fading. The feeling was too familiar.

She sat curled in the wingback chair, all the lights in the palace doused except for the one candle at her side. Reading, again. If she read it enough times, she'd find out what was so damned important it had been worth dying for... he'd only left the safety of the library to find her, to share this text with her... it had to be important...

Gwen snapped back to the present, her spine crackling as she jerked upright. Spilt tea marred the southeastern corner of the map, obscuring the entrance to Wolf Bay. It was too far away to figure into any of her calculations anyway. She pressed her palm into her eye, trying to rub away the exhaustion.

Movement flickered in her periphery. Gwen reached for the knife she'd left on the table by rote, even though she doubted that any of the humans lodged in the house would even imagine harming her. They were all too busy being scared shitless.

"I beg your pardon," Sylva said from the doorway. Her thin night rail billowed around her, catching the breeze from the window Gwen had left open. The mug in her hand steamed with freshly brewed tea. She arched one gray eyebrow at Gwen. "The solar is usually deserted at this hour."

The house was packed to bursting with humans whose homes had been destroyed in the earthquake. Any structure still standing had been converted to housing, the business of shops and eateries happening around stowed bedrolls and piles of salvaged belongings.

The fae refugee camp was even worse.

As a village elder, Sylva had been among the first to offer her home. Gwen had accepted a bed in the pantry at the back of Sylva's kitchen.

She'd considered lodging at the elemental camp. But while she'd become a familiar presence among the elemental courtiers who'd resided in the goldstone palace, to the commoners she was a strange, polarizing figure. A terrestrial—the one who had been in command of their city when it fell to the succubus.

It was all torture. She might as well be close to Sylva so she could seek her counsel in bringing the humans together.

Elora had left earlier in the day, her small band of elemental soldiers at her back. There were no more communication crystals to pass around. She would either return through the rift with the remains of the elemental army or she would disappear into the dunes along with their hopes.

Gwen had barely seen Sylva. The woman had been busy organizing space for the elementals, arranging food to be shared, and then eventually distributing the limited store of amorite that Veyka had promised in return for giving her subjects refuge.

The elderly woman looked tired, the age lines around her eyes carved even deeper than usual. But she did not retreat. She took her tea and circled the table where Gwen had spread the map, coming to stand beside her.

"I did not mean to wake you," Gwen said. Though if she'd thought of it, she might have, instead of puzzling over this alone.

She constantly had to remind herself that humans exhausted easier and needed more time to recuperate. Sylva was running the village essentially on her own, for all the help that the two remaining members of her Council of Elders seemed to provide.

"The older I get, the less sleep I need." Sylva sipped her steaming tea. "By the time I'm as old as you, I'll have plenty of time for it." Because she'd be dead, her life snuffed out by her mortal lifespan. If the succubus did not come for her first.

Sylva chuckled over her mug.

Gwen did not.

"You must have memorized that map by now." The woman's gray brows arched in question.

"Yes." Gwen nodded. "But memorizing it is not helpful without context." She'd learned that much from Parys' book, *The Travelers*.

Flashes of the nightmare clawed at the edge of her mind. Gwen pushed them back resolutely. They already haunted her in sleep. She could not allow them to find purchase in waking as well.

Sylva matched her nod. "Then it is a good thing I am here."

Gwen could not concern herself with the woman's wellbeing. If she insisted on spending her only free hours consulting instead of sleeping, then so be it. She turned her attention back to the map, forcing her eyes to refocus through sheer power of will. "There are six human villages within range, that fae messengers could reasonably reach and return in time."

"I wasn't aware there was a deadline."

"Every minute is borrowed." Gwen had already done the calculations, but she verbalized them anyway for the human's sake. "It will take the Queen and King a week to reach Cayltay. Perhaps another week to muster the terrestrial army and get it moving. Add another week for things to go awry. Any longer than that and I expect this thing will start talking to me." She motioned to the white communication crystal, acting as a paperweight to hold down the curling edge of the map.

"So, whoever we seek to rally, we must reach them, convince them, and assemble them within three weeks' time," Sylva summarized.

"Assemble them here," Gwen clarified. "If what Arran said is true and the succubus are attracted to Veyka, then this is where she will end up."

The woman's dark gray brow furrowed. "Why here?"

"Baylaur is her home," Gwen said simply.

Veyka's memories of the goldstone palace and the city below might be mixed; the Ancestors' knew that Gwen's feelings about her own home in Wolf Bay were complex. But it was the place that had made her. No matter how far she went, she'd always feel drawn back to where it had all begun. And in her warrior's gut, Gwen knew that the same was true for Veyka.

She cleared her throat. "It also makes sense from a tactical perspective. The queen's ability to open portal rifts is new. If it fails, or is exhausted, we need to have our forces assembled near an existing rift so that we can move freely between realms and meet the succubus on whichever battlefield will end this war."

This would not be a war of endless battles. Gwen had fought alongside Arran in wars like that, waged on distant continents for gold and guts and glory. The succubus would not pause to regroup; they had no need. Their strategy would be to overwhelm. They gained nothing from surrender. If every battle must be fought until the absolute destruction of the enemy, there would not be many battles at all.

Sylva tugged a stool over to the edge of the table, settling herself as she examined the map over the rim of her steaming cup of tea. Several minutes of silence passed while she considered. Gwen held her silence. She'd learned patience early in her quest for queenship.

"Wraithwood, Emberhaven, and Thornbriar are all close enough that you could send a human envoy along with your fae representative. It will make the alliance easier to swallow. The other three are too far for anyone but your soldiers."

Gwen picked the villages out on the map easily, considering the damn thing was burned into her brain. "Then we concentrate our energy on those three."

"Ferndale is the largest." Sylva pointed to the city on the far western coast of the continent. "They are the closest thing the human realm has to a city—and proud of it. They will expect to be treated with due respect and dignity."

A larger village meant more soldiers.

It was also the farthest.

"I can't waste an entire delegation to appease them in the hope they will join us. One fae warrior is worth at least twenty humans when facing the succubus in battle. Maybe more."

Sylva did not argue. She took another sip of her tea.

Gwen mulled it over in her mind again. No, she would not waste valuable fae warriors on a fruitless mission. Her stomach twisted, but she held firm. Arran and Veyka had left her in charge once, and she'd lost Parys and Baylaur.

She would not fail them again.

"A fae messenger will have to be enough. They will accept our invitation, or they will die."

25

ARRAN

Veyka could have brought us right into the middle of Cayltay. As much as I would have enjoyed the expressions of shock and watching Veyka put down anyone stupid enough to challenge her, it was tactically unsound. I wanted to know the disposition of the troops in the war camp on the other side of Wolf Bay before walking into the fortress. They were mine to command; had been for the better part of three hundred years, even before I'd been crowned High King of Annwyn. But I had not walked among them in months.

Veyka brought us to the foot of the mountains south of the Spine and we made the rest of the journey on foot. I could tell that it pained her to go so slowly, when she could have opened a portal rift with a flick of her wrist. But that was my other reservation.

She was spending more and more time in the void. A few months ago, I'd have been elated to see her embracing her power. But the carelessness with which she expended it nagged at me. She acted like a female with nothing left to lose.

Even with the possibility of the grail and the power of uniting the Sacred Trinity, I could tell that her belief had not shifted. Veyka still believed that the cost of banishing the succubus would be her life. The hope that I'd felt flare within her when Merlin spoke had dwindled. Or she'd snuffed it herself. Not willing to believe. To hope.

I could hope enough for the both of us.

After me, Cyara was the other person who loved Veyka the most. She was clever and observant and resourceful. If anyone could find the grail, it would be her.

But until Cyara returned, I had my own role to play. Securing the terrestrial troops, arming them with amorite, and holding off the succubus long enough to give Veyka a chance at life.

I'd do it all.

"Stop thinking so loudly," Veyka said aloud, nudging an elbow into my side.

I did not retaliate. We were supposed to be laying still, spread flat on our bellies on the edge of a mountain looking down on the war camps below. Overhead, airborne terrestrial shifters soared through the air. If we moved too much, even the tree that I'd shifted to give us cover would not be enough to hide us.

Still, I cocked my head in her direction. If she'd truly been able to hear my thoughts, she would not be smiling that wicked smile of hers.

"Hear something you liked?"

Her smile deepened at the corners.

"Are they always like this?" Barkke said from Veyka's other side.

"Yes," Isolde and Lyrena said in unison.

"Inconsiderate," Barkke muttered, shifting his midsection just enough to be awkward.

Except it made Veyka laugh. That alone kept me from tearing into him. My mate deserved every bit of laughter she could find.

We turned our eyes back down to the army, each of us making our own calculations. Isolde was surely marking out where the medical tents were; Lyrena probably wondering how many terrestrials she could take out with her fire power. But Veyka... I was tempted to slide along the bond between us and see if I could deduce where her mind had gone.

"I count twelve thousand," Barkke said, revealing the direction of his own thoughts.

Veyka's swallow was audible. "We don't have enough amorite for every male in that army."

"Not to pierce their ears or to arm them," Barkke agreed.

That was what she weighed—the worth of their souls versus their killing strength. And I was about to make the calculation harder.

"There are twice as many," I said, shifting closer to my mate until her rounded hip met the hard muscles of my thigh. "The arrangement is meant to be deceptive. There are more men in those tents than you realize. They move in and out rotations to obscure their numbers. And over that hill." I nodded to the horizon. "Another three thousand are lodged in the sea caves along the eastern edge of the bay."

"A lot of subterfuge within your own base camp," Lyrena noted. She did not bother to conceal the admiration in her voice. She'd never commanded troops in battle, but I could feel the fire inside of her, the desire. The warrior's need to test herself against yet another challenge.

"Most battles are won or lost before either side steps foot on the battlefield." I'd set up this camp. I'd modified it over the decades, changing tactics and updating the layout. I'd made mistakes and learned from them.

Veyka cleared her throat softly. "And this one? If this army faced the succubus today? What would happen?"

My eyes swept over the army again, assessing battle readiness, weapons reserves, patrols—every tiny intricacy. It still wasn't enough.

"We don't know how the succubus organize, but the legacy of the Great War tells us they do eventually create a mass that can be faced in battle. Do you remember the carvings in the water gardens?"

I felt Veyka's nod.

"The fae forces were depicted in organized formations, as you'd expect. What we believed to be humans—actually the succubus—were haphazard," I explained. "Facing them will be different than any other foe I or anyone living has encountered."

Lyrena shifted subtly on my other side. Isolde's claws clicked together faintly. Barkke muttered a curse under his breath.

Veyka pulled her elbows under herself and turned away from the army camp below. To face me. "You did not answer my question."

"I don't know." We'd made vows of truth between us. I would not break them now.

Veyka held my gaze, her blue eyes dull and flat. "Have you seen what you need?"

"Yes."

"Then let's go."

26

VEYKA

The fortress of Cayltay was damn depressing.

Unlike Baylaur, with the goldstone palace perched on the mountainside and the city sprawling across the valley beneath it, there were no buildings or residences radiating out from the high stone walls. There was inhospitable marshland and trees whose branches did not start until a hundred feet in the air, making them impossible to scale.

The fortress itself was a mess of gray stone, with a dizzying array of turrets and crenellations that seemed to make no sense to an outside observer. Maybe that was the point—to disorient any foe trying to decide where to concentrate their attack. I counted at least seven towers rising above the tangle of stone, every one a different height. The tallest of them rose until its spire disappeared entirely into the fog that seemed to cling to the place.

It was not the sort of place that welcomed visitors.

"What is the best way in?" I asked, tilting my head to consider. Of course, there was my way. But Arran had already vetoed that.

"There is only one," Arran said grimly. He took the first steps into the marshland and the rest of us followed.

"What about the lake? Surely there is a port of some kind,"

Lyrena asked, falling into step off my shoulder, on the opposite side as Arran. I rolled my eyes, even though no one was paying me any kind of attention.

Arran had his battle axe already in hand. "It would be a point of weakness. There is only one way into Cayltay. And two ways out."

I opened my mouth to say something sarcastic, but when Barkke beat me to it, there was no mirth in his voice.

"The way you came in, or death," he said.

Barkke had never been south of the Spine, by both his and Arran's accounts. But he knew the legends of Cayltay. They must be pervasive in the terrestrial kingdom—and carefully concealed from elementals.

"And you terrestrials think we've got a flair for the dramatic," Lyrena laughed. Like Arran, she had her weapon in hand. In her other, flames danced. "What about magic?"

"Stone doesn't burn, Lyrena," I said, flashing a grin over my shoulder.

"But flesh does," she winked back.

Arran's beast growled at our insolence. "The wards here are different than the ones on the goldstone palace. Because the royal line does not pass through families, it repels certain types of magic instead. No vines can climb the walls."

"And let me guess—no airy terraces that could be infiltrated by shifters?" I said, turning my saccharine smile in his direction and ignoring the fact that my boots were now wet with stagnant marsh water.

He'd once complained about the balconies of the goldstone palace. Coming from a place like this, I could begin to understand how he'd found the elemental palace deficient by comparison. At least in terms of defensibility. This place would win no accolades for beauty.

"You want to linger outside in this?" As he said it, he caught my hands between his. I'd shucked my gloves so they wouldn't be in the way if I wanted to grab my weapons. As we walked, he lifted one hand to his mouth, cupped between his larger ones, and blew several long puffs of hot air. When he was satisfied that one hand was warm, he changed it for the other.

A wasted effort in cold like this. But I did not stop him.

Nor did I pull my hand away when we reached the gate.

For a fortress so imposing, the gate was anything but—wooden, with metal posts joining the crossbeams. I could see right through to the other side, where a crowded inner bailey was already filled with curious onlookers. But to do so, I had to look over the shoulder of the guard standing in the dead-center of the gate.

"One guard? Arrogant," I said, flipping a dagger in my hand to stem the nervous energy.

I wasn't afraid of the terrestrials. I was afraid *for* them. If they were as obstinate as those north of the Spine had been, then many more would die. Unnecessarily.

Arran kept his eyes pinned to the singular figure before us.

"The Dolorous Guard," he said. "You must kill the guard on duty in order to be admitted to the fortress."

I caught the dagger in my palm. "Barbaric. I like it."

"I've always wanted to try my hand against the Dolorous Guard," Barkke said, cracking his jaw and swinging his mace.

"Any rules? Weapons, magic?" Lyrena asked. Her eyes already had that feral glint that meant blood, and she'd flicked her braid back over her shoulder.

Arran was not the type to roll his eyes. But he did sigh. "Terrestrials train their entire lives for the honor of joining the Dolorous Guard. Hundreds of years. Some serve longer than a thousand."

My smile matched Lyrena's. "Even better."

I felt the flash of desire shoot through Arran—*oh, that wicked smile of mine really did do things to him*—but he did not act on it. Instead, he stepped ahead of all three of us, battle axe ready.

"I've done this dozens of times over the last three centuries."

"Bragging or reminding us you're an old male?" I said, stepping to my place at his side. "I'll do it."

His beast rewarded me with a growl that had me pressing my thighs together. He coveted my wicked smiles. I reveled in the possessiveness of his beast. The male stared down at me, an argument forming in his onyx eyes.

I cut it off.

"This tattoo might symbolize something north of the Spine. But here? They won't believe I've earned it."

I'd been thinking about it constantly as we made our way south. The Terrestrial Kingdom of the Fae had accepted an elemental ruler for seven thousand years, but as a figurehead. The High King and Queen ruled from Baylaur; the terrestrial heir, be it queen or king depending on the generation, might occasionally travel back here to Cayltay every few hundred years. But I was asking for something different—demanding it. I would walk through that deceptively simple gate as Arran's equal, bearing the mark of a terrestrial. A Talisman was sacred. The terrestrials of Eilean Gayl had not bestowed it upon me lightly. But I also knew that some here in Cayltay would see it as a rallying cry—and not to join our cause against the succubus.

Not that there should be any debate about joining. These were our troops to command.

Fucking politics.

I squeezed Arran's hand harder where it was still hooked around mine. I wanted to reach for his face, to kiss him—fuck it. I deserved all the kisses I could get.

I molded my body against his, claiming his mouth for every onlooker to see. I was not just the Queen of the Elemental Fae. I was Arran Earthborn's mate. This place had made him hard, these people had hurt him and his mother, Elayne. But now he belonged to me, and soon they would learn the full meaning of that.

By the time I lowered my feet to the ground, Arran was hard against me and I knew I'd won even before I said— "Let me show them."

The ring of black fire around his pupils gave me his answer.

"Remember, you only need to kill the one."

I flicked my other dagger into my palm. "What fun is that?"

✣ 27 ✣

ARRAN

The Dolorous Guard waited for Veyka, still and silent. Anyone who approached understood the cost of entry. If they did not, they'd learn quickly.

Veyka was unhurried as well. In her left hand, she held one dagger with lethal casualness. In her right, she flicked the other blade over hilt. Anyone watching would assume that the left was her weaker hand, based on the movements alone. But it was a trick, I knew. One I'd seen her use against many opponents. She was just as good with either hand. And good was a dangerous understatement.

The walls of the fortress were designed to hide the numbers of those within, just like the army camp across the bay. But I'd stood on those battlements enough times to know that by now, news of our approach had spread. There were surely thousands of eyes on Veyka.

Above my head, a buzzard circled the gate tower before perching on the edge. Crows cawed. Real or shifter, even the animals watched as Veyka disappeared.

And reappeared an inch in front of the Dolorous Guard.

Watching her took my breath away. She did not bother to slip in and out of the void after that first blow. Yet I knew that there were those questioning if she did, trying to make sense of how she could be so incredibly fast.

Years of torture and training.

She'd honed herself into a weapon as formidable as any in Annwyn. Even me.

The Dolorous Guard kept up, but only just. He had yet to land a blow or to make an offensive parry. Every swipe of his massive greatsword was defensive. Veyka danced in and out of range, forcing him to extend himself and leave his body exposed. Then on the next turn, his arm. She slashed into his face, then his arm. I heard the reverberating crack of bone. But she did not go for the kill, even when she knocked his helmet free and exposed his neck.

She was toying with him.

She could have landed her killing blow in the first second she appeared from the void. Ripped off his helmet, slit his throat, and been done with it.

But this... it was not just for the show. Veyka did it because she enjoyed it.

My wolf howled his appreciation inside of me. Ancestors, as if I wasn't already hard for her.

Is that for me? Veyka's sinuous voice slid into my mind.

I shifted my weight on the marshy ground. *You know it is.*

She did not even break stride, slashing across the Dolorous Guard's chest with a clever blow that used the weight of his own armor to knock the air from his lungs. *Such a needy beast. Does watching bloodshed make you wild?*

Only when it involves you.

I was too far away to hear her laugh, but I felt the rumbling of barbed joy as it rose inside of her. She spun away from a blow, that wicked smile on her face. *Have they realized it yet?*

That you could have killed him ten minutes ago? Her only response was to keep fighting. *Even terrestrials are clever enough to figure it out.*

Good. Because I'm hungry. Veyka lunged forward, plunging a dagger low in the Dolorous Guard's belly. He stumbled, she forced him to his knees. She crossed her daggers at his throat, and a second later his head hit the marshy ground with a muted *thud*.

The response was resounding silence.

Then, as Veyka wiped the thick scarlet blood from her blades on the trousers of the downed body, a creak echoed across the marsh and up into the forest beyond. Veyka rose to stand in time with the gate.

She sheathed her blades and shot me a look. "Come and show me around, Brutal Prince."

Lyrena and Barkke flanked us on either side. Isolde sheltered directly behind Veyka, on her orders. Of the five of us, Isolde was the most defenseless. I'd seen her wield those wicked claws, but she was a healer, not a warrior. And here she would be a fascinating oddity. Already I marked the gasped inhales as the crowd of terrestrials parted to make way for our party.

Expressions ranging from awe to outright scorn appeared on the faces of the terrestrials around us. My kind did not bother to hide their emotions, not in the practiced way the elementals did. We sneered at bloodlines and nobility. All that mattered in the terrestrial court was strength. Veyka had been right to insist she fight the Dolorous Guard.

For all that I was the supposed strategist, commander of armies, my mate was learning. Fast.

My compatriots, however, were slow to learn.

Every eye was upon us. There could be no doubt who we were.

But not a single knee bent.

Not a word of reverence was uttered.

Veyka's face was impassive.

But my rage was alive.

The outer walls of the fortress were enchanted to keep outside vines and branches from penetrating. But inside, ancient trees grew within the bailey, their tops reaching up to join the worn gray towers. Ivy coated the walls. A flora-gifted terrestrial's playground. And I was the strongest terrestrial in millennia.

If they noticed the trees bending to my will or were too transfixed by the arrival of their king and queen, I did not care. There was no escaping the vines that crawled along the ground or the branches that reached across the battlements. I did not have to lift a hand to command my power. The terrestrial flora bowed to me. And every single one of the terrestrials would bow to my mate.

"Bow," my beast growled.

It was not a warning, nor a request.

A thousand sets of knees crashed down onto the stone and dirt. I forced every single terrestrial watching to the ground—where they belonged, kneeling before their queen.

Veyka watched, her face still unreadable. A few of the terrestrials wobbled, grabbing at each other to keep themselves upright. Veyka laughed when one fell face-first against the flagstones. Dagger in hand, she approached the female nearest to her. She dragged a fingernail along the back of the female's exposed neck.

"Should I slit a few throats to drive the point home?" Veyka asked, her voice bored.

"As you wish, my queen." I made sure that every terrestrial, subjugated down to their knees, heard my words.

They were no longer the recipients of my protection, the benefactors of my generation-shattering magic. Veyka was. And it was time they all knew it.

Veyka stepped back from the female. She opened her mouth to say something else, but another sound echoed across the inner bailey. A single staircase rose along the far wall, ragged stones jutting out of the wall itself. At the top, a door groaned as it opened.

A willowy female appeared at the top of the staircase, her dark skin and darker hair framed by the stone archway behind her. She wore a deep sapphire gown, simple in the way favored by terrestrials, cut close to her body except for the slit that ran to her hip, revealing the matching dark blue leather leggings beneath—and the dagger strapped to her slender thigh.

Recognition. Knowing. Supreme confidence edged her motions as she tossed her halo of tight black curls over her shoulders. Her eyes marked Veyka, but it was me she addressed.

"Welcome home, Arran Earthborn."

28

VEYKA

"Where are you taking us?" Lyrena asked, raising her voice to be heard from near the back of our entourage.

The female had introduced herself as Morgause. And since the requisite 'Your Majesty's' were completed, she'd spent too much time looking at my mate. I'd have to be blind to miss the glowing umber ring in her brown eyes.

"To the Dyad," Morgause answered, pausing on the next landing until Arran was at her side. Then she immediately began to move again, up the narrow stairway. It was only just wide enough for them to walk abreast. But she made no move to step ahead.

Covet him all you like. He's mine.

Arran's eyes were everywhere but on me, assessing threats and rightfully assuming I could take care of myself.

"The Dyad are the stewards of Cayltay," Morgause explained. "The most powerful flora-gifted terrestrial and most powerful fauna-gifted terrestrial form the Dyad that rules the city."

"And here I thought I'd married the most powerful flora and fauna gifted terrestrial in the kingdom." As I spoke, my thumb traced over the ring on my finger. Elayne's ring. Then Arran's. Now mine.

I hadn't been taught about the inner workings of the terrestrial kingdom. Those lessons were saved for Arthur. But Arran and Barkke, and before them, Elayne, had given me a slapdash course in how things ran here in Cayltay.

Though they'd all left out the Dolorous Guard. What other details had they missed? And what nasty surprises awaited because they had?

Arran paused on the stairs. "I've never sought a place with the Dyad. I prefer actions to words. Battlefields to politicking."

Morgause stopped a step later. She waited for him to join her. He waited for me. Let me pass him. Then took up his place a half step behind, one hand on the small of my back.

Ancestors, I fucking loved him.

Our guide's smile was pinched. I enjoyed the sight.

"Come now, Arran. There is plenty of blood to be shed on the way to the Dyad's thrones," she said.

She did not wait for me to join her on the next stair.

Nor did I move from mine. "Kings and queens have thrones."

Do I need to kill her as well? I asked Arran's beast.

"Seats," she amended. But Morgause's gaze did not linger on me. It slid over my shoulder and settled on Arran, standing of a height with me a stair below.

She could not have disguised the glow of desire in her eyes if she'd tried. The curse of our passionate race afflicted the terrestrials and elementals indiscriminately.

Arran's voice did not radiate into my mind.

Oh.

Oh.

This female did not just *want* my husband. She'd *had* him before.

Do not kill her yet, Arran's beast growled into my mind.

Apparently, I did not make my point clear when I kissed you outside of the fortress. I was not jealous. Jealousy implied some sort of fear of losing, of competition. I'd watched Morgause's bony ass all the way up the first two flights of stairs into the dark heart of Cayltay. I'd felt Arran's love for me through the bond before I could recognize my own.

Jealous was the wrong word.

Pity—no, not quite. She was much too smug to pity.

Anger, certainly. Maybe even rage. Arran was *mine*. Any being, elemental or terrestrial, who thought to challenge that deserved to die.

The pressure of Arran's hand on my waist increased, nudging me up the stairs.

Morgause resumed her climb. Up and up and up. We had to be going to the highest tower, the one whose tip was hidden by the clouds from the ground outside the fortress. One of the Dyad was probably a bird shifter who liked to roost.

I was laughing at my own joke as Arran's dark rumble continued to explain terrestrial governance, more for Lyrena and Isolde's benefit than mine. "They kill their way to the top. The last one of each type standing is granted a seat on the Dyad."

Isolde was quiet, but Lyrena, sword still out, questioned. "And they keep their seat until..."

"Someone challenges them for it and wins," Arran answered.

"It sounds delightfully chaotic."

I knew if I turned around, I'd see Lyrena's gold tooth glinting through a massive grin. She'd be drinking with the terrestrials in the kitchens of Cayltay before the week was out. Fortress or no, my golden knight could charm—and disarm—anyone.

Just like the gate into the massive fortress, the door to the Dyad's meeting chamber was unremarkable. Plain wood. No engravings. No jewels. Not even the tasteful tapestries and gold gilt frames that Lady Elayne used to decorate Eilean Gayl. The only thing that mattered in Cayltay was power and strength. The stark appearance, inside and out, was a reminder of that.

The chamber inside was equally bare. But for the first time since entering Cayltay, the austerity worked to enhance the impact of the space. The walls were not made of stone, but glass, rising up in straight, triangular planes to where they met in a pointed dome high above our heads. Outside the windows, clouds encircled the tower in a swath of white.

In the center of the room stood a round table—less grand than my own, made of wood rather than stone—several matched wooden chairs, and two wooden thrones. Like everything else, they were plain, their only decoration the sheer size of them. And the fact that there was no other furniture in the room.

Seats. Morgause had the right of it the first time. The Dyad imagined themselves kings and queens in their own kingdom.

Maybe I'd have Lyrena burn the thrones before we left Cayltay as a reminder.

Neither throne was occupied. But a massive male stood beside them, his yellow gold eyes marking every one of us as we passed through the door. He was shorter than Arran, but wider. Despite the cold, he wore a sleeveless leather tunic that left his massive biceps, nearly the size of one of my thighs, bare except for the weapons strapped to them.

He was the only occupant of the room. Which meant—

"I am the flora-gifted half of the Dyad," Morgause said. She moved over the stone floor like liquid, her dark blue gown shifting around her. Unlike most of the terrestrial females, she'd opted for heavy silk and velvet instead of wool.

She'd been building to this since the moment she appeared in the inner bailey. Arran made no sound of surprise; nor did Lyrena or Barkke. They'd both likely suspected as much, though each for their own reasons. Lyrena was an elemental. Reading between the lines was beaten into her from birth. Despite having never traveled to Cayltay himself, Barkke was a terrestrial. Even as removed as Eilean Gayl was, they surely received news about major changes in government officials.

Only Isolde made a little mewl of displeasure. Despite her gentle healing magic, the faerie could be fierce when provoked. And she recognized the game as well as the rest of us. Clearly, she did not approve.

My instincts told me that this female did not command vines

the way my mate did. Her gifts would be subtler. Poisonous, perhaps. There were many ways to kill and not all of them were loud and demonstrative.

I wondered if Isolde sensed that as well. She was an unmatched healer, preserving life as much a part of her identity as the white braids that dangled around her shoulders or the porcelain-tipped claws she clicked together in displeasure. The magic of the Faeries of the Fen was ancient, not governed by the rules of elemental and terrestrial fae heritage. It was entirely possible that she sensed something about Morgause that the rest of us did not.

But there would be no private conversations in the glass tower we'd been led into.

Morgause dismissed Isolde and the rest of us, focusing her attention on Arran. Ancestors, she was *obsessed* with him.

She gestured to the massive male at her side, though stopped short of actually touching him. "You recall my husband, Orcadion?"

Arran lifted one dark brow. "No wonder you've chosen the Cloud Tower for your meeting chamber." Then to me, "Orcadion is an eagle shifter."

And a ruthless killer, Arran added just to me. *He has never been defeated in combat.*

Then he's never faced you.

Arran's beast answered my observation with a growl of approval.

I wished I'd said my earlier jest aloud. But I had another observation ready in lieu of a greeting. "We have eagles in the Effren Valley. They are scavengers."

Morgause narrowed her eyes on me. Which meant they were off of Arran. *Good.* "Here they are creatures of opportunity."

"We are not here to debate particulars. I am taking command of the terrestrial army and preparing them to fight the succubus. Veyka will oversee the distribution of amorite. As of now, it is the only weapon we know of that can slay a succubus and prevent it from stealing into a male's mind," Arran said, severing our staring contest.

He said he disliked political maneuvering, but he was good at it.

It was not so different from commanding bloodthirsty troops, except that the conflicts were with words. I rolled my shoulders, the weight of Excalibur resettling between my shoulder blades. Maybe not *only* words.

Morgause sank down onto her throne, bringing her quietly hulking husband down with her. She ran an idle finger along the wooden arm. "Yes, we've heard about your succubus."

"Heard," I repeated. "You've been unscathed. No attacks." I did not form them as questions, and I modulated how much of my surprise I allowed to show.

Morgause shrugged her slim shoulders. "We have maintained control."

She did not question the succubus' existence or ask for an explanation of what a succubus attack meant. She was posturing. "An illusion of control," I scoffed.

Morgause folded her hands in her lap. "So often, it is only the illusion that matters."

My kingdom was falling apart, my people dying and murdering each other while their souls leaked from their bodies in trails of noxious black bile, and she pretended like it was nothing.

"Yes. For instance, you might imagine that the way I disappear and reappear is an illusion." I stepped into the void, reappearing on Arran's other side. Morgause's eyes widened, her head snapping to the side to follow me. "However, I promise you that my command of the void is very," in and out, now behind her, "Truly," I appeared just in front of the thrones, dragging my dagger across her brown knuckles, "Real." I reappeared beside my mate.

Morgause did not move. Blood welled and dripped down the arm of her wooden throne.

"Your queen is impressive," she said. This time, her eyes were firmly on me.

"Our queen," Arran corrected. He did not need to interrupt our staring contest. I held Morgause's brown eyes with my own as droplets of her blood fell from the tip of my dagger and splattered on the bare stone floor.

"The army is yours to command, of course. But without the support of the Dyad, there will be difficulties. You could spend months rooting out dissenters and trying to establish loyalty." She had fought her way to that stupid throne, and for that, she had a tiny bit of my respect. Despite the subtler methods I guessed were her preference, she did not flinch from the wound I'd dealt her. But I could bargain.

"Months we do not have," I said, wiping her blood on my skirt and returning the blade to its jeweled scabbard at my waist. "What do you want?"

"We've heard of the prophecy made about Lady Guinevere's Round Table."

"*My* Round Table." I was getting sick of correcting her. "Mind your tongue or next time I'll go for it instead."

Morgause tightened her hand to a fist, the blood that had finally started to clot flowing once more. "Seat another terrestrial at it. That is our only condition."

Arran growled. "There are no conditions. The terrestrial army is ours to command—

"Done."

Veyka, his beast warned.

We do not have time to argue, I shot back.

This will not end the way you think.

Morgause stared at us hard. She hadn't figured out the secrets of the mating bond. Lyrena snorted into her hand at the confused look that the terrestrial exchanged with her male counterpart.

A knock broke the silence.

Morgause straightened, the sanguine smile back in place on her lips.

"Enter," she called.

A male entered carrying a tray of wood-carved cups and a flagon of wine. I'd have preferred food, but wine would fill my stomach for the time being. There was something strangely familiar about the cupbearer.

"My son, Mordred," Morgause said, accepting the wine that he served to her first, even before his king and queen.

My. Not *our*. Not related to Orcadion, then. From the surprise Arran had felt but did not let show when Morgause had announced her marriage, I could glean that the union was recent. The male bore no resemblance to Orcadion, his shoulders square and strong but lacking the brutish width of the eagle shifter. His skin was a paler brown than his mother's, his black hair clipped too close to his head to discern if he'd inherited her tight curls.

But the angle of his eyes was entirely different from hers, as were the heaviness of his brow ridges. And the color.

"Thank you," Lyrena murmured, lifting a golden brow and then collapsing it into an impertinent wink. Perhaps Mordred would be her next conquest. It could prove useful in managing the Dyad. Though I hoped that once we left Cayltay with the terrestrial army in tow, I'd never have to see Morgause again.

"To new alliances," I lifted my cup.

"And old ones," Morgause added. She took a deep drink from her cup.

The rest of us did the same, the male taking up a spot against the angled glass wall of windows. He watched us intently, though there was nothing unusual about that. It was not every month—or even every decade—that the High King and Queen of Annwyn came to Wolf Bay. Let alone with a faerie of myth for a companion. But the intensity of his stare drew my eyes back to him.

Arran finished his wine and turned, ready to get the hell away from Morgause. A solid plan. But the aforementioned headache stopped us.

"You truly do not recognize him, Arran?" She passed her wine to Orcadion, who drained it as she stood and approached the male, Mordred. She laid a possessive hand on his arm.

"Who?" Arran asked, already halfway to the door.

Morgause waited until he turned back to look at her. Once she was satisfied that she had his attention, she turned those conniving brown eyes to me. "Mordred. He is your son."

❧ 29 ❧

CYARA

They had two options before them. Scale the mountains of the spine, or whatever the human equivalent was called, facing ice and snow and most likely injury. Or find the hidden tunnel into the caves of the Faeries of the Fen.

Two full days had passed, and even with all four adults spreading out, the search had thus far been fruitless. They'd passed close to Avalon. Although they'd not actually seen it, Cyara could feel its radiating tendrils of power. Neither Percival nor Diana remarked on its nearness.

Maisri floated between the adults at will, peppering them with questions or demanding attention for her flowery antics. More and more, she chose Diana as her companion.

Cyara watched from atop a hilltop, sheltering from the winter wind beneath a towering pine. She shivered despite her layers of wool, leather, and fur. She could pile layer after layer on her body, but so long as her wings were exposed, she would be cold. But she'd die before she tried to cover them. With wings, the world was infinite. Not even Veyka, with her formidable void power, could soar above the trees.

Cyara let her eyes flutter closed, savoring the crispness of the breeze even as she shivered again. Maybe she ought to search from the sky, see if the terrain was any more recognizable from above.

She drew her wings together, tensed her thigh muscles.

Snow crunched behind her.

His scent hit her nose a second ahead of the harpy.

She'd never envied the terrestrials' elongated canines before. But she'd have liked to gnash her teeth and have it mean something just then.

"Sneaking up on a harpy," she hissed through her straight, flat teeth. "Foolhardy, even for you."

Percival lingered in the shadows.

"I had the impression you'd rather have this conversation in private."

"You think I am keeping secrets." Cyara's wings stayed tight, their curved tips nearly touching. If Percival was able to read her, then she'd no hope of deceiving Osheen.

"I was there on the hilltop in Eldermist. The Queen does not believe the grail is worth her time."

The Queen is afraid to hope again.

Cyara kept the thought locked safely inside her mind. Percival was not as terrible as Veyka believed. But that did not mean he deserved to be privy to Veyka's confidences, spoken or unspoken.

"It will not take all of us to convince the Faeries of the Fen," Cyara said.

She slipped one near-frozen hand inside her heavy fur-lined parka, searching for the weight of the communication crystal. They possessed three—the two used by Igraine and Gorlois and the one Percival had stolen from the festival.

Gwen kept one in Eldermist. Cyara had been given another. Veyka and Arran possessed the third.

She wanted to hear her friend's voice. To remind herself that this was not a betrayal.

But there was nothing to report. Nothing to do but plan.

"Where do we begin looking for the grail?" Cyara asked, eyes fully open now.

"You guess is as good as—"

"No," she said sharply. Snow crunched beneath Percival's feet again as he shifted his weight. "Where?" she repeated.

"How long was Merlin unaccounted for?"

"Months." Cyara's mind had already traveled this path. "She made it all the way from Baylaur to Eilean Gayl. She possesses water magic, but no other powers that would have hastened her journey. Still, it is more than enough time, even if she detoured to hide the grail."

Percival exhaled slowly behind her. Too slowly to be insignificant.

"You have an idea," Cyara breathed.

Below them, a peal of laughter announced Maisri's arrival. Diana stumbled out of the thicket behind her, blowing out rapid puffs of warm breath into the frigid air. A blanket of snowdrops erupted through the thin layer of snow, catching Maisri as she fell giggling to the ground.

More crunching snow and Percival was at her side, watching the pair below.

"Fae, human, and witch came together to craft the Sacred Trinity. Excalibur went to the fae. The scabbards to the humans. And the chalice to the witches," Percival recited.

Cyara clenched her teeth together to stop herself from chewing her lower lip. "Then, after the Great War, the priestesses took the chalice."

Percival nodded. "But what if Merlin returned it?"

Cyara shivered again. "The witches are all but extinct."

"But magic lingers. You must have felt it when we passed by Avalon."

She said nothing.

She could see where the logical series of conclusions led. A month ago, even she would have thought it impossible. But then Percival had told her about the human sacrifices to the witches. Merlin had appeared and given her hope. Why should it surprise her when her understanding of the world shifted once again?

"Tirbyas," Percival said, eyes still pinned to his sister.

Tirbyas. The Isle of the Dead. The Witch Isle. Percival and Diana's birthplace.

"She would have had time."

Cyara's face remained still as her mind raced beneath. Yes, Merlin would have had time. But how had she gotten there and back? What dangers had she faced? She should have had this conversation with Percival before leaving Eilean Gayl, with Merlin still at hand. But there had been no time. There was never enough time. The succubus was not coming; it was already there.

And Cyara knew that if she did not find the grail and return before Veyka found the Ethereal Queen...

Veyka would not wait. She would give her life to banish the succubus.

There was no time.

Tirbyas was on the other side of the continent.

Osheen appeared in the clearing below. They were too far away to hear, but Cyara recognized him giving direction to the woman and child, the beginnings of making camp for the night. Maisri began digging in the snow, searching for hard ground beneath on which to build a fire. Diana started for the edge of the forest, sent for firewood.

She was still prone to hysterics, but there was more confidence in her steps. Cyara felt a surge of pride and affection for how much the woman had grown and healed. Diana was not the same woman—

"Diana," Cyara whispered.

Percival's head whipped around so fast that his neck cracked. "What about Diana?"

Diana was the answer.

But even Cyara winced at the thought. "You are not going to like it."

❧ 30 ❧

GUINEVERE

There were no festival celebrations to mark the approach of spring. Celebrations spoke of hope—an emotion in short supply in both the human and fae sections of Eldermist.

Winter showed no sign of loosening its grip on Eldermist, though a thin layer of frost and occasional dusting of snow was nothing compared to the feet and feet of it that still buried the terrestrial kingdom. Still, neither the humans nor the elementals were used to prolonged cold. At least they did not have to worry about fuel. Now pierced with amorite and no longer under constant guard, the human men of Eldermist had made short work of the buildings damaged by the earthquake. What could be salvaged was set aside for rebuilding. What could not be was broken down for firewood. The elementals, of course, need only flick their wrists to start a magical fire.

But even the slums of Baylaur were superior to the camp they'd constructed on the edge of the Eldermist. The slums, at least, were their home. Here, the fae could not take a step without having it marked by the humans.

Gwen told herself she was accustomed to it. She'd come with

Arran to Baylaur for his Offering. She'd felt the heavy threat of hatred and violence from the eyes of every elemental courtier.

At least a dozen sets of eyes watched her as she walked through the village from Sylva's home to the central square and her destination beyond, the makeshift elemental camp. Gwen forced herself to keep her own eyes forward.

The envoys and messengers had been sent out. Elora had not returned. The communication crystal that Gwen carried with her everywhere was silent. But she'd be damned if she'd sit and wait for something to happen.

Despite their raggedy camp, there were able-bodies among the fae refugees from Baylaur. And now that the male half of Eldermist had been returned to safety, the women no longer required to shoulder every burden on their own, there were fighters available from that quarter as well.

If all that remained to her were weeks, Gwen would use them. She'd organize a fighting force to join up with the terrestrial army— and the elemental, if any part of it had survived. If Elora ever returned. Too many 'ifs' to linger on them. There was a task before her now, and she'd accomplish it. Execute one task and move on to the next. *Just. Keep. Moving.*

Being alone with her thoughts and emotions was where the true danger lurked.

The sounds of the village changed as she moved through the streets. The sun's progress toward the horizon marked the time as late afternoon. The sky would turn to the gray of evening soon. But instead of the sighs of a work day drawing to a close, there were urgent whispers. Doors clicking shut and latches scraping across wood.

Gwen let her eyes stray.

A curtain whipped over the window of the house to her left, hiding the occupants from view. On her other side, a woman stumbled in her urgency to get into her half-ruined house, a man gripping her upper arm and dragging her the last couple of feet.

She knew the humans were wary of their new fae neighbors, even fearful.

This was outright *terror*.

It followed her the last dozen yards to the village square, where a command station was set up. Sylva had overseen its staffing with half a dozen of the village's warriors, those not on patrol with the contingent of fae guards that Elora had left behind. Not *with*, Gwen corrected. Separate patrols.

The purpose of the stall was to organize offerings of food and supplies from the humans and redistribute them as needed to the fae refugee camp. Gwen hoped that once the elementals were settled and could turn their attention to tasks such as hunting and gathering, the trade of supplies would begin to flow both ways.

But that was naïve.

The command was deserted.

The ground was compacted and frozen over with frost, tracks difficult to make out. But that wasn't the only sense at her disposal. Even in her fae form, she maintained the dark lioness' sense of smell. Blood stained the air, coppery but not thick. Human blood. And those were drag marks.

Gwen drew her sword as she turned, following them around the command stall and to the other side of the square. Shallow, close together... something—or someone—small.

The scent of blood intensified. She was close, the trail ended— in a closed door.

Blood was not the only scent that hung in the air. The tang of terror was so thick Gwen could nearly taste it. She was a terrestrial, more animal than fae, from the pointed tips of her elongated canines to the rising roar she could feel building in her chest. The elementals were cunning, indeed. But terrestrials were beasts in fae skins.

Gwen knocked on the door.

Silence.

She knocked again.

Furniture shifted inside, followed by a sharp cry. Someone

running into something. Even with her sharp hearing, she could not discern precisely who and what. But she caught whispers—frantic ones.

She knocked a third time. "I want to help."

More whispers. An argument. Two females.

Gwen did not want to break down the door. It would only worsen the fear that poisoned the air. She did not need the humans to like her. But if they would not trust her, they would not follow her commands. And if they hesitated at the wrong moment they might die.

She lifted her hand to knock a fourth time, flattening the planes of her face into the calm mask of composure she'd perfected when she'd believed she would one day rule all of Annwyn.

But before her knuckles hit wood, the door creaked open, no more than the width of a finger. A single brown eye seated in a pale face appeared.

"What happened—

"My son didn't do anything wrong," the voice belonging to the eye rushed out. "Please, just leave us alone."

The woman tried to close the door but Gwen was faster. She slid her fingers into the gap, just enough to keep it from closing. The woman inside flinched, the door slipping from her grasp, gaping wider, and then slamming shut again as she realized.

The wood tried to latch around Gwen's fingers but was denied.

The woman inside whimpered, eyes growing at least two sizes as they filled with terrified tears, waiting for Gwen's vengeance.

Gwen did not move an inch, not her fingers nor her face.

"I don't understand," she said. "Tell me what happened."

Another door opened to her left, this one swinging wide on its hinges.

"You heard her. The boy didn't do anything!" a gravelly voice aged by hardship admonished. Gwen jerked her head to the side, to the hunched woman glaring at her from the doorway of the next dwelling.

A matching old man appeared over her shoulder. "Agnes, stop."

Then a younger man, middle-aged, his beard wild to match his eyes. He grabbed the older female by the shoulders, starting to lift her into compliance. "Mother, you'll get yourself beaten like the boy, or kill—"

"Who." The word reverberated through the square. Gwen turned back to the woman before her. Even open just a crack, she could smell the blood—the trail she'd followed ended here.

Tears spilled out of the woman's eyes. Gwen forced the door open a few more inches. Just enough to see inside, to where another woman cradled a small boy in her lap. He was crying, but conscious. One arm was bent at an unnatural angle. His lip was split and blood leaked from his ear.

Gwen felt the ropes of control that held her composure in place begin to fray.

"Tell me who harmed your son."

The woman did not move. Frosted ground crunched. New terror lit in the woman's eyes—light brown, set into a face whose angles were softened by age and child-rearing. Terror not for herself, but for the child. The door slammed, and this time Gwen let it.

The elderly woman and her family had retreated as well.

But across the square, a trio of fae males loitered, their laughter echoing off the closed doors and deserted ground.

A thread of control snapped.

"Did you touch that child?"

She did not need to cross the square to command their attention. The three elemental males turned. She did not recognize them; unsurprising, as she'd spent almost no time in the city of Baylaur itself. But she saw the fire dancing at the fingertips of one, felt the unseasonably warm blast of air from another.

There was no telling how powerful they were. Unlike the terrestrial kingdom, where strength corresponded to status, in Baylaur bloodlines reigned. A strong elemental born to an undistinguished family would spend their life on the outside, regardless of the depth of their power.

Gwen crossed the square. All signs of elemental magic winked out, the trio assuming a casual air. They were dirty, sporting wounds of their own. Males who had been confined by their female elemental counterparts for the last several weeks since their escape from Baylaur. Amorite winked in each of their ears. They were free —and hunting a new sort of prey.

"Did you touch the child?"

The tallest of the three, whose fingers had flickered with flames, sneered. "The sniveling human?"

Another snap.

"The child."

One of the other two shrugged. She could not be certain which had wielded wind, nor what the power of the third was. But it did not matter.

"He stole from the rations they'd assembled for us," the third said, lifting a lazy hand in the direction of the abandoned command stall. "In Baylaur, the punishment for stealing is loss of a hand. I was merciful."

I was merciful.

Gwen did not try to rationalize. That the child did not understand, that human customs were different than fae. More details that did not matter.

"We are not in Baylaur." She resisted the urge to shift, drawing her sword instead.

The two who had not admitted guilt stepped back. They did not know her personally, but they knew of her. Guinevere the Graceful, for her grace and calm in combat. The terrestrial heir who had slaughtered dozens of other females to win her title. The dark lioness.

They understood punishment and retribution.

"Take his hand," the fire-wielder suggested.

"His hand will regrow." Gwen's control snapped entirely. "But his head won't."

Ice shot from the male's fingertip to impale her like blades. But she evaded them with feline grace as she swung her sword, cutting through bone and sinew in one single, brutal swipe.

The two remaining males stared at her, awaiting justice. The desire to dispense it hummed through her, the control she'd so famously cultivated laying in tattered shreds of rope and restraint at the bottom of her consciousness.

Someone coughed behind her.

Sylva stood in the center of the square beside the deserted stall. Three human warriors, all heavily armed, flanked her. They'd deserted their post to retrieve the village elder. Gwen had somehow missed them on her way into the village.

But that was another thing that did not matter. Her punishment would have been the same.

Gwen held her sword steady. "He—"

"I know what he did."

"He had to be punished or more violence will follow." But she lowered her sword. The two remaining elementals retreated, careful not to show her their backs as they scurried for the perceived safety of their camp. As if she could not find and execute them there.

Sylva remained. "You said it yourself—we need every able body to fight the succubus. Human and fae."

Gwen stifled her sigh, internally tying knots and putting her restraints back into place. "You think I was wrong to distribute justice."

"I think if you kill everyone who carries prejudice in their heart then we will not have much of an army left."

Gwen did not have the heart to tell her that any group they hoped to assemble... human, fae, some tortured alliance of both... it was not an army. Not even close. Nor that killing was the only thing that gave her solace these days.

Over Sylva's shoulder, Gwen watched as doors that had creaked open to watch the exchange closed. She marked the sound of heavy furniture being dragged across the floor to block the doors.

31

EVANDER

Just because he knew the two males waiting for them on the beach did not mean he trusted them. And he certainly did not *like* them. The only being in the world he truly liked was the female standing at his side. The side where she promptly poked him.

"Stop glowering," she chastised.

She did not give him much time to comply—not that he would —before lifting the arm that was not looped through his in greeting.

"Good tides," she called, her smile widening with every step.

Agravayn's eye twitched, which was his equivalent of an effusive welcome. Gaheris, the conciliator, offered a bow to Mya and a respectful nod befitting a consort to Evander.

"Thank you for your quick response," Gaheris said. He offered a hand to Mya, escorting her higher up onto the beach.

Evander let her go, but only because he knew that she needed to touch Gaheris without being weighed down by him. If she touched more than one person at once, it could become difficult for her to parse motivations and intentions. Evander would not risk a mistake on behalf of his own possessiveness. Letting her go was the best way to protect her in that moment, he told himself. Again.

"You are worried," Mya said, glancing back over her shoulder.

Gaheris did not deny it. "The succubus will not stay away forever."

Evander reached for his shortsword by instinct. He'd given up all his other weapons but this. Small enough to allow him freedom of movement in the water, but still deadly sharp.

"What have you heard?" Evander demanded.

"Nothing," Agravayn answered. The oldest of the brothers angled his body, never fully turning his back on the sea. Even after signing an alliance with the new queen, he had not eradicated a life-time of distrust of the Aquarians.

"Messages stopped arriving from Baylaur weeks ago," Gaheris elaborated.

"You've been ignoring their missives for months. What did you expect?" Evander countered.

They'd ignored them because the brothers had suspected treachery from the crown, Evander knew. Rightfully so, after word had come of Gawayn and Roksana's betrayal. And then the death of their third brother, Gareth. Evander did not linger on the events of the past few months. That was a luxury the current situation did not afford them.

But if Baylaur had stopped sending any communication at all...

"We sent a runner. A wind wielder, using the breeze to hasten his steps." Gaheris looked at Evander as he spoke. Evander also wielded wind, though his was so cold he only used it to touch another's body in battle.

Mya gasped, jerking her hand away from Gaheris' arm. She could not read his thoughts. Despite most interpretations of the prophecy, that was not how her ethereal powers worked. She sensed intentions and emotions. Her light blue skin turned grayish as she paled, reeling from whatever she'd felt from Gaheris.

"Baylaur has fallen to the succubus," Agravayn said. "The war has begun."

Mya reached for him. Once, he would have pulled away. First, to hide his emotions from her. Then, to shield her from them. But theirs was a true marriage of souls. There was no hiding from her now.

Evander tried to sort through his own emotions so he could understand what Mya was able to with a single touch. There was fear for what this meant for his new Aquarian home. Anger that Agravayn and Gaheris had not found a way to tell them sooner—unreasonable a response as it might be, it was there nonetheless. He expected to find regret. But though the loss of an entire city meant something to him, he truly held no affection for the gold-stone palace itself. He did not regret any of the actions which had brought him to Mya.

There was guilt. It was strongest, and Evander knew Mya felt it by the way her sapphire eyes softened at the corners.

"My forces are ready. General Ache has command and has agreed to serve alongside your troops. Not under them," Mya said, looking specifically at Agravayn. The Aquarian scouts had reported he'd gathered his own force from nearby elemental estates and towns.

For seven thousand years, the Aquarians hid beneath the surface of the Split Sea, passing away from all fae memory. There was no human realm or fae realm in the sea. It was a single shimmering, ever shifting entity all its own. Those ever changing, opening and closing layers made them more vulnerable to the succubus. They were nearly decimated by the Great War. With the succubus banished, they'd wiped away all record of their existence and disappeared into the watery depths to recover.

Until the succubus returned and Mya was elected Queen of the Aquarian Fae.

"I have sealed the sea." Mya folded her arms across her chest, drawing herself up to her full height. Not tall, but solid. Strength. A regal bearing that had existed within her long before she was elected queen. "The Aquarians are trapped here in Annwyn until the succubus are defeated."

She'd agonized over the decision. Sealing the sea meant that for the first time in history, the Aquarians could not travel at will between Annwyn and the human realm. She'd altered the magic of the sea itself, because every shimmer of light in the water was a sort of rift, an entry point for the succubus.

"And under my command, we will defeat—"

"I do not think you understand, Lord Agravayn, what I mean when I say I have sealed the sea," she cut in sharply, needing no weapon but her iron will. "The equivalent might be cutting off both your arms. Or banishing the very clouds from the sky so you cannot wield them. I have separated my people from a vital source of their power. I have nearly crippled them—so that the succubus cannot use our kingdom to enter yours."

She extended her hand into the space between them. "We will fight as equals or we will not fight at all."

Gaheris rumbled something between a cough and a sigh.

Agravayn stared at Mya's proffered hand like the threat it was.

Her meaning was clear. Submit to her conditions, offer his touch so she could validate the sincerity of his agreement, or the Aquarians would disappear into the Split Sea for another seven thousand years.

Evander saw it for what it truly was—a bluff. When Mya had made the agonizing decision to seal the sea, she'd also decided to fight. But how and when and with who remained to be seen. The terrestrial kingdom waited on the other side of the Split Sea. She could offer her aid there instead, leave the elementals without her valuable reinforcements—and Agravayn without the glory and status he'd achieve by securing their alliance.

If it were Evander's decision, they'd walk away.

But in the aftermath of Gareth's death, Mya had clasped hands with both Gaheris and Agravayn. Whatever she'd seen and felt then was enough to bring her back to the shore today.

Agravayn took her hand.

Mya smiled. Soft, like her. Kind, down to her watery essence.

Whatever Agravayn felt, he stepped back the instant she released him, putting several feet of distance between them.

The curves of Mya's smile flattened out into a line of grim

determination. "Well, then. It is time for us to find Veyka Pendragon."

❧ 32 ❧
VEYKA

"Your son?"

The door clicked shut behind us. I could still hear Morgause bristling—*how dare she banish the Dyad from our own chamber*—as Lyrena and Barkke dragged her none-too-gently down the stairs.

Hopefully, she'd fall and break her neck. It would probably not be enough to kill her, but I could see to that later.

"You have a son?" I asked again, staring at my silent mate.

Arran blinked at me, his onyx eyes more dazed than I'd ever seen them.

Fucking great.

They locked on me. *I didn't know.*

I knew that. I could feel his shock, even more visceral than my own. A male who'd scorned love, connection, and emotion. Earned the title of Brutal Prince. Now saddled with a mate and offspring. And that offspring's terrible mother.

It was a good thing I had not eaten, because even the few sips of wine I'd drank threatened to reappear.

Fuck that. I grabbed the flagon that Mordred—*Arran's son!*—had left behind and drained it. I already felt ill; I couldn't make it much worse.

Arran did not move from the center of the room. Tall, slanting glass windows surrounded us on all sides. I could see the latches where they would open to accommodate Orcadion's winged beast form. Outside, clouds obscured any view of the surrounding landscape. On a clear day, I had no doubt that the Dyad could see all the way to the army camp on the other side of Wolf Bay.

We'd come to Cayltay for an army, only to gain a thus far unspecified Knight of the Round Table. And a son. Arran had gained son.

I threw myself down onto the throne that Morgause had vacated. Arran's eyes stayed with me, but they were unseeing. Distant.

"How long?"

Arran's beast growled low in his throat. "Thirty or forty years. I think."

I pressed my palm to my forehead, exhaling a laugh at the absurdity of it all. "Your son is older than I am."

"Morgause left Cayltay after..." After he ended things between them, whatever that had been. "I have not seen her in decades. The last I knew of her, she was languishing on her mother's estate on the eastern border of Annwyn."

Raising her son and waiting for the perfect moment to use him to her advantage.

Arran's shock was ebbing, but I could not disentangle the maelstrom of emotions that followed. The mating bond between us was not logical, it was visceral. Strong emotions, tortured thoughts, intense, glowing love. They moved along that golden thread unpredictably.

But I did not need the connection to recognize what my husband felt. I read that in his eyes, in the frozen lines of his body. In the mask he only allowed to slip because it was me that sat before him.

He was in pain.

I extended my hand. "Come here, my love."

Part entreaty. Part command. Arran came to me.

He sank onto the throne at my side. He did not speak, but he also did not release my hand.

I stared at where his dark bronze skin contrasted with the pale white of my own. I'd never considered what our children might look like. It had always seemed like a luxury beyond reach.

I raked my teeth over my bottom lip. "I never asked you whether you even wanted children."

Arran stared at our joined hands as well, as transfixed as I was.

"It is our duty to produce an elemental heir," he said, syllables scraping across his throat.

I snorted. "When have I ever been concerned with duty?" Arran did not laugh. I squeezed his hand. "Aside from duty. What do *you* want?"

Arran's fingers tightened around mine. He lifted our joined hands to his lips, pressing a kiss to every single one of my white knuckles. Then he pressed his mouth to the back of my hand, dragging his tongue in claiming circles over my skin.

A shiver of need slinked through me.

The desire to let Arran fuck me right there on Morgause's not-a-throne spread through my veins.

But my mate needed something else from me first.

Arran exhaled over our hands, warming me right down to the fingertips.

"I want everything with you, Veyka. Wailing babies, willful adolescents. I want to fuck you in every position discovered and create a few of our own. Taste every food on your tongue. When we are ancient and gray and bent, I want to leave this world wrapped in your arms. I want a thousand years."

"And a thousand more," I whispered back.

I wanted all of it and more. But that future was not ours to want. Not with the succubus looming and the grail a distant hope.

"I do not begrudge you your son," I said quietly. It needed to be said. I was not angry at Arran for having a life before me.

I was plenty angry at Morgause for ambushing us with Mordred's existence.

I watched my words sink into Arran. They were the truth. If I was destined to die, then I was glad he had the opportunity to be a father. The pain in his eyes, the questioning... he wondered if he was fit for the role. What darkness he might have passed on. The curse of his unmatched power. The specter of fatherhood brought every painful thought he'd had about himself right to the fore.

It began to overwhelm him. The rush of conflicting emotions, the questions, threatened to crush him to dust.

This I could help with. I could distract him.

I dropped our joined hands to my thigh and let my legs fall open in unmistakable invitation.

Arran's beast rumbled in appreciation. "Your jealousy is showing."

Even as he said it, he was dropping to his knees.

"I am not jealous," I insisted, lifting my leg very accommodatingly and hooking it over the arm of the throne. "I am reminding your former lover of her actual status."

Arran huffed a laugh against the inside of my knee. I wore a layered wool skirt, slit to my hips to make for easier movement. To compensate for the cold, I'd donned thick stockings pulled up to mid-thigh, well above my boots.

He caught the top of one stocking with his thumb, dragging it down my thigh, digging his nail into the soft flesh as he went. He slid his tongue over the line of subtle pain. Up from the corner of my knee to the apex of my thighs, where my pussy pulsed with need.

"Veyka," Arran growled from between my legs, his hot breath torturing my clit. "You seem to have misplaced your undergarments."

His face was too busy to see my wicked smile, so I gave him a wicked laugh instead. "We were short on fuel last night. I burned them."

A hum of approval vibrated against my pussy lips. "Burn them all," he said. Then he dragged his tongue up the seam of my cunt.

Neither of us was thinking about Morgause or her son anymore.

33

ARRAN

She tasted fucking amazing. The saltiness of sweat, earned when she battled the Dolorous Guard, mingled with the sweet plum and primrose that was uniquely Veyka. She tasted like life.

I slid my thumbs back up her thighs, passing the boots still on her feet, until I reached her burning core. With one thumb on either side, I pulled back her pussy lips to expose her fully. Wet desire slid down her seam, gathering at the deep 'v' before falling to coat the soft skin just above her puckered rear hole.

What a fucking invitation.

One I intended to exploit. Fully.

"So wet for me, Princess," I growled.

I'd taken her on every corner of this continent. But never here in the court that had made me into the Brutal Prince.

Veyka's choice of location was not accidental. Morgause had made a mistake. The Dyad was powerful. But only one female in Annwyn sat on a throne. And the next time Morgause came to sit on this one, she'd find its wood soaked with evidence of Veyka— and the way I worshipped her.

I caught that bead of wetness and the one that followed. My

knuckles kneaded that soft inch of skin before circling her tight hole. Too tight, still. I'd happily do the work to prepare her.

I buried myself in her cunt fully. Breathing was unnecessary. Not when her musky scent filled my nostrils and her juices flowed freely to my lips. I worked my tongue deep into her, curling it into the most sensitive parts of her channel. It wasn't quite as effective as my fingers, but I had time to ignore efficiency.

When her hips began to buck off the throne, I knew she was close. A second later, she threw her head back and wetness flooded my mouth. I circled once more, then slid my thumb into her beautifully puckered ass. She tensed for half a second, her body resisting the intrusion. Then she yielded, welcoming my touch with a moan. I would never tire of possessing her like this. Every corner of her body, every facet of her soul.

"I'm burning all my clothing," she huffed, taking carefully controlled, deep breaths as I eased my thumb deeper inside her. Her come provided all the lubrication I needed and more. So beautifully pink, she gave herself to me fully.

"Tell me what you want, Princess." If it was in my power, it was hers.

Veyka's hand landed on my shoulder, curled up the nap of my neck to tangle in my hair.

"Everything," she gasped. "I want everything."

Deal.

I plunged my tongue into her pussy in time with the penetration of my thumb. If I could have reached her mouth, I would have rammed my rigid cock down her throat.

Next. After I made her come around my fingers and all over my face.

In the distance—in another realm entirely—I was conscious of the sound of footsteps. If Veyka noticed, she gave no sign. She'd gone to that feral place of pleasure that made me wish she'd been born a terrestrial just so I could see her beast form.

She screeched more fiercely than any hellcat, her claws so sharp in my scalp that I caught the tang of my own blood in the air. I tried to draw it out, determined to block out the world of responsibilities as long as possible. But my demanding queen was having none of it. She gripped the sides of my head, forcing my mouth over her clit and holding it there. Who was I to deny her?

I sucked her clit into my mouth, flexed my thumb inside of her, and it was all over. She came careening into her climax, pussy pulsing against my mouth and her insides gripping me with insistent demand.

Fuck, I needed to be inside of her.

But I'd barely stumbled to my feet, face still slick with her pleasure, when the door behind us swung open.

Lyrena stood in the doorway, eyes glazed over with residual lust from overhearing our fucking.

"If you've quite finished," she managed, garbling the words. "The fighting has already begun."

Veyka followed Lyrena out of the Dyad's roost at the top of the Cloud Tower, the stairway slithering away below us like a serpent. The haze of lust cleared with every heavy step on unforgiving stone, leaving behind a new reality.

I have a son.

Mordred had not flinched when Morgause made her declaration. He'd known I was his father. I had grown up with the curse of my power, knowing that the specter of my birth hung heavy over my mother and my family. Mordred had lived his three or four decades alone with that curse.

Ancestors, I did not even know how old he was. A great fucking father I was going to be.

That was how inconsequential my interactions with Morgause had been. I could not even pinpoint between which war or conquest they had happened. My years as the Brutal Prince, my life before Veyka, it was a patchwork of death and blood and an occasional fuck to take the edge off of my physical needs.

Veyka had asked what I wanted and I'd given her the truth.

Before her, the concepts of love and family were more than foreign. They were abhorrent. A weakness. Another way I could be hurt and completely antithetical to the identity I'd chosen for myself as the Brutal Prince. But loving Veyka, choosing her, changed everything.

I'd expected her to rage. I had no doubt that she would punish Morgause for springing Mordred's existence upon us. But with me she'd been... gentle. Loving. Perfect.

I had ripped the sheets from her bed and burned them because Parys had dared to even lay on them. That felt like a lifetime ago. I could not say that my reaction would have been any different now.

Veyka, Morgause, Parys... my mind tried to distract me from dealing with the feelings in my heart. I had a son.

Not with Veyka. Not a child. Grown. Whole. Perfect.

Perfect? I had not even exchanged a full sentence with the male. But I wanted to.

A year ago, if Morgause had sprung Mordred upon me, I would have walked away. Perhaps arranged for him to go to Eilean Gayl and spend time with my mother and father, if I was feeling particularly generous. But a year had changed everything. I was High King. Husband. Mate. I knew how to love. And despite the inconvenience of it, I wanted to love my son.

Which was precisely why Morgause had chosen this moment to drop the knowledge of Mordred's existence upon me—when she could use my son as a weapon.

34

VEYKA

I knew that in the terrestrial kingdom, the heir was determined through battle. Gwen had briefly described how she'd fought dozens of other females to the death to win the honor. Only to have it all taken away when Arthur was murdered.

I'd even heard the grumbling in Eilean Gayl about how Arran had circumvented the traditional process. Our engagement had been rushed to ensure the security of Annwyn, and only one male in the terrestrial kingdom merited no challenge.

But I knew nothing of the Pit.

The smell alone was enough to defeat many warriors. Thousands of years of blood and decaying bodies had sunk so deep into the stone that there was no washing it away. And it was right there in the center of Cayltay, where no one living within the fortress would be able to avoid it.

At least it was open to the sky above.

At the top, the roughly circular pit gaped about a hundred feet wide. Three levels descended concentrically, each smaller than the last. The final level was at least forty feet below the flat ground of the inner bailey.

The edges of the Pit were already lined with terrestrials.

"I was promised a meal," I groused as we descended the final level of uneven stairs from the Cloud Tower.

"My apologies, Majesty. Once word spread of the place of honor at your Round Table, your subjects were eager to prove their worth." Morgause's words were perfectly respectful and correct, but the hatred on her face betrayed her.

I rolled my eyes and walked past her. Hatred I could deal with. Especially in someone so terrible at concealing it.

Arran was at my side a heartbeat later. I threw out a hand in the direction of the descending levels opening from the ground like hell itself. "Care to explain?"

"Fighters enter the Pit. When half remain, they descend a level. Only the final two descend to the lowest ring."

He wore his taciturn battle commander's face. He had fought and killed in the Pit. Just like the fortress itself—one way in, two ways out. Victory or death.

Isolde appeared at my other side. The terrestrials pressed in closer, eager for a look at the strange creature the High Queen had brought into their midst. I resisted the urge to put my arm around her tiny shoulders. It would only make her look weak, and then she would be more of a target.

Lyrena was at my shoulder, as always, and Barkke had taken up on Arran's other side, inserting himself between Arran and Morgause. My affection for the fauna-gifted terrestrial grew.

Assign Barkke to watch over Isolde, I said through the mating bond.

Arran did not respond, but his gaze marked Isolde at my side before he turned and spoke to Barkke. His old ally moved immediately, positioning himself directly behind the faerie—and shoving away several disgruntled terrestrials in the process.

Now I was able to focus.

"What does the victor win?" I asked Arran. But Morgause answered.

"Whatever is put up as stakes. Castles. Weapons. Females. The occasional male."

I fucking dare you. I let my control slip. Morgause flinched.

I licked my lips and flashed Arran a grin.

"A seat at your Round Table," Orcadion said. Thus far, he'd been content to let his wife try to spar with her betters. Now he wanted his turn? Fine.

"Let's get on with it, then. Someone bring me a chair and something to eat, and they can have my Ancestors'-damned throne."

Chairs appeared. Food, too. It looked more delicious than it had any right to, coming from a place as bleak as Cayltay. I had no doubt that Morgause, the flora-gifted half of the Dyad, had a talent for poisons. But I was too fucking hungry to care.

I devoured roasted lamb in cherry wine sauce and herb root vegetables while the terrestrials organized themselves. Arran made a comment about my plump, round ass, his eyes glowing with black fire for emphasis. I called for second servings.

There were no desserts or chocolate croissants. But by the time the terrestrials lining the uppermost level of the Pit had thinned, I was fully sated. Only those that would actually enter and fight remained at the edge, weapons of choice in hand.

Males, females, and those who identified as neither. An assortment of weapons just as impressive as the array I'd seen at Eilean Gayl—swords, daggers, axes, flails, spears, and even a mace tipped not with metal spikes but some sort of razor-edged animal tooth. A shame that so many formidable fighters would die.

Today, we'd endure this barbaric tradition. Tomorrow, we'd raise an army.

I tried to mark out Talismans where I could. Most concealed them, not keen to give any hints about the power that lived beneath their skin. But surely most of these combatants already knew each other.

One female, wearing nothing on top but a leather bustier I was instantly envious of, had membranous wings etched across her back. A bat shifter, maybe. Another had blades of grass tattooed on his neck, reaching up to graze his jawline. I remembered how Arran had subdued the skoupuma in Baylaur using thousands of blades of grass.

That one caught my gaze and sneered openly. I blew him a kiss.

"Let's start this," I said.

Morgause rose. "Of course. The victor shall earn a palace at the Round Table, as Knight and councilor to the High King and Queen." She turned her eyes to us. "Tell us which of you will enter the Pit, and we shall begin."

35

ARRAN

Morgause was going to get herself killed.

Decades ago, we'd entertained a passing entanglement. It could not even be termed a relationship. There'd been no affection, only fucking. Mutual release followed by retreats to our separate quarters. And from it, a child had been born.

But Mordred was not my concern in that moment.

It was my mate and the mess we would be in when she killed Morgause and left the Dyad one short.

Veyka had learned self-restraint as a means for survival. But she had a wicked temper, and a quickly mounting list of reasons to want the other female dead. Morgause thought she was flexing her power. Stupid, foolish female.

"We have heard that only the most formidable warriors are granted seats at your Round Table. What better way to test them than to battle them yourself?" As she spoke, Morgause stroked a vial that hung at her waist. She had not been wearing it before, when she'd escorted us up to the Cloud Tower. But the finger-sized vial could only hold one thing—what Morgause was known for. Poison.

My stomach lurched, the meal we'd eaten suddenly heavy. She

would not be stupid enough to poison us outright like that, when the act could so easily be linked to her. But there was nothing innocent in the way she stroked that vial nor her proposal that Veyka or I enter the Pit.

"You have heard incorrectly. More than one Knight of the Round Table are not warriors at all," Veyka said with feigned disinterest. After months of knowing and watching her, I could note how her eyes slid casually over the candidates, covertly assessing them.

"I have never seen a harpy myself. But I hear they are quite lethal." Morgause stroked Orcadion's arm. "Would you like to match yourself against one, husband?"

Veyka's pupils dilated just slightly at Orcadion's willing grunt.

Someone in Eilean Gayl had been reporting to Morgause.

We'd anticipated as much, but it still rankled to have it confirmed.

"Will you be competing for the Knighthood?" Veyka said with saccharine sweetness. Her smile matched her tone, but her storm-cloud eyes made a different kind of promise. She hoped that Morgause would enter just so she'd have an excuse to kill her.

My cock hardened instantly.

The option to ignore all of this and drag Veyka into my lap sounded infinitely better than political posturing.

Morgause matched Veyka's smile. "Alas, I have surrendered that honor to my son."

The crowd lining the Pit shifted to accommodate the arrival of one more. Mordred stepped up to the edge, the warmth of his light brown skin heightened by the gray leather armor he wore. Just like in the Cloud Tower, his expression was stoic, focused. He held a hatchet in one hand. Vines curled around the other. That answered one lingering question, at least. Not a shifter.

Over Veyka's corner, Lyrena laughed, making an easy mockery of the entire spectacle. "And how is that supposed to work? Battle the King or Queen to the death for a chance to serve as a Knight for the King and Queen? Terrestrials aren't known for their cleverness, but I'd thought you'd at least understand how to follow your own rules."

Veyka's golden knight was brilliant. A few brash sentences, and she'd made Morgause look a fool while also clarifying the terms of the competition.

Morgause's smile melted into a sneer. "The final round will be to first blood."

I felt Veyka's pulse of appreciation, matched it with one of my own. Lyrena deserved a new gold tooth or two. In one supremely elemental twisting of words, she'd also managed to remove the possibility of fatal harm to either Veyka or myself. Not that any of the terrestrials stood a chance against me or my queen.

But talking was getting tedious. If we let Morgause keep going, she'd conjure up some other complication. I stood from my chair, drawing the axe from my belt and shrugging off the heavy cloak I'd worn while we traveled.

"Let's get on with this."

Veyka lifted one impertinent white eyebrow. Something else white flashed behind her, but it must have been a lock of her hair shifting.

"So eager for bloodshed, Brutal Prince?" Veyka purred. "Maybe I'd like a try."

"You've already done your share for the day," I countered. "It's my turn."

Veyka's smile grew, her eyes sliding past me to the terrestrial challengers. Pity shone in those clever blue orbs. But they widened, suddenly.

Her head jerked to the side, where curved white claws closed around her shoulder.

"Majesty," Isolde hissed. "You must not fight."

There was no privacy in the middle of a thousand terrestrials. Nowhere we could go to have an unheard conversation—except down.

Veyka jumped into the Pit without hesitation. I helped Isolde down one level, expecting to see my mate waiting. Nope—Veyka had already descended two more levels, into the very heart of darkness.

This deep, the cloudy light from the open sky overhead bled away to almost nothing. The scent of dried blood filled every pore, oppressive as any battlefield. The lowest level of the Pit was meant to disorient, to steal away one's senses and strip them down to their basest self.

`If Veyka noticed, she did not show it. She turned to Isolde, her voice low even forty feet below eager ears. "What is wrong?"

Isolde clicked her claws together, her white braids trembling against her shoulders. "I... I do not think you should fight, Majesty."

Addressed to me, not Veyka.

"What do you mean? Why not?" my mate asked anyway, as if I were not even there.

"I could be wrong." The faerie could not hold back her trembling any longer.

Veyka lowered a hand to the tiny female's shoulder. "I trust your instincts, Isolde. Tell us."

Her gentle command seemed to calm the white faerie. At least enough to get the words out. "His Majesty, Arran," she stumbled over my name. "You may not be fully healed."

"What?"

"I am fine."

Veyka's eyes pinned me with accusation. I felt her presence in my mind as she wrapped herself around the golden thread between us and tried to search for some sign of weakness. The beast inside of me began to growl.

"I am fine," I repeated.

"Then you will allow Isolde to examine you," Veyka commanded. I wanted to throttle her. Or fuck her.

She did not flinch from the ire in my eyes, nor from the growing rumble of my beast's growl.

"We need to know either way," Veyka insisted.

Fine.

She nodded to Isolde, who lifted her hands to my chest. Veyka stepped in front of us, blocking the white light that emanated from Isolde's hands so that the terrestrials above us could not see what we were doing. She understood better than most that perceptions were the first half of any battle.

For two agonizing minutes, Isolde moved her hands up over my shoulders, then back down to my abdomen and to my chest once more. I counted every second. Finally, Isolde dropped her hands. The light snuffed out, and Veyka turned back to face us.

The faerie wasted no time with her diagnosis. "You emerged too soon from the healing sleep on Avalon. Had you remained, perhaps the gaps would have closed."

I had no words.

Veyka said one for both of us. "Gaps?"

Isolde nodded her sharp little chin. "It is not a precise description. But when my light touches your power, it is as if there are gaps in it where the pieces are not fully connected. There are suggestions of congruence; as if it was once whole, and now it is not."

Gaps in my power. What in the Ancestors' hell did that mean?

Nothing good, I thought. I did not know if my mate heard it. There was only silence in my mind. And a persistent bead of recognition.

"I had visions of Accolon while I slept," I said slowly. "He showed me things—the past. The final battlefield of the Great War." I swallowed. "And he told me that it was time to wake up."

She needs you now.

Accolon's final words echoed in my memory. I had not realized who he meant when he said it, all my memories of Veyka stolen from my mind in exchange for healing from the near-fatal blow. Accolon had known it was not enough time, but he'd also known that Veyka needed me at her side.

My mate watched me carefully, her eyes searching my face. But she did not press into my thoughts, giving me space to sort through my reactions.

She waited, expecting me to say more.

Sensing, without meaning to, that I was keeping something from her.

But I would not tell her about Accolon's final words. She carried too many burdens. I would not let her shoulder the guilt for this as well.

After several heartbeats without a response, she swung her eyes begrudgingly back to Isolde. "What do these gaps in his power mean? Will they heal?"

Isolde started quivering again. "I don't know."

Veyka turned to me. "Can you feel them?"

"No."

She growled in frustration. "So someday you'll reach for your power and... it won't answer? Or you'll suddenly no longer be able to shift?"

The beast roared inside of me.

"I am fine," I said again. As much to myself as to her. I'd sensed no gaps in my power. Since waking in Avalon, it had behaved exactly as I'd always expected and experienced since I'd first learned how to control it hundreds of years ago. "Morgause cannot be trusted."

Veyka rolled her eyes. Twice, for emphasis. "Obviously she had this planned from the moment she asked for a seat at the Round Table. I do not believe her explanation about the new terrestrial proving their worth. She watched me battle the Dolorous Guard. She knows you. She knows we will best anyone who enters that Pit."

The thought of poison entered my mind again. Morgause had

not poisoned our food. She knew we would not die in the Pit. So what were all these machinations about, then?

Veyka offered no possible explanations as she rolled her shoulders back to stretch.

"Well, best order some more wine," she said, unsheathing Excalibur from her back. "I will be the one fighting in the Pit. Enjoy the show."

✦ 36 ✦

EVANDER

"How do you move in these?" Mya spun to examine the back of her garment in the mirror. "These laces are impossible."

She'd chosen fitted silver trousers and a flowing blue tunic. The laces at the back were meant to cinch in her waist and accentuate her figure. It was a relatively simple ensemble. But considering Mya's clothing usually consisted of a woven brassiere and a tail...

"Stop smirking," she ordered at his reflection. She considered the laces for another few seconds before sighing and turning to face him. "You don't have any laces."

Evander finished buttoning the tunic he'd selected. Gaheris had sent his trunk from the seaside estate where he had abandoned it months before.

"No, but I have these." He buckled the shortsword to his belt. But that was just the beginning.

Mya's eyes dropped from his, following each motion as he added several daggers to the bandolier across his chest. Then the quiver of arrows and a bow.

"I forget, sometimes," she said softly. She reached into the space between them, trailing her fingertips across the straps of leather now in place over his chest.

She found an expanse of open chest and covered it with her hand. Evander could not feel her in his mind—he never could—but he recognized the gesture. She was anchoring herself in him. Mya's ethereal powers allowed her to access the feelings of others. In doing so, she incorporated bits of them into herself. Too much, too fast, could make her lose all sense of herself and her own motivations. Her identity.

Evander breathed in and out, giving her all the time she needed. The growing clamor outside of their tent could wait. Agravayn's war camp was immaculately organized, but enough soldiers in one place would always be loud—and only seemed to be getting louder.

Mya's eyes finally opened. She kept her hand pressed to his chest, but her shoulders relaxed and a soft smile turned the corners of her sensuous lips.

"Thank you," she hummed.

"Always."

Her smile deepened, her light blue skin flushing slightly across her cheeks. "If you'd been half this accommodating to your own queen and king, they would not have sent you away." He'd been sent away to assist Gawayn's brothers with investigating the disappearance of elemental children. But he took her meaning just fine. No one at the elemental court had missed him.

Evander snorted. "Wait until you meet Veyka Pendragon before passing judgement."

Mya reached for her sea glass crown, leaning down in front of the mirror to adjust her black curls around it.

"I am certain I will adore her," she insisted.

"You adore everyone."

"Mostly," she agreed, straightening. The eclectic mix of blue, turquoise, and white sea glass shimmered softly in the muted daylight the white canvas tent allowed in. "Tell me something about her that you like."

Evander's dark brows nearly disappeared into his hairline. "Her Brutal Prince cut off my arm."

"I did not ask you about him." Mya reached for her own accessories.

Unlike Evander, she bore no weapons. She'd trained as a healer of sorts, using her ethereal powers to help other Aquarians sort through difficult feelings and learn how to cope with them.

"Your queen," she prompted as she fastened a string of seashells around one wrist.

"You are my queen," Evander huffed.

He never tired of watching her. She was singularly unique. Not her pale blue skin, characteristic of all Aquarian fae. Nor the way she adorned herself in the symbols of her home and its denizens. It was her quiet, fluid grace that always captivated him. Even on land, she moved like the sea. Steady. Constant.

She snapped her last accessory into place—a golden medallion that symbolized her office as Queen of the Aquarian Fae—and turned back to face him.

"One thing, Evander."

He ground his teeth, but couldn't hear the sound over the din of the camp outside. "She is unbothered by the expectations of others."

Mya tilted her head to the side. "Interesting. See, that did not hurt quite as much as you thought."

She patted his shoulder as she walked by. Evander caught her arm, dragging her against him. Mya's mouth was still curved in a smile when he pressed his lips to hers. He was about to undo every careful preparation she'd made when a body came crashing through the tent flaps.

37

CYARA

Cyara stared at the parchment in her hand. The small square was nearly covered in ink, a series of words blotted out. Some scribbled, some written with infinite care. Every sentence destroyed by a wall of black. She'd been trying for the last hour to come up with the correct words. She'd tried an apology. An entreaty for understanding. An emotionless elemental missive.

She crumpled the parchment in her hand. A second later, it was cinders.

A note was the coward's way out.

Whatever she'd become over these last few months, she would not let herself be that.

She released her fist, letting the remnants fall into the snow at her feet. Bits of ash clung to the legs of her gray leggings like a reproach. Cyara ignored them. She'd already set things into motion. Months ago, really. When she first began researching the Sacred Trinity at Veyka's urging. Then when she'd poisoned Percival. Accepted Arran's quest. Pressured Diana until she was in tears. The kind, gentle female she'd been was gone, slaughtered with her sisters, her friends, her father. She was a harpy now, inside and out.

After today, Osheen would no longer cast her those sidelong

glances. She'd never catch him watching her as she bent near the fire, admiring her figure. Nor feel the warmth of his smile as she sat hip to hip with Maisri, the child of his heart. After today, he would hate her.

She could accept that.

If Veyka lived, she could accept anything.

Wiping her hand on her thigh, she walked back into camp.

Osheen's eyes flicked to her from where he bent over the fire. Behind him, the entrance to the faerie caves hid beneath a bramble of thorns. Osheen would make short work of them, she knew, securing safe passage for himself and Maisri. They'd only paused to camp here so that Osheen could finish skinning the wolf he'd killed earlier in the day, intent on bringing an offering of fur to the faeries as a gesture of goodwill.

Cyara paused long enough to take stock of the camp. Osheen was back at work. Diana and Percival had removed themselves to a log set well back from the fire, just as they'd planned. It was not unusual for the brother and sister to find moments of privacy along the trail, and Cyara had seized upon that opportunity. She'd also asked Maisri to help her untangle the skeins of yarn she'd carried in her pack for knitting night after night. Ever vibrating with unspent energy, the daisy fae had them lined up on a barren stump, working away diligently.

Her heart lurched in her chest.

Careful to keep her steps steady, to raise no alarm, she circled the edge of the firelight. She forced her arms to swing casually at her sides, to keep her wings loose, to not stare across the fire at the pair, male and child, who she'd unwittingly given slices of her heart.

She took her place behind Percival and Diana, facing the camp, her back to the darkness.

As one, the siblings rose, stepping over the log and joining her to form a circle. Diana knelt, arranging the pile of stones on the ground between them. The snow crunched beneath her feet. Osheen looked up. Froze.

"What are you doing?"

Cyara swallowed down the lump of cowardice in her throat. "We must go."

Osheen straightened. Maisri was at his side now, too, a skein of neatly raveled yarn in one of her small hands.

"We must make common cause with the Faeries of the Fen." Osheen's voice cracked over the words, though he tried to maintain that lieutenant's command.

The stones were in place. Diana stood and began chanting, joining hands with her brother. Diana was the one with the power of prophecy, the witch-gift in her blood that allowed her to unmoor her mind the way her full-blooded witch ancestors could.

"You have your orders. I have mine," Cyara said. She'd written some variation of these words on her note a dozen times, scratching out every iteration. They were just as insufficient coming from her lips as the end of her quill.

Diana began to tremble, her eyes rolling back in her head. But just like the spell she'd cast in the temple at Eilean Gayl, her lips continued to move, repeating the chant again and again.

"Do not do this," Osheen implored. He started toward them, long strides eating up the snow-covered ground. Maisri trailed behind them.

Cyara pulled her wings in tight, shoving the harpy down, lifting her hand to send out a blast of fire instead. It struck the ground between them, bringing Osheen up just a yard short of Percival's back.

Osheen shoved Maisri behind him, to safety from the raging wall of flame.

A familiar tingling began in her limbs. Not quite like Veyka's ability to move through the void, but close enough that she could see the comparison, understand how Gorlois had manipulated Diana's gift to allow the short movements between realms and over land. The same way she forced Diana now.

Maisri's lower lip trembled, a pair of tears sliding down her cheeks. Osheen tugged the child against his side, his eyes dark.

Cyara thanked the magic that was pulling her away before she could see the light in his eyes fully die.

"I'm sorry," Cyara said, knowing that the words were not enough. That they might be stolen by the wind and the flames. Knowing that she was hurting him. "I cannot let her die."

Her flames winked out.

But before Osheen could cross the line of scorched earth, they were gone.

🦩 38 🦩

GUINEVERE

It was a terrible idea. Truly, the worst she'd ever had.

The aftermath of beheading the elemental who'd abused the human child was mixed. The humans were still scared of her, but she encountered no open hostility. The same could not be said for the elementals. Some barely acknowledged the incident. After so much loss, what was one more death? But others broke their elemental masks and glared outright.

Fine. As long as they'd fight to defend themselves.

Which brought her back to her truly terrible idea—to integrate the human and elemental volunteers.

The idea had entered her mind after two patrols, one human, one fae, had nearly slaughtered each other in the mountains outside of Eldermist. Each thought the other was an infiltrating force. Two humans died, one water-wielder was injured.

Sylva's words rang in Gwen's head. *If you kill everyone who carries prejudice in their heart, then we will not have much of an army left.*

Killing each other would have the same effect.

In her stupid, stupid attempt to focus that lethal energy on the succubus, she'd called the volunteers to the hilltop outside of Eldermist, in view of the standing stone that marked the rift to Annwyn.

It was the largest expanse of flat space she'd been able to locate in the nearby mountains without descending into the valley itself, which would leave them not only too far from the village, but exposed to any approaching enemies.

The other benefit was that the space was too small for the two groups to remain separate. But Ancestors, were they trying.

The elementals took up more than their share of the hilltop, their superior size and general menace warning off the humans. While wary, the humans who'd climbed to the hilltop to volunteer were not the same ilk that hid in their doorways at the first sign of violence. These were the women who had fought for their families, learning to hunt and fight while their husbands and sons were kept under constant guard. Now, they were joined by the men who had been forced to watch, useless, as their brothers and fathers and sons were taken by the succubus. They all *wanted* to fight.

Gwen told herself that she had mustered troops under worse conditions.

"Stop glaring at each other and form up. Straight lines of ten," she barked. The human half of the contingent jumped, though they did not move to form up. The elementals continued glaring at her.

"You are not our commander, terrestrial."

She tracked the voice—female—to somewhere near the back of the assembly of elementals. But it was impossible for her to pinpoint it. It could have come from half a dozen females of the more than two dozen glaring at her.

Dressed mostly in rags, they were at least upright. Their flight from Baylaur had been fast and cruel, the intervening weeks more of the same as they'd fought the succubus who crept into their camp. And they'd still climbed this hill to volunteer to fight. These were the type of warriors she wanted to command.

If they would follow her Ancestors'-damned commands.

"It is not a discussion. The High King and Queen have given me command of the fae in Eldermist. What remains of the Council of Elders have put human volunteers under my command as well. First, you spar. Then I will put you in formation."

"And if we think one of us would be a better leader?" The same voice as before. Gwen had been watching; she narrowed the possibilities to three.

"You are free to take it up with Veyka Pendragon or Arran Earthborn when they return."

No one had a response for that, not even the mysterious female instigator. Humans and fae alike feared the High King and Queen of Annwyn. "Move!"

This time they did. It took only one inhale and exhale for Gwen to realize what was happening—and not happening—right before her eyes. The exact opposite of what she'd intended.

"No—pair up. Human with fae." She had to stop saying elemental. It only gave the refugees a reason to point out the differences between them and her. "We are going to become one fighting force. We start that now."

The human volunteers who'd come forward flinched, except for the warriors. Gwen recognized some of the band that had surrounded her and Lyrena in the pass above Eldermist. Good, it would not all be novices.

"Are they allowed to use magic?" the red-haired woman who'd led the patrol called out.

"Yes." Gwen watched the ripple move through the crowd, but she'd anticipated this. "But any injury that incapacitates a human and prevents them from fighting will be punishable by death."

More murmurs. Now *everyone* was glaring at her.

Ironic as fucking hell.

The elementals should be the ones mistrusting her.

But the humans were just as skittish.

Ancestors, just kill me and be done with it.

They all hated her. At least they had one thing in common.

They'd all had their lives ravaged by the succubus. That was another.

The red-gold haired warrior who had cornered Gwen in the mountains stepped across the breach of space, pointing a finger at a fae male with a dagger in a makeshift scabbard on his belt. "Let's go."

Her words were the first hole in the dam.

Next her lieutenants stepped forward, selecting fae opponents. Some of the fae began to step up as well, jerking nods to the humans.

Slowly, but in a steady flow, the matches were made. Sparring began.

There was not much space, but that was fine with Gwen. Battles were sometimes fought in tight quarters. It was never like the training ring, just you and one opponent. On the battlefield, there were always other bodies to be concerned with, whether they be friend or enemy. With these first blows, the training had begun.

Gwen walked slowly between the matches, ducking punches and flinging bodies. The humans were outmatched. Of course they were. But the fae held back, unwilling to risk their own lives by injuring the humans after they'd already survived so much terror at the claws of the succubus. She assessed their restraint and control, both vital on a battlefield as well.

All magic had a cost, and if the fae spent their magic too fast, those consequences would be dire. They might pass out from exhaustion in the middle of the battlefield, and then they'd be easy fodder for the succubus.

As she moved through the crush, she catalogued every movement, every error in form and every carefully controlled torrent of power. An ice-wielder who threw daggers of ice, but couldn't aim them. A human who was so fast, they'd pose a worthy opponent to Veyka herself.

Gwen had seen Arran do it dozens of times. It was part of what made him a brilliant commander—his ability to assess the strengths of those under his command and use them to offset one another's weakness while simultaneously reinforcing each other's strengths. He'd done it with flora and fauna gifted terrestrials. She'd do it with humans and fae. A single discrete task she could lose herself in, hide from the nightmares and guilt of her own emotions.

She neared the edge of the hilltop, where one female waited. She was slight—could have been mistaken for a human, if not for the pointed tips of her ears. She was not waiting for an opponent. She was waiting for Guinevere.

"You killed my brother." Gwen did not have to ask who she meant.

She didn't bother to reach for her sword this time. She was the only shifter here, but she would not be the only one once Arran and Veyka arrived with their army. This group of would-be warriors would have to learn how to maintain their composure when there was suddenly a beast fighting alongside them.

"He survived the succubus long enough to make himself into a villain." Gwen let the lioness shine out through her amber eyes. "He got what he deserved."

The female lifted her chin in defiance. "And what about you?"

"My punishments have already been wrought by the Ancestors." There was not much space around them. But it would be enough. "You are welcome to try to improve on their methods."

The female's eyes flashed. She was no more than an adolescent, Gwen realized. Her hands shook, the emotionless façade that all elementals were trained on from birth threatening to shatter completely.

Compassion—that was the unexpected feeling roaring to life in Gwen's chest. Maybe it had been left there by Parys. The Ancestors knew it had never existed before her arrival in Baylaur.

Gwen shifted her stance into a fighting position. They were the only two unmatched volunteers.

"You can die like your brother. Or you can learn to live."

The young female stared at her. Eyes flashing between hatred and grief. Emotions that Gwen understood all too well. Her clothes were tattered, but her thick braid was recently washed and carefully plaited. As she stared Gwen down, shards of ice rose in her hand.

"I want to live," she said, and stepped up to meet Gwen's challenge.

Gwen drilled them every day. A week. More. She counted the hours as the winter sun tracked across the sky. Then the days. No responses came to the human and fae envoys she'd sent to Ember-haven, Wraithwood, or Thornbriar. The communication crystal was silent.

On the first day of the third week, she hiked up into the moun-tains north of Eldermist. She wanted a sense of how long it would take the band she'd assembled to reach the Effren Valley, either through the pre-existing rift or through a more direct, portal rift approach.

But when she reached the pass, all the air deserted her lungs.

An army marched along the perimeter of the valley, moving closer and closer with each blink.

She was too late.

❧ 39 ❧

EVANDER

"Ancestors below—"

"I don't think your Ancestors are going to help us just now." Mya stepped out of his arms, extending a hand to the male on the ground in the middle of their tent. "Are you injured?"

The male pulled himself up easily. No significant injuries.

"I..." His mouth fell open as he caught sight of her face. He jolted backward, recoiling from her touch, fear lighting his eyes. "You are—"

"Queen of the Aquarian Fae," Evander cut in, hand on the hilt of his shortsword. He recognized the expression on the elemental male's face. And if the male even thought about acting on it, Evander would run him through without hesitation.

Instead of bowing or even uttering a word of reproach, he ran.

"What the—" Evander cursed under his breath, but Mya was already out of the tent after him. He pulled himself up just short of running into her where she froze, not even a full step past the tent flaps.

"Fucking Ancestors," Evander swore again. He'd marked the rising ruckus, but he had not heard it for what it was.

Not the regular din of an army camp—but the next thing to a riot.

The male who'd come flying into their tent was already back in the fight, his fist swinging in a vicious uppercut that caught the chin of an Aquarian female. She staggered back, crashing into a brawling trio of two elementals, both fire wielders—whose every blast was parried by a powerful Aquarian's wall of bubbling water. One of the elementals hit the ground, sending a blast of flame into the jeering crowd. Screams rent the camp as elementals and Aquarians both started to burn.

"Disperse!" Mya commanded, reaching for one of the Aquarians nearest her. Evander caught her wrist just short.

"No." He was her shield in battle. Her sapphire eyes sparkled with calm ire. "You will not stop them that way," Evander warned. He'd been a Goldstone Guard. He'd lived through the chaos of Arthur's murder and the assassin's attempts on Veyka afterward. These fights were to the death. If Mya involved herself, the elementals would not care that she was a queen.

Water sprayed on the other side of the fighting, dousing the crowd and quelling the flames. A familiar figure pushed through, her trident hovering above the heads of the crowd.

Mya saw her as well. "General Ache, stop this."

"I am trying." The general swung her trident in a wide arc, sending a powerful spiral of water from the lethally pointed tips. It knocked half a dozen of the fighters down, but those still on their feet did not even pause.

Evander unsheathed one of the daggers from his bandolier, his shortsword already in his other hand, ready to wade into the melee. But Mya's hand on his arm stilled him.

"I will stop it."

The glint in her sapphire blue eyes changed, the power of the Split Sea itself rising like a tide around her. Around them all.

A strange pulse rippled through the crowd. Elementals crashed into each other, into Aquarians, as they tried to dodge the droplets of water that the Queen of the Aquarian Fae pulled from the very ground itself.

Drops were all she needed. Drops turned into ribbons that grew into streams. They swirled high above the heads of the crowd, above the army camp. The tendrils of water curled around each other, coalescing into a massive, undulating orb. The fighting slowed as even those engaged in violence were distracted. But it did not stop entirely.

In a sudden flash, the water magnifying the winter sunlight above, the orb of water burst. Hundreds of waves crashed out from it. Except they were not waves, but creatures of the deep. Massive sea serpents, fanged otters, whales that the Aquarians called the wolves of the sea—made of water themselves, they swam and swirled into the crowd below, pushing apart the last remaining rioters, pushing the Aquarians and elementals apart and bringing nearby tents down as the dissidents tried to retreat. A few tried to run down the avenues of tents, only to be chased back by Mya's water creatures.

They circled and snarled until there was not a single sound. Not a single movement.

There were water-wielders among the elemental fae. Fire, wind, ice, water, storms—all were among the powers elementals claimed as their birthright. But the Aquarians were something else. Water was not merely theirs to command; that salty sea brine flowed in their veins right alongside their fae blood. They were the water and the water was them.

And when Mya was elected and invested as their queen, every single creature in the Spilt Sea had offered up a kernel of its magic to her.

She stepped into the breach of space left by the fighters. Some were still on their knees. Others had retreated into the crowd.

"Enough." On the second syllable, the army of water predators dropped away, dousing the crowd of soldiers in water. "Lord Agravayn."

Evander had not seen him appear, too transfixed by Mya's display of power. The male stepped forward.

"General Ache."

The general lowered her trident, burying the base in the dried-out earth below their feet. "The elementals attacked—"

"I do not wish to hear excuses, General Ache," Mya said sharply. She turned to the cluster of Aquarians, glaring at the elemental soldiers. Some of the Aquarians even smiled, reveling in the power their queen commanded. Mya did not return those smiles.

"The Aquarians are a peaceful civilization. We do not fight unless it is absolutely necessary. I do not know what slights you all imagine were leveled at you, but I can tell you with certainty that this violence was not absolutely necessary. You have weakened and bloodied not only yourselves, but our allies as well. I am shamed by your behavior."

She rounded on the elementals, where Agravayn had moved to the fore. "Lord Agravayn. Is this how you propose to command?"

"No, Your Majesty," he growled. The smirks melted off the faces of the elementals as well. "My shame of my compatriots matches your own."

"Queen Mya will do," she corrected. "I have no need of your honorifics. Only of your alliance."

"You have it." Agravayn inclined his head in acknowledgment. The elementals behind him murmured, but they did not refute him.

Mya stepped back, addressing the entire assembly. "We have one enemy—the succubus. Remember that, or we will all be dead by the end of this."

Her gaze roved the crowd, pausing to meet the eyes of elementals and Aquarians both. Pride surged in Evander's chest. Not once since bending his knee to Mya and pledging his allegiance to the Aquarians had he questioned his decision. Nor would he ever. Even if Veyka Pendragon considered him a traitor because of it.

Slowly, the crowd began to disperse. The injured were hauled towards where the healers had set up. If the Aquarians and elementals each sought their own healers, at least they did not squabble along the way. General Ache worked her way to Agravayn's side, her trident bobbing above the heads of the crowd. Evander followed it with his eyes—until they snagged on something odd. Like a fish trying to swim upstream, a single tow-head pushed against the retreating tide of soldiers.

The elemental female pushed her way to Agravayn's side, rising on her tip-toes to whisper into the commander's ear. His cunning elemental mask did not slip, but his eyes zipped straight to Evander's wife.

"Your Maj—Queen Mya. The scouts are bringing in a messenger," Agravayn said. Evander paused just short of sliding his short sword back into its sheath. "The humans are calling for aid."

40

VEYKA

In the end, it did not matter what Talismans marked their skin or whether they were flora or fauna gifted. All of those terrestrials except one were going to die. I would not be responsible for all of them. I was not quite that cocky.

I could open a portal rift and shove them each through it, one by one, eliminating my opponents in the Pit by sending them for a frigid swim in Wolf Bay rather than killing them. I could do that. But I wouldn't.

There were times for mercy and times for strength. In the terrestrial kingdom, strength was the only measure of value. They would not think my mercy a strength.

If the cost of a seamless transition of power was the terrestrials in the Pit, I'd pay it. I'd come to fear many things in the months since Arran pulled me from my apathy. Love meant fear. I loved Arran. I loved my friends. I even loved my kingdom. And to save the thousands, I would sacrifice the few. I was afraid for my kingdom. But I was not afraid for myself or my soul. It had turned black a long time ago.

I left Excalibur sheathed across my back. I was tall enough that no one would have enough of a height advantage to take it from me. If they stupid enough to try. I palmed my daggers instead, the jeweled scabbards secure at my waist, their secret known only to my own party. The amorite swirled blades reflected back the light of the white-gray clouds above, the wolf-heads carved into the hilts caressing my palms.

The low rumble of Arran's beast raised the hairs at the nape of my neck.

Do not worry, Brutal Prince. This is what I do best.

If he had an argument for that, he held it back. Morgause snapped her fingers. All around me, terrestrials leapt down into the Pit. The fight for the Round Table had begun.

Two terrestrials waited just below, blades raised and ready, eager to match themselves against me. What they hoped to gain by killing their queen, I did not know nor want to. It was absurd that the same terrestrials who sought a knighthood by my hand wanted to draw my blood.

If I could kill them, then they did not deserve that knighthood.

Bloodshed did not have to make sense. Not among our kind.

I jumped—and disappeared into the void. I reappeared behind one of their backs, sliding my dagger up beneath his armor and straight through his kidney. A killing blow.

The male across from him watched his partner fall. He did not turn away from me, lifting his axe to attack. My respect for him rose a notch—only to disappear entirely as a massive bear rose up behind him and ripped his head from his body, tossing it into the second level of the Pit.

I laughed.

And began.

Arran did not exist. Nor Lyrena or Isolde or Barkke. Nor even Morgause, though I was certain she preened over the scene like the queen she imagined herself to be.

There was only that moment, the swipe of my blade across the flora-gifted terrestrial's throat, severing his blades of grass and his arteries in one slash. I felt the gush of blood as it splashed across my face, savored its warmth before spinning and lodging my knife in the shoulder of the same bear shifter from moments before. The beast roared, swiping with his mighty claws. But it was huge and bulky, while I was swift beyond reason. I flayed open its belly and leapt over its entrails as they spilled onto the dark stone floor of the Pit.

I did not pause to count, but I could feel the contenders around me thinning. There was less movement at my back, less to keep track of in my peripheries. Still, I kept moving. Moving was the best defense in a battle like this; Arran had taught me that. It was different than the sparring ring, where I only had one opponent. In close quarters like this, with so many opponents, slowing down for even a breath meant presenting an easy target.

But I did not need to take a breath. My lungs burned with excitement, not exhaustion. I hardly needed to plunge myself into the void. I was capable all on my own. *You are strong, and you are powerful. And every realm should be trembling at the strength of the new High Queen of Annwyn.*

Arran's words were a memory that fueled me through the next kill. A hawk shifter I relieved of one of his wings. A flora-gifted who found her thorns could not make me bleed, even when she wrapped them tight around my wrists.

I stabbed, slit, swirled—and then stopped.

A hatchet met my dagger.

So similar to the weapon my mate wielded, but smaller. Though its blade was no less deadly. And unlike Arran's axe, the head of the hatchet shone with swirls of amorite.

Mordred.

Morgause had sent her son into the Pit.

A table of destiny.

He held his weapon strong against the push of mine, not giving an inch.

Five shall be with you at Mabon.

We could not remain like this, locked in a single hold. We were too vulnerable. I could not kill Mordred. It might neutralize Morgause. But it would destroy Arran. He had not shared his feelings with me, beyond shock. But I knew my husband. He was attached to his parents, he'd grieved his brother's death and the part he'd played in it. I could not kill Mordred.

One is not yet known, but the bravest of the five shall be his father.

The bravest of the five was Arran. Of course, it was. Arran, who had loved me even when I was nothing but a shell. Who had sacrificed himself for me again and again. Who had chosen me, even when his memories deserted him, even when the easier thing would have been to walk away.

But if that part of Merlin's prophecy was true, then did that mean the rest was as well? Her cunning voice echoed in my mind.

When he comes, you will know that the time for the Grail is near. The last is the Siege Perilous. It is death to all but the one for which it is made—the best of them all—the one who shall come at the moment of direst need.

Morgause had heard the prophecy and decided that her son would be the one to fulfill it. If I believed that we had any choice in such things at all.

I did not know what I believed.

But I was spared the decision. A flash of silver moved over my shoulder. I moved by instinct, digging in to find more force within myself to push away Mordred and his hatchet, then to spin and meet the blade with my own. I caught the female's forearm with my other hand and swung her up over my head, bringing her down with as much force as I could manage. The sound of her neck snapping as she hit the second level echoed through the Pit.

Everything around me came to a standstill. Far above, outside of my consciousness, I heard Morgause's voice give the next command: "Descend."

I leapt down to the second level of the Pit, my feet crunching on the broken body of the female I'd thrown down moments before.

41

ARRAN

I shifted. There was no way I could control myself, not with Veyka in such endless danger. She was formidable. She was one of the best fighters I'd ever seen, in any kingdom. I'd only ever seen her defeated by two—Gwen, and myself.

But still, I shifted.

My beast was faster. Even with the huge trees and ivy laden walls inside the fortress, my beast was faster.

"You cannot interfere," Morgause purred as I paced the edge of the Pit.

I did not need her to tell me. I'd fought in the Pit dozens of times over the centuries. Sometimes over real things—a female who'd used my mother's name in dishonor. Other times for less noble reasons, like the fact that my beast had not killed in a few weeks and was hungry for blood.

Logic deserted me as I paced back and forth around the circular Pit. Terrestrial spectators backed out of my way, edging back into place once I was several yards away. I did not notice any of them, my attention focused on the flashes of white as Veyka fought her way around the Pit. The first level was only ten feet wide. The next level narrower still.

Her knife locked with Mordred's hatchet. My beast threw his head up toward the sky and howled his displeasure. I had no feelings that I could parse. Not like this, with the wolf fully in control.

But as quickly as the stalemate occurred, it ended as Veyka spun to bring down another attacker. The herd had thinned. It was time for next level. But Morgause did not move.

I snarled, bounding along the edge of the Pit. I was before her in a second, saliva dripping from my fangs, bared and brutal. I would rip out Morgause's throat and deal with the fallout later.

I shifted only long enough to snarl— "Call them down to the next level."

I punctuated the command with another snarl from the jaws of my wolf.

Every second that the fighting in the Pit continued, Veyka was vulnerable. She could not bleed, that was true. But there were other ways to kill her. If that was Morgause's plan—to eliminate Veyka in a way that absolved her from any blame, she was a fool. She did not understand me at all.

Morgause's eye twitched, but she didn't delay any longer. She called down into the Pit: "Descend."

Mordred jumped. So did Veyka and a half dozen others.

Mordred turned away from Veyka and engaged the female shifter on his left.

Veyka kept her back to the wall, limiting her opponents' angles of attack. She'd always been formidable, but she'd spent these last months getting even better. I recognized techniques from Gwen's arsenal as well as my own. Even a particular twist and kick combination that Barkke had patented when we were young together in Eilean Gayl.

But she'd already fought today. And no matter how good she was, she was not invincible.

A male I did not recognize, who'd eschewed his shifted form in favor of a brutal set of claw-like metal knives protruding from a gauntlet across his knuckles, landed a swipe across her abdomen that would have gutted her if she hadn't danced back just in time.

As it was, she should have bled. Her bodice was in tatters. But the scabbards kept the blades from even breaking the skin.

She spun, burying her dagger to the hilt in the center of a huge female's chest. She did not pause to pull it out, her other hand already flicking her other knife toward the male who'd swiped at her stomach.

Mistake.

I realized it a second too late. *Mistake! Veyka!* My beast roared. But she was already crumpling.

The massive female twisted Veyka's wrist, dislodging the knife. Veyka couldn't get traction in the puddle of blood. Her opponent flipped her, slamming her down onto the stone floor hard enough that the ground beneath my paws shook. But that was not the sound that echoed in my ears.

It was the snap of bone.

She could not bleed. But her bones could still break.

Two screams twined together as they ripped out and over the Pit, Veyka and her opponent both powerless to contain their pain.

I did not think. I leapt—only to be slammed back by a pulse of magic.

The wards kept me out, kept me from her. The Pit was as old as the fortress itself, built by forbearers whose existence had passed out of memory. No one alive knew how the wards around the Pit worked, only that they prevented outside interference.

Fuck that.

I leapt again, the force sending me rolling as it knocked me back from the invisible barrier.

Again and again. It made no difference. I could not reach her— not physically.

But that was not my only pathway to Veyka.

My beast roared his dissent, but I forced myself to shift back into my fae form. Veyka was still screaming. Only seconds had passed. Maybe less... one heartbeat? A full minute?

Veyka was still screaming.

I wrapped myself around the golden thread that linked our

souls, sinking into the primal connection that evaded all reason, including time and space. Even the void bowed before the power of our mating, that bond between us the only thing that tethered Veyka and prevented her from being lost in the void.

The ancient wards of the Pit were no match.

I felt them yield.

I shifted, bounding down the first level and onto the second in one leap. Veyka was already shoving the massive female off of her, her opponent clearly incapacitated. But there was no space for reason over the roaring in my head. I ripped the female's head from her body. Then her arms, her legs, until she was nothing more than pieces. Pieces that would never be able to harm my mate again.

Veyka stared.

For once, there was no blue ring of desire in her blue eyes. But they were certainly burning.

What have you done? she hissed without moving her mouth.

The roaring ebbed. A low growl replaced it, vibrating against the fur in my chest. Veyka stood, but she did not reach for the beast.

They will think less of me. That I'm weak. That I need you to protect me.

All the other fighting had stopped. Only two contenders still stood. Veyka and, pressed against the wall on the other side of the Pit, Mordred. My son.

The growl started to build again.

Veyka's eyes darted around the Pit, then back to me. *You should not have come down here.*

If you're waiting for an apology, that's too damn bad. I told you—you belong to me. I will not sacrifice your life for Annwyn, nor for anything as trivial as a seat at the Round Table. Wards and traditions be damned.

Her eyes narrowed, but the fire in them banked.

"Get out," she said. *We will fight about this later.*

I recognized a promise when I heard one. I tensed the muscles of my haunches and leapt the thirty feet out of the Pit in one bound. Our audience jumped back to make room, but they did not wait for me to shift before scrambling back to the edge. I could not miss the way they watched, different than before. One eye on Veyka... the other on me.

Fuck, she was right.

I'd lived in this court for three hundred years. How could I be so fucking stupid, to sacrifice the integrity of her victory for my own selfish, unfounded fears. She would have won—there was no other outcome. Veyka could stand a few broken bones. She'd withstood much worse. I forced myself to flick my ears away from the Pit, to listen to the words spoken around me. To gauge the level of damage my pride had done...

But those were not the whispers circulating around me.

"—enough to overpower ancient magic—"

"No one has seen power like that in thousands of years..."

"—above the laws of nature itself."

I let the words slide through my consciousness, across that golden bond, down to where Veyka stood quivering on the edge of the Pit's second level. Neither she nor Mordred waited for a signal from above. They met each other's gazes and they jumped.

I emptied my thoughts, clearing the whisperings and any lingering guilt or rage. Veyka needed none of that now. She needed a clear mind as she approached the last round of the Pit.

The final descent.

42

VEYKA

"To first blood."

His voice was achingly similar to Arran's. My chest flooded with emotions, the killing calm deserting me. I could not allow that. Not now, when every swing and stab was fraught with meaning and consequences. My heartbeat throbbed in my arm. The pain was easier to block out than the feelings. I'd spent twenty years blocking out physical pain. Tucked in at my side, stabilized against my body, was the best I could do for my broken arm.

I forced a slow, confident smile to climb my face as we circled, mirroring each other's footsteps. "Are you reminding me or yourself?"

Every twitch sent a lance of fire through my body. For a few seconds, I debated. I could call this whole thing off. Mordred was the only terrestrial left. He'd earned the seat at the Round Table that I'd promised to Morgause. There was nothing to be gained from continuing—except that the other terrestrials had all heard Morgause's snide comment about proving his worth—and understood that it had really been about proving mine. And now they'd all seen Arran jump into the Pit to defend me.

Broken arm or not, I had to fight.

Mordred tossed his hatchet from one hand to the other and back again. "I have no wish to harm you, Majesty."

We were deep enough in the Pit that no one could hear us, not even the crowd of fae ears overhead. I might never have this opportunity again.

I drew my dagger with my good hand and tossed it without pausing.

It sailed past Mordred's head, close enough to prick the raised collar around his neck. He moved easily to avoid it.

"I do not believe you," I said simply.

I stepped in and out of the void, retrieving my dagger before he could. I threw it again—disappearing again—narrowly avoiding his hatchet, flying head over shaft, and catching my dagger on the other side of the Pit.

One handed was no way to fight. But at least I could still move through the void.

Mordred turned, walking backward to retrieve his hatchet, careful not to show me his back. The distrust was mutual.

"You do not wish to kill me either," he said. "Unless your prowess with these blades has been overstated."

Well noted. He recognized that if I'd wanted to kill him with those throws, I could have.

I tossed again, appearing behind his shoulder just in time to catch the hilt of the dagger I'd sent sailing over it. "It hasn't," I whispered.

He had the good sense to leap out of reach. I let him go.

"You could choose not to hate me," he said quietly, chest heaving.

Was he tiring already? Or trying to curry my favor with a show of emotion? He needed a better education on what impressed elementals.

"I do not hate you," I said, coming to a decision. I slid my dagger back into its scabbard. "But I do not trust your mother." I drew Excalibur.

Mordred sighed. He adjusted his hold on the hatchet and lifted a wrist toward the opening above us. The unmistakable slither of vines reached my ears.

"You are wise not to trust Morgause." Another casual toss of his hatchet. The vines cleared the first level of the Pit. "But would you be judged by the actions of your mother? Or would you rather stand alone?"

I'd been judged by and against my mother my entire life. But just because Mordred knew how to twist the invisible knife he'd shoved into my gut changed nothing.

How did he know? Morgause had spies. We already knew as much from the comments Morgause had made about Cyara's harpy. I'd made a spectacle of Igraine's execution, and word of it had reached Cayltay ahead of us.

"I killed my mother." Vines slithered down over the edge behind me, in my periphery, everywhere. "Would you be willing to do the same?"

He held my gaze, hatchet held fast. Ready. His eyes were not quite as dark as Arran's. More brown than black, with flecks of paler gold and even blue. An unusual color for an unusual male. The son of a king, but not his heir. Flora-gifted, like both his mother and father, but his power clearly resembled Arran rather than Morgause.

I lifted Excalibur.

Mordred inclined his head the barest fraction of an inch. "I would do as my queen commands."

I lunged forward, swinging Excalibur for his knees. But he was ready, sending vines twisted at me from every direction. Pushed back on the defensive, I sliced through vine after vine, twirling in a circle as I went, faster than he could summon new ones to replace those I destroyed.

Excalibur was heavy and unwieldy in the compact space, but the reach was longer, allowing me to keep my broken arm pinned to my side. I darted over the ground, knowing from experience that if I lingered too long in any one place, those vines would ensnare my ankles and drag me down.

But Mordred was quick as well. He hurled his hatchet at the shoulder on my uninjured side. Slow—I was too damn slow with the injury. Even as I shoved the grimaces down, they distracted me. I threw myself into the void, coming crashing out a few feet away, landing hard on my broken arm.

My scream reverberated against the walls of the Pit. Arran's beast growled, but I could not afford to look to see if he'd shifted again or if it was just in my head.

I kept screaming even as the pain ebbed. Mordred's vines did not creep any closer. They curled, ready and waiting to strike. A stupid mistake. He was not as ruthless as his mother, and he would pay the price. He'd learn.

I screamed through the pain as I leapt from my back to my feet, exactly as Guinevere had taught me. Using my momentum, I slashed through the wall of vines Mordred had erected around himself. The hatchet was back in his hand. He parried the tip of Excalibur as it sliced through the vines he tried to rebuild. But not fast enough.

Mordred's eyes were wide. I was still screaming. He thought I was going to kill him.

Excalibur cut away the last of the vines, but caught on the downward swipe, sending my hand ricocheting back and pain radiating through my arm and into the rest of my body. The force of my fist knocked the hatchet from his.

Then there was nothing between us but air, and my sword pressed to the column of his neck.

Killing him would be easy. So deliciously easy. It was even logical. If I slaughtered the last terrestrial in the Pit, I could declare that none of them had proved themselves worthy and take my army with impunity. I'd have to kill Morgause. But that was likely necessary, anyway.

I could kill him.

The slightest pressure of Excalibur's amorite-swirled blade and he would be dead. Another threat disposed of—when had I ever hesitated? I'd killed for less, and often.

Arran's son.

This was the reason that Morgause had insisted that either Arran or I entered the Pit. Because in either case, victory could be hers. If Mordred won, he would earn the coveted Knighthood of the Round Table, extending Morgause's influence beyond the Dyad. Had Arran entered the Pit and faced Mordred, he would have been forced to injure his own child—potentially creating a divide between them that Morgause could then exploit. And if I was overcome with wrath, if I used the opportunity to punish her by killing Mordred... I would forever drive a wedge between Arran and myself.

My head swam. I had not lost any blood, but the pain in my arm radiated out. I'd compounded the break by falling on it. Maybe a couple of ribs as well.

I swallowed down the whimpers of pain, shoved those tendrils of fire back into my arm, concentrating and imagining it as nothing more than a pinprick. A pinprick of pain was nothing.

"You said you did not want to kill me," Mordred said, his mouth barely moving for fear of slicing himself on my blade.

"I said I did not hate you," I corrected.

A part of me did want to kill him. A selfish, horrible corner of myself did not want this added complication to the short time that remained to me and Arran. I'd told Arran I did not begrudge him his son—and in that moment, faced with my mate's needs, it was true. But here, in the depths of the Pit, where the layers of myself had been stripped away, I was who I had always been. Selfish.

But that was not all I was. Not anymore.

I lifted Excalibur from Mordred's throat to his cheek. With control fueled wholly by adrenaline, I drew a shallow cut from the outer tip of his eyebrow down to his jaw.

Mordred's throat—notably intact—bobbed. "First blood is yours."

I stepped back, not even attempting to sheathe Excalibur. I wasn't sure I could without further injury to my throbbing arm and side.

"That is your first lesson you should take to heart as a Knight of the Round Table. How I feel and what I want are inconsequential to what I must do."

I loved Arran more than myself. For him, I would ignore the selfish parts of myself.

Swallowing back a sigh, I kicked Mordred's hatchet toward his feet. "You're responsible for getting yourself out of here."

He frowned in confusion, but I did not wait to explain. I used the void to take myself up to the top, to Arran's side. It took every ounce of my remaining strength not to collapse into his arms.

"Isolde," Arran demanded.

I shook my head. "Not here."

Arran growled in my ear, but he slipped his arm around my waist and started toward the stairs.

Overhead, a fractious caw split the air. A single raven swooped down from the sky, passing the battlements, aiming for the inner bailey. Everyone knew what to expect, clearing away a landing zone. I was too addled to realize what was happening.

The raven landed, shifting into a petite female with blue-black hair that matched her raven's wings. Another female reached out to steady her, but she threw out a hand to hold her at bay.

I'd never seen her before in my life. But she knew exactly who we were as she gasped the words out. "Word from Outpost! The Spit is under attack!"

43

VEYKA

"How old are these reports?" Arran peppered the soldier with a steady stream of questions as we climbed. Stair after stair, up and up and up the spiraling tower. At least these were wider than the ones at Eilean Gayl. The two males could easily walk abreast.

"A day or two, at least. It would have taken that long for the human to reach the rift, pass into the Shadow Wood, and then make their way here." To Outpost, the terrestrial fort perched on the edge of the continent overlooking the Spit.

The Spit was neutral territory, belonging to neither the elemental nor terrestrial fae kingdom. The terrestrials watched for treason from their tower, dubbed Outpost. The elementals did the same in the west from Skywatch.

I rolled my shoulder as we climbed, half-listening to Arran's briefing as I assessed the hasty healing Isolde had done. I hadn't even bothered to change out of my blood-stained clothing. As soon as I could bend my arm without screaming, we were on our way to Outpost.

We reached the top of the tower. But even from there, it was impossible to see all the way across the Spit from this tower to its elemental twin. Still, I braced my hands against the stone sill and leaned, eyes straining to see what was not there.

Skywatch did not appear through the clouds. Nor did the succubus' dark specter mar the stretch of unclaimed land. The only sounds were the waves crashing against the shore and the call of birds—some of them surely shifters on patrol.

Waves.

"The Split Sea," I croaked, hardly believing what I saw with my own two eyes. "It is moving."

The terrestrial jerked his chin in confirmation. "For a few weeks now."

Weeks. A few weeks ago we'd been in Eilean Gayl, rescuing the refugees from the goldstone palace. That could not be a coincidence, could it?

I leaned further, looking north to where the Split Sea stretched out. The soldier was right—the waves were not contained to the shore. The entire sea was a roiling tempest of gray and blue.

A low growl told me what Arran and his beast thought about how far I was leaning out the window. I settled my weight on my forearms and let my toes lift off of the stone floor.

The soldier gasped. I guess that growl wasn't just for me.

I ignored the look Arran leveled me as I put solid stone beneath my feet once more. I still needed to punish his stubborn ass for what had happened in the Pit.

"Have any of the males under your patrol succumbed to the succubus?" I addressed the soldier. He wore the typical wool vest favored by the terrestrials, buttoned at an angle across his chest that terminated at his shoulder. He wore his hair cropped close to his head, which made the awestruck looks he kept shooting Arran even more apparent.

Fear wasn't the only thing my Brutal Prince inspired, it seemed.

"Two in the last hour," the soldier admitted.

We'd never used any kind of mechanism to measure the rate at which the succubus stole the minds and then the bodies of their victims. Once they had taken over, we'd seen how they degraded, expelling the soul within in torrents of black bile until all that remained was a skeletal husk that felt no pain and could only be felled by amorite weapons.

I caught my lower lip between my teeth. "Do you think it has to do with proximity?"

The soldier's mouth fell open in confusion, but the question was not meant for him.

Arran answered by crossing his arms over his chest and stepping to the side so he could see past me and out the window I'd dangled myself from moments before.

"They are in another realm," Arran pointed out.

"But the realms... they exist like layers on top of one another. Some places they are thinner than others." I'd felt it when moving between them. Sometimes, it felt like a single step. Less, even. A blink to move from one realm to the other. Then others, a leap or a lunge was required. At first I'd thought it had to do with my own reserves of power or control. But the more I stared at the Spit, the more I *felt* it in my bones. The wrongness in the air. "If there is an army of them right there, but in the human realm..."

"Proximity," Arran finished.

I nodded, palming the hilts of my daggers by habit. "How much amorite do we have left?"

"The stores we collected from the Baylaur refugees are almost depleted."

That was the agreement we'd made. The small jewels, already fit for piercing, would be put to that purpose. The gems mined from Castle Chariot would be smelted into weapons. The survivors from Baylaur had brought through a decent stash, but I'd dispersed some of that to the villagers and elementals in Eldermist as a show of goodwill.

The terrestrial army was tens of thousands of fae strong. How would we decide who received the life-saving amorite piercing and who did not?

"Just because we give them an amorite piercing does not mean they will live. Nor does putting an amorite weapon in their hand. Even those that have both will die. Thousands of us will die."

Thousands of my subjects. Even more of the humans.

I need to find the Ethereal Queen.

Arran's posture tightened. *I need you in this battle. Then we will start raiding the library in Cayltay.*

"Flattery will get you everything," I said, flashing a grin. The poor terrestrial soldier frowned in confusion.

You cannot delay forever.

I said it—thought it—to remind myself as much as him.

But the other end of the bond was silent.

44

CYARA

The limitations of Diana's magic made Cyara miss Veyka even more. Diana could only take them a few hundred miles at a time, with rests to recover in between. Those rests became longer each time she cast the spell. Every new line of fatigue that appeared on Diana's face sent Percival raging. Cyara forced herself to endure it without a single word in her own defense.

She had her reasons. But she could not expect Percival to share them. He only remained for Diana's sake. Diana, who even after all she had endured, insisted she would help. She refused to remain in the safety of Eilean Gayl, cloistered away with the priestess and healers. What Cyara admired more was the unimpeachable goodness inside the human woman—while her own understanding of herself continued to crumble.

After three agonizing days, Diana was not the only one buckling under the ever-present weight of exhaustion.

But then, the Isle of the Dead materialized around them.

Diana sank to the ground, sucking in one ragged breath after another. Percival kneeled at her side, rubbing wide circles across her trembling back. Only Cyara stayed on her feet.

The isle was barren, not a single stalk of plant life visible anywhere. But Cyara could not banish the sense that, despite that, the island was very much *alive*. Magic was here. Strong, like Avalon, but different. Sinister. An irrepressible urge to flee took root in her chest, blooming as it stretched out into her limbs and curled its tendrils along the intricate network of her veins.

"We should not be here," Cyara whispered.

"Too fucking late for that," Percival sneered, tugging his sister to her feet.

Diana was calmer. "It is the vestigial magic of the island," she said. "It pushes you to leave, but to me... it calls."

Cyara shivered despite the humidity that hung in the air. They were at the far southern end of the continent, on what would be the elemental half of the realm, if they could open a rift to Annwyn.

"Do you feel it, Percival?" Diana wandered forward a few steps, toward the center of the island.

Her brother frowned, scrubbing a dark red-brown hand through his already unkempt tangle of black hair.

"Maybe." His hand rubbed across the stubble darkening his chin. "Following it could be dangerous."

"This entire place is dangerous," Cyara murmured. Percival's face contorted into a scowl.

She should not have said that, not after all she'd asked of Diana in order to get them there. But the compulsion to flee was visceral, embedded in that place in the center of her back, below her nape and between her wings, that ruled with instinct rather than logic.

The urge to take flight back to the safety of the continent, to leave her companions behind...

"We are here," Diana said with uncharacteristic calm. "We must follow."

One hand gripping her heavy purple robes, she started into the interior, all exhaustion seemingly forgotten, lost to the compulsive call of the island. Percival ran to keep up with her, no hesitation.

Cyara's wings tensed. Her thighs. She could shoot into the air and be away from this place. She pinned her hands to her sides to cut down on resistance—but one collided with the hard bulge in her pocket.

The communication crystal.

Her wings sagged, realization and relief coursing through her. She'd almost lost herself to the witch magic. Never again.

She must remain in control.

She dug her feet into the sandy ground, running to join the pair of humans.

She must save Veyka.

45

ARRAN

I'd been away from Wolf Bay for nearly a year, but walking into the army camp shocked my senses into thinking mere minutes had passed. The scents were the same—roasting meat and blood and unwashed bodies. I'd missed the sounds. Maybe that was why I'd struggled to sleep these last few months. Even a busy palace was quiet in comparison to a city with walls made of canvas.

Veyka and I split as soon as our feet landed in the thick mixture of mud and snow. Lyrena appeared at her queen's side, armed with information about the layout of the camp and a proposal for how to distribute the amorite gems remaining to us. Barkke waited for me, Orcadion and three other lieutenants I recognized at his side. I'd swallow the presence of the Dyad; at least Morgause was nowhere in sight. Poison was not an effective weapon against the succubus.

I started down the central artery of the camp, the three males and two females falling into line on either side of me. "The latest word from the humans is that the Crossing—their version of the Spit—is swarmed. The succubus are pushing inward toward the land mass that corresponds to the Terrestrial Kingdom."

"We do not know how they reached the Crossing, whether this is the same force that took Baylaur or another wave entirely." I laid out the information we did have in succinct, factual sentences, trying to remove all bias.

"The queen will open a portal rift to the bluff to assure we have the high ground. We'll attack in a standard formation. Three columns, head on." I pivoted when I reached the sheer cliff face, dropping straight down from the mountain towering overhead. Veyka had selected this spot to open her rift. But not just yet.

I turned to my lieutenants. The two females and their male counterpart had served under me for a combined total of two hundred years. Orcadion was married to Morgause, but he was also very good at ripping out throats. Barkke deserved a chance to lead after the services he'd rendered to me and Veyka in Baylaur.

"Concerns."

The first female lieutenant, a blonde flora-gifted terrestrial with a particular affinity for trees, stepped forward. "If we push them across the Spit—the Crossing—what is to stop them from spreading out once they reach the other side and ravaging the humans there? It might be better to drive them into the sea."

"They will not retreat. Not with Veyka there."

"You are certain?" she pushed. I let her. When I asked for my subordinates' concerns, I meant it. If there were holes in my plan I wanted them to find them before the enemy did.

"I wish I wasn't. What else?"

Barkke twirled the end of his ridiculously long beard around his forefinger. "Could we try to surround them? Use Veyka's magic to take a few companies and catch them from the rear?"

"We do not know the size of the horde or where the rear is." If there was one. "I will consider it if the situation changes or we gain new information."

None of them suggested leaving the humans to die. That was a victory. In what was bound to be a day of defeats, I would take even the smallest one.

I assigned them each to one of the three columns, giving Barkke a rank of second in command to the blonde female. She'd let him flex his leadership skills while managing any disasters. If we lived through the day, there would be another battle. And another. If this was an opportunity to train Barkke for command, I would not waste it. Who knew how many of the six I had before me would still be alive when the sun rose tomorrow.

Orcadion I kept for myself.

"You have your orders. Call your troops into formation."

The others nodded and broke off. Only Orcadion remained, eyeing me speculatively. "I thought you'd send me as far away as you could."

"I want you scouting overhead."

The male's fingers contracted as if he could feel the talons that were not there in his fae form. "Scouting is a job for a child. Not the Dyad."

"The Dyad are stewards of the court. Here you are another weapon to be used. And in either position, you answer to me."

He wanted to argue.

If I had to put him down, I would.

My wolf began to rumble—Veyka was near.

"I will accept your command—if you will take Mordred into it as well."

These were Morgause's words. She may not be on the battlefield, but she was waging her own personal war. She'd negotiated the terms for the Knighthood of the Round Table and ensured that Mordred entered the Pit along with Veyka or myself. Now, she was shoving her son closer still. *My* son.

Fuck. I did not have time to think about what that meant to me. Morgause's objective was easy. She wanted power and she intended to use Mordred to get it. If we were all still alive in a month, I'd deal with her then.

"Fine. Join the others." I was already striding for my mate as the words left my mouth.

Veyka emerged from the left, Lyrena a half step behind her. Her golden knight fell back as Veyka approached, stopping just short of launching herself into my arms. The feeling was more than mutual.

I wanted to bury myself in her—to shut out the coming battle; to give me the strength for it.

I'd fought in hundreds of battles over the last three centuries. In plenty of those, I'd led an army that was outmatched. I'd walked onto the battlefield expecting to die. But I'd never truly entered it hoping that I would live.

Instead of dragging her against me, I settled for taking her hands. "Use the void, but stay with Lyrena. If you're going to go out of reach, take her with you."

"I do not need to be minded like a child."

She was still angry that I'd intervened in the Pit. But that was not the battle we'd chosen to fight today.

"She is your Goldstone Guard, Veyka. The only one left. She has sworn her life to protect the throne of Annwyn. Let her do it." I knew that Veyka was capable of handling herself. I raked my eyes over her body, checking for the hundredth time in the last hour that all of the bones in her body were fully mended. But the female before me was indomitable, and it had nothing to do with the strength of her body.

After too long, she finally nodded her acquiesce. "If you need me to open a rift—"

I know how to find you.

That earned me one of those wicked grins that had my cock tightening instantly. *After*, I promised myself. Because there would be an after. For both of us.

I could not hold myself back. I dragged her against me, pillaging her mouth for one last taste to take me into battle. She was the reason I wanted to live. And I'd give her a damn good reason to feel the same way.

The sound of twenty thousand footsteps falling into line forced me to pull away.

"I love you," Veyka said before I could. By the smile that curved her lips, she knew it.

"Make them pay, Princess."

❧ 46 ❧

EVANDER

"This is taking too long."

"Armies do not move fast." Especially ones that were so skittish around one another. But at least there had been no more physical altercations. The columns marched side by side, one robed in flowing white and pastels, the other draped in colors of the sea that matched their pale blue skin. The elementals had even agreed to give the Aquarians preference when passing through the rift.

That was what had slowed them down. They had to walk through it one at a time. The only other option would have been to split their forces between the two nearest rifts, the one in the northern dunes and the one nearest to Skywatch—the one they'd used. But Mya was not going to split them up when she'd just scared everyone into getting along.

They were scouting ahead of the small army. The bedraggled human messenger remained back with Agravayn and General Ache, who grilled the poor man for every detail as they formed their battle strategy.

Mya walked silently at his side, keeping up easily despite the fact that she had to use her least favorite form of transportation— her legs. She was stunningly fast in the water. Evander had accepted early on in their relationship that he'd never be able to keep up with her underwater. That powerful tail of hers was made for those depths in a way he never would be, at least in his body. In his soul, he knew exactly where he belonged.

Wherever she was.

The pale winter sun reflected off of the Split Sea to their left, the undulating golden plains of the human realm to the right. In Annwyn, they were covered with sand. He'd never seen the Barren Dunes, but they were supposedly a death trap. No water, no plant life or game. Just endless red-orange sand. By comparison, the knee-high pale gold grasses felt welcoming. But it was impossible to miss the direction of Mya's eyes... ever to the left. To the sparkling sea.

"Was sealing the sea a mistake?"

Evander blinked in surprise, wondering if he'd imagined the question. How long had it been since he'd had a sip of water?

"Are you questioning a decision? *After* it has been made?" He'd watched her agonize over the decision—and many others. It had only taken watching her rise to power and rule the Aquarians for Evander to realize he never wanted to wear a crown.

But when she made a decision, she did not waiver. She moved to the next and the next, ever steady. Evander reached for her hand, only to have it swatted away.

"I am not infallible," Mya said through pursed lips.

"You had me fooled."

"Husband." Another swat.

He took it readily. His eyes continued to scan the horizon, the sea, the plain, for any sign of the succubus horde. But the scenery was deceptively peaceful. He took the opportunity to slide his arm around her waist and pull her closer. Once the battle was joined, he might not see her for hours. "Why do you ask?"

Mya dropped her head to his shoulder—the only sign of exhaustion she'd shown in the last few days, and only because they were alone.

"If I had not sealed the seas, we wouldn't have had to go through the rift." The Aquarians wouldn't have, but the elementals would still be land-bound. But he did not interrupt. "General Ache would *be* there already. None of this ridiculous land crossing."

Evander tightened his hold on her waist. "If you had not sealed the seas, General Ache might not have any soldiers left to command."

The sea was too temperamental. Rifts opened unpredictably amid the shifting ripples of light and energy. The Aquarians would never have made it out of the water. They would have died defending their home, until the succubus overran them entirely.

He did not say any of that. Mya understood better than he did the benefits and costs of sealing her people into just one side of their home. She'd used the power vested in her as Queen of Aquarians to hobble an entire facet of their water magic, changing the very nature of the sea itself. She believed that when this was over, she'd be able to free it once more. Evander prayed to the Ancestors and any other deities who might be listening that she was right.

They continued in silence. Mya spent so much time in the minds of others, he knew that she sometimes struggled to know her own. These moments of quiet were essential for her, without the demands of others pressing in on her.

Once, he'd abhorred silence like this—inaction.

He, too, had not known himself. Only what others expected and wanted him to be.

Now, the silence did not scare him.

And he hated that just a few minutes later, he had to break hers.

He released Mya's waist, drawing his short sword. She wasn't armed, but by instinct she took a step closer to the water. She could dive into it or draw from it, Evander reminded himself. She could protect herself.

"There it is." He pointed ahead, to where the rolling slopes surrendered to a continuous rise. "Over that bluff we should see the Spit."

"They call it the Crossing here," Mya corrected him quietly. But her eyes were not on the rise he'd pointed out. "I have never seen it from this view."

Not the land—but the sea.

They'd walked along its edge for the last hour, but here she could see clearly where it separated from the land, stretching out toward the horizon. Logically, he knew that the other half of the continent lay on the other side. But from where they stood, the sea looked beautiful and endless.

"How far behind us are the troops?" Mya squinted as she spoke, her eyes focusing on something he could not see.

"An hour or two. Agravayn's forces will push in from the west, while General Ache leads from the sea." They had not given him any more particulars. His task was to assess the disposition of the enemy—the succubus horde that had attacked the humans who'd taken up residence on the Spit in the last several months.

There had been no sign of the darkness as they crossed the plains. No ruined bodies—not the skeletal black monsters that the succubus became once they'd inhabited a body long enough, nor the eviscerated remains of their human victims. The absence was almost eerie. How many humans were on the Spit, that they could keep the horde occupied for so long? The humans could not possibly be holding them back. Did that meant that succubus were... feeding?

Evander suddenly wished he'd remained back with the army to hear the human's report in full.

But Mya had begun to move. Up the bluff, her steps steady despite the miles they'd walked. She reached the apex—the sound she made sent a knife of fear straight into Evander's gut. A terrible gasp. A keening. Mourning.

He closed those feet between them in seconds.

If he made a sound to match Mya's, he did not hear or notice it.

"You asked if sealing the sea was a mistake."

He should have known. He may have never fought in a war—he'd been a Goldstone Guard, not a solider. But he understood what it meant to be outmatched. He'd fought against the succubus enough to know that even joining forces with the elementals, they were fighting a war that they were destined to lose. Their enemy did not tire. They did not retreat.

Below them, the bluff dropped down in a sheer cliff face. The natural barrier was the reason they had not seen any destruction. Evander could just make out the trail down, but it was winding and narrow. He could see why the succubus had not bothered to scale it. There were plenty of humans to feed on below, on that narrow strip of land that stretched out like a finger into the Split Sea until it disappeared into the distance.

Or at least, there had been.

As far as he could see was darkness.

Evander reached for Mya's hand. "No, I don't think it was."

47

VEYKA

Void.

Rift.

Portal.

I went through the void. I brought others through a rift. I created a portal.

I was the darkness of the void between realms and the light that waited on the other side. I was infinite, spinning through the darkness and then commanding it, bending the realms to my will to create safe passage not for one, but for thousands.

I was power.

The first portal I'd opened in Eilean Gayl was difficult—painful, even. I'd felt the weight of each body that passed through. But it became easier each time.

The cost has already been paid. Arthur had died for me to have this power. I would not waste it.

Arran did not hold any of our forces back. All twenty-some thousand terrestrial troops came through the portal rift I opened on the hillside above the eastern end of the Crossing. I did not ask his reasoning because I did not want to hear the words spoken aloud. If we were defeated here, there would be no second battle.

But if this war ended with our loss—our deaths—at least it would be in defense of life.

The female who'd raged against the humans, who'd tried to murder a messenger in her own throne room, was gone. The queen who'd taken her place... I was still not sure that I truly knew her and all her facets. But she loved and was loved in return—a reality I could not have fathomed even a year ago.

If I died defending the humans, then so be it.

But I wanted to live.

As the last line of terrestrials stepped through, I let the portal close behind them. Only Lyrena and I remained in the deserted war camp.

She lifted one golden eyebrow. "Fancy a nap?"

I burst out laughing. Only my golden knight could have managed such a thing, with the tension coming off of me in waves. "Maybe later," I smiled.

She took my hand without hesitation, and I brought us to the Crossing. Arran's army was already in motion below us. We were familiar with the terrain from having crossed it ourselves months before in our quest for Avalon. Arran and his lieutenants had gone on about the high ground and waves of attack and strategic advantage.

I was not a commander. A queen, yes. I'd accepted that. And a warrior. My place was on the battlefield, not trying to command it.

I expected to hear Arran in my mind, but it was eerily quiet. The golden thread of our mating bond was strong, the connection taut but not strained. He was not far. But his attention was elsewhere, as it should be. Worrying about me would only distract him —and I was more than capable of taking care of myself.

Lyrena and I stood above the army on the tiered bluff that eventually gave way to the thick, jungle-like forest where we'd been attacked by the succubus ourselves and then saved by Isolde.

I sent up a silent prayer to the Ancestors to protect the faerie. She was back in the war camp, convening with the terrestrial healers and preparing for the injured. She'd tried to come with us;

I'd refused. Leaving her with the terrestrials, healers but also strangers, made my heart twist uncomfortably.

She'll use those claws if she needs to, I consoled myself. The Faeries of the Fen had survived for thousands of years without help from the fae. Despite them. Isolde would be fine. She had to be. I did not know if I could stand the loss of another loved one.

Lyrena's voice pulled me back to the reality unfolding before our eyes.

"It doesn't seem real." Her sword hung limp at her side, all the humor drained from her lovely face. "I've imagined it... but never as bad as this."

I was not the only one who had nightmares about the succubus.

I followed her gaze down the graduated tiers of sheared off rock, past the mass of terrestrials clad in browns and greens. Most of the fauna-gifted among them had shifted. Wings and claws and gaping maws surged forward—forward and forward and forward towards the black mass that had overrun the narrow land bridge the connected the two sides of the continent.

It seemed impossible that we'd been here only months before.

What had once been a thriving human festival was now a wave of black death. Even staying awake through the night, refusing to sleep or let their minds become vulnerable, the succubus had eventually found them. *If only we'd known about the amorite then...*

And what would I have done? We'd carried none with us. Nor would I have been willing to spare it to protect *humans*.

Yet here I stood, ready to die for them.

I imagined I could see the spot where I'd stood in Arran's arms, kissing him while colorful fireworks burst overhead. My fingers curled into fists, remembering the way we'd painted each other's skin. For a brief moment, we'd been free.

Ancestors, I had not yet told him I loved him when we were here before.

The colorful tents were barely visible through the churning waves of black. Where before there had been music, now screams competed with the clash of metal. The latter was losing.

Lyrena exhaled slowly beside me. I recognized the careful, measured way she released the breath and then drew in the next. She was trying—failing—to steady herself. My heart rate increased, pounding wildly in my chest.

I drew Excalibur from across my back. I would not risk losing the precious amorite-swirled daggers by throwing them, and the great sword would allow me to kill the succubus while keeping as much distance as I could.

Lyrena's grip on her own weapon tightened. "Where do we even begin?"

"The village." We'd carefully avoided it when we made our way over the Crossing the first time all those months ago. But if it was still standing, then that was our first task. "We clear the village so that the survivors have somewhere to retreat."

Lyrena was good enough not to question whether there would be any survivors.

She extended her hand, her golden rings winking up at me. I knew that by the end of this day, no matter what happened, they would be coated in black.

There were survivors in the village.

Their screams told us that there would not be for long.

It was smaller than Eldermist. Even once cleared, it would not provide much shelter. I counted no more than two dozen buildings and only half of those were residences. If we could fill all of those with human survivors it would be nothing short of a miracle.

Lyrena swung her sword in a circle, loosening her wrist. "Stay close—"

"Never farther than an arm's reach," I finished for her.

She thought it was for my protection. I knew it was for hers.

There was no village square, only a single wide road and haphazard alleys crisscrossing off of it. The first alley was empty. The road was not. Four women tried to fight off a single succubus—

a male, recently turned from the fact that most of his body was still intact. One of the women was crying, sobbing, *begging* the others to stop.

One word cut through the melee. *Husband.*

I ended him with a single swipe of my sword. Not him—*it.*

The woman collapsed on the ground. Lyrena kicked open the nearest door, shoved the group of women inside, and slammed it behind her. More screams beckoned a few doors down.

We turned the corner—a group of them, more succubus than I could easily count, surged up the alleyway. A few broke off to feed. We could not help those humans. But we could try to stop the advancing pack.

Lyrena and I developed a rhythm. Her sword could not finish the succubus, but her fire slowed them enough that I could slice their heads off with Excalibur.

We cleared the alley. I grabbed Lyrena's arm and took us through the void to the next one, parallel, leaving the handful of human survivors to find their own refuge.

Alley after alley. If we cleared the alleys, they could not make it to the main road where all of the doors were. Behind the doors hid most of the humans.

Until we followed screams through a door, where a mother stood at the stairway to an upper floor, fighting off a succubus by herself with a frying pan while her children cried behind her on the landing.

She died. At least the children lived.

I told myself that we were making a difference. That this mattered. If Lyrena and I were able to clear the village, then surely the army down on the land bridge was able to defeat the horde of succubus. But my brain knew what my heart protested—the reason we were able to fight so effectively was because the horde had not yet reached the village. We were not facing a wave of black death, but a stream. A stream we could manage without drowning.

Arran.

I did not want to distract him. I just needed to know that he was uninjured, still in command and fighting.

The connection remained silent.

I could not afford to close my eyes, but as I swung again and again, the motion becoming almost routine, I let a small piece of my consciousness seek out the bond between us. I found it quickly —golden bright and shining.

Arran might be too distracted to hear me, but he was more than alive. He was fighting.

I breathed a little sigh of relief.

Lyrena had finished shoving the last of the surviving humans into one of the structures. I did not pause long enough to examine whether it was a house or something else.

"Separate your men; choose the strongest among you to guard them," she advised. With a grim nod, she added, "Protect your children from your husbands and fathers and prepare for the arrival or survivors."

Then she slipped her hand into mine. We needed no words between us.

There was only one place for us to go now.

❧ 48 ❧

ARRAN

Where the fuck is Orcadion?

The eagle shifter with the stubbornness of a bull had not returned in nearly an hour.

I ripped the throat from the succubus in front of me, shaking my head violently from side to side until the body broke free from the head and flew across the battlefield, joining the ever-growing mess of carnage of the ground. The black bile that spewed from the severed head tasted even worse than it smelled. The heightened senses of my beast made it nearly intolerable. But the wolf also dulled my thoughts. In this form, my primary concern was killing. I'd have to shift back to talk to Orcadion. I'd be able to take stock of the battle and send him to relay orders to the other lieutenants. But that would require him to return.

My beast threw his head back and howled, sending the sound up in the air above the fray. Clouds had begun to roll in during the first few minutes of engagement. Rain had not yet begun to fall, but the deepening gray overhead told me it was only a matter of minutes.

If we'd had the elemental army, I would have called for the weather-wielders to clear them. Or maybe they'd be using lightning to strike down succubus from the sky. It was not an approach we'd ever tried before.

My mind was in no place to file away information. Just that logical strain of thought was nearly too much. *Kill*, my beast urged.

I obliged him.

My massive jaws shredded the flesh from a newly turned succubus. Ripped off the arm of one that tried to claw out the guts of one of my soldiers. I always went back for the head. Just like a fae, removing their head was the only way to keep them down. An amorite weapon could do the job as well. Any mortal blow would do, so long as it was delivered by an amorite weapon. There were no fire wielders among the terrestrial troops—it was an elemental power. But somewhere, I knew Lyrena was using her flames to slow them down.

Lyrena.

Veyka.

My beast howled again, calling out for her through the bond. But she did not answer.

Terrestrial soldiers littered the ground around me. But we had not lost ground, either. The horde of succubus had not reached the mainland. Why—when they'd overwhelmed Baylaur so easily?

Because these were humans, I realized as my teeth sank into another skull. Humans turned by the succubus were easier to kill than fae who'd turned. Their bodies were smaller, weaker. Even with the insatiable nature of the succubus, the human bodies they occupied were easier for the larger, magic-wielding fae to hack apart.

We were only holding our own because we were not facing our own.

The beast shook his mighty head, blood and gore raining down around me.

Veyka?

The plea turned to a snarl. *Where are you?*

I could feel her, but I couldn't reach her. Ancestors, what was happening? My beast usually had a stronger connection to Veyka than even my fae form. She was *his* mate, *his* to protect.

I shook my head again, trying to clear it. The fog of killing had overtaken me. There was no room for feelings or emotions when all that mattered was death—raining it down upon our enemies and evading it myself.

Back to my fae form—maybe that was the answer. The beast was too far gone to reach her, too deep in that place of killing and death. The connection between us had always defied logic—how else could a connection driven by a mating bond exist even before we were truly mated? It was forged by emotion, by my beast's recognition from the beginning that what existed between us was beyond the constraints of reality. It was why I'd been able to defy the ancient magic of the Pit.

I shifted so I could search the battlefield with different eyes—

No.

My hands were still paws, massive and tipped in shredding black claws.

I sank my teeth into my lower lip, using the pain to anchor myself. But those were not my elongated canines, but fangs.

Shifting was natural. Even the first time the beast had emerged, when I was a child locked in a torture chamber, it had happened without thought. It had taken me three hundred years to accept that my beast was me, that the two were not inseparable.

I shifted.

Except I did not.

I was trapped in my beast form.

I threw back my head and howled again, rage consuming me.

Gaps in my power. That was how Isolde had described it. Was this what she'd meant?

I plunged into a knot of succubus feeding on the remains of a bear shifter. My beast tore them apart, ignoring heads or dismembered limbs.

Trapped—I'd never been trapped. Not since those torturous months in my youth, when I'd been stolen away for the power that thrummed in my veins. I'd fought on hundreds of battlefields, but I'd never been captured. Now I was a prisoner within my own body, within my beast.

Veyka, where are you? My beast snarled. I could fucking feel her. The glowing golden bond between us was practically vibrating with energy. Why couldn't I hear her?

My mind raced, but my fangs and claws tore and maimed. The black bile, the souls of the taken, filled my jaws, coated my tongue and slipped down into my stomach. It matted my pale fur until I could not tell from looking down that it had ever been white.

Veyka—

Claws sank into my back, digging past the thick fur and raking down a vicious line an inch from my spine. I threw my head back, the bellow of pain mingling with the howl, a cry for help. I twisted violently, trying to dislodge the succubus. But its worn-down nubs of fingers were speared deep into the flesh of my back. It was only half a human, the entire bottom half of its body missing—where I'd ripped it apart moments before. I'd done this to myself. I'd lost control and now Veyka might lose me.

No, that could not happen. Without me to hold her back, she would sacrifice herself even more willingly. She would *die*.

I twisted again, throwing myself back onto the mass of bodies beneath me, trying to break the succubus's aching grip. Pain seared up my spine, but the monster felt none of it. It clung to me, lowering its jaws to add its teeth to the torture. I snapped my jaws, determined to rip its head off once and—

A swirled blade sliced through the head, so close to my snout that I felt the whoosh of air against the sensitive black pad of my nose. Expertly wielded, the hatchet severed the succubus's head. Two more swings and the body fell away as well.

I shifted.

And this time, my power answered.

My knees hit the ground, the black bile and churned up dirt sinking into the knees of my trousers. A raindrop fell on the pale brown hand that extended in front of me.

Mordred. My son had saved me.

I took his hand. Tugged myself to my feet. Refused to acknowledge the pain in my back. I couldn't count the wounds; the pain was too intense. Nor could I parse the scent of my own blood from the rivers of it that flowed around me.

My eyes flicked upward. Orcadion was nowhere in sight. But Mordred stood in front of me, his chest heaving up and down in a rhythm that my own echoed back.

Arran?

The force of relief nearly brought me back to my knees. *Veyka.*

What's wrong? Are you injured? she demanded, her worry flooding the connection between us. But if she was worried for me, that meant she was not scared for herself. Wherever she was, she was whole.

I gritted my teeth. I could not say the same for myself—but I also did not need her distracted with my wellbeing. *I am fine.*

Silence filled my mind.

I did not need her words. With the connection restored, I could feel her response. She did not believe me.

49

VEYKA

Arran was lying to me. I added it to my list of grievances to punish him for later. We would survive to have that argument.

"We need to scout ahead," I told Lyrena, fighting at my back. "Can you grab my arm?"

"Arrrggggh!" Lyrena cried out, her back leaving mine, pushing me back with the momentum she needed to charge forward. A heartbeat later, she was back, her breath coming in uneven gasps. She stank of the black souls the succubus expelled; we both did.

"Scouting?" she managed between breaths.

My chin stabbed an uneven nod as I parried, swinging Excalibur wide across the gut of the very same succubus she'd driven back with her flame seconds before.

The monster dropped. Lyrena swallowed hard. Her smile was more of a grimace as I grabbed her arm. "Let's go."

❦

It was the hardest thing I'd ever done. Whenever I fought, whether it be sparring in the training ring or facing the first massacre of Baylaur, my mind descended past thinking into a place of visceral control. But in that place, I could not reach Arran.

Our bond was emotional. It appeared that if I shut down my emotions, then that part of my heart that belonged to him, that allowed us to communicate as if we were one soul split into two bodies, that was also blocked.

How was I supposed to kill and feel at the same time?

The human woman's screams echoed through my mind.

My husband.

I shoved Excalibur through what had once been the heart of a human adolescent.

I can still see the eastern cliffs. The succubus are thinning here, I told Arran.

Grabbed Lyrena's arm. Through the void.

Two of the monsters converged on me. One latched onto my arm, sinking its sharpened teeth into my thick leather armor. But I couldn't bleed. I swiped for my dagger, dragging it across the knuckles to get the succubus to release me. But succubus didn't feel pain. I rammed the dagger into its throat instead. I didn't let go, not when every amorite weapon was precious. The succubus reeled backward, taking me with it, bringing the second one down atop me. I pulled my knees to my chest, only to be enveloped with flame. Lyrena ripped the succubus off of me. I sprang to my feet and drove Excalibur into its gut in two coordinated motions.

There are so many of them. You need to send more forces toward the center, I told Arran. Maybe he would follow my suggestion; maybe it made no sense at all and he'd know better.

Grab Lyrena's arm. Through the void.

Women screaming and screaming and screaming. *My husband.*

The sea was wilder now that we'd passed the center of the Spit. The Crossing. Whatever the fuck it was called. From this position, I could just see the cliffs in either direction through the now steady rain.

Lyrena fought at my side, but all the succubus around me were on the ground. Where—how? There were no terrestrials. Was the sea swallowing them up? How could that be? Did the monsters drown? We should have started pushing them into the sea months ago.

"We need to go farther," I yelled to Lyrena. But the wind and the rain stole my words. Or was it the roaring of the sea?

The waves attacked the edges of the narrow strip of land, vicious and driving. A torrent of water spiraled upward, then plunged down, taking a succubus with it. How—

I don't understand.

I felt Arran's jolt. I hadn't meant to say that. I reached for Lyrena, halfway into the void already. My fingers touched her wrist —but there was nothing there.

The world spun around me, a second of darkness and then a burst of gray and clouds. I was alone. I'd left Lyrena behind.

Fuck, fuck, fuck.

Arran. Lyrena and I are separated.

But I was not alone.

I was surrounded by strange blue creatures. And directly in front of me were two faces I'd thought I would never see again. Two males whose faces could only mean my death.

50

CYARA

Night fell quickly on the Isle of the Dead.

Cyara wondered if the stars would even dare to shine their light on the forbidden island of Tirbyas as she followed Diana and Percival for what she thought was the third hour. She had not thought the island to be big enough for that. But as far as she could tell, they were not walking in circles. Just continuing over the unremarkable, barren ground. Eventually they'd come to the sea on the other side, she supposed.

Prayed was more accurate.

Cyara prayed to Nimue, to Accolon, to all the other Ancestors. They'd left a mess for Arran and Veyka to sort through, it was true. But she still trusted them more than the witches that had occupied this island and the eerie magic they'd left behind.

Diana and Percival were both quiet, speaking neither to her nor to each other. But whatever call Diana answered, it must persist, because the woman did not hesitate in her steps. She did not stumble, not once.

Cyara kept her wings tucked in tight, ready to take flight at any moment. She'd seen the Gremog leap out of its tunnels in the Effren Valley to protect the goldstone palace. There was no telling what sorts of protections the witches had left behind to guard their ancient island. Or what sorts of tests Merlin had contrived, if she had indeed stored the grail on the island to await its worthy wielder.

The moon had just appeared over the horizon when Diana stopped. Percival came to her side, his head tipping back to admire the stars. The first of those had appeared as well, hanging midway in the pale purple sky.

Cyara pushed down the knot of unease that had taken up residence in her chest, forcing herself to take the steps to come stand beside them. The sand made no sound beneath her boots as she—

"Ow!" Cyara screamed, her forehead colliding with stone. She fell backward, crushing her wings at an awkward angle behind her, sending a slice of pain up the left one. She tried to roll, ripping out her own feathers in the process. "What in the Ancestors?"

"What is wrong with you?" Percival squatted down at her side, his eyes drawing together until his thick black brows formed a single line across his forehead. Diana only half turned, gave Cyara a cursory glance, and then turned back to the sky she'd been looking at before as if it held the answer to every question she'd ever wondered about.

Cyara squinted over Percival's shoulder at the pillar of crumbling stone "It just appeared out of nowhere."

One second, there had been nothing but open space in front of her. The next, she was on the ground, her head throbbing and wing aching, and a half-tumbled down white pillar stood in the space directly next to where Percival had been standing.

Percival's unibrow shot upward, his dark eyes blowing wide. "How hard did you hit your head? What do you think we stopped to look at, the two stars that are just barely visible?"

Cyara blinked. That was exactly what she thought. But as she got back to her feet, mindful of her aching wing and the bruise already forming on her backside, she was forced to reconsider.

"I don't think she can see it, Percival," his sister said quietly.

Dreamily. Just above a whisper, but not like a secret. There was almost a melody to the cadence of her words.

The ball of unease that had lived in her chest since they're arrival on Tirbyas sent a tendril snaking down her spine.

Percival watched Cyara shiver, then looked back at his sister. Then back at Cyara. "What *do* you see?"

Cyara rubbed her forehead. "Until I smacked into it, I didn't see anything. Just the sand and the gray. And two stars," she said with a hint of sarcasm. "Now... I see ruins. A mighty temple once stood here. There are... five pillars. But only one of them looks like it is still at its full height. They look like sandstone, maybe."

"Moonstone," Diana corrected.

Cyara squinted through the falling darkness. She took a tentative step forward, then another. No new structures sprung up to knock her back. The ones that had appeared remained sedentary. But once she was close enough, she could confirm. Definitely *not* moonstone. At least, not to her eyes.

Diana hummed low in her throat.

"You see something different," Cyara realized. She spun back to the ruined temple, trying again. But it appeared exactly as it had a moment before.

Diana swayed gently on her feet to the rhythm of a music that only she could hear.

"I see a glorious temple. A reservoir of magic. Five pillars, just as you saw. But they stand tall, supporting arches between them engraved with the most beautiful carvings. There is no ceiling, it is open to the heavens. And it is glowing."

Her eyes had gone dreamy, misty—like they had when they'd found the circle of standing stones left behind by Accolon and Nimue. Her gift was foresight, the ability to let her mind travel through time and space. They'd exploited that very gift to allow them the painful little jumps to get to the island at all.

Cyara swallowed. "Percival?"

He frowned. "I see what Diana sees."

Cyara nodded; she'd expected as much. They were witches. This was a witch temple.

"So, which is it?" Percival asked, crossing his arms over his chest.

Cyara reached out to touch the pillar of sandstone. She paused, glancing to Diana to see if the woman would protest. But she continued to hum away dreamily.

The stone was cool, like the air around it. Smooth beneath her fingers. The pale stone reflected the rising moon, but it certainly wasn't glowing. Not like it would be if it was moonstone.

"Does it have to be one or the other? Maybe we are seeing different plans of existence," Cyara mused. Either the unease in her chest was subsiding or she was getting used to its constant presence. At the very least, she no longer had the urge to immediately take flight.

"So we command the void now to?" Percival scoffed.

Cyara shrugged, then regretted the motion as her a jolt of pain shot through her wing. "Not all magic can be explained." Like the harpy within her. Yes, it had emerged after her sisters' brutal murders. But how had it survived in her bloodline at all? According to her mother, no family lore mentioned the harpy. The females of their line carried wings, but those were beautiful and white feathered. Nothing like the monster that Cyara became when she needed to protect those she loved.

"Magic does not owe us an explanation," she said.

Percival snorted and turned away. Cyara breathed in softly, hesitant to disturb Diana's endless murmuring.

Except that she'd stopped. It was silent.

"It calls to me."

The unease sprang back to life. But it awakened the other seed that Cyara had been carefully nurturing these past weeks—hope. "The chalice?"

Diana did not answer. She stepped forward into the ring of pillars that formed the exterior of the temple, moving toward its center. All Cyara could see was more barren sand. But by now, she had stopped trusting her eyes. Mindful to keep her hands extended in front of her, she stepped past the worn pillars.

It felt like stepping through a wall of water. Inside, the pillars were the same. Crumbling, unremarkable sandstone. But at the center of the temple stood a matching altar.

Diana and Percival approached it as well. Whatever they could see, it was similar enough to draw their attention.

"What do the carvings mean?" Percival asked, leaning in closer to the flat circular top.

"I don't see any carvings," Cyara admitted. She skimmed her fingers over the stone rim where Percival focused his attention. "If there were any here, they've been long since worn away and obscured. At least for me."

"I see them," Diana confirmed. Her fingertips caressed the strip of stone tenderly, tracing patterns that Cyara could not see. "They are instructions."

Cyara held her breath.

"They tell us how to find the grail."

🐾 51 🐾

ARRAN

"The water came to life," I repeated. I'd pulled back to near the neck of the Crossing, where it joined with the land.

By sheer numbers and a heavy dose of luck, we were going to prevail. If this battle had been against fae taken by the succubus, the outcome would have been different. If I'd left any of the troops back in Wolf Bay, the outcome would have been different. If Orcadion had listened to orders, it might have been over sooner.

"It must have been an elemental," Barkke said. He sported a split lip and a deep wound to his shoulder that he's sustained in his dog form. But he was upright and had earned a nod of respect from the blonde female lieutenant I had assigned him to shadow.

"Has there been any sign of Elora?" That was the only explanation that made any sense. The humans must have sent messengers into the western half of the continent as well and encountered what remained of the elemental army that was under Elora's command.

Barkke shook his head. He didn't know the female well, but I trusted him to at least recognize her from making her acquaintance in Eilean Gayl.

Maybe the elemental army had made their way to the Crossing on their own, but had not yet met up with Elora.

Veyka would be back any moment with Lyrena and a more comprehensive report from further down the land bridge. From this side, I could not see to the other. But she'd been working her way down when last I'd heard her silken voice in my mind.

I began to reach for the golden thread of the bond when a familiar hulking presence appeared in my periphery.

"Orcadion!"

For half a step, he looked like he would ignore me. Then his stepson—my son—leaned forward and murmured something I could not hear. Orcadion turned, the heavy brow-ridge that imitated the ridges of his eagle form turning his yellow eyes a deeper, nasty gold.

"Your Majesty." Orcadion stepped on the bodies of fallen terrestrials as if they were nothing. He did not bother with the facsimile of a bow or even a nod.

"You deserted your duty." Part of me had expected it. Orcadion had always been a ruthless bastard, and a position of power on the Dyad was not likely to change that. But I had changed more in the last year than even I could account for. Some stupid, naïve part of me had hoped he would as well.

He rolled his shoulders, the nostrils of his wide, flat nose flaring. "I was detained."

"You disobeyed direct orders from your commander and king, and you neglected your duty to mentor your stepson in his first battle." It was more than enough to deserve death. Maybe I had changed more than even I realized. "You are confined to the fortress at Cayltay. I have no use for disobedient soldiers in my army."

His upper lip curled, but he did not acknowledge the order. "The whelp saved your life, I believe."

"My son acquitted himself well." The words rolled off my tongue easier than I expected. "He may remain."

Orcadion's arms flared out from his sides in a clear threat. He wanted to shift, to use his sharp beak to tear out my throat.

Let him try.

But his arms dropped back to his side. The sneer remained in place. He turned away from me, back in the direction he'd been walking before—towards where the remainder of my troops were organizing.

"One last thing."

He stilled, as did everyone around us. A handful of human survivors. Two dozen terrestrial soldiers within earshot. Three of my lieutenants.

"Kneel, Orcadion."

He did not turn, but I heard his words just fine. "You did not fight in the Pit for that crown of yours. You are still nothing more than the Brutal Prince."

He was lucky that Veyka was not there to hear his disrespect. She would not have bothered with his knees. She'd remove his head from his body for such words.

"Kneel, or I will cut off both your legs at the knee." They would regrow. But it would be slow and painful. And there was nothing to stop another fauna-gifted terrestrial from challenging him for his seat on the Dyad while they healed.

Orcadion took one step. Bones crunched beneath his feet. Another step. He would not meet my eyes, but I did not need his respect. I only required his submission. As he kneeled, he kept his eyes fixed on those just behind me.

I waited until both of his knees touched the ground. I would not do him the honor of waiting for him to rise. But before I could life my foot, something closed around my ankle. Barkke lunged, but Orcadion threw his meaty body in the way, letting the monster drag me down into the water.

I recognized the blackened limbs that tangled around my own. The succubus *could* survive in the water. Of course they could. They did not need air, they did not fear the beasts of the deep. One pulled me down, another joining it. Even with the weight of the water slowing my movements, I got my amorite-swirled knife free from my belt. I stabbed blindly, water rushing up to obscure my view.

One succubus fell away, but another replaced it just as quickly.

It clawed up my body, ripping open the still-oozing wounds on my back with a fresh torrent of blood that mingled with the seawater.

I stabbed with the amorite dagger, but there were too many of them. The amorite had to land a fatal wound. Stabbing it in the shoulder or cutting off their arms wasn't enough.

My feet kicked wildly, trying to force me back up to the surface. My boot connected with something, and I pushed off, but it gave way. Not enough leverage. I gulped, but more water than air filled my lungs.

Realization spread through me with the saltwater.

I was drowning.

Drowning was the worst-kept secret in Annwyn. A fae could heal from almost any injury if given enough time. Limbs would regrow. Wounds would knit, so long as the blood could be staunched long enough to replenish. Most humans believed that the only way to ensure a fae did not rise was to cut off their head.

But drowning was just as effective. Once the water filled the lungs and breathing stopped, there was no return.

This was how Igraine killed Parys.

Veyka would break...

She would sacrifice herself...

I tried to summon the strength, but it ebbed away from me with my lifeblood. The water swirled with red and black as the light from above dimmed to nothing. My last view of this realm would be the mixture of my own blood with a soul stolen by the succubus.

I'm sorry, Veyka. I tried to reach for the bond, but I knew my own hold on it was fraying.

Something hit my back, ramming into the already gaping wounds. But I was beyond feeling pain. As my eyes drifted closed, a lovely face appeared in the water. The fading light turned her white hair dark in silhouette, her eyes a darker blue. But at least I saw Veyka's face... *one last time*...

52

CYARA

"Tell us." Cyara used every decade of her elemental upbringing to keep her voice even so she did not spook Diana. Although the woman had been uncharacteristically calm since their arrival on the island, Cyara was loath to push her. The pressure might break at any moment, and who knew how long it would take for her to recover.

"A witch at your mercy must answer three questions truthfully," Diana said as her fingers moved slowly along the perimeter of the circular altar. Percival's expression was more than skeptical, though his eyes followed her fingertips, clearly tracking her progress. Whatever she felt or saw, it had meaning to her. That was enough for Cyara.

"The seeker of the grail must put themselves at the mercy of the witches who forged it. To prove yourself worthy, you must offer three truths freely."

Cyara's wing twitched, but she did not feel the pain. "And then?"

"That is all it says."

Cyara swallowed, turning over the instructions in her mind. The witch-altar was a sort of vengeance for the curse in their blood that required the witches to give truth against their will. In order to gain their most precious object, the Grail, the seeker would have to offer freely what the witches had been forced to give again and again for thousands of years.

"Any truths?" Percival lifted one dark brow, the moonlight softening the red undertones of his ochre skin.

"Three truths offered freely," Diana repeated. She folded her hands neatly in front of her, as she always did. Cyara suspected it was an affectation learned in Avalon, reminiscent as it was of the priestesses.

"They must be significant truths. Hard truths," Cyara mused. Otherwise, there would be no challenge.

Merlin had said that only the worthy could retrieve the grail. She had also implied that it did not have to be Veyka herself who retrieved it in order to wield the Sacred Trinity in its entirety. Which meant that Cyara would not leave the cursed island without it.

"The chalice was forged by and entrusted to the witches," Cyara said. "Originally." Before the fae Ancestors had stripped them of power and their sacred object. "One of you should try first."

Perhaps that was the reason Diana had felt called to this place. Perhaps it was her destiny to retrieve the grail. With every moment that passed, as the moon climbed in the inky blue sky and the stars appeared in full force, it was more and more difficult for Cyara to suppress her excitement. Her stomach bubbled, her wings twitched. A lifetime of elemental training was quickly melting away.

She was trembling as she laid a hand on Diana's forearm. "You are strong."

It was the truth. But it also felt like a manipulation. Cyara needed to keep Diana from faltering in this moment more than any that had come before.

Diana licked her lips. "Before I was stolen from Avalon, I was apprentice to the Lady of the Lake."

Cyara's mouth popped open.

That was a truth. And one she did not plan on telling Veyka about.

Percival harrumphed, his disapproval clear. But Diana continued.

"I am banned from returning. But I still wish to be a priestess."

Once, Cyara's heart would have broken. But now the painful admission only kindled hope for her own friend in her heart.

Diana laid a hand on the flat sandstone top of the altar.

"I still have nightmares of the months I spent in," she paused, her throat bobbing. "In captivity."

Cyara's breath caught in her throat. She waited, expecting... something. Anything. For the stone to start to glow, for the altar and the temple to transform into the glowing, magical edifice that Diana had described.

But nothing happened. The surface of the altar remained unbroken. No grail appeared.

Cyara looked up at Diana, then Percival, hoping that perhaps they saw something she did not. But the latter jerked his head to the side.

Cyara braced herself for Diana's reaction, curling her fingers into her fists and tightening her wings. But the woman simply stepped back and turned her face to her brother. "You must try, Percival."

Percival stared at her as if she had suggested he sacrifice himself on the altar, lifeblood and all.

Cyara lifted a brow in challenge. There were two ways to get Percival to do anything—for Diana, or for his own pride. "Afraid, Percival?"

The stare he'd given his sister turned to a glare just for Cyara. She took it easily, without even a flicker of her wings.

"I abhor chocolate."

Diana made a little squawk of disapproval.

Cyara carried a small knife attached to her belt. It was her only weapon, other than the talons of her harpy. Her fingers *itched* to stab it into Percival's smug face.

She waited for the reaction, for the softer part of herself to respond to that urge for violence. But her anger only sharpened.

"Take this seriously, or all of your sister's suffering has been for *nothing*."

His upper lip curled, but Cyara did not miss the color draining from his cheeks, leaving his skin ashen in the cool-toned moonlight.

But he did not flinch from meeting her eyes as he gave his second truth. "I dream of what it would feel like to kill every person who has dared to hold my sister captive."

The harpy inside of her screeched, tearing at the surface. How dare he threaten Veyka, Osheen, Arran, Lyrena, even her? There would be no stopping the monster this time. Cyara felt her wings flare wide, her fingertips curling at the push of the talons—

"These truths are meant to be painful," Diana said softly. Her hand landed on Cyara's arm, soft and light as a feather, but still *there*.

The harpy receded instantly, leaving a hollowness in her place. *She* was the one who'd fallen apart—and Diana had provided comfort. Her reality had been shifting for months now. But as Diana's hand fell away, Cyara felt the final pieces begin to slide into place. She listened through a veil as Percival offered his last truth.

"The fate of this realm does not concern me. Only that of my sister," he sucked in a breath, "And myself."

No one moved.

The grail did not appear.

Cyara did not wait for the surprise or disappointment, because she had not expected Percival to be successful. If either of the siblings was capable of earning the grail, it would have been Diana. But the chalice had not come forth—they had not been judged worthy.

The only thing that Cyara felt was panic.

If they were not enough, then she certainly was not. A year ago, she would have felt differently. Before she'd lost her sisters and her father, before the harpy had awoken within her, before the soft, pure parts of her soul had withered away to darkness.

Her mind began to jump ahead. When she failed, she would have no choice but to use the communication crystal and admit to Veyka that she'd disobeyed her orders. She would beg her queen to come here, to this cursed isle. Maybe if she begged, Veyka would listen. Maybe if Veyka understood what her death, her obsession with sacrifice, would mean to those who loved her... maybe she would be willing to try for the grail herself.

Veyka would never regard her the same. But Cyara could bear that shame. She could not bear her friend's loss.

One hand slid into the pocket sown into her gray tunic, finding the thick shape of the communication crystal and closing around it.

Neither Percival nor Diana had been able to retrieve the grail. Cyara had thought that their witch-blood would give them an advantage, a natural affinity. But maybe the opposite was true. Maybe it would only answer to a non-witch.

Or to someone whose soul had fully descended into darkness.

There was only one way to find out.

"I have poisoned, betrayed, and lied in service of my queen. My first truth is that I do not regret any of it."

Cyara's voice shook, but somehow she managed not to trip over the words. That precious elemental calm deserted her completely, replaced by every emotion she'd kept carefully suppressed for the last year. They gnawed their way out, insistent, demanding, until her lips trembled and tears spilled down her cheeks.

"My second is that she did not ask it of me. Every action I have taken has been of my own free will."

No one had forced her to become the harpy. Gawayn murdered her sisters. But when the harpy awoke inside of her, Cyara had welcomed her. She'd been fire and light her whole life. When the darkness came, she let in willingly.

She lifted one hand—the one that did not clutch the communication crystal—and laid it on canter of the sandstone altar. Her lids lowered until they closed. A thousand truths swam behind her eyes, each more terrible than the last. Each a fragment of a broken soul. But there was only one worth giving.

"I will sacrifice everyone on this island to get the grail and save my queen."

She felt Percival shove Diana behind him. Heard the woman gasp as the female she'd considered her friend gave voice to the betrayal that had become a part to her. But Cyara did not move.

She did not have to.

The altar did—bathing her in a blast of warmth, lifting her hand.

Cyara did not dare to open her eyes, afraid that what she felt under her fingers was another trick. But the gasps of the two humans told her the truth. The rim she felt beneath her fingers was real.

She opened her eyes to watch her own fingers curl around the grail.

53

GUINEVERE

Too late. The dark lioness ran fast—faster than any two-legged beast, human or fae. Faster than the Brutal Prince's wolf. The only beings faster were those that ruled the skies. But as her stride stretched out, eating up the mountainous dirt and blurring the scrubby trees around her, she felt certain that even the fastest winged shifters would have struggled to keep up.

She had to be fast, because already it was too late. The succubus had come. A horde of them crawled across the valley, ever closer to the humans and elementals waiting unsuspecting in Eldermist. The patrols did not go this far; they would not see the enemy until they were too close, too late. There was nowhere to run. Through the rift into Baylaur there waited only more death.

The communication crystal—Gwen had to use it now.

Not now. Soon.

She had to know how many. How fast. How soon. She had to get all the information she could, even knowing that it would come too late. Who knew what other horrors Arran and Veyka had encountered in Wolf Bay. If it came to a choice between saving their own realm or the human's, she could not fault them for choosing Annwyn. They were its anointed rulers. But Gwen would stay and fight here. She would die *here*.

But not just yet. Not until she had the information she needed.

The sand shifted beneath her paws, sending her sliding down the side of the mountain. She turned it to her advantage, let the momentum carry her to the next outcropping of stone, used it to brace her footing, and leapt over the next dune entirely.

She'd circumnavigated half of the valley now. In a few minutes, she would be just above the horde. She must get close enough to assess numbers, strength, and speed. From what she could tell from her first look, they were moving in a tight group. That information would be vital to forming battle plans. They'd only faced the succubus in massacre scenarios, where they overtook the unprotected males at such a speed that those remaining could not hold them back. But what would it be like to face a horde in the open field of battle? They did not have commanders as far as any of them had been able to tell, did not follow a strategy of their own. Ancestors, they did not need one. Not when they did not tire, did not feel pain.

They were drawn to Veyka. That was the most telling bit of information thus far.

Veyka was on the other side of the continent, in another realm entirely. What had drawn the succubus horde to the valley?

Thoughts changed and formed and changed in time with the cadence of her own bounds and leaps. But they all faded away as she cleared the next rise—the one that would bring her into direct view of the advancing horde.

They would be able to see her as well, but she was far enough and fast enough for it not to matter. Besides, she would appear as nothing more than a lion of the mountains, hunting for prey just like them...

It couldn't be.

She shifted, not believing her lioness's eyes. But the sight she saw now, the details in sharp relief, was the same.

Not a succubus horde.

She counted, doubling, stretching, estimating. One thousand. Two thousand. Three. Her heart stretched and groaned, unused to the emotion that pushed aside the worry and fear.

Not a force of darkness, but of light.

Elora marched at the head of the remains of the elemental army. And at her side, in perfect formation and keeping pace despite their smaller stature, was a company of a thousand human foot soldiers.

54

VEYKA

"Traitors." Anger seared through me, hot and bright even through the driving rain. I expected to see lightning coming down around me, even though I'd shown no affinity for storms. The force of my anger was enough to defy all logic. "I knew you'd come for me one day. But I will admit, I did not expect it to be today."

The resemblance only made it worse. Agravayn conjured images of his brother, memories of the guardian who'd been the next thing to a father to me in those months after Arthur's death. Just the memory was enough to set the blood in my veins sizzling dangerously.

"We are no threat to you." Agravayn lowered his weapon, sheathing it at his belt and showing submission by offering his hands palms up. I gripped my weapons tighter, savoring the weight of Excalibur in one hand, my familiar dagger in the other.

"Save your lies. Your brother was good with them, too. I have learned my lesson." My eyes scanned the flat expanse behind him. There were two more brothers, no doubt lying in wait to support Agravayn.

"You haven't learned anything. You're the same self-centered princess."

Fucking Evander.

Ancestors. I'd managed to forget his existence for the last few months. Gwen had told us that communications stopped coming from the estate belonging to Gawayn's brothers on the edge of the Split Sea. But with the liberation of the survivors from Baylaur, then the settling of those from the mountains into Eldermist and reaching the terrestrial army.... Evander had been a blip unworthy of my attention.

Until now, when he stood before me gripping a short sword and sneering at me, hate shining out of his dark eyes.

The feeling was utterly, completely, and overwhelmingly mutual.

"I always knew you wanted to kill me, Evander. I did not realize that by ridding myself of you, I was sending you into the arms of the traitors lying in wait in my own kingdom." But it was a mistake I could rectify now, quickly. "You finally have your wish. Kill me."

It would give me the ultimate pleasure to put him down.

The battle around us ebbed. The screams died away from the urgent sounds of imminent death to the longer groans of agony that belonged to the wounded. By sheer numbers and luck I was not going to question, we'd defeated the succubus this day.

There were carcasses behind the two traitors. Human and succubus. Which meant they'd fought their way across the bridge. Were those blue bodies as well?

Before I could follow that line of thought, another male appeared, wading through the carnage to stand between Agravayn and Evander.

"The killing is done for today, Majesty." Gaheris—the most reasonable of the brothers, after Gawayn. Or so I'd thought. I could remember with perfect clarity the day they'd stood before me shoulder to shoulder in the throne room of the goldstone palace.

I'd been amused and intrigued to meet Gawayn's brothers. Before their brother murdered my handmaidens, tried to kill me, and aided the female who'd orchestrated Arthur's death.

I had been horrified when they'd described the children gone missing from their shores. Had that, too, been a lie? A ruse to rob me of my Goldstone Guards?

Agravayn was the angry one. That was also easy to recall. And he deferred easily to his brother, the conciliator.

"Come to convince me of your goodwill? Your loyalty?" I lifted a brow at Gaheris. Nothing they could say would convince me. Not after what Gawayn had done. The primal need for vengeance mingled with the adrenaline of battle, driving away all reason. I would kill them where they stood—

Except I didn't. The anger was there, alive in my veins. But my feet did not move. I did not swing Excalibur or throw my dagger. I waited, giving them a chance to say something, to convince me, to change my mind.

Mordred's words from the Pit came back to me, when he'd beseeched me to judge him for himself, rather than the actions of his mother. There was a chance, ever so slight, that Gawayn's brothers had not conspired to overthrow my throne. That Evander, hated and vile as he had always been to me, had a reason for his prolonged absence.

Gaheris mirrored his brother's stance—feet apart, palms up in supplication. "We came because the humans called for aid. But our eventual goal was to find you and join our forces with the elemental army."

"There is no elemental army. The succubus took Baylaur. Where was your aid then?"

Actions. That was what would convince me now. They'd come to the aid of the humans at the Crossing but left Baylaur to be overrun? Where was the loyalty and duty in that? They should have done both. They should have been fighting and losing loved ones the way I had been. They could not possibly be loyal.

"We heard of the fall of Baylaur. The succubus has not spared us, nor the estates nearby. We secured our own homes and we came," Gaheris explained, his voice steady and reasonable. The consummate elemental.

But I did not want to deal with him, with reason. I threw my snarl at Evander, his sneer shifting into a frown, the hatred in his gaze softened to something more difficult to identify.

"You do not step up to defend your queen," I accused, although neither Agravayn nor Gaheris had offered any real threat. But I wanted to provoke. I wanted him to swing that shortsword, so I could finally let out my anger and put to bed the reason that kept trying to take control. "You have abandoned your vows."

But his sword arm dropped instead. "I did not abandon them. But I am bound by new ones more powerful."

He would not advance. Neither did I. "And what are those?"

"Marriage vows."

Laughter bubbled out of my chest, wild and unhinged. "And how am I to trust anything you say? You, the brothers of a traitor." I threw my hand wide, sweeping in front of the three men. "And you... the hatred still shines in your eyes."

But they were spared a response by the crashing of water upon the shore. We turned as one as a pale-blue figure emerged from the water. A female, her dark curls sticking to her shoulders as she dragged herself up onto the shore. She wasn't alone. I recognized the torso she gripped beneath the arms, hauling it out of the water. I knew the knot of dark hair and the stubbled bronze cheek. My heart stopped—his chest was not moving.

Then Arran heaved a massive cough, water ejecting from his lungs and spattering across the front of his leather armor and down onto the ragged rocks that broke the land from the sea. My eyes clung to his chest, watching every gasped rise and fall as he forced his lungs to function normally again.

I counted those rises and falls, the rich sapphire blue of the sea behind him slowly coming into focus. Until it wasn't the sea. It was a tail. And it belonged to the pale-blue skinned female who'd dragged him out of the water, who now looked up at me with a smile so wide, it almost reached her delicately pointed ears.

Evander's harsh laugh swept in along with his cold wind. "Because my wife is the Ethereal Queen."

55

ARRAN

Sleeping felt like a waste of time. Not for Veyka, whose white skin was marred by dark bruises beneath her eyes. Exhaustion that she could not hide and Isolde could not heal.

I had not told her about being trapped in my beast form. Nor about Mordred's role in saving my life. I did not want to admit to myself that I had needed saving not just once, but twice. Arran Earthborn, Brutal Prince, was supposed to be the most powerful terrestrial in millennia. Until that power failed. Until I nearly drowned.

Only to be saved by... the Ethereal Queen? Who was also Queen of the Aquarian Fae, a third race of fae that had wiped themselves from memory after the Great War? It was too much to think about. No wonder Veyka was exhausted.

I was, too.

Isolde healed the wounds on my back. I'd managed to clear the salty sea water from my lungs all on my own. Usually, I never slept better than the night after a battle. But tonight, I just wanted to watch her.

There might not be enough nights left to savor the feeling of her in my arms, completely surrendered and unguarded. Not now that we'd found the Ethereal Queen. The other half of the prophecy.

I'd forced her to sleep before the argument could be made and vocalized. Introductions were all that was necessary for me to realize that the asking and answering of questions needed to wait. Gaheris and Agravayn, the males I'd met only once, whose own brother had helped orchestrate the massacre of the goldstone palace and the deaths of Cyara's sisters. Evander, the wind-gifted male whose arm I'd cut off in anger when I first arrived in Baylaur, later deployed to assist Gawayn's brothers on the shores of the Split Sea, and now married to the Aquarian queen?

It was too much after a battle we'd barely survived.

The fact that Veyka had not argued with me illustrated just how right I was. She'd curled into my arms and fallen asleep without hesitation. Without reaching for me in heat or even kissing me goodnight. I would give her whatever she needed, no matter how big or small. If she just wanted me to hold her every night for the rest of our lives, I would do it.

My cock twitched in a protest I chose to ignore.

What I could not ignore was the dread settling into my chest.

The Ethereal Queen was no longer a mystery. She was a female, complete with a sapphire blue tail that turned into muscular legs and a consort at her side. She had the allegiance not only of Evander and her own people, but of the force of elementals that Agravayn had assembled as well.

Evander had referred to her as the Ethereal Queen. While we'd not yet discussed the prophecy or seen any exhibition of her powers, the words said enough. They meant that Evander and his new wife were aware of the prophecy's existence. Did they know the final line as well, the one that required the sacrifice?

A small ray of hope lit in the night.

Maybe she would not agree.

I already knew Veyka's mind. I'd felt her terror while she fought the succubus horde in the village and then on the land bridge. I'd heard the gasp she tried to hide as we picked our way back across the Crossing to where the terrestrials were setting up camp on the eastern cliffs.

She would not wait.

She understood what I'd known all along—why I'd pushed so desperately for the amorite weapons. The war with the succubus was not just dangerous. It was deadly. Our kingdom would be decimated, even if we eventually emerged as the victors. Annwyn would suffer. Every being in Annwyn would be touched by the darkness in one way or another, whether it be the loss of their own soul to the succubus or those of their loved ones.

And Veyka could spare them all.

But only if the Ethereal Queen—Mya, that was her name—only if she agreed. The carvings on the standing stones depicted both queens. *Together they must stand, to defeat what once thought dead. Together they must give, if any shall live to the end.*

Accolon's final words before he'd woken me from the enchanted sleep were clear. To banish the succubus required the sacrifice of both the Void and Ethereal Queens.

But maybe Mya would not agree.

Maybe Evander would not allow his new wife to make the sacrifice.

That thought tasted bitter in my mouth. If Mya was anything like my own wife, he would not be able to stop her. Even in sleep, Veyka made demands of me. She nestled her calf between my legs, held my fingers laced tight with her own.

I would go with Veyka gladly, abandoning this realm to fight for itself against the succubus. I would go *anywhere* if it meant that she would live. But she would not leave. The heart she'd tried so hard to protect, to ignore, had grown too much. She loved too deeply. She would die for those she'd sworn to protect.

It was one of the reasons I'd fallen in love with her.

56

VEYKA

I woke in the dark hour before predawn. Just before the shift, where the promise of tomorrow did not yet linger in the air but the worries of yesterday had faded. I lay still for several long minutes, waiting to see if Arran was still awake. Every time I'd rolled over or reached for a sip of water, I'd found him watching me. He did not even pretend to sleep. Merely pressed a soft kiss to my lips and pulled me tighter against him.

But his breathing was even and steady. When I fluttered my eyes open to examine him from beneath my lashes, his own were closed despite the footsteps only a few feet from the opening of our tent. I'd learned quickly that an army camp was not a quiet place, nor a dark one. With so many bodies encamped together, there was always someone up seeking a place to relieve themselves or a bite of food. Or slipping from one warm bed to another. Then there were the patrols. Flora-gifted sent vines to creep around the perimeter, while the fauna-gifted patrolled on four legs or from the air.

I suspected Lyrena had taken a shift outside our tent. This one, at least, was roomier than the low-slung, single-poled contraption we'd used when traveling across the continent for the first time. A proper army camp called for a proper tent—especially when it housed not only that army's commander, but its king and queen.

Sliding from the bed was easy. Disentangling myself from Arran was harder. I'd barely managed to get off my clothes before falling into our bedrolls. I tugged on a pair of trousers—failed to get them past my hips—*nope, those are Arran's.*

A little more digging and I found my own more generously cut leggings. I pulled on the first tunic I found, a small purr of appreciation sneaking out of my lips when I recognized Arran's scent clinging to the wool.

"Where are you going?"

My teeth sank into my lower lip, stopping just short of drawing blood. If Arran caught a whiff, if his beast scented my blood, I'd never make it past the tent opening.

A low, sleepy growl brushed against my consciousness. "Veyka?" he hummed.

The urge to reach for him was physical. A tug at the center of my chest, radiating through the sinews of muscle to my hand. My fingertips curled for the silky tendrils of his hair, my palm heating for the burn of stubble across his jaw.

But I forced a fist.

"Not far," I promised.

"Hold on," he rolled over. "I'm coming with you."

No! "Camping does not leave much dignity. At least let a female relieve herself in peace."

That earned me another growl, less sleepy this time. But he did not stand.

"I will be back," I promised, careful not to append the word 'soon' out of habit.

The Ancestors must have decided to pay attention to me for once, because Arran did not move again as I slipped out of the tent.

Barkke had taken Lyrena's spot just outside. He sat in his huge hound form, hind legs folded behind him and front two straight, his proud head on a constant swivel, ears perking now and then at distant sounds.

I forced my hand to remain at my side. I'd never asked whether terrestrials found it offensive if you stroked their beast forms. I had simply touched Arran because from the very beginning, he'd belonged to me, no matter what form he took.

Giving the same excuse to Barkke as I'd given to Arran, I headed for the small gap between our tent and the one Lyrena was sharing with Isolde. Though I doubted I'd find the white faerie inside; she'd been busy with the other healers when I'd come into camp earlier. While the terrestrial healers were skilled in their use of plants to create tinctures and salves to treat the ailments our soldiers would eventually heal from, only Isolde possessed the true power of healing. She was invaluable in battle, and even more so after it.

I waited a few more steps, for the darkness beyond the camp to swallow me fully, before stepping into the void.

The temptation to linger was stronger each time I stepped into that glorious swirling dark. Without the pull of Arran, the golden thread that connected us through all the realms of creation, I knew I would have given in a long time ago.

The witch in the Spine had told me the price of my magic was already paid. But there was an element to the power of the void which she did not understand. The power itself had built steadily since that first time I'd been flooded with it in the moments after my Joining to Arran. First my own ability to move through the void, then to take another along with me, until it culminated in the portal rifts that allowed me to move entire armies from one realm to another. It was a mighty gift, and I did not face a coma like Lyrena or aches like Cyara in the wake of using my power.

But it was not entirely without cost.

To have access to so many realms, beautiful and dangerous and infinite, but be unable to linger in them for as long as I desired— that was a cost all its own. To be constantly saddled with the knowledge that there were worlds beyond the ones I knew, to see them and taste them, but never fully experience them, because there was the tether, always pulling me back.

Unless I brought Arran with me.

That was not a choice.

Or... I supposed it was. But I was prepared to pay the cost the prophecy required of me to save my kingdom. Even if my mate was not ready to let me go.

Tonight was not for that.

I slid out of the void and into a world of endless golden sand. Two suns hung in the sky, rather than one. They glinted off of the turquoise blue water, more vibrant than any natural color I'd seen anywhere in Annwyn. I laid in the sand, letting the tiny granules fill the space between my toes, soaking the heat from those suns into my delicate skin. When the heat began to burn, I slipped into the void once more.

This time I emerged into a world drenched in rain and mist. But unlike the cold gray that had enshrouded us during the battle with the succubus hours before, this world was made wholly of light. Rainbows formed all around me, curving and swirling. I reached out into the mist, eager to feel if it was cold or warm. It was neither—it was *alive*. I trailed my fingers through the haze, leaving furrows that turned to rainbows in that glorious ever-shifting light. But I did not remain long in that realm, either.

Back to void. Enjoying, savoring. But always searching for the one realm I had not yet found.

57

VEYKA

Fully healed, fully dressed, and fully ready to draw blood. Just another morning.

Arran walked at my side, the tension of barely contained violence wafting off of him like it had an actual scent. Not an hour before, he'd had me on my back, moaning loud enough to wake the entire terrestrial army camp. But his edges were just as sharp as they had been upon waking. If I was lucky, he'd point them at our new allies.

As much as I hated Evander and mistrusted Agravayn and Gaheris, the picture of the battle had become clear as reports came in over our evening meal. We had not defeated the succubus on our own. Pale blue bodies littered the western half of the Crossing. There were dozens of reports of fire being wielded against the succubus. The elementals and the water fae had fought *with* us.

Water fae? Ancestors, I thought I'd dreamed it. But as we approached the midpoint of the Crossing, halfway between our camp and theirs, reality insisted on smacking me right in the face.

Agravayn and Gaheris stood side by side, the former still in warrior's armor. Where was their third brother, Gareth? The laughing one who'd looked so much like Gawayn that my stomach flipped just at the memory.

Sleep appeared to have done nothing to improve Evander's mood nor his opinion of me. He wore his shortsword and a dagger, tucked into his belt. The dagger shimmered with swirled amorite. They understood how to fight the succubus.

At his side stood Mya, looking every inch the queen she purported to be. She'd dressed in shades of aqua and silver that complimented her pale blue skin as well as the delicate sea glass crown she wore perched atop her dark hair.

As we approached, she jabbed her husband in the side with her elbow. I was inclined to like her.

I leaned into Arran as we walked, hoping the casual contact would dull the need that hummed constantly along our mating bond.

"In another decade, we would have been here anyway," I said casually. He did not respond, too focused on the group ahead. "The Summit?"

"Is that how you would have preferred to meet Morgause?"

"Someone in that court would have killed her by then, I guarantee it." I flashed a grin. His jaw ticked almost imperceptibly. My smiled widened. "Possibly her own son," I added, glancing over my shoulder.

Mordred walked with Lyrena a few yards behind us. It must be horrible for her, having to decide between staying at my shoulder or keeping within arm's reach of Morgause's son. But as the newest Knight of the Round Table, we couldn't very well leave him behind.

As we took the final few steps, a tall water-fae female stepped up to Mya's other side. I recognized her for a warrior instantly, and it had nothing to do with the massive trident she carried. Where Mya's face was soft, her posture easy and open, the new female was rigid and firm as the weapon she held. And the only part of her that moved were her eyes, scanning each of us up and down like the threats that we were.

The void tugged at my consciousness while my fingers drifted to my waist. The urge to test myself against her in combat was as potent as any physical hunger. Except for the hunger for chocolate croissants. Still no sight of one of those. Mysterious water fae? Sure. Delicious, flaky golden pastry filled with chocolate? None.

I muffled my sigh and slid on the bored, slightly sarcastic mask that was becoming less and less comfortable to wear. It turned out that hiding my feelings had always been easy because I had not let myself fully feel them. Fall in love, make friends, decide to care about my kingdom... and all of the sudden, that mask did not fit quite so well.

Arran stopped three yards short of the other party. Plenty of room for bloodshed. One of the many things I loved about him.

Mya stepped into the breach immediately. "Good tides. This is not my land to offer welcome, so instead I offer my thanks for your willingness to speak with us."

Arran said nothing. I supposed the politicking fell to me, then. I didn't match her step forward, but I made my hands fall away from where they'd lingered not-so-accidentally near my weapons. "Thank you for fighting with us yesterday. Our losses would have been much more severe without your help, Your Majesty."

The blue-skinned queen nodded gracefully. It was easy to imagine how she'd move in the water. "We do not use honorifics. My position is not hereditary. I was elected to the queenship. Queen Mya, or just Mya, will do fine."

"Elected? You water-fae really are a breed apart," Lyrena quipped from my shoulder. Apparently with so many potential enemies, she needed to be close.

"Aquarians," Evander corrected, glaring at his former fellow Goldstone. "She is the Queen of the Aquarian Fae."

Ancestors, he was still fucking irritating. But the intensity in his eyes was aimed squarely at Mya. It seemed he made a better consort than Goldstone Guard.

"And how did an entire race hide for so long that we—who can live a thousand years—forgot your existence?" I addressed my question to Mya. If I talked to Evander any more than absolutely necessary, I was likely to fling a dagger at him.

"By doing precisely that. Hiding." Mya still stood in the space between us. Evander drifted to her side as she spoke, but Agravayn and Gaheris did not, setting themselves apart. Interesting.

"Our numbers were depleted dangerously after battling the succubus in the Great War. Fearing extinction, our ancestors retreated into the depths of the Split Sea and forbade any water-dwelling creature from breaching the surface."

They already know about the Great War and the succubus' role in it. Perhaps they had never forgotten, like we had. Arran's hand brushed against mine, a silent offer of comfort. I resisted the urge to curl my fingers around his. We could communicate with our minds. There was no need to show these newcomers any softness.

I was still unconvinced that Gaheris and Agravayn did not nurture some other nefarious purpose.

"Much can be forgotten in seven thousand years," Mya said.

That truth fucking burned.

Do you think she speaks true? Arran's beast growled into my mind. I recognized the timber of it. The low threat of a stalking predator.

Her skin is blue and yesterday she had a tail. I'm not sure how much she could be making up.

The Faeries of the Fen hadn't existed to me a few months ago, either. What was another mythical being? Elemental, terrestrial *and* Aquarian fae? It was not the most fantastical thing that had happened in the last year by anyone's measure.

Arran was trying to mask his feelings, but though the Brutal Prince's façade remained staunchly in place, he could not hide his mind from me. Skepticism mingled with desperation and quickly fading hope.

"What do you know of the Ethereal Queen?" Arran demanded, wasting no time on pleasantries.

Mya dipped her chin. "I am the Ethereal Queen."

"Prove it," Arran said, brows rising. He threw out a hand in the direction of the lone male off of our right flank, two steps behind—Mordred. "Who is he?"

We had not bothered to introduce anyone else in our party. And though the resemblance between them was there, it was not obvious.

Evander sucked in a breath, a protest on his dangerously sharp tongue. But Mya reached for his arm, leashing him with a single soft touch. Impressive. I'd never quite managed to bring Evander to heel.

Arran's feelings blurred with my own. He wanted her to fail. Because if Mya was the Ethereal Queen, there was no more reason to delay the sacrifice that would bar the succubus from Annwyn forever. *Oh, Arran.*

But the Aquarian queen had no reason to lie to us. No one would claim a power whose inevitable conclusion was death. But even depleted, Arran's hope was a constant white flame, burning the same color as my hair and his beast. I was suddenly glad I hadn't gorged myself on croissants. They would no doubt be trying to make a reappearance now.

Mya approached Mordred but did not reach for him. "May I touch you?"

His face was an eerie mirror of Arran's, his jaw ticking in an identical motion that could only be inherited. But he was not as good at masking his emotions. Terrestrials valued truth. Strength. They were not schooled to dissemble the way elementals were. Trepidation took up residence in the crinkle of his brow, discomfort in the pucker of his lips.

But he nodded.

The Aquarian queen lifted her hand to cup his face. I watched for some outward sign of her magic. *Twice blessed, the realm of shift and mist, when comes the awaited queen who shall possess ethereal might. With a touch, she will feel the heartbeat of her subjects and she will unlock the secrets they guard within.* But all I saw was the contrast of her pale blue fingertips against the deepened bronze of his cheek.

Mya spoke softly. "Assured in his prowess as a warrior; perhaps a bit cocky. Determined to prove his loyalty. He fears that he will not be able to escape the reputation of his mother. Your son." She dropped her hand as she turned back to look at Arran, eyes searching. Then they came to me. "But not yours."

I stifled my sharp inhale. Clever, brilliant mate of mine. By challenging Mya to use her ethereal powers on Mordred, he'd verified two vital truths at once—Mordred's loyalty and Evander's veracity.

But those realizations dimmed in comparison to the other. Mya was the Ethereal Queen.

A light inside of me flickered out.

Arran's son shook his head, dislodging Mya's hand. "Mordred. My mother is Morgause, of the Terrestrial Dyad in Cayltay."

A flash of a golden cape, and he no longer stood alone.

"Lyrena Lancelot. Goldstone Guard and Knight of the Round Table. Try that trick on my queen and I'll cut your hand off." She punctuated her threat with a wink. *Oh, Lyrena.*

The Aquarian warrior was at Mya's side in a flash. "Try it, and I'll show you what real water power feels like,"

Fire flared to life at Lyrena's fingertips.

"General Ache," Mya said, giving Mordred space and coming back to address me and Arran. "Commands my small army."

Arran's onyx eyes narrowed. "How small?"

"About a third the size of your terrestrial forces, if my scouts were correct in their estimations based on what they observed yesterday," General Ache said with a bite that immediately had Arran's beast growling. Thank the Ancestors I was the only one who could hear him.

A sarcastic remark played across my mind, but if Arran heard it he showed no sign. He only nodded, then looked over Mya's shoulder to Agravayn and Gaheris. "And your force of elementals?"

"A quarter of that," Agravayn said.

Arran nodded again. "More troops are coming from north of the Spine. The commanding general of the elemental army is rounding up what remains after the siege of Baylaur, and Guinevere seeks to build a human coalition."

We do not know if we can trust them, I hissed at the feral beast. But the wolf was already off and running in the opposite direction.

"Even with these reinforcements coming, it would only take a horde twice the size of what we faced yesterday to destroy us. I cannot overstate the importance of your forces joining with ours. The need could not be any direr than it is in this moment," Arran said, dividing his attention between Agravayn and General Ache, commander to commander.

"Ancestors," I breathed, realization slamming into me.

Even at a whisper, all eyes swung to me.

"She is the Siege Perilous,"

Arran tensed beside me. I knew Lyrena and Mordred would understand. The latter had just fought for his position at the Round Table based on that same prophecy. But our new allies stared at me openly.

"Another prophecy, this one made by Merlin, the priestess in my court. It speaks of the Round Table, gifted to me by Guinevere, and the Knights who will sit around it," I explained, hating that I remembered it so well. "*The last is the Siege Perilous. It is death to all but the one for which it is made—the best of them all—the one who shall come at the moment of direst need.*"

I exhaled, letting the words of the prophecy settle. "It cannot be a coincidence that Queen Mya and the Aquarian Fae have appeared now, after seven thousand years in hiding, at what can only be described as the moment of direst need—driving the succubus from Annwyn."

"She is a queen in her own right, not a knight to be seated at your table," Evander snarled.

"So literal, Evander. I'd think you'd been spending time with terrestrials," I bit back.

The insult landed, sending the male a step in my direction. Arran swung his battle axe, the growl that had been just for me spilling out. Evander, wisely, stepped back.

My emotions churned too fast for me to smile genuinely, but I flashed my wicked smile just the same. "We'll call it an honorary knighthood, then."

"I accept," Mya said readily, her smile softer and infinitely more genuine.

The growl in Arran's throat turned inward.

So we believe in prophecies now, do we? he growled.

When your life hangs on one, you're entitled to whatever opinion you like, changeable as it might be, I snapped back.

Mya glanced between us, sapphire eyes sparkling. The prophecy said she must touch in order to access thoughts and intentions, but there was a knowing in her eyes that told me she'd at least guessed at me and Arran's private conversation.

"Evander, you did not tell me how entertaining your queen is," she said around a smile.

"*You* are my queen," her husband said through gritted teeth.

"General Ache has agreed to lead the Aquarian forces. She will work with you, Your Majesty," she nodded to Arran. "But not under you."

Arran did not quibble; I did not expect him to. His goal had always been to assemble an army big enough to defeat the succubus without having to fulfil the void and ethereal prophecy.

"And what of us?" Agravayn interrupted.

Apparently the reprieve from dealing with traitors was over.

"Your brother betrayed his sacred sworn duty and facilitated the deaths of hundreds of elemental courtiers—including my own friends. Unless you can prove your loyalty, you shall meet the same end as he did." I did not mention that Arran's beast had ripped off Gawayn's head with his jaws. If they did not know, letting them imagine was even better. "Where is your baby brother?" I'd seen no sign of Gareth.

Gaheris dropped his gaze. Agravayn held it.

"Dead, Your Majesty," the latter answered.

I did not need ethereal magic to detect the pain that limned his words.

"Queen Mya can vouch for our good intentions. She has put her hands on us more than once to assure we mean the Aquarians no harm." Gaheris paused, but I did not fill the space. "Our only desire is to protect Annwyn. We will fight the succubus until the prophecy is fulfilled and they are banished forever."

They knew about the prophecy—and what would be required of me and Mya in order to fulfill it. They'd bow to me as their queen, knowing I would not be alive for long. If it meant the succubus were gone, it would be worth it.

"You will subordinate your forces to Arran, as Elora will be expected to when she rejoins us." I hoped that was not just lip service. "We are not the elemental and terrestrial armies any longer. We are one." I lifted my finger to tap the swirling black tattoo on my cheek. "And we will fight as one."

I held each of their eyes. Gaheris, Agravayn. Then Evander, Mya, and General Ache. I did not possess Mya's ethereal gift. I could not see their intentions or guarantee their loyalty. I'd been betrayed by those close to me again and again. But choices were deserting me one by one. If creating an alliance would save my kingdom, I'd do it.

And then my pocket started to glow.

❧ 58 ❧

ARRAN

Veyka had chosen a unique blend of elemental and terrestrial styles for our rendezvous with the Aquarians. It was still winter, so she could not discard her leather entirely. She wore embroidered leather and wool sleeves that covered most of her arms and tight-fitted leggings that disappeared into her boots. But the gown she wore was made of layers and layers of iridescent gray fabric the glinted in the sparse winter sunlight we'd been granted. An improvement over the driving rain of the day before, at least.

But it was that transparent gown that gave her away. There were pockets concealed in all that drapery, but once the communication crystal started to glow, there was no hiding it.

"You still have them," Mya breathed in awe as Veyka pulled the palm-length white crystal out of her pocket.

"Ours was broken," Mya said, leaning in to examine the crystal. "Thousands of years ago, the rulers of each kingdom possessed one. They used them to communicate across continents and even—"

"Across realms," Veyka finished. "Remarkable."

It *was* remarkable. Objectively. But remarkable had faded to normal and often downright dreadful, given the current circumstances. There was only one reason that either of our Knights would use the crystal—something very good or something very bad.

"Speak," Veyka said, her eyes fixed. Lyrena stepped closer. I held my ground at Veyka's side.

Several heartbeats of silence passed, but the crystal did not flicker or fade. Finally, a voice emerged.

"Your Majesties," Gwen's voice stuttered out of the crystal. "Arran? Veyka?"

"Guinevere!" Veyka gasped, halfway to a laugh or a sigh of relief. "Gwen, I am here. We are here. You may speak freely."

That was debatable. But the look I tossed my mate was lost by her concentration on the crystal. Her eyes wrinkled in excitement, her lips tilting in the first real smile I'd seen her wear in days. She missed her friends.

I'd been so focused on keeping her hope alive, on retrieving the terrestrial army, that I did not think about what this separation meant to her. She'd regained Guinevere, only to see her go again. She'd never been parted from Cyara, not since she emerged from the water gardens after her father, Uther's death.

Veyka was measuring the remains of her life in breaths, and the majority of those were separated from the ones she loved most. Fuck, my heart ached for her. And for myself. When that crystal had begun to glow, all thoughts but one drained from my head—the grail.

But it was not Cyara whose voice spilled from the crystal

"Elora has found the elemental army," Gwen said.

Veyka's eyes flew to mine, a mixture of relief and guilt clouding the blue irises. She carried the guilt for what had happened in Baylaur close to her heart. I had not told her that I nursed my own share as well. If I had not lost my memories, or if I had chosen to believe in Veyka again sooner, we might have made it back to Baylaur in time to prevent disaster.

But her soul was already fracturing under the strain of responsibility. I could carry my guilt on my own, rather than burden her with it. At least for now. I stepped closer to her, leaning over the crystal.

I listened as Gwen detailed their condition and number, explaining that they were now camped in the valley on the other side of the mountains from Eldermist. A short march to the rift that would take them into Annwyn, were Veyka unable to open a portal rift for them.

Veyka waited as I clarified a few points, but I knew which question came next.

"What about the humans?" Veyka asked.

The crystal caught Gwen's heavy sigh. "One detachment of humans joined ranks with the army on its march here. The others..."

"Tell us," I said, my mind already racing ahead. There was not enough time to integrate human and fae forces to fight together. But we could still be strategic with how we deployed the forces of our steadily growing army.

A growing army. An army that could face the succubus—and maybe prevail. Or at least stall them long enough for Cyara to return with the grail.

Gwen hummed from the other side of the crystal's connection, the sound infiltrating my thoughts. "They've called a council of sorts in two days' time to decide."

"To decide what?" Veyka asked in disbelief, her blue eyes wide.

"Whether to aid us in the fight against the succubus."

Veyka blinked. When her lids lifted, her eyes burned with ire. "We are at the Crossing now. We answered a summons to come to the human realm and aid *them*. Terrestrials, elementals, and Aquarians. And they are still trying to decide whether or not to join us?"

"Aquarians?" Gwen's voice dropped.

"Later," I cut in before Veyka could lose her temper entirely. Communication crystals left something to be desired where nuance was concerned. The Gwen that had left us in Eldermist was a different creature than the one who'd traveled with me to Baylaur. She could not handle the weight of Veyka's emotions. I needed

Gwen in control—to convince the humans to join our army. To save my mate.

I kept my voice crisp and authoritative. Commander to lieutenant. "Gwen, you will convince them. In two days, I expect an updated report. Troop strength, disposition, rations, and marching speed."

"Yes, Your Majesty. Two days."

59

ARRAN

Two days to convince Veyka not to sacrifice her life.

Once, I'd cut off Evander's arm. Now, I needed his help. I was not so naïve to believe that every marriage was built on the same foundation as mine. But I'd watched how Evander interacted with Mya, how his eyes tracked her as she interacted with each of us, his body moving in answer to the questions she did not even realize she asked.

I watched Veyka as she tucked the communication crystal away, but I also watched Evander. I looked for any sign that he, too, recognized those two days as the dreaded countdown that they were.

His face was stoic. An elemental by upbringing, if not by choice.

Veyka brought her hands to her hips. "I assume you all heard that. In two days, Guinevere will report back on the strength of the human alliance. Whether or not we gain their alliance, your objective does not change. Together, you will hunt down any succubus who remain in Annwyn or the human realm."

No. Do not say it. Do not think it. Begging couched in command. But Veyka did not respond to the thoughts, though I knew she must hear them. She was not touching me any longer, either, had carefully withdrawn her hand.

"You are aware of the prophecy—in its entirety?" she asked Mya.

"*Together they must stand, to defeat what once thought dead. Together they must give, if any shall live to the end.*" Mya's voice matched her movements, graceful and liquid as it slid over the syllables.

She knew the prophecy. Every last word.

Evander remained silent at her side.

Veyka nodded once. I reached for her, but she stepped out of my grasp, closer to the Ethereal Queen. "Then you know what we must do."

She did not want me to touch her, because she knew it would shake her resolve. But I was as stubborn as she.

"We can wait two days," I said. "The healers need time to do their work." A thin excuse. If they weren't already dead, the fae soldiers were already nearly healed.

The look Veyka gave me said she knew it.

"We have not heard from Cyara and Osheen. The Faeries of the Fen could make a considerable difference in this fight." That was desperation in my voice. The world had narrowed to me and Veyka. I no longer cared what Evander or Mya had sorted out between the two of them. I knew my mate. If she was determined to do this, she'd convince Mya as well. Evander had no hope. And mine was rapidly being smothered.

"What fight, Arran? There does not need to be a fight. If Mya and I fulfill the prophecy, then all of this ends. Everyone gets to live," Veyka said, nearly choking on the last word. *I want to live,* she'd told me.

"Cyara searches for the grail to unite the Sacred Trinity. If she is successful, you would not have to fulfill the prophecy." She did not listen when I begged silently. If going to my knees before the entirety of Annwyn was what it took to convince my mate, I would do it. For her, I would beg. For the future we should have had, I would crawl. "Please, Veyka."

Mya made a sound in the back of her throat. Evander was at her side in a second. Now I had his attention.

"What is the Sacred Trinity?" he demanded.

Veyka's eyes darkened. I did not look away, but I did not allow myself to be cowed by their intensity either.

I held her gaze as I explained. "Ancient objects forged by the fae, humans, and witches. Excalibur, Veyka's scabbards, and the grail—a chalice hidden by Merlin. Even now, Cyara searches for it."

"Cyara is with Osheen, securing the alliance of the Faeries of the Fen. There is no way she has had time to search for the grail," Veyka said. Her voice promised all kinds of violence. Normally, my cock would have tightened in response. But I was fighting for her life, and we both knew it.

I did not flinch from Veyka's ire. "She is not with Osheen," I said.

"And what power do these objects grant?" Evander asked. Beside him, Mya had gone silent.

"What do you mean, she is not with Osheen?" Veyka's voice dropped to a dangerous whisper.

But I answered Evander's question, not hers. "The Sacred Trinity grants the bearer the power to defeat the succubus."

"Maybe," Veyka interjected. Her hand was on her dagger.

"There is a chance to stop the prophecy," Evander repeated, as if he could not believe the words. I knew that if I looked his way, I'd see the cracks in his elemental mask. I'd see the male who'd fallen in love with a doomed queen, and the first flickers of hope stirring to life.

But Veyka's glare did not let me go. "Where is Cyara?"

Pale blue flashed in my periphery. "We will leave you, now. We have our own wounded to tend to," Mya said, steering Evander away.

"If there is a way to stop the prophecy—"

"This is a private argument," Mya said. The quiet strength in her voice told me that she and Evander were about to have one of their own. But that was not my concern. The only thing that truly mattered to me stood three feet away, looking very much like she was contemplating where to fling her dagger first.

Agravayn and Gaheris retreated as well. Lyrena escorted Mordred back the way we'd come. Veyka and I stood alone, on the center of a narrow spit of land at the center of the world.

She stared at me just as she had for the last several minutes, her blue eyes turned dull and fathomless. She stared, but she did not see me. Veyka may as well have been in the void for how far away she felt in that excruciating moment.

We'd once vowed honesty to each other. I was not ready to let her go. I would do anything to save her. That was my honest truth.

"Where is Cyara?" she asked again, the words rough and pained.

"I sent her after the grail," I said honestly. "She took Percival and Diana with her. They know more about the Sacred Trinity than anyone, having grown up in Avalon. They are searching."

"And the Faeries of the Fen?"

"I assume that Osheen and Maisri are with them now." I hoped so, at least. There were not enough communication crystals to go around.

"You assume," Veyka echoed. "If Cyara had found the grail, she would have called."

Another truth.

"We can give her two more days."

"The succubus could return for us. They are drawn to me."

I held her gaze, but I felt my heart beginning to crack. "Isn't your life worth waiting a few more days?"

She blinked. And then completely unraveled. As if I'd snapped the bonds holding her in place. "For what? Another disappointment?" She threw out her hand, spinning on the spot, gesturing to the armies encamped in either direction. "What are their lives worth, Arran? Why is my life worth more?"

I grabbed her shoulders. I could not stand another second without touching her, not when the world was determined to steal her away from me. My eyes *burned*. Burned with tears. I blinked them away, angry that my body dared to blur what might be my last image of her.

I shook her, harder than I should of, because it did not seem possible that she did not understand. "Because *you* are mine."

She was still shaking. Not me, but her. Her entire body shook as sobs rolled through her, tears that matched my own streaming down her cheeks. "And you are mine," Veyka whispered. "But so are they."

How had I ever called this female selfish? How had I not seen from the first time I met her the beautiful, singular soul that waited beneath her layers of self-crafted armor?

I had, that was the answer. I'd always suspected who she was at her core. What I had not expected was how deeply I would love her. The depth of the love she would give to me. To her friends.

Her friends.

I knew what I had to do, then. The last weapon I could deploy against my mate.

Fuck, she's going to hate me.

"Will you deny your Knights the chance to say goodbye?" I asked.

Veyka wrenched out of my grip as if I'd struck her. But even that did not stop me. I knew I was hurting her, but I could not stop myself. Not if it gave Cyara a chance to find the grail, to find us, to save Veyka's life.

I struck the last blow, hard and true. "Haven't they lost enough already?"

Veyka stumbled back another step.

She was still shaking, but no fresh tears tracked down her cheeks. "Two days. Then we summon Cyara and Gwen and we end this."

I was not surprised when she disappeared into the void rather than spend one more minute with me.

🕸 60 🕸

VEYKA

I wanted to go far. To the Spine. Beyond, past the lakes of Eilean Gayl to the uncharted north. Or to the far south, where the fabled witch isle waited off of Annwyn's southwest coast. I wanted to go as far and as fast as my power could take me.

But I'd promised Arran. On the bridge outside of Eilean Gayl, I had promised that we would not be parted again.

I was going to break that promise in the end. There was no way to avoid that. But in the meantime, I would do everything I could to keep my word. So I took myself up to one of the striated ledges of the cliffs overlooking the Crossing. But I chose one high above the terrestrial camp, where no two or four-footed fae would be able to reach me. Arran could if he tried hard enough. There was nowhere I could go to escape him, he'd made that clear months ago.

No place but one.

But it got cold up on the cliff and I did not have a cloak. I wasn't ready to go back to our tent and retrieve one, even for the brief second it would require. I ended up exactly where I'd started hours before—in the middle of the Crossing, looking out over the Split Sea. This time I sat down.

The waves lapped at the stone, a deep gray blue that mirrored the sun as it began its evening descent. I'd never dangled my legs over the lake at Eilean Gayl. The snow was a decent deterrent. The beasts that lurked beneath the surface an even bigger one. But here, I was unafraid. If sweet, even-tempered Mya was not afraid of these depths, I would not be either.

I removed my boots and rolled up my leather leggings, but I stopped just short of actually dipping my toes beneath the surface.

"I won't bite. But I cannot speak for the other denizens of the sea."

I snorted. I should have known she was lingering nearby. "Isn't that precisely what you do with your ethereal power?"

A splash split the water and Mya emerged fully, pulling herself up onto the shore. It took more than a little maneuvering to get herself up to where I sat on the edge of the land bridge, but she did so without shifting to legs.

This must be what she considered her true self. It was more than impressive. Her thick sapphire blue tail was covered in tens of thousands of tiny scales. Each one shimmered as she moved, iridescent in the light.

She braced her arms behind her, leaning back and letting her eyes become heavy, but not close entirely. She had limited days remaining to her, just like me. Of course she'd want to spend them staring out at her home.

"I must physically touch individuals in order to gauge their heart and intention. But for large groups, or the sea itself... it is more of a feeling that builds." Mya dug her fingers into the sand as she explained. "It has gotten stronger in the last few months."

Probably in response to the growing strength of the succubus. And my own powers. "How long have you had your ethereal powers?"

Mya's eyes opened enough for her to look at me. "I was born with them."

I did not explain how my void power had awoken. None of them—Agravayn, Gaheris, Evander—had questioned that I was the queen of the void. If word of my power had spread ahead of me to the terrestrial kingdom, then it had certainly reached them as well.

The conversation ebbed, but I made no effort to revive it. I stared at the sea. The sea stared back. The tips of Mya's fin skimmed the water, sending out rings of gentle ripples that were swallowed by the ever-present waves.

Emboldened by her presence, I slid one foot down toward the water. The next wave came, up and up and up, cresting just below my toes. My heartbeat quickened, but I held my foot in place. The next wave came, faster than the one before. It would reach me. Up over the sand it climbed, closer and closer and closer—until it crashed past my toes, curling up and around the arch until it reached my ankle.

It felt... fucking cold. And also glorious.

But then there was another, coming up faster, at an uneven interval. It splashed right past my foot, curling up my leg and wetting my leathers. I jerked my foot back, shrieking.

Mya laughed, flicking her fin in the water.

"Are they always so unpredictable?" I said between laughs. I was just brave enough to slide my foot back down and allow my other to join it.

Mya's smile softened. "No. It has only been like this since I sealed the seas."

Sealed the seas? "I do not understand."

Mya's smile disappeared entirely, her lips drawing together. It was difficult to see in the falling light, but I thought that the blue color on her cheeks deepened slightly.

"On land, you pass between realms using rifts," she said. "But the sea is ever moving, ever changing. The rifts are not static, nor are the realms really separate. There is the human realm, and the fae realm, but there is one sea."

Now I understood. She'd closed the rifts—changed the very nature of her kingdom. Sacrificed. There could only be one reason. "You sealed the sea to prevent the succubus from using those ever-changing rifts."

She nodded solemnly. "My ancestors refused to seal the seas and it nearly cost them everything. Our population was decimated in the Great War, and we did not fight a single battle on land. All of it took place beneath the waves. I understand why they did not take that last drastic step. Sealing the seas limits the full breadth of my magic, and the magic my people command. I call to the sea to summon my power, but only a small fraction of it answers."

"You did what is best for your kingdom." A statement, not a question. From one queen to another.

But Mya's eyes were no longer on me. There was no more laughter. Her eyes drifted out to the horizon, where the sun was just about to kiss the edge of the water.

She did not ask about the grail or the Sacred Trinity and I did not speak of it. I would not dangle a fool's hope in front of her. Not when I expected she'd already accepted her fate, as I had. Was trying to.

"Arran does not understand." I said it without expecting a response. Mya did not know me. She owed me nothing. I did not want to know what conversations she and Evander had endured on the subject. But I still could not stop myself from letting the words out, from saying them to the one being in the entire realm who had a chance at understanding.

Mya exhaled slowly. "Does that surprise you?"

"Yes. When he first came to Baylaur... he accused me of being lazy and selfish. He told me I'd failed in my duty to Annwyn. And he was right." The worlds spilled out of me, and I began to realize how afraid I'd been to say them, but how desperately I needed to. Everyone around me was so intent on saving me, on protecting me. I could not be honest. My hands curled to fists, sand squeezing out of them as anger sharpened inside of me. "How can that same male ask me not to do my duty? To be selfish and choose my own life over the very existence of my kingdom?"

Mya waited. I thought she might reach for me, to try and use her power to find an answer for the questions that were unanswerable. But after several loaded moments passed, she only shrugged.

"You changed," she said quietly.

So did he, my heart finished.

"How can you be so calm?" Because she was. I was the Queen of the Elemental Fae, a race famed for our ability to control our emotions even to a fault. And yet I was coming apart at the seams, while my Aquarian counterpart was the picture of composure and grace. It made me like her just a tiny bit less.

"There is no other option," Mya said.

"Ha! I am anything but calm."

One corner of her mouth lifted into a slight but still lovely smile. "Fulfilling the prophecy is the only option. It is the only way to save my kingdom. I never imagined that my queenship would end like this," Mya admitted. "But if this is my one real act as queen, then it is enough."

Yes, I understood her perfectly. I'd never imagined ruling at all. First, because there was Arthur. Then later, because I'd planned to leave Annwyn rather than saddle the kingdom with a powerless, dangerous queen. Now... now I would die to save my kingdom. And somehow, it was enough.

Except for Arran. There would never be enough time with him. Not even if we had a thousand years. But less than one seemed like a cruel bargain.

"I don't want to die."

"Neither do I," Mya admitted. "But I am not thinking of it as dying. The prophecy refers to a sacrifice. Perhaps it will require something else. Something other than my life."

I laughed, because the idea she posed was preposterous. Of course, our lives were the price. The carving on the standing stone had been clear, even if the words of the prophecy were not. Those two queens depicted on the stone were there, and then they were gone.

"That is quite a risk to take," I said quietly. Not with her life, but with her heart.

She smiled and I recognized it for what it was—the lie she told herself to make it okay, to give herself the courage to go through with it. She knew. Of course, she knew.

That sad smile lingered as Mya turned back to the sea, quickly blending with the sky in an endless black expanse. "Your Arran will not want to trust Evander. I have heard the history between them and seen your own mistrust. But I am intimately familiar with the depths of my husband's soul." There was that slight change in the blue of her cheeks again. "He can be trusted, Veyka. I promise you."

I swallowed the lump of emotion in my throat. Hearing her speak of her husband made me long for mine. I'd been gone long enough. "I will tell Arran."

I pulled my feet through the sand, leaving deep channels that filled with water as I stood. Mya made no move to leave. Part of me hesitated to leave her here alone. But the sea was her home. She was much safer here than I.

"Veyka."

I paused, boots in my hand.

"I... I can help you, if you wish. It is what I do... what I did, before I became queen. I helped people. By laying hands on them, I was able to see the emotions and fears they could not articulate for themselves and help them sort through them." She turned to look up at me, blue eyes turned almost black by the night. "I can help you, before... before."

Before we died.

Instead of waiting for her to touch me, I reached out and squeezed her shoulder. "I know who I am, for better or worse. And I know what I want." *Who I want.*

Mya nodded in understanding. "In two days, we will go."

I huffed a sigh. "I suppose we can use those two days to figure out where and how. We do not even truly know what to do, how to make this sacrifice."

"No," Mya agreed, her eyes already back on the sea. "But I know who to ask. We must go back to where this all began. Avalon."

❦ 61 ❦

GUINEVERE

"Here." Something warm appeared in the vicinity of her hand—the one that was not occupied rubbing at her temple. Her gaze dropped, but she struggled to comprehend.

Gwen stared into the steaming cup of tea that Sylva slid in front of her for long enough that the old woman added, "For the headache."

It was going to take more than tea to sort this lot out.

They were in the Sylva's small parlor. It had seemed like a good idea when the woman posed it. With the guild hall long since destroyed, there were limited places in Eldermist to convene a large group of people.

This group wasn't even that large. But with all of them shoved into Sylva's house, the noise was intense. And only growing.

Gwen expected something similar to the way the Knights of the Round Table conducted themselves. Even the bloody terrestrial Pit would have been preferable to this... disaster. Complete and utter disaster.

Six representatives crowded the room, if Sylva and Gwen were included. It was a better response than Gwen had hoped for. All three of the villages where she'd sent paired human and fae delegations had returned with a force of human soldiers in tow. Gwen did not stretch to call them warriors, but at least they were willing. Sort of. Although Wraithwood, Emberhaven, and Thornbriar had all sent soldiers, only the delegates from Emberhaven had actually agreed to join the fight.

The representative from Ferndale, the largest of the human villages, located on the far western coast, said their troops were a week behind. But again, he was unwilling to commit them to a fight.

The humans had been squabbling for the better part of an hour.

"We have enough troops to overpower them. We take the amorite to protect our males and supply our warriors, and then we retreat further into the mountains."

"Only to have a horde of succubus-infested fae pursue us?"

"You've heard the reports. The fae here will be called away to purge the succubus from Annwyn. We would be perfectly safe."

It took Gwen several seconds to even comprehend what they'd proposed.

"You do not have the troops to overpower us," Gwen ground out, a feline hiss slipping out between her words. She was just barely keeping her lioness under control. "If any of you are stupid enough to believe that, then you have no place in this discussion."

That stunned them into silence for a solid minute. But then they dissolved into arguing again. The citizens at large were still avoiding Gwen as if she carried an infectious parasite. But their leaders, apparently, had gained too much familiarity. To their detriment.

"It might be faster to dispose of these ones and see who the remaining humans offer up in their places," Gwen grumbled under her breath.

Sylva did not disagree with her. The old woman merely sipped her tea.

She should have asked Elora to join them. She'd at least earned the respect of the Emberhaven leader. From the long glances Gwen had observed between the two, she'd also invited the woman to her bed. At this juncture, Gwen was not inclined to quibble over the *how* so long as it served the *when*.

"If it were just the refugees, perhaps you would be correct, Helene. But we marched with the fae army for more than half the journey here. They are well-trained and absolutely lethal without even needing to touch a weapon. We would need to outnumber them ten to one to have a chance—which we do not," Elora's bedmate said, calling the leader of Thornbriar to account. "Emberhaven will fight."

"And ask for nothing in return?" the grizzled gray man from Wraithwood spoke.

"In return, you get to live to see the summer," Gwen growled.

"On the contrary, Lady Guinevere," he just barely contained his sneer. "If we wait for the succubus to come, some of us will die. If we fight for your queen and king, all of our soldiers will."

"Maybe," Sylva finally interjected. "But those who have volunteered to fight would die first. If we await the succubus, it will be your women and children who die, massacred at the hands of their own husbands and fathers."

"They could give us amorite," Helene countered. The woman who'd proposed stripping the fae of their protection and hiding in the mountains.

"There is no more amorite," Gwen said. "Not now, at least. All that we brought to Eldermist has been distributed, and it will not be taken back because you have decided to be greedy. The humans of Eldermist gave our citizens refuge, and the amorite was a gift from the High Queen."

She was going to do it. Shift, eat the two loud ones for a snack, and give the man from Ferndale one last chance to decide if he wanted to cooperate or become dessert.

"Then you'll leave us to die," the Wraithwood man sneered openly.

The Emberhaven woman across the table sighed dramatically. "You are doing this to yourself. Join the fae or scurry back to your village and wait to die. You are a man. The succubus will come for you eventually."

The man's eyes narrowed. Gwen had anticipated they would hate her. What she hadn't counted on was the distrust the humans bore for each other. There were no kingdoms or unity in the human realm. Only scattered villages too caught up in their own self-preservation to realize they hobbled themselves with their idiotic refusal to develop any sort of inter-dependence.

"Perhaps you should show us that knife in your belt. Not all of us have used our sexual wiles to secure an amorite weapon," he sneered. "Fae-fucker."

The woman surged across the table, her hands around the man's throat before he could get out another insult. Gwen was inclined to let her at it; one less human to convince. But Sylva intervened.

"Release him, Tally. His brother will not forgive the loss," Sylva said.

For a moment, Gwen thought the woman from Emberhaven— Tally—would ignore the older woman's appeal. But what Sylva said must be true, and Tally must have realized it. Gwen could not even remember all of their names. Meanwhile, Sylva understood the political machinations from a decade serving on the village's Council of Elders.

Tally slid back across the table, but she kicked her chair out from behind her instead of resuming her seat.

"Say it again, and I will slit your throat," she promised, addressing the table at large, before storming out. The force of the door slamming shook the entire house.

Bruises were already forming around the Wraithwood man's throat.

"Come. Hot tea and a poultice, or you won't speak again for days." Sylva left the room without waiting for the man. He glared at Gwen, but eventually followed, as did his Thornbriar counterpart.

Which left Gwen and the Ferndale delegate, who'd yet to say a single word.

"If we do not fight, we will die," Gwen said. She did not have any fancy words or promises to give. She didn't even have any more amorite to bargain away. Maybe she'd been wrong to stay behind in the human realm, to even think this was a possibility.

A minute later, the delegate from Ferndale stood without speaking and returned upstairs to the room he'd been given.

Gwen's forehead dropped to the table. She owed Arran and Veyka a report. But only one word repeated steadily in her mind.

Failure.

62

ARRAN

Sleeping without her was impossible. I kept close watch on that golden thread between us, monitoring its strength. It was steady, which meant she had not gone far. But despite the visceral need in my chest, building with every breath, I did not reach out to her with my mind or try to follow the connection to find her.

I was being selfish and I knew it.

But how could she even ask it of me... to sit by and watch her give her life... and do *nothing*.

A better husband would have held her hand and supported her. I could have asked how she was feeling and held her while she cried. But I did not need to ask—I could feel her as easily as I felt myself. Veyka did not want to die.

Yet she was willing to, because that was the cost demanded by the power in her veins and the prophecy made thousands of years ago in Avalon, by a priestess who'd been too cowardly to choose life for herself.

Fuck prophecies.

Fuck all of it.

I stopped myself just short of charging out of the tent to find her.

Be what she needs. At least for tonight.

I forced myself to undress and climb between the furs of our bedroll. Then I forced myself to wait. It was fucking agony. There was absolutely no sleeping. Not without her. I recalled those nights I'd slept alone in Eilean Gayl, my faulty memory robbing me of precious nights I should have spent sheathed inside of Veyka.

I rolled to my back, my traitorous cock lifting the bedsheets up and away from my body. Ancestors, I needed her. Not just physically, though that demand was growing with the minute. But I needed her soul wrapped around mine, her words warm in my ear.

It was too much to resist. Maybe if I took the edge off now, I'd be able to think beyond my own selfish physical desires when she did come to me. My fingers gripped the base of my cock, stroking up to the tip and back down again in a motion I'd perfected over the last three hundred years.

As I stroked myself, I thought of her.

Those leather leggings she wore beneath everything now that it was winter were absolute torture. The revealing gowns she'd worn in Baylaur were bad enough, but to see that leather gripping her thighs, curving around her ass? I was jealous of fabric. Ancestors, how was that even possible? And her hair... I'd enjoyed wrapping the waist-length braid around my wrist and yanking her head back when I had first fucked her. But now the ends were just long enough that they brushed her nipples. Even when clothed, all she had to do was move, the ends of her moon-white hair swishing, and all I saw in my mind was the dusky pink of her nipples begging for my mouth.

I was going to come hard and fast. My fingers pinched the tip of my cock, trying to slow the building pressure. My balls were already throbbing with need. I imagined how Veyka would drag her tongue over them, sucking one into her mouth while she palmed the other—

The tent flap opened. A second later, the scent of plum and primrose reached me.

My grip on my cock tightened by reflex, but I forced my fingers to relax. I couldn't do much about the arousal; my body was vividly aware of her closeness as she moved through the tent in near silence. But my ears and mind were attuned to every sound. The heavy thump was her boots dropping to the ground. The supple slide was leather as she pulled down her leggings—then a little mewl of annoyance as her foot tangled in one of the legs. The diaphanous material of her gown whispered against her skin as she peeled it away.

Last was her jewelry. Cyara had wrapped and packed it carefully, and Veyka put it to good use, bedecking herself as a queen should. The metal of bracelets and armbands jangled against one another. The soft click of a necklace being shed. Another little growl of frustration as the small diadem she'd worn tangled in her hair. She'd leave her earrings. She always left her earrings.

I lifted my hand to touch the one in my own ear. A single amorite stud to protect me from the succubus. Veyka had traced it with her tongue more times than I could count.

The furs lifted, a quick cool breeze sneaking in ahead of Veyka, but it would have taken all the snow in the Spine to cool my ardor. She settled herself on her back, kicking her legs to untangle the blankets, stretching her arms overhead and bringing her nipples close enough to my mouth that my beast began to growl. Which made my wife take even longer.

Cruel princess.

She laughed, low and sensuous, the heat of her breath filling the space between us as she rolled to her side, pressing her body against my hip. I noted the weight of her breast as it settled onto my chest, the soft rolls of her stomach where they curved around my hipbone. And the soft mound of her pussy, already hot against my skin.

"You've started without me," she purred. "Were you worried I wouldn't come back?"

It was dark, but I fucking *heard* her licking her lips. Ancestors, save me.

My hand was still on my cock. I tried to pull it away, but Veyka caught my wrist, encircling my fingers with her smaller ones.

"I hope you were thinking of me," she breathed against my throat, stopping just short of grazing the stubble with her lips. This female was going to kill me.

"You are all I think about."

She rewarded me by dragging our hands up the length of my cock.

"Tell me, Arran. Tell me what you thought of while you touched yourself." She was already breathless as she made the demand.

Cruel, cruel princess.

"These," I leaned over and nipped her breast, cursing the angle that prevented me from reaching her nipple. "So round and full, especially now that you're eating properly again. I imagined burying my face in them and licking every inch of your skin until your nipples are hard enough to slice."

Those same nipples hardened against my skin where she pressed into me.

I thrust into our next stroke.

"More," Veyka urged.

Ancestors, I'd been close before she even came into the tent. Another minute, and I'd spill myself all over our blankets.

"You were taking off your leggings, and all I could think about was how unfair it is that they hide you from me all day. I want to watch your muscles contracting and the wobble of that round ass of yours as you walk through camp, demanding worship like the goddess you are."

She ground her pussy against my hip as she guided my hand up and down, up and down. A feral little whimper escaped her lips. She was just as tortured as me.

"More," she demanded.

I'd give her more. I'd give her every last drop of me.

"I was wondering how I could give you what you need, agonizing over it. But I know what you need, Veyka. You need my cock buried inside of you, stretching and filling you until you don't know where I end and you begin. You need to forget every name, every word, every worry but me. Until I am the only thing in your body and your mind. I know *exactly* what you need, Princess."

"Arran," she moaned, her hips grinding in time with her hand.

"I'm going to come all over you, Princess." It was the only warning she'd get. She answered by covering my mouth with hers, pouring herself down my throat with a vigor matched only by her hand.

I came apart in powerful spurts that coated her hand, my cock, the juncture of my hips. Veyka stroked me through it, thrusting her hips in time with my orgasm until I collapsed onto the bedroll in sticky mess of my own exhaustion.

I only needed a minute, and then I would repay her in kind.

But my wicked princess did not give me a minute. She lifted her soaked hand to her mouth and began to lick my spend from her fingers one by one in long, loud sucks.

The next sound was the thump of her back hitting the bedroll. Her hips were wide and full beneath mine, a perfect match for the long lines of my own body. I'd fill that time I needed to recover well.

I plunged my fingers into her, the wet heat of her pussy and the come coating my fingers more than enough lubrication. Veyka arched her back, a feral moan echoing beyond the linen constraints of our tent for the entire terrestrial army to hear.

Yes, my queen, let them hear the sounds of your pleasure, my beast growled. My mouth was too busy for words now that I had full access to her breasts. The hand that was not pounding into her pussy cupped one breast, pinching the nipple up to my waiting lips. I circled it once with my tongue before sucking it between my teeth, nipping hard enough to elicit another cry of pleasure from Veyka. She was such a magnificent creature, my mate. She did not hesitate to be exactly who and what she was. She did not hide herself from the world or apologize. She let them hear me worshipping her because she knew that she deserved it.

Already her pussy started to pulse. Torturing me had driven her to the edge as well.

I curled my fingers inside of her, over that textured cluster of nerves that ornamented her inner walls. Once more. Then I withdrew my hand, coated now in the mingled nectar of both our pleasure.

Veyka's next cry was followed by a string of reproachful curses, but I only smiled.

My cock was ready.

Pulling away from her was a physical pain, but I took the two desperate steps to the free-standing lamp a yard from the bedroll. I'd never envied elemental powers until that moment, when I could have stayed with my hand buried inside her pussy and simultaneously lit fire in the lamp.

"Brutal... fucking... prince," she huffed, rising up on her forearms.

I grabbed her hips and dragged her to the edge of the bedroll. The wooden platform of our bed was a definite improvement to sleeping on the ground. Now we'd see just how sturdy it was.

The fire I'd lit in the lamp flickered, throwing undulating light across the tent. But I could see her pussy clearly, and that was all that mattered. I watched as my own fingers dipped to spread her pussy lips, my other hand curled around the base of my cock as I guided myself to her entrance.

She was watching, too. Braced on her forearms, we watched together as her pussy lips stretched around my cock, taking the head and then resisting. A low growl built in my chest as I pressed forward, past the slight resistance until my shaft started to disappear into her as well.

Veyka's sharp inhale, the desperate sound she made as I slid in that last inch, was almost enough to make me come again. I slid my gaze up her body, savoring the sight of her stomach, curled up into rolls of delicious soft flesh as she leaned forward to watch me take her. Then her breasts, wobbling with each shaking breath. She was so desperate for me, she didn't even meet my eyes at first. She was too busy rolling her hips, fitting me in as tight as she could, hungry for every tiny fraction of an inch I had to give.

"Such a needy thing," I murmured, watching her watching us.

Her eyes snapped to mine, the blue rings of desire burning bright enough to light the tent all on their own. "I will always need you."

She held my gaze for another second, then she planted her hand on my chest and shoved me backward. I hadn't even realized that I'd leaned forward, so eager to be close to her. But the demand was clear. She wanted to watch.

I hooked my arms under her knees so I could fuck her harder.

Every stroke into her was better than the last. Then I withdrew, saw my cock glistening with her juices, and I took her again. The tension was building with every beat of our hearts in time with our thrusts. Veyka slid her hand between us, touching her swollen clit. I tried to reach for her to do it myself, but she shoved my hand away, returning it to where it had gripped her thigh. She'd have marks in the morning from my fingertips, but I knew we'd both look on them with pleasure.

She arched against me, her eyes flickering closed. She was close —so close she'd almost forgotten.

"Watch me come inside of you, Veyka," I ordered. "Do you see how your pussy takes me, every inch? I can't..."

Fuck, I was losing control. I tried to hold it back, but it was impossible. I ground myself into her, my thrusts turning small and desperate, my orgasm completely taking over all other thoughts.

Veyka threw back her head, her fingers stilling over her clit as she whimpered through her own climax.

I lost control.

Veyka's response to that thought was a low, sultry laugh that I felt in the corners of my mind and warm against my skin.

Maybe she'd already realized what I hadn't until that moment. With Veyka, I was never in control.

"Veyka? Veyka, can you hear me?"

It was still dark outside.

"Go away," Veyka groused, burrowing deeper against my chest. My beast growled in agreement, but I ignored him.

It took me several seconds to orient myself. My battle axe was in my hand before I'd even consciously thought about grabbing it, three hundred years of battle and bloodshed conditioned to a point beyond thinking.

But there was no disturbance outside our tent. The camp was quiet—as quiet as an army camp ever was.

"Arran?"

Not Veyka, but another female voice. And it was not coming from outside the tent, but within. From where Veyka had tossed her clothing over the camp chair in the corner before coming to bed. I followed the faint white light, my heart stuttering and tripping over itself while I dug through the folds of her gown to find the communication crystal.

It shined brightly in my hand, the glowing white length pulsing with magic.

I lifted it closer to my face. "Have you found it?"

Several beats of silence. "Yes."

The world stopped.

The human realm, Annwyn, the Split Sea, any others that existed. Everything stopped. The only thing that mattered was that one word, this one moment in time, this one answer.

My entire chest filled with light. Bright, moon-white hope.

The bedsheets rustled behind me, the wooden platform groaning. I turned, lifting my palm so that the white glow of the communication crystal shone into the space between us. Veyka sat in the bed, the lines of her dimples and rolls of soft skin silhouetted by that pale glow.

"Yes," Cyara said again. "I have the grail."

I looked to Veyka, expecting her to say something. But she shook her head.

She had no words. But I could speak for us both. In the moments before we'd fallen asleep, she'd whispered what Mya had confided in her. "We are going to Avalon."

🎜 63 🎝

GUINEVERE

Wraithwood, Emberhaven, Thornbriar, and Ferndale. Gwen recited the names as she walked through the village of Eldermist, now completely overrun by a mix of human residents, visitors, fae refugees, and elemental soldiers. They mostly kept to their own camps. Mostly.

Some mingling was inevitable as supplies were collected and distributed.

Gwen's own mixed company battalion was in charge of that task. They could at least stand one another after a couple of weeks training together.

Tonight she owed her report back to Arran. Which meant that today, she had to secure an alliance worth reporting. Or rather, four of them. Her eyes twitched as she walked, the slight burn of a sleepless night beginning. But sleep would have to wait. She'd spent the entire night in conference with Sylva, planning.

Veyka and Arran had given her what amorite they could spare and leeway to negotiate. Sylva had armed her with information.

Helene of Thornbriar wanted amorite.

She found the woman in the village square, negotiating at the command stall for rations of sugar in exchange for salted beef.

Gwen waited until the conversation finished, noting the woman's stance and tone. She was tall for a human woman and rail thin. Her once blonde hair was liberally sprinkled with gray that lent a certain gravitas, but it was the sharp hawk nose in the dead center of her face that drew the eye.

"What do you want?" Helene asked, not bothering to lower her voice despite the prevalence of pointed fae ears in every direction. At least the woman in the command stall was already busy with her next visitor.

Gwen kept her own voice pitched low, so that only Helene would hear it. If Helene required no pleasantries, then neither did she.

"I cannot arm all of your soldiers. But I can spare four amorite weapons—enough for your lieutenants." Gwen used the term loosely, as the human fighting force had no formal structure. "And one amorite stud—for your son."

That was the true price of her alliance, Sylva had guessed.

The woman's eyes blew wide, the whites showing all the way around dark brown irises. Gwen did not flinch. Once, she might have worried about the appearance of favoritism. But this war would be over before each of the human leaders stopped arguing long enough to compare the price of their allegiance.

Helene swayed—like she might fall over with a gust of wind. The end of her hawk-nose twitched as she considered, but Gwen could taste victory. She reached into her pocket, the amorite already at hand, and pressed it into the woman's palm.

"Yes?"

Her hand closed around the amorite stud. "Yes."

"I will inspect your forces tomorrow morning." Gwen turned and walked away before the woman could argue or attempt to add any caveats to her cooperation. Her last target had not left his room on the upper floor of Sylva's house, though there had been a steady stream of visitors who he welcomed behind his closed door.

Wraithwood, Emberhaven, and Ferndale, Gwen recited again as she retraced her route through the snow, now churned into a muddy mess by foot traffic.

Elora had already secured the alliance of Tally of Emberhaven. Even with the Wraithwood leader's disgusting words, Emberhaven's allegiance had not waivered. Elora must be very persuasive in bed.

Wraithwood. She left him to Sylva. Gwen knew enough about prejudice to understand that she would not be the one to convince him. Any promise she made would not be trusted, anyway.

Inside the house, she discarded her heavy fur cloak but left her weapons in place. Winter in Baylaur was supposed to be mild; but in the human realm, just through the rift, the weather more closely matched the terrestrial kingdom. Though there was something to be said for a few inches of snow, rather than a few feet of it.

Sylva appeared at the door to the kitchen, gray hair neat as always and steaming cup in her hand. She offered it to Gwen immediately.

"Ferndale still upstairs?"

Sylva nodded. "I've got Wraithwood convinced. Coerced," she amended. "But Ferndale..." her eyes traveled up the stairwell.

"One of Elora's scouts spotted their approach this morning. As big as the forces the other three sent combined, and then some," Gwen said grimly.

Sylva had admitted to not knowing much about the delegate from Ferndale personally; but she'd confided there was one thing that the town was known for—greed.

Gwen could use that.

She thanked Sylva and climbed the stairs. The door at the end of the hallway was closed, as it had been since the man's arrival. He'd only opened it to attend the meeting downstairs the day before and to receive food and guests. As far as Gwen knew, those guests had ranged from residents of Eldermist to Helene, the leader of Thornbriar. But no fae had been invited over the threshold.

Gwen knocked but did not wait for an invitation.

She closed the door behind her with a resolute *click*, pressing her back to it as her eyes scanned the room. It was sparse by elemental standards, but better than many places Gwen had slept over the years. Including the last few weeks, when she'd taken up residence in Sylva's pantry.

A real, wood-framed bed stood in the corner. Too short for fae proportions, but adequate for most humans. A dressing table in the other corner, with a pitcher and basin for water. Embroidered curtains hung at the window, where a single wing-back chair held the room's occupant.

He was round and dressed for cold despite the roaring fire in his hearth. Unlike the headache from Wraithwood sitting in the kitchen downstairs, there was no hate in the man's dark eyes. Gwen struggled to place human ages, so different from how the fae aged, but she guessed he was at least a decade younger then Sylva. Experienced but not yet elderly.

"I wondered when you'd come." He tilted his head to one side as he considered her, the thick black hair on his head shifting with the motion. "You are welcome to sit."

There was a single wooden chair across from him.

"I'll stand."

"As you wish."

Gwen folded her hands neatly in front of her, a trick she'd learned in her youth when she'd dreamed of being High Queen of all Annwyn. It kept her from fidgeting.

"You have voiced no objection to joining your forces to ours," she said. "But you have not agreed, either."

"That is correct." The man—Ferndale, her mind dubbed him— tilted his head the opposite direction, as if that would give him some new information.

"What will it take to secure your alliance?" Gwen asked. She did not have time for anything but honestly.

Ferndale's head straightened to attention. "I see that what I have heard of the terrestrial fae is true. You do not favor the clever, cunning machinations of your elemental brothers and sisters."

"I am tired and the battle will soon be joined," Gwen said. If her hands had not been clasped, she would have crossed them over her chest. "The time for cleverness and cunning have long since passed."

Ferndale's chin dipped a fraction of an inch. "What will you offer me for my alliance?"

Your life, her lioness purred.

She needed to go hunting. After, she promised the feline that lived just beneath her skin.

"Gold, jewels, protection," she listed the most obvious choices.

His head did not tilt, nor did his chin move.

But the left corner of his mouth lifted. "Amorite?"

Gwen had anticipated this question. "I'd have to take it from my own males to give it to you. Your fighters are valuable, but they are not trained fae warriors."

One amorite stud, she could lose. But not even the elementals that Elora had found in the mountains were protected from losing their souls to the succubus. As it was, female warriors all over Eldermist and the outlying areas, human and fae alike, guarded the males who could turn deadly in an instant.

"Once we join forces with the High King and Queen, it is possible—"

Ferndale lifted his hand. "Do you know why there are no mighty human cities left? Why we've been reduced to struggling villages?"

Gwen clenched her jaw. She would not give him the satisfaction of shaking her head.

"It is because of your Ancestors. They destroyed everything during their Great War. You say it was never about fighting us, but about defeating the succubus even then. But the fae who came and burned our cities did not do it to protect themselves. They did it simply because they *could*."

She could not argue with him. Maybe it had been a mercy—trapping the humans taken by the succubus and burning them alive in hopes of extinguishing them. Or maybe it was a brutal way of controlling the human population should the succubus become a threat once again. Humans reproduced much more quickly than fae. Or maybe it was exactly as he said. But those truths were lost to history, and they would not help them live through today.

"Ferndale is not a great city yet, but it will be soon. Our port allows us to trade all across the continent. We do not need jewels or gold. We need to survive. But without your precious amorite, the humans will be nothing more than charnel for your fae to sacrifice to the succubus as a shield."

"I will retain command of the human forces. I will not let that happen," Gwen vowed.

But Ferndale did not even dignify that with a response. He turned and stared out the window.

It was unacceptable. She could not atone for her Ancestors. They were the reason all of them, human and fae alike, were battling this monster from another realm. Ancient massacres and prophecies could not be given so much power over the present, not when the very future was at stake...

The future.

It was the only thing more powerful than the past.

"A place in Baylaur." Gwen dropped her hands to her sides. "When this is over, the world will be different. We... we will renegotiate the treaty between our realms. Humans will have a voice in the fae court."

She would never have considered it if she were in Veyka's place. Humans had slaughtered Arthur—Veyka's twin brother, Gwen's betrothed. But those humans were not these humans. Those humans had been commanded by Roksana, and manipulated by Igraine and Gorlois, from the recounting Arran and Veyka had given back in Eilean Gayl.

These humans just wanted to live to see another dawn.

Ferndale tilted his head to the side. "Your King and Queen will honor this promise?"

"I am a Knight of the Round Table and her Majesty's Goldstone Guard. Before that, I was the Terrestrial Heir to the throne of Annwyn. They will honor it."

He nodded once. "So be it."

Gwen's shoulders sagged with relief.

"Close the door behind you."

She could have done with a *please*, but her goal was secured. The calculations began to shift and rearrange themselves within her head. This would be her command. Arran was not a meddlesome commander; he would not interfere with however she decided to organize it. She would use the humans, but she would not sacrifice them unnecessarily.

The tiredness that had plagued her evaporated, leaving a sizzling energy in its wake.

The door opened just as her foot hit the landing, letting in a blast of frigid air.

Elora rushed through it, the emissary from Emberhaven on her heels.

"A succubus horde," Elora gasped, her breath scissoring in and out of her chest. "In the valley."

Gwen shook her head. She'd made this mistake before.

"It could be humans from the sixth village." The one that had not responded at all to her envoy. Gwen could not recall the name, but Sylva knew. Gwen had been wrong before.

But the lines around Elora's mouth only deepened. "In a few minutes, you'll be able to scent their bile from here."

The sizzle of anticipation in Gwen's veins turned to dread. "You could pull your troops up into the mountains. I can call for Arran using the communication crystal. Retreat until we can join our forces with the terrestrial army."

Elora's nostrils flared. The door still hung open, making it impossible to tell if the chill came from outside or from Elora herself. "Or we can fight."

Gwen recognized the vengeance in the female's eyes. In Baylaur, she and Elora had fought side by side, lost the city inch by painful inch. Elora wanted retribution. She wanted victory. She wanted to feel like she was not an Ancestors'-damned failure. Gwen understood her completely.

But even though she'd just told herself and Ferndale that she would take command of the human forces, she found herself looking to the other doorway.

Sylva stood, hot tea in hand as always, framed by warmth and firelight that glinted and turned her gray hair a striking silver.

"We have been running long enough," the human woman said. "This is our realm. It is time we fight to defend it."

⚜ 64 ⚜
VEYKA

I'd hoped to never visit Avalon again. The instant my boots touched the lush green grass, the memories of Gorlois, Arran—

His hand curled around mine. *I am here*, his beast growled just for me.

Once, I would have been horrified at how easily he accessed my emotions. Now I was just grateful.

My hand was steady as I lifted it, a spiral of light appearing instantly. I did not spare time for greetings, though my eyes prickled uncomfortably at the sight of Cyara.

"We cannot linger here or we will quickly lose our senses," I reminded everyone. "Through the rift." Only once we were all safely on the mist-shrouded island did I take another full breath.

Mya peered around, nose crinkling as she realized we could not see more than a few feet in any direction. "Evander, can you do anything about this?"

He lifted his hand, cold whipping up at his command. But my focus narrowed before I could judge his effectiveness. Cyara gripped my hand.

"Your Majesty." She dropped to her knees, bowing her head over the hand she held. "Forgive me."

My throat threatened to close. She wore her usual gray tunic and pants, a thick cloak against the cold like the rest of us. Her copper hair was neatly arranged in its customary plait. But Cyara had never prostrated herself before me. Ever. Even when we first met. She'd curtsy and show the utmost respect. But this... it made my heart ache.

"We've talked about this," I said around the lump in my throat.

She lifted her turquoise eyes to mine, glowing with unshed tears. "I know. I did not complete the quest you set for me, I betrayed your trust, and I will surrender my Knighthood willingly." She did not offer an apology.

I'd told her to go to the Faeries of the Fen and secure an alliance. Instead, she'd abandoned Osheen and Maisri and run off with the humans, Percival and Diana. The two currently lingered at the edge of our group, eyeing Mya's blue skin with wariness and a heavy dose of fear. The dutiful but honest handmaiden I'd known had changed.

But none of that could touch the love I bore for her.

"Veyka. You call me Veyka," I reminded her, pulling her to stand.

Cyara blinked.

I tried very hard to keep my voice steady. "You followed your king and your heart. I am lucky to call you my friend and my knight."

Her wings wobbled, and I knew she was very close to collapsing again. I pulled her tight against me—the oldest, truest friend that remained to me. Forgiving her was easy.

"Do not be angry with him," Cyara said into my hair.

"Anger," I laughed at the absurdity. "Such a simple word cannot even begin to touch what is between us." I'd forgiven him, too.

I was ready to give up my own life to save Annwyn. But the simple truth was I did not know how I would react if the roles were reversed. If the prophecy had asked for Arran instead of me... part of me said that I would let him go. That I would still choose Annwyn.

But another part screamed in protest.

"Here," Cyara said, pressing something into the space between us. Large, metal, and rounded. The chalice.

There it was. The grail. The final item of the Sacred Trinity. I'd dripped my blood into it not once, but twice. All three sacred objects had been there in Baylaur and I'd had no idea. *But Merlin did.* She'd known all along. Punishment would come for her, now that I had the chalice in hand. Though Arran might have to be the one to deliver it. Even with the metallic gold of the grail against my palm, I struggled to believe.

No footsteps alerted us to her coming, but I felt the Lady of the Lake's approach all the same. The magic of Avalon was intense and wild, and it all centered around her. She pulled the force with her as she walked, appearing from the mist that Evander had managed to push back by several feet.

Mya glanced in my direction, looking for confirmation. It was strange to see her wrapped in fur, the warm browns and golds so contrary to the cool tones of her skin and clothing. She said she did not feel the cold of the water, but by the slight tremble of her hand, she could feel it in the air. That must be the reason that ever-steady Mya was trembling.

"Morgyn le Fae," I confirmed. "The Lady of the Lake." My half-sister. And utter pain in my ass.

"I am the Ethereal Queen," Mya said steadily. Evander held her hand so tightly it could not tremble with the cold, or anything else. "We have come to fulfill the prophecy."

Morgyn's response was to ignore Mya completely and look at me instead. My perfect half-sister was as composed as ever—her curtain of brown hair fell in a straight line to her shoulders, the only ornamentation a braid that started at each temple and framed her beautiful face. Her blue eyes matched the ones I saw in the mirror each morning, the ones I'd adored when set in Arthur's smiling golden face.

She looked at me because she *knew*.

Pain. In. My. Ass.

I broke away from the group—Lyrena and Arran at each shoulder, Cyara close by as well. I walked right up to the Lady of the Lake, pulling Excalibur from its sheath across my back, unbuckling the belt that held the scabbards, the grail's golden shimmer dulled by the mist.

"Not quite yet." I dropped all three of the sacred objects in a heap at her feet. "Tell me about the Sacred Trinity."

The tiniest of divots appeared between her eyebrows. "You treat our sacred objects as if they are nothing."

"They all belong to me now," I said, planting my hands on my hips. "Tell me what it means to be master of death. Don't leave out any details."

Morgyn was an expert at appearing completely unruffled by my antics. It was more than annoying. But her eyes stayed with me—as if everyone else who'd come to her island, including the prophesied Ethereal Queen, did not matter at all.

"Only when wielded as one can they serve the purpose for which they were made," Morgyn began. I recognized the words that Gwen had recited, the ones Parys had found in the library in the goldstone palace. "Fae, human, and witch united to create the Sacred Trinity. Only when united again can the three be wielded to defeat the darkness by becoming the master of death."

I wanted to stab her. But my daggers were inconveniently in the scabbards at my feet. "You are still talking in riddles."

Morgyn did not engage with my complaints. "All magic has a cost."

And this one had not been paid.

I knew that Arran listened to every word, the hope that he'd kept alive a tiny flame between us. Precious. And still flickering, still alive. He did not understand.

"What is the cost to become the master of death?"

Morgyn held my gaze, as she had from the moment her eyes landed on mine. Just once before, I'd caught a flash of emotion in her blue orbs that were such a strange reflection of my own. She did not try to hide it now. That was sympathy that turned her irises a shade lighter, that softened the smooth plane of her forehead.

"Your soul."

I did not want her sympathy. "You knew all along."

Arran's beast howled, snarled, growled—he was losing control. His shift was imminent. He understood.

"Of course. I am the Lady of the Lake." Any feeling that had shone for that brief second was gone.

"You should have told me months ago," I snarled. It wasn't wholly me—some of it was Arran, clawing his way across the golden connection between us. "Spare me your prattling about Avalon's neutrality. You should have told me."

Mya gasped. She understood now, too. Another few seconds, and my Knights would work it out as well.

Morgyn dipped her chin. "Rage at me if you like. I know who you are really angry at."

Arran shifted. He was with me in a single bound, his head beneath my hand, his wet snout shoving into my stomach. Trying to reassure himself that I was still here. That what Morgyn had implied could not possibly be true. But it was.

That precious ember of light Arran had so lovingly cared for died.

There had never been any hope for me. To fulfill the Void and Ethereal Prophecy and banish the succubus would require my life and Mya's. To unite the Sacred Trinity and wield it against the succubus would cost my soul.

I was doomed either way.

65

VEYKA

"She will die either way. Why should you sacrifice yourself as well?"

"It is my life to give, Evander."

"I should slit your throat just for saying—"

"What does it mean? Losing a soul could be..."

Their words blended together in a sonorous cacophony. The snarling wolf joined in, circling my legs. I kneeled down, grabbing the scruff of thicker fur around his neck and tugging him to me.

We will find another way, he growled.

One second, my face was buried in thick white fur. The next, the spice and earth that filled my senses was all Arran, my face tucked into the eternal warmth at the crook of his neck.

"We will defeat the succubus by strength of numbers," he said against my hair, stroking his fingers through it.

I let myself linger there longer than I should have. Too long, and that hope inside of him would rekindle. He'd think I had changed my mind.

I forced myself to pull away, to stand. Arran moved with me, hands cradling my face, his black eyes searching my features for any sign of what I might be thinking. So easily, he could access my mind and my heart. But now they'd became a torrent too big for even me.

"Wait for me here," I said.

I'd meant it for Arran, but I felt the weight of all their eyes landing on me. Cyara and Lyrena, my loyal Knights. Diana and Percival, acolytes and humans, always on the outside. Mya and Evander, a new friend and an old enemy.

Arran grabbed my hand. *Stay.*

I will return, I promised him. "There is one thing I must do." I pushed the communication crystal into his hand. "Call for Guinevere. There is not much time now."

It was harder than I'd thought to walk away. Only the promise of where I was going kept my feet moving forward.

66

VEYKA

For weeks, I'd snuck away whenever I could to search. But the truth was that I'd been looking for him for over a year. In the beginning, I searched for him in the past. I refused to live in the present because it meant being alone. If I refused to move forward, to accept my new reality, then I did not have to let him go.

Then Arran came, and I was no longer alone. But I searched for him still. Every time I stepped into the void, a part of me cried out, waiting for an answer that never came. Only in the past few weeks, when I'd come to accept my fate, had I begun the search consciously. I passed through realms of light so bright my eyes were not evolved to see. I slipped between the fabric of the universe, searching for that one place that I knew he would be waiting.

I walked alone through the mist, trusting the Ancestors to guide me. Nimue, so far removed that she seemed nothing more than a character in a book—one that had been written about my life before I was even born. But I could feel her with me now. She steadied my steps through the mist until I was far enough away from those I loved to make this one final journey. She held my hand as I stepped into the void.

She only let go once I finally found what I'd been looking for... but not *who* I'd been looking for.

The after realm looked suspiciously like the library in Baylaur.

And sitting right there on the floor, books and wine spread all around him, rich brown curls glinting in a late afternoon sun, was my dearest friend.

I did not know if I fell to the ground or if he stood. The laws that governed this realm might be wholly different than my own. But I was in his arms, his familiar scent wrapping around me, his smaller frame disappearing into my own.

"Parys, I am so sorry."

Tears streamed down my face. His or mine? Could spirits cry? What *was* he, even? I didn't know, and that made me sob harder. But he was real. Solid. His arms around me, curls brushing my cheek, the familiar scent of books and wine flooding my senses and drawing forth chest-wracking sobs.

He let me cry, rubbing small circles on my back. Ancestors, I could *feel* his smile against my cheek. He drew back to look at me and I could see it. Feel it, as bright as the sun that shone impossibly from outside of the two-story-tall windows.

"No wonder you never let anyone see you cry. You are absolutely hideous."

I dragged the back of my hand across my face, wiping away the snot and tears and disbelief.

"I am so sorry," I said again, this time in a broken whisper.

Parys tugged at the end of my braid, no longer waist-length. His warm brown eyes studied my face. I expected him to frown at the changes he must see there, but the corners of his smile only deepened.

"You have nothing to apologize for," he said.

I choked on another sob. "My mother murdered you."

"The Dowager never was particularly fond of me," he joked. He looked whole and healthy, no physical signs of how he'd died. I wasn't sure what I'd expected... perhaps for his hair to be wet, water leaking from his mouth. But his curls bounced merrily at his shoulders, no sign of his watery death anywhere to be seen.

I reached out, fingering the edge of his collar to reassure myself this was real. As real as it could be. I was not even sure how I'd come here—and deep inside of the soul that I might very well sacrifice before the day was done—I knew I would not be able to come here again. This was a gift from the Ancestors, from Nimue. To help give me the courage I needed.

Parys' closed his fingers around mine, then tugged them up and pressed a kiss to the knuckles. I laughed at the intimacy that only he had ever claimed. But Parys, as always, saw through me.

"I am fine. See," he gestured to the spread behind him. "Plenty of books and wine."

"You are dead," I reminded him.

Parys shrugged as if that fact meant nothing, and not *everything*. "This realm is not so bad."

I looked around. "All the places in the universe you could choose, and this is it, huh?"

Parys waggled his index finger at me. "Ah, you are focused on what you do see. But think for a second about what you don't."

It took me several seconds to realize. "There are no librarians."

"Exactly!" Parys smacked his thigh and laughed, the sound reverberating through the stacks.

I let the vibration settle in my chest, savoring it. "It is so wonderful to see you," I whispered.

Parys quirked a brow. "But I'm not the one you were looking for?"

The guilt climbed my cheeks in streaks of heat before I could tame it.

"I expected you to be together."

"Who says we aren't?" Parys countered.

I glanced meaningfully around the very empty library.

"You should know better than anyone that time and space do not always work in the way that we expect."

Indeed.

"How do I find him?" Then I added, with more force than I'd intended, "No cryptic answers. I've had enough word play to last a dozen fae lifetimes."

Parys only laughed.

"Try the doors," he suggested, nodding over my shoulder.

I did not want to let him go. He still held my hand. But the pull was growing. Different from the compulsion of the mating bond when Arran used it to tether me and pull me from the void. This feeling was older, seeded in me from birth.

Parys brushed another kiss over my knuckles and then released my hand, giving me a little push. I backed away, unwilling to give up even a second of him before I absolutely had to. But too soon, I was at the massive library doors. I reached behind me for the handle.

Parys dropped back down among his books and wine. But he did not look away.

"Tell Gwen it is not her fault," he said instead of goodbye.

I smiled. "I already have."

He grinned, and I tried to burn that image into my memory. He was exactly where he belonged. I could leave him here knowing that.

I pushed through the door to find who I was really looking for. Who I was really angry with, as Morgyn had so infuriatingly pointed out. The one who I'd been searching for all these months.

"I knew you'd come one day."

Arthur.

I punched him.

67

VEYKA

"Parys gets tearful embraces, and I get a black eye," Arthur groused, gingerly touching the eye in question.

Thank goodness he was solid and not some strange ephemeral spirit. That would not have been nearly as satisfying.

"Not much of an afterlife if I can hurt you here." My own hand ached, a small split appearing in one of my knuckles. The tiniest line of blood rose to the surface. I was bleeding. The scabbards were still back on Avalon. And apparently, I could bleed in the after realm. Interesting.

"The living are not supposed to be here at all," Arthur commented. He'd stepped back when I punched him in the face. Now he used the distance to look me over.

I stared right back at him, righteous anger overcoming more than a year's worth of longing. "Yes, well. It turns out I am something of a special case."

A soundless chuckle lifted his chest. "You always were."

His chest led to his neck, which was firmly attached to his head. Thank the Ancestors. Though after seeing Parys fully intact, I'd expected as much. I inhaled every detail of him, from the top of his overgrown golden hair down to—was that an amorite earring in his ear lobe?

"You lied to me."

"Veyka—"

"Every day of my Ancestors-damned life, you lied to me! And then you died. You died on purpose. You left me alone to—"

"To do what you were always destined to do, Veyka."

"Fuck that, and fuck you, Arthur." I spun on my heel, determined to get away from him. Then I remembered that he was the whole reason I'd been sneaking away from Arran in the dead of night to search the void. Morgyn was not the only irritating sibling I would be dealing with today.

"Would you like to hit me again?" he offered.

I did not answer.

"I deserve it. Every bit of your anger."

That... deflated me a bit. I turned back to face him. Arthur extended a hand, and I accepted, letting him lead me to sit on a log at the center of the clearing.

We were in a—where were we?

It was a forest clearing, but I did not recognize it. Not anywhere near Baylaur, the trees were all wrong. Thick green leaves spread out in a canopy overhead so that the sunlight that did reach us was dappled. Wildflowers dotted the grass below our feet. Birds chirped. My brother had created quite the idyllic little paradise for himself.

He sat beside me on the log, stretching his long legs out alongside mine. Ancestors, even our legs were the same length. I'd never noticed that. I'd always been so busy cataloguing all the ways we were different—the ways I was less than.

I'd wasted precious time comparing myself to the one person who'd never judged me at all. Arthur, the source of all things good in my world for the first twenty-five years of my life. There were so many questions I yearned to ask, so much I wanted to tell him. But all of it seemed inconsequential when I could just *be* with him, soaking in his presence.

"Do you know what makes me the angriest?" I said after a while. "You chose Annwyn over yourself. Over staying with me."

He uncrossed and re-crossed his legs. "And don't you plan to do the same for your kingdom?" A long exhale. "To your mate?"

Irritating sibling. "What if I said that it is different."

"I'd ask you to tell me how."

"If you had lived, Arran would never have become the Terrestrial Heir. I would never have fulfilled the prophecy and the succubus never would have come to Annwyn." And Arthur would have lived.

Did that also mean that I never would have found Arran? Would never have recognized him for my mate and fallen in love? Even the vague possibility of that made my stomach clench with terror and protest.

But Arthur was shaking his head.

"The succubus would have come either way, Veyka. They were already here, even before my death, slipping through the rifts that Gorlois opened in his selfish quest for power. Eventually, they would have found another way through. But I was not the one destined to stop them. If you'd never gained your power, the succubus would have overrun Annwyn and that would have been the end."

Fuck. I'd asked for the truth and he'd given it. Maybe I liked the lies better.

I leaned into him, resting my head on his shoulder. For once, he did not wear any golden armor. It was just his shoulder beneath a white silk tunic. If I listened hard enough, I imagined I could hear his heartbeat. "It isn't fair, Arthur."

"I was only king for a short time," he said. "I suspect that you understand even better than I can that life is rarely fair. Ruling a kingdom is even less so."

I elbowed him in the ribs. "You were always such a comfort."

He exhaled a long sigh. "You speak about me in past tense, even as I sit beside you."

I shot upright. "Arthur, I'm sorry—"

But he caught my shoulder, keeping me beside him on the log. "No. I am glad of it. It means you have accepted my death and that you have moved on."

I wanted to argue with him, but... I couldn't. Fuck. When had that happened?

"Tell me about your mate," Arthur said once I'd finally relaxed enough to rest my head back on his shoulder.

"He's an overprotective ass."

"Good to hear," Arthur snorted.

"Is this place not all seeing?"

He shrugged. "I find that I am thankful for the things I do know, and do not lose heart wondering about the things I do not. It is peace, I think."

Peace. I could not even fathom it. But I could answer his question.

"Arran is... everything." A word that was supposed to encompass enormity and that felt pitifully small. "He sees me. From the very beginning, he has seen me. I don't think that anyone has ever looked into my soul like that, into the very depths of who I am, even the parts I am scared and ashamed of... and loved me for all of it. Not even you."

It felt like a betrayal to say it. But when I looked up, Arthur was smiling. "You should go back to him, Veyka."

I wanted to. I needed to. "What do I do?"

My life or my soul. Was one worse than the other? What did it even mean, to live without a soul? Was that just another way of describing death? Or something worse—because both Parys and Arthur's souls seemed perfectly intact, even though they were dead.

Arthur stood, but he tugged me against him as he did. Time to go.

"I cannot tell you what choice to make. That was not your purpose in coming here," Arthur said. He planted a kiss against my hair, then released me. Stepped back. The log was gone, now. The chirps of birds faded away.

My heart stuttered in my chest. "Will I be able to return?"

Arthur nodded. "You would not have come here if you'd truly doubted it."

"Not to Annwyn." He was right. Even now, I could feel Arran tugging on the bond, reassuring himself that I was still his. "To you," I whispered.

The void began to tug at me, calling me back. Arran, using the tether to rescue me from the darkness.

Arthur did not reach for me, letting me go back to where I truly belonged.

"We will see each other again, Veyka," he promised.

Then he was gone. Nothing more than a memory.

🕸 68 🕸

ARRAN

It was difficult to measure the passage of time enshrouded as we were in the mist. Evander and his Aquarian queen, Mya, disappeared for what might have been an hour or could have been two or three. When they returned, Evander's face was set in a harsh mask. The puffiness around Mya's eyes told me that she had been crying.

Percival and Diana sat on the grass, occasionally speaking to one another but mostly silent. A lavender-draped priestess appeared from the mist to offer water and bread. I should have used the time to strategize with Lyrena or to question Cyara about her journey since leaving Eilean Gayl. Instead, I passed off the communication crystal and let the two of them contact Gwen.

I watched Veyka go, and then I *felt* her go. Through the void. She did not emerge for a long time. The bond was still intact, still strong, but it was as taut as I'd ever felt it. Wherever she'd gone, it was not in the human realm. My instincts told me she had not gone to Annwyn, either.

Where else... she'd mentioned the succubus realm once. When recounting those terrifying trips through the void, when her power overwhelmed her at our Joining, she'd mentioned a realm of darkness and death. A smell and chill she later attributed to the succubus.

She would not go there alone, I told myself. Not when she could have taken me with her, when we could have battled together. Not without saying goodbye.

But the longer she was gone, the less sure I felt. She was *beyond*, of that I was certain. The bond was intact but the pressure built in my chest minute by minute. It was almost painful.

I'd never tried to reach her when she was in another realm. I had no idea if the connection between us would reach that far. But I had to try.

Veyka, where are you?

Nothing.

My beast howled inside of me. I tried again. *Veyka, come back.*

My mind flashed to the temple in Eilean Gayl, when Diana's mind had floated unmoored through space and time, and Percival had used his bond as her brother to pull her back to him. I did exactly what I'd described to him. I wrapped myself around that golden bond, tugging, an insistent demand.

For a few heartbeats, I thought it wouldn't be enough. Then I felt her on the other side.

The mist obscured everything, but I knew my mate was near.

She walked on silent feet out of the fog, but by the time she'd fully emerged, everyone in the small circle that Evander held clear was on their feet.

Veyka's eyes tracked around the circle, holding the gaze of each person in turn. Everyone except me.

No footsteps sounded over my shoulder, but Veyka's expression told me who had joined us again from behind the wall of mist.

"I am ready," she said to the Lady of the Lake.

"There is a succubus horde in the valley below Eldermist," Cyara said. "Humans from five villages prepare to fight in coalition with

Elora and the remnants of the Elemental Army. Gwen cannot leave them."

Cyara's hand shook around the communication stone.

"Thank you." She hugged Cyara close. Then Lyrena.

This was unacceptable.

She reached Mya and Evander. She glared at the latter. But she grasped the Ethereal Queen's hand.

"It is not your decision alone, Veyka. My life is mine to risk," Mya insisted.

Veyka shook her head. "There is no reason for us both to sacrifice our lives when my soul will do the trick."

I watched the weight lift off Evander's chest and felt it settle on mine.

I'd known what she would choose. But it was still wrong.

She reached me where I stood over the items of the Sacred Trinity, still on the ground where she'd dropped them. The jewels on the scabbards were dulled by the mist. Excalibur's blade was buried six inches into the dirt. The golden chalice lay carelessly on its side. They did not seem special at all in the white mist. Just *things*. Things that would take my mate from me.

Veyka nudged the sword with her toe. "Can you be any more descriptive about what it means to trade my soul for the ability to wield the Sacred Trinity?"

Morgyn le Fae stared at her sister. I resisted the compulsion to step back and give the two females space to speak privately. If these were Veyka's last moments, I was selfish enough to hold on to every single one of them.

"I have never wished you ill, Veyka," Morgyn finally said. "If the ones who originally forged the Sacred Trinity knew the cost, they did not pass it down to us."

Veyka nodded silently, as if she'd expected that answer.

"How?" Her voice was small and quiet.

"Don the sword and scabbards. Dip the cup into the water of the lake, and drink."

A simple way to die.

Veyka leaned down to retrieve the scabbards, but I reached for them as well. I closed my hand around hers, drawing the belt to her waist. Together, we secured the straps. I checked her daggers for her. I lifted Excalibur from the ground and stepped up to her so our bodies were flush. She was so tall, so perfectly matched for me. The inches I had on her were just enough to allow me to slide the sword into place across her back.

Neither of us reached for the grail.

Veyka needed both her hands to hold my face. If she hadn't, I'd have chucked the blasted chalice into the lake. But when she held me, I could not pull away.

"When you lost your memories, there were times that I thought it would have been better if you'd died. But I was wrong. Any piece of you, no matter how small... I was grateful for it. For you."

She was asking me to love her, no matter what was left. *You do not have to ask, Princess.*

Without my soul, who am I?

I savored the warmth of her breath against my skin, the scrape of her thumb over the stubble on my jaw.

I spoke aloud, desperate for the sound of her voice. "Whoever you are, whatever you become, I will love you. This realm, any other. Whether you live or die. You are mine, Veyka, and I am yours."

Two tears slid down her cheeks, one from each eye. The right one amplified the darkness of the Talisman inked on her cheek. My beautiful, brave mate.

She leaned into me fully, pressing her lips to mine. A kiss that meant everything, and yet would never be enough. She dipped her tongue into my mouth, tasting and twirling. I let her have her way, trying to be what she needed.

Veyka needed me to let her go.

She broke away and I did not pull her back. More tears spilled down her cheeks. "I love you. And if even a fragment of my soul persists, here or in another realm entirely, it will always belong to you. For a thousand years."

"And a thousand more."

She stepped out of my embrace, picking up the chalice. The mist had cleared without me noticing. Her path to the edge of the lake was open. She dipped the cup, turning to look back one last time. One last burst of love, shining there in her eyes bright and clear.

Then she closed her eyes and drank.

For a few brief seconds, I thought that maybe her willingness to make the sacrifice would be enough. That it was a test. But then those seconds passed, and I was wrong.

At our Joining, when our blood mingled together, she'd exploded with light. Now, she became a phantom of darkness. The mist was gone completely. Overhead, the sun was nearly gone as well, twilight upon us. But the shadows... the darkness that marked the coming night... they *moved*.

Shadows raced across the landscape. All of the darkness around us yielded itself up to her, entering her body through her eyes and nose and mouth. The force of them lifted her hair off of her shoulders, swirling around her abdomen, wrapping around every limb.

Just as quickly as they'd come, the shadows disappeared. But not back from where they came. Veyka inhaled them like air, taking the darkness into her body.

She fell to her knees, knocked down by the force of power. A hand went to the ground to steady her.

I watched, unsure of what had happened—what might still be happening. Slowly, Veyka lifted her hand from the ground, opening her palm to examine it.

A cut had broken open on her hand, dark liquid sliding out of the small wound.

She wore the scabbards—she could not bleed. But what came out of her was not blood. It was black, and thick, and leaked a scent so distinctive that all the hairs on my body rose in unison.

That was not blood leaking from her wound. It was her soul.

Her gaze lifted from her hand. But the female that looked up at me through soulless black eyes was not my mate.

Veyka was a succubus.

69

VEYKA

Kill.

My entire life, I'd been starving. The darkness inside of me ached to feed, but I'd denied it again and again. A slashed throat here. A dagger shoved there. They were nothing more than bites of sustenance. Only one thing would sate that need inside of me, the need I'd spent a lifetime denying. I needed *death*.

Why had I ever denied myself?

Already I could sense the lifeforce of this place. Oh, yes, it was rich with magic. I sucked in a breath, savoring the scent of rich magical blood all around me. *Yessss*. Even the humans were tinged with something special. Something I needed to taste.

There was more... a tingling at my fingertips that I vaguely recognized as familiar, as mine. Power, that's what it was. I was powerful. And I was hungry.

My legs bent under me, pushing me to my feet. Legs—I had those. Arms, too. A cut across the back of my hand. But I did not bleed, I could not bleed, I remembered. Viscous black leaked from the wound. The soul, expelled. That insistent light, finally purged. Too long I'd done battle with the light inside of me. Now, I could let it all flow away.

There were weapons strapped to me. I could feel their weight. But I did not need weapons, not when I had hands capable of ripping flesh. Not with this glorious power rippling through my veins, crying to get out.

But what could this power do?

I let it unravel, watched as tendrils of darkness emerged from my fingertips and wove their way around my arms. They caressed my cheeks, sweeter than the touch of any male, the touch of my—

Mate.

My eyes snapped up.

I recognized him. The dark hair, pulled back into a tight knot at the back of his head. The persistent bits that escaped, falling forward to brush a jaw shadowed with stubble. I knew the feeling of that stubble. I could imagine how it felt scraping over my skin.

"Arran," I gasped.

He had me before I could inhale my next breath. Powerful hands gripped my upper arms, holding me in place as his black fire gaze burned down into me, searching my face.

"What happened?"

I swallowed, trying to make sense of it. My hands, raised in the space between us, were no longer wreathed in shadow. But I could feel it, that power crawling just beneath my skin. The darkness that lurked in my mind. I'd shoved it back—Arran had shoved it back. But not forever.

"I don't know." I blinked at my hand. My hand, which was bleeding. Except not, that was not blood. That was... my nose wrinkled, my stomach turning over violently.

I dropped my head, retching onto the grass between us. Arran did not flinch. He held my hair out of the way and let me empty my stomach onto his boots. I hung there even after the heaving stopped, struggling to breathe normally, eyes shut tight against the world. But that only left me with my own mind, which was currently in possession of...

"What..." The vomit on the ground. It was not my last meal. It was black. Just like the bile that leaked from the cut on the back of my hand. My eyes flew to Arran's—and I saw what he tried to hide. Fear. He was afraid of me?

"Am I a succubus?" I whispered.

But Arran was not the one that answered.

"Yes, Veyka," said the Lady of the Lake.

70

ARRAN

It was *her*. Her eyes were black instead of blue. She bled black bile. But I could feel her, right there—in my hands and in my mind. I could feel the mating bond between us. That thread of connection was still intact, was still gold. But it was weaker.

Where once it had been hundreds of fibers all wrapped together in a strong, unbreakable thread, now it was... less. It felt as if the majority had been stripped away, leaving only a few strings twisted and braided together to hold the connection between us. It felt wrong.

"She cannot be a succubus," Cyara protested, walking up to Veyka as if nothing had changed. Ancestors be thanked for her elemental upbringing; she did not flinch an inch. "She's not trying to rip us to shreds. She is talking. She is *reasoning*."

"But I wanted to," Veyka said, her voice trembling.

She was afraid.

Of course she was fucking afraid.

"I wanted to feed on the magic of this place." She looked around at the rest of the group. "On all of you."

Evander stepped in front of Mya. Percival mirrored the motion with his sister.

Lyrena did not retreat, though she kept one hand on the pommel of her sword. Morgyn actually stepped forward, as composed as ever.

Veyka looked over my shoulder at her sister, but did not make any attempt to remove herself from my hold.

"This bile... it is my soul," she said.

Morgyn nodded in confirmation.

We'd figured that out months ago, in Castle Chariot with Palomides.

"The succubus cannot physically travel from their realm. They come to the most vulnerable minds, the males, when they are at their weakest, while sleeping," Morgyn intoned.

Again, all information we already knew. And not an answer for how my mate could stand before me, when seconds before she'd been wreathed in shadow and hungry for my fucking blood. And not in an erotic way, for once.

"They take over their bodies and expel the soul until all that remains is a physical husk, with the female succubus inside," Cyara finished, her impatience showing as the tips of her wings clicked together.

"So it is only a matter of time until I expel my soul completely and then I'm fully a succubus?" Veyka's voice rose as she spoke. Her eyes might have been black, but her emotions flashed in them just as they always had.

"You are not male," Cyara said, braving another step. She put herself between Morgyn and Veyka. It did not take Cyara's wit to figure out who the knight blamed for the current state of Veyka's soul.

Morgyn did not advance another step, respecting the boundary that Cyara had silently drawn. But she did nod. "A wakeful female mind is infinitely stronger than a sleeping male one."

"Great. So I'm only a danger while I'm asleep," Veyka seethed. But as she did, something in her shifted. Her stance tightened, her hands going slack in my grip where before they'd been clenched into fists. She tilted her head to the side, as if seeing me anew.

"Fight it, Veyka," Mya said.

I had not even noted her approach, much too focused on my mate. Evander was there too, trying to pull his wife away. But she shook him off by sending a splash of water into his face.

Mya laid a hand across Veyka's arm, ignoring the snarl that ripped from Veyka's bared teeth. "There is darkness within you. But you can control it. You have always controlled it."

Veyka's hands flexed into action, she tried to twist out of my grip. But Mya's hand did not move, her voice dropping to a murmur. "Reach for the light, Veyka. Reach for Arran."

I watched in horror and then amazement as the darkness faded from her. Shadows that I hadn't even marked fell away from Veyka's shoulders, and her posture changed, a heavy exhale that seemed to steal all of the strength from her body. Suddenly, I was the only thing holding her up.

She stared up into my eyes. "Kill me now."

"No," Evander cut in. "You did this to have the power to banish the succubus—to become the supposed *master of death*. If we kill her now, it will all be for nothing."

"She is not a tool for you use," my beast snarled at him through my mouth. "She is my mate."

"Being your mate is why she is still here," Morgyn said. "Part of her soul resides within you. That part is safe. That is the part that allows her to exercise some control over her mind, to keep the monster inside of her at bay."

Veyka ignored Evander, her eyes fixated on me in what could only be described as a plea. "Please."

Even I could not say what she asked for—the reprieve of death, or help staying in control long enough to banish the succubus. Because as I looked into my mate's eyes, changed but still her, we both understood. Defeating the succubus horde on the battlefield was one war. But it was the one that raged inside of her that was most dangerous.

71

VEYKA

Mya kept one hand on my arm, monitoring. I thought Evander hated me before. Now that I was a succubus—possessed by the succubus? Part succubus? Ancestors, it would have been easier to be dead.

Evander looked like he'd be more than happy to take care of that, standing in front of me with an amorite dagger ready and one hand on his wife's shoulder, ready to shove her away.

"The humans need us now," Mya said, somehow able to hold a conversation and use her ethereal powers to keep track of what remained of my soul. She was damn impressive.

Arran stood at my other side, no longer touching me. Afraid to? Fuck. There was not enough time in the world to analyze those feelings. Certainly not with a horde of succubus crawling across the valley toward Eldermist.

"Your forces are already nearly there. With the elementals under Agravayn's command, it might be enough," Arran said.

If what Gwen had told Cyara was true, it wouldn't be. Arran knew it, and so did Mya.

"We need the terrestrial army," Mya countered. I tried to feel her inside my mind, any sort of additional awareness or intrusion.

But I felt like me... except for the darkness prowling at the edge of my consciousness, waiting like a predator for the scent of blood.

"It would be shortsighted to deploy all of our forces on the western half of the continent..." Arran's eyes slid to me. "With Veyka here, and so..."

Unpredictable? Dangerous? Evil? I used the bond to speak to him for the first time since I'd sacrificed my soul. I was both relieved to find it intact and horrified that he did not answer me.

"Do you still have your void power?" he asked aloud instead.

"Yes," I answered immediately. I could feel the void calling stronger than ever. "And a fun new one." The shadows that the succubus inside of me had summoned did not appear.

No one laughed at my jest. Not even Lyrena.

"We cannot leave the humans to die," Mya said again.

Arran's fingers curled at his side. If we were alone, he'd have already scrubbed his hand up over his face and through his hair. But here, as the commander? His face was hard as stone.

He won't want to be alone with me anymore.

The thought slid into my head, and even though I knew the darkness from whence it came, I could not push it away entirely. Arran had vowed to love me... but what if I wasn't me any longer?

Arran and Mya were still talking, still debating. I lost track of the conversation.

If he doesn't want me, then there is no need to hold on. The darkness was right there, calling to me. If I gave into the succubus, I would not have to feel this rising fear, this pain in my chest that told me again and again that Arran could not possibly love a succubus. I'd become a monster to protect my kingdom, sacrificed my soul to the very beings we were trying to destroy, and I'd lost my love because of it.

I am more than that, I tried to remind myself. *I am a friend. A queen. A sister.*

I shook my head hard, erratic enough that they all stopped talking and stared. They'd never stopped, really. How could they, when I was now a monster among them?

"We could draw them away," I choked out. I coughed hard, but I refused to spit out the black bile that filled my mouth. If that was truly my soul being forced out by the succubus now occupying my body, I would not make it easy to expel.

"How?" Mya questioned, her sapphire eyes gentle. Her hand still lingered on my bare arm.

"Not far. Just to the Effren Valley." I swallowed. "If I fight, they will come. They have wanted me from the beginning. I thought it was for my void power, but maybe... maybe it was because they recognized this darkness inside of me and saw me as one of their own."

"You are not a succubus," Arran grabbed my hand at the same time that he reached out along the golden connection of our bond, now reduced to meager threads.

That was precisely what I was. But I understood why he said it —he needed to. He needed to remind himself that I was still there, that the fragment of my soul that I'd given to him with our mating was enough.

Enough for what... that was not a question I wanted to hear the answer to.

"I'm not fully *me*, either." I squeezed his hand back, thankful for that connection he'd given us. "I sacrificed my soul, let myself become this monster, to save Annwyn and the human realm. If we don't use me, then it was all for nothing."

I could feel the tension in him, his hand unmoving in mine, his mind trying to hold itself together by the force of his indomitable will. "Fine."

72

GUINEVERE

She'd always known her death would be bloody. She was a warrior. Even her title as Terrestrial Heir had been earned through bloodshed. But Gwen had not expected it to come so soon. Eight hundred years, maybe even a thousand.

At least she would die fighting.

The mixed human and fae formation she'd put together held for the first two hours. But they broke in the third. Maybe if she'd had three months, instead of three weeks. They fought so well. A human whose name she scarcely remembered fell back, only for a wind-wielding elemental to step up and battle the succubus before it fell upon her and began to feast. But another of the monsters pushed in from the side, sinking its sharpened fingers into the elemental's flesh. The rush of air faded with its wielder. The human regained her feet, but now she was surrounded on three sides.

Gwen slashed through one succubus, removing its head. She reached for her belt, for the amorite-swirled knife sheathed there. But her hand stopped, cocked halfway behind her head, as a succubus ripped out the human woman's belly, spilling her innards on the red floor of the valley.

She spun in the other direction so she would not have to watch it devour her.

Behead with her sword. Stab with the amorite knife, but only a mortal wound. Keep fighting. She had to keep fighting. If she stopped, if she let herself fall, then the cause was lost. The humans would flee.

For every one succubus that fell, it took a dozen humans with it. Gwen had known the cost from battling in Baylaur. But at least there, she'd been protecting the living, focused on getting them to safety. Here on the battlefield, she lost track of the why and the who. She just killed. And killed. And killed.

But not enough. They'd met at the midpoint of the valley. But the succubus gained ground every hour. Relentless. They did not tire. They did not pause. Gwen spun to stab a succubus that tried to take her from behind, only to find the mountains mere yards from where she stood.

This was the end.

The communication crystal was with Sylva. She'd given her brief instructions on how to use it, but Gwen knew that the possibility of the human woman being able to access the crystal's magic was slim. The crystals worked on intent. Gwen was the intended recipient of any messages that Veyka, Arran, or Cyara might send using their crystals.

If help was coming, it would have arrived by now. Gwen knew that.

If Veyka had not opened one of the portal rifts, she was not going to now. Maybe the queen was dead... she was going to sacrifice herself to banish the succubus. She could have tried and failed, and been lost in the process. Gwen's heart clenched at the thought. Arran would never come back from losing Veyka. Never.

The humans fought valiantly, the elemental fae, both soldiers and commoners, among them. But it was not enough. The succubus would push them back against the mountains, and they would all die.

Gwen looked down the line of warriors remaining, marking the faces of those still standing. Not far from her stood the female elemental whose brother she'd killed for harming the human child in Eldermist.

There was no defiance left in the young female's features. The rags she'd worn the first time Gwen met her were in an even worse state now, splashed with the black bile of the succubus. It was too far for Gwen to see if the female trembled.

Gwen met her eye and inclined her head. She tried to infuse every bit of strength in that one exchange. She could not offer hope. But she could share the little strength that was left to her. Gwen lifted her sword and turned to face the enemy. In her periphery, she watched the ice-wielder lift her hands and turn as well.

But just as the next wave reached them, light and water and fire began to rain down from overhead.

Gwen's head snapped up, trying to make sense of what was happening.

Tiny creatures hung off of the mountainside. They were too far away to read their features—no, they truly were that small. Half of Gwen's size, maybe. They moved quickly, the motions of those new to a fight, fresh bursts of magic raining down up on the succubus, slowing them. One zoomed overhead, and Gwen got a look at the pointed ears peeking out from a head of fiery orange hair.

Fae... but unlike any she'd ever seen. They were a rainbow of colors, brilliant blue and deep burgundy red all the way to a black so dark it would have matched her dark lioness. And some of them were airborne. Not as shifters, but they had wings attached to their back. Not unlike Cyara, but smaller.

Not fae, she realized. Faeries.

The Faeries of the Fen had come to fight.

But this battle was nearly over, and Gwen recognized the feeling of defeat. But with the faeries overhead, the humans that remained might live to fight another day.

"Retreat!" Gwen screamed. Around her, humans and fae alike started to disengage and pull back. Too many couldn't—they were already bleeding to death on the ground, their throats ripped open by blackened jaws.

Gwen shifted into her dark lioness form and lifted her head to the sky, roaring loud enough that it echoed across the valley. More heads turned; more soldiers turned and ran. The faeries covered their retreat from the air, the small, winged legion sending down bolts of lightning, blasts of water, and wickedly pointed arrows.

It was enough, just barely.

The dark lioness patrolled one end of the line to the other, roaring and ripping apart the succubus as they tried to follow. But the mountain was the one place that the human and fae forces had an advantage. They succubus scrambled, not caring for the pain of scrapes or falls, but they didn't take care with their footfalls, didn't think critically about climbing through already churned up mud and clay. They slid back and back. Eventually, they'd make the summit. Gwen could only hope that by then, what remained of her scattered little army would have made it to the next mountain.

73

ARRAN

"Any final words of wisdom, sis?" Veyka tossed the words to Morgyn without even looking at her. She was already focused on the stretch of ground in front of her where she would open the portal rift.

The Lady of the Lake was as immovable as every other time we'd interacted with her. "You have what you need," she said.

"You should be fighting alongside us." Veyka leveled the accusation with equal coolness.

"Don't bother with 'Avalon is neutral' and all that or I might have to let the succubus out."

Evander's trepidation ratcheted up toward anger with each sarcastic comment Veyka made. He thought she was serious. I knew her better than that. She was a second from breaking, and the thinly veiled sarcasm was the only thing keeping her from shattering into a million pieces. Or worse, losing control of the succubus.

Mya soothed her husband with a hand on his arm and a word whispered in his ear. Fine. Evander was not my concern. Veyka had all of my attention.

I hardly dared to touch her. Not because I feared the monster now residing behind Veyka's eyes. I could never fear Veyka. But I was afraid of what I might do to her, if I caused even the tiniest fracture in the tenuous glass wall of control she'd thrown up.

I did not give a damn what Morgyn le Fae said. I could feel Veyka's soul. Maybe it was broken, maybe it was only a tiny fraction of what it had been before. But I could feel it. Maybe what I was feeling was the bit of it that resided inside of me, protected by our mating bond, as the Lady of the Lake had said. But it was still *her*.

And that piece of her was still damn stubborn.

"I am going with you," I said, stepping up to her side but carefully not touching her.

"I can do it," she said, lifting her hands. "You would not have doubted me before."

It was a fair observation... and so fucking unfair at the same time. I would not have doubted her ability to open rift after rift after rift to rearrange an entire continent's worth of armies. I might have worried about the cost, her exhaustion, but I would have encouraged her and stood by her side. Now?

I was terrified of what it might do to her. Would the succubus inside of her take over? She was fighting off a monster from another realm with only a tiny shred of her own self to cling to, and we were asking her to open half a dozen massive portal rifts. Entire armies, that's what they were asking of her. After she'd nearly died.

I did not want to doubt her. But it was there all the same.

"Here to the Crossing. Terrestrials to the mountains above the Effren Valley. Then the Aquarians and elementals. Last, Eilean Gayl to the Effren Valley," I repeated the plan.

From Avalon, we would take everyone assembled back to the Crossing. Then Lyrena and Cyara would go with the terrestrial army through Veyka's rift to the mountains above the Effren Valley, near the natural rift that connected Annwyn and the human realm, but not close enough to Baylaur to draw the attention of the succubus squatting within. Veyka would open another rift for Mya's Aquarians and Agravayn's elementals, sending them to set up camp alongside the terrestrials in the mountains. And finally, Veyka and I would go to Eilean Gayl to collect the forces my father had been tasked with raising north of the Spine.

I would be at her side for all of it. The vow we'd made to stay together seemed even more important now, when Veyka waged battle within her own mind.

Her hand hung in the air, like she was about to open a rift. But no spiral of light appeared.

"What do you need?" I asked, pushing away gentleness and trying for the even voice of the battle commander. She wanted me to treat her as capable and whole; I could force myself to do that.

Her head tilted to the side. Her fingers contracted into her palms, forming fists. I tried to meet her eyes, but they were closed.

Alarms began to ring inside of my mind. *Veyka*, I tried to reach for her. But instead of her bright and brilliant mind awaiting me on the other side of our mating bond, I felt only fathomless dark.

Her head snapped up. She shook it from side to side, eyes popping open. Still black, but focused.

My heart tightened in my chest.

"Let's go," she said. A second later, light appeared, spiraling outward in a circle and then a gateway. I recognized the outlines of the terrestrial camp on the eastern edge of the Crossing. There was our tent, where I'd held and kissed my mate thinking it might be the last time. How had the world suddenly become infinitely more complicated?

She is alive, my beast snarled.

There was nothing complicated about that.

Cyara led the way. Then Lyrena, still armed. Evander practically shoved Mya through. Then the humans approached. We'd given them no role, assigned them no part in the upcoming conflict. They'd stood by silently as Veyka decided to sell her soul for a victory that felt anything but assured.

Percival took a step toward the rift.

"Diana stays."

The man's mouth fell open, his foot a second from crossing over, his sister's hand gripped tightly. "What—"

"We did not agree to this," Morgyn le Fae said. Her voice was even, but she showed the same tells of annoyance as Veyka. The tightening of her mouth, the way her shoulder shifted back in the subtlest defensive stance.

Veyka looked to Diana. "You helped us. You deserve to stay in safety." Unlike her sister, she did not bother to hide her annoyance with Morgyn. "Welcome to life on the outside of your precious island. Sometimes, you do not get to choose."

Morgyn did not argue.

There was no question of Percival staying. Whatever reason Veyka had for leaving him out of her last-minute machinations, she did not share it with me. We had not shared a single thought through the bond since her sacrifice.

The bond was intact, so that must be as well. But now was not the time to test it, not with sweat already sliding down from Veyka's temple. This was only the first of many rifts she'd open in the next few hours. Her internal battle with the succubus was costing her.

"Be quick about your goodbyes," I ordered. I had already vowed to stay by Veyka's side through what would be a hellish few hours. My role was now to make this as efficient as possible, for her sake.

Percival hugged his sister, but for once he did not argue. Diana dissolved into sobs, but she did not protest. He stepped through the portal, then Veyka and I followed. I tried not to notice the tear that slid down Veyka's cheek as well.

It was too much. The look Mya shot me as she followed her troops through the portal rift into Annwyn only deepened my conviction. This had to stop.

Sweat was not the only thing pouring off Veyka. The cut on her hand had opened into a gaping wound that leaked black bile continuously. The soldiers noticed. But thankfully they were too in awe of their queen to question.

But I could not stand by and watch her soul leaking from her body. Every drop that splatted to the ground was a knife to my heart. What would be left when this day was over? Was the transformation ongoing... and the flow of that darkness literal? Was I watching my mate lose her soul drop by drop, right before my very eyes?

It had to stop.

She closed the portal with a bright flash, stumbling backward from the force of the magic tearing from her body. I tried to catch her, but she brushed me off. Our hands did not even touch. She did not even pause for a drink of water before lifting her hands to open a rift to take us to Eilean Gayl.

I didn't miss the fact that she did not reach for me to take me through the void with her, as she'd done a hundred times in the past. She moved to open a portal rift, which would not require any contact at all.

I did not have to touch her to block her. "It can wait until tomorrow."

She huffed out a haughty exhale. "There is a succubus horde in the valley now. The humans might not be alive tomorrow."

I don't give a damn about the humans. But I kept that thought to myself.

"And what about you?" I said, stepping into her space but not reaching for her. "I can see you fighting."

She couldn't hide the flashes of darkness. When her posture changed, when the expression that crawled over her face did not belong to her. But the harder she pushed herself, the more frequent those little battles became. Little was the wrong word. I knew there was nothing small about the battle for her soul that Veyka was now waging with every breath.

"I am in control. This *thing* cannot have me," she snarled. At least that was all Veyka.

"You are tired. You heard what the Lady of the Lake said as clearly as I did. The mind is weaker when you sleep."

"Then it is a good thing I am not asleep."

She'd traded sarcasm for anger. Anger was her last line of defense before despair.

I searched her black eyes for the female I loved. I tried to let her see all of the emotion in my own, the fear for her. If she would not rest for her own sake, maybe she would do it for mine. "Wait until tomorrow."

Another battle, that's what I'd forced upon her. I wished I regretted it. I watched the battle in her eyes. And knew the moment I lost.

She stepped around me and opened the rift. I had no option but to follow her through it. Guards waited on the other side on the bridge that connected Eilean Gayl to the mainland. Their eyes flared with surprise, but not fear. They'd known to expect us, at least. It was the work of another hour to find my father and give the word for the troops now camped on the lakeside to break their camp and prepare to march. My mother spoke quietly with Veyka. I did not try to intrude on their conversation.

When the northerners were ready, Veyka opened the last rift. I did ask her if she was well enough to do it. We both already knew the answer to that. So I stood by her side and tried to be a pillar of strength. If she reached for me, I would be there. I would always be there for her.

My father led the first column through. A line of black leaked from the corner of Veyka's eye. Vera had command of the second column. Veyka coughed, but she could not press a hand to cover her mouth. I saw the droplets she tried to hide by angling her body away. I would have rather she coughed up blood than bits of her soul.

By the third, she had to hunch over, supporting her elbows on her knees.

"Stop this." I did not know how much longer I could stop myself from touching her.

"There are only a few more."

A few dozen more.

"It is enough."

"It is not."

"Stop." The wound on her hand was nearly gushing. She couldn't do this anymore. I reached for her hands, but she jerked away.

"*I do not belong to you,*" she hissed.

I tried to grab her shoulders, but she twisted away from me. Even at the breaking point of exhaustion, she was so fucking fast. But the movements were disjointed. They lacked her usual grace.

She tripped over her own feet and careened into the line of soldiers. But instead of trying to regain her feet, she turned and sank her teeth into the male who'd caught her.

She did not need the elongated canines of the terrestrial fae to tear him apart. She ripped a chunk free from his neck, thick red blood spurting out and spraying her and the soldiers around us. They couldn't scatter fast enough, the bright light of the rift illuminating the horror on their faces.

Somehow, the rift was still open.

Inside, Veyka still fought.

"Get through the rift!" I yelled, closing in on her.

I tried to wrench her away from the male, but she fought me with a strength that did not belong to her. The succubus was in control now. I had to get to her skin, to her mind. I ripped away her cloak, grabbing her shoulders hard enough that there would be bruises. There was only darkness on the other end of our mating bond.

Veyka, this is not you. My beast snarled into the darkness.

A second later a voice came. Veyka's, but not. A hiss in the night. *This is me. This is us. This is who we have always been.*

That *we* did not refer to the two of us.

She is mine, my beast howled back. *You are mine,* I told my mate.

I ripped her away from the male, breaking contact, the severed artery at his throat spraying both of us with blood. We crashed into the hard ground, frozen by months of snow and ice. Pain shot up my leg. Veyka cried out horribly. But it *was* Veyka.

"Get him through the rift!" I yelled to whoever would listen.

I did not wait to see if they complied. I lifted Veyka into my arms and carried her through, her fingers still up, still holding the way, still shaking terribly.

Three bodies stumbled through after us. I looked away from Veyka only long enough to confirm that everyone was through. I grabbed her hands in mine, pulling them down. The portal shook and then closed.

"Take him to Isolde," I ordered, aware of my father's appearance. But I did not hear him. I lowered Veyka to the ground. I was shaking, too. I needed to check her for wounds. She had to be okay. Those were her eyes looking back at me. Black, but hers. Her lips trembling. Her tears, clear and heartbreaking, flooding down her cheeks.

No words came to me. What comfort could I offer? This was the price.

I'd imagined a thousand different possibilities in the hours Veyka had gone away through the void, leaving us to ruminate on Morgyn's word. The cost of uniting the Sacred Trinity was Veyka's soul.

I'd pictured her death. I'd pictured a husk of a person, blank eyes and mechanical movements. Ancestors, I'd even pictures an ephemeral spirit. But I'd never imagined this... watching my mate struggling for control of herself, to keep the shred of her soul that remained intact, only to lose.

This was worse than death. This was torture on a level neither Veyka nor I had ever experienced, even after everything we'd survived together and apart.

And those shadows that Veyka had manifested... those must be tied to banishing the succubus. The key to ridding our world of them lay within Veyka, within the monster now inhabiting her body. To rid us of the succubus, she had to become one.

I had no words, because there were none. Nothing I could say would make this better.

I held her, rocking us gently back and forth on the ground as night fell and the army she'd brought together made camp somewhere behind us.

Veyka's mouth moved against my throat, forming words I couldn't quite hear.

I eased her forward, steeling myself against the mix of blood and bile and tears that coated her pale face. "What was that, Princess?"

"Take my weapons," she rasped. "Bind my arms and legs."

I shook my head. "You will be defenseless."

"I am a succubus, Arran." She was shaking again. Ancestors, I'd only finally gotten her to stop minutes before. But she got more words out. "I can still use my void power. But at least disarmed, with my hands and ankles tied, whoever I attack will have a chance."

"Veyka." She was going to make me beg.

But her eyes had drifted beyond me, over my shoulder. I followed her gaze, found the line of soldiers who'd been stationed to watch over us. Or guard the camp *from* us.

"It will make them feel better," she murmured. "Feel safer."

I refused to look any closer at the warriors behind us. I did not want to see the worry or fear or scorn in their eyes. Seeing all of those things in Veyka's had already broken my heart. She shifted again in my arms, her eyes begging mine, just like I'd predicted.

This is wrong. "Bring the shackles," I called over my shoulder.

Veyka reached up and stroked my face.

"It will be all right," she whispered.

"You should not be the one comforting me."

Solid metal clanked to the ground beside me. Footsteps retreated. Veyka disentangled herself enough to reach for the shackles, slipping them into my hands. Then holding up her own.

No. I can't.

She pressed her lips to mine. *Do it. Please.*

I pressed the thick metal pin into place, and it felt like I might as well have closed it around my heart.

✣ 74 ✣

VEYKA

For the first time since Baylaur, all of the Knights of the Round Table were present. Cyara, Lyrena, Gwen, Arran, and I took the same positions we would have at the actual table. But we were not in the goldstone palace, with that mighty stone creation to anchor us, names in glowing golden scrollwork.

We stood in the center of a massive command tent, on a compacted dirt floor where a circle had been sketched out, and within it, two identical maps. One of the Effren Valley, one of the valley below Eldermist that the humans called Camlann.

Osheen took the spot that would have belonged to Parys. I could think of none among us more deserving. I tried to smile at him, but it must have come out as something else, because the terrestrial winced and then nodded in acknowledgment instead of smiling back at me. I'd cleaned the blood and black bile from my skin. But that did not make me any less of a monster, and after that display with the rift, we all knew it.

Mordred and Mya held the other two positions. Standing, rather than sitting. *One is not yet known, and the bravest of the five shall be his father.* Arran's son, and the Siege Perilous.

Others listened and waited on the outskirts of the circle. Elora,

Agravayn, Evander. The human called Sylva and another human leader I'd never met. Taliya and Isolde stood on opposite sides of the tent, the Faeries still not keen on one another.

The first true meeting of the Knights of the Round Table. And if I could not keep this monster inside of me under control, quite possibly the last.

I understood what I needed to do to banish the succubus back to their realm forever. None of the others had asked it of me yet, though it had to be on their minds. Every moment I lingered in this form I was a danger. But whether it was out of respect for what I'd offered and now endured, out fear of Arran, I did not know.

The realization of what I must do had come to me during the long day, opening rift after rift, battling the succubus for control of my mind. Letting this thing inside of me had bestowed a new power—the shadows. Tendrils of the void that I could pull into this realm with me and wield like weapons. I'd paid with my soul for this new power, so it must be integral to banishing the succubus.

But if I could not keep control long enough to do it, then the sacrifice would be for nothing and Annwyn and the human realm would fall.

"How much time do we have?" Mya asked.

I'd been so busy in my own mind that the debate had begun without me.

"Not much. The succubus in the human realm are trying to scale the mountain. Thus far, the Faeries and our archers have been able to pick them off before they make much progress. But there are too many for us to hold them off forever," Gwen said. *Our. We.* Gwen spoke of the humans as her own. I expected a mixed reaction from myself, but found only a surge of pride.

"The Aquarians and remaining elementals will go through the rift and join you in the fight there. The Faeries of the Fen will fall back and protect the rear. We need fresh troops at the front," Arran said, using Excalibur to draw corresponding marks on the maps. He was the only one I'd trusted to hold it. I still wore my scabbards, for all the good they'd do me, but they were empty.

Shackling me wouldn't mean much if I still had access to my daggers.

"Would it not be wise to split the terrestrial army instead? They are more seasoned and used to fighting as a unit," Elora questioned. "They would help steady the myriad groups already in the human realm."

"No—"

"You are sending your weakest forces to the human realm and keeping the best for yourself." The unnamed human leader had decided they were entitled to an opinion.

I have not yet tasted human blood...

No. The only blood I needed to taste was Arran's. And not now. Not with this monster lurking inside of me. Exhaustion clawed at my mind and the succubus took advantage. I forced myself to gulp down the tea that Cyara had prepared, safely warm in the special cup that Osheen had fashioned for me months and months ago. It seared my throat on the way down, but that was a small price to pay for the stimulant she'd ground into the brew.

Arran lifted Excalibur. Not a threat—it was much too loose in his hand for that.

As if he needed a blasted sword to be lethal.

The human's eyes widened.

A nightingale swept into the tent, gliding over our heads and shifting into a slight female form just behind Arran's shoulder. I was at his side, but even I could not hear what she said. Arran's face showed no hint. He whispered a response, she shifted, and then was gone again.

"The horde forming in the Effren Valley is bigger," Arran said simply.

The group erupted at the news. There had never been a true hope of hiding an army of this size. The succubus had found us—found me. I wondered if the pull was stronger now that one of their own squatted within my body.

The human kept arguing. "The fae are stronger. You'll last longer against them—"

"If your alliance cannot hold, then it is not an alliance at all," Arran countered.

"Enough." I may not have the actual Round Table, but I was still the High Queen of Annwyn. And according to Arran, my eyes were now an eerie black. If the crowd would stop for anyone, it would be me.

The human stepped behind the elderly Sylva. I rolled my eyes, black as they were. At least he was silent. As was everyone else.

"We need the terrestrial army here in the Effren Valley to hold off the succubus," I said. I hated the rasp in my voice, but I kept going. "They must hold the succubus back long enough for me to reach the Tower of Myda at the center of the valley."

Where all of this had begun, less than a year ago. Or seven thousand years ago.

"What about your void power?" Mordred asked. He had not been among those who'd witnessed my loss of control, but I was certain everyone had heard of it. The High Queen of Annwyn is a succubus. Hotter gossip had never been spread.

Enemy.

"I cannot touch my void power, not until the last moment." That realization had come later, while Arran rocked me back and forth on the ground. Opening the rifts was dangerous. Going into the void gave the succubus in my mind too much power. If I was going to maintain control long enough to drag the succubus back to their realm, I could not use the void until the very last possible moment. "The void, the shadows... they are too closely intertwined with the succubus." My head began to tilt to the side, but I snapped it back forcefully.

Mordred is not my enemy. Mordred is precious to Arran, whether he realizes it yet or not. Mordred is not my enemy.

The darkness receded. All eyes were still on me. Worried faces, all. I could hardly blame them. I took another deep drag of tea.

"Uniting the Sacred Trinity has made me the master of death. The succubus *are* death. I am High Queen. I will use my power of the void and the new powers this thing has given me, and I will rip them from these realms forever. The tower is the highest point in the valley. From there, I will open a rift and force the succubus back to our realm."

Our.

I could not even control my words. Suddenly, the shackles and my wrists and legs did not seem like enough. The monster was going to get out. I was going to kill everyone, feast on their flesh, taste their souls and open the way for my sisters—

"I will stay at your side." I hadn't even noticed Mya moving. But her hand on my arm was warm, her sapphire blue eyes clear and unafraid.

"You will not—"

She silenced her husband with a wave of her hand and a few droplets of water. "I have spent my entire life helping my people face the darkness within themselves. That is how I have used my ethereal gift. I can help you, Veyka."

She'd said as much before, but I hadn't really understood. Now, I was desperate. I jerked my chin in a nod.

Her eyes softened around the edges, the lines of determination less prominent but by no means gone. She leaned in so only I could hear. "I have learned to stay grounded in myself, dealing with so many others' emotions. You can do it too, Veyka." She squeezed my arm a little tighter, the pale blue of her grip lightening. "I know you can."

She knew, because she was inside of me now. She could see the light and the darkness. Surely she could see that I was losing, the monster a wrong word from wresting away control and devouring the remaining shards of my soul.

"We will have to fight our way across the valley," I said.

"Not alone. I will accompany you." Evander's tone brooked no argument, and I was not going to give one. Mya may be confident, but I wasn't. She would need protection. Not just from the succubus horde, but very likely from me.

"And me," Lyrena said. Her golden sword had been in her hand since Avalon. Goldstone armor, golden hair, golden rings, a flash of a golden tooth. My faithful golden knight. I could not refuse her.

Arran captured the attention of the group before it could dissolve again.

"This is the war," he said, looking around at each face in turn. "There will be no more skirmishes or battles. The last battle of the Great War was fought in the Effren Valley seven thousand years ago. This is where it all ends. This is the final battle."

He reached for my hand, holding it even as the shackles rubbed against our skin. "Tonight is for final preparations. In the morning, we must be ready."

✤ 75 ✤

ARRAN

I ducked out of the command tent, leaving Veyka reluctantly. She was bent over the map with Mya, Evander, and Lyrena, plotting a course for the next day. I had to see to the terrestrial forces, speak with my father about integrating his northerners. Lyrena would stay with her until I returned, I knew without asking.

But it still felt like torture.

"Your Majesty," a deep voice called, footsteps digging deep into the cold-hardened ground to keep up. There may not be snow on the ground in the elemental kingdom, but it was far from hospitable.

My mind supplied the answer before my eyes—Mordred.

The young male ate up the distance between us easily, moving on long legs that I recognized as the mirror of my own. He was not quite as tall as me, but nearly. Mya had reassured us of his loyalty, but it did not change what I saw when I looked at him.

Morgause.

"A word, Majesty?" he said, coming alongside of me, breaths even despite the exertion. He was strong.

My first instinct was to turn him away. His mother may have secured him a spot at the Round Table, but that meant nothing for the relations between the two of us. If he had an objection to the plans we'd made, he should have laid it out in the command tent with everyone else.

Veyka was not there, but I heard her voice in my head. *I do not begrudge you your son.* Even then, with everything else happening, she had recognized the importance of that connection.

I'd only known him for a few days. We'd never spoken privately. But he was my son. I could spare him a few minutes, couldn't I?

"As I walk," I said, not breaking step.

"You assigned me to the fight with the northerners."

Ah. I should have anticipated this argument. "I cannot afford to babysit you. The Lord of Eilean Gayl is a worthy leader. You will learn much from him."

"Respectfully, Majesty, I do not need minding."

No, he didn't. But that was not the true reason I'd assigned him to fight with my father.

"I am leading an army. I cannot afford distractions."

He stumbled a step.

Maybe it was cruel to characterize him as such. But I could not let him be any more. Not now. If I cared about him, if he fought at my side and I allowed myself to worry, then he was just another person that I stood to lose.

I was already in danger of losing my mate.

If my son fell on the field while fighting beside me? What would happen to me then? Would my beast recognize it? Would I be heartbroken? Or worse, would I feel nothing?

We were almost to where the northerners were encamped alongside the rest of the terrestrial army. I waited for Mordred to offer more argument. I expected it, but I had no right to. I did not know this male. We shared blood, an especially strong flora-gift and the color of our skin. But beyond that... not tonight. I could not let myself go there tonight.

Not with Veyka's soul hanging in the balance.

I do not begrudge you your son. She'd been so damn gracious about the whole thing, so uncharacteristically level-headed—

Because she'd expected to die.

Ancestors' fucking hell. She'd expected to die, and that Mordred was all I would have left. She'd thought he would be a consolation in the wake of her death. Now that she'd sacrificed her soul to the succubus, her feelings were likely unchanged. But her soul survived, a precious piece of it, safe within me, tied to our bond. Once the succubus was banished, she could push it out. She could regain what she'd sacrificed.

What if she cannot beat it?

I banished the thought. If I allowed it purchase in even the tiniest corner of my mind, I would not be able to walk onto that battlefield come morning.

I wished there was more of me to offer my son. But I barely held what remained of myself together. What I could give him was the best male I knew—my father.

I stopped us on the edge of camp. My insides screamed at the impulse, but I lifted my hand to grasp his shoulder. "Serve with Pant. He is the best teacher you could have. He was mine, after all."

Mordred didn't quite smile but he nodded his acceptance. And I recognized that as mine as well.

❧ 76 ❧

CYARA

She fought the urge to follow Osheen out of the tent. He had not spoken to her when they'd gathered the Knights of the Round Table, and he left the second the meeting concluded. She was not self-centered enough to believe that his behavior was wholly about her. He was likely checking on Maisri. Finding his place in the ranks for the next day. Setting up his tent, if he hadn't had a moment yet.

Or he was avoiding her.

But with mere hours left before the fight, she could not hold her peace. Her mother was with the healers. Her queen was with her Aquarian counterpart, Lyrena guarding her back. And Cyara... she was alone.

It took some asking, but eventually she located him on the outskirts of the terrestrial camp. He'd volunteered himself for perimeter patrol even though it would mean he had less sleep than most of the other warriors on the battlefield come the morning. It did not surprise her at all.

He walked a slow but steady line along a northwestern stretch of the camp, between two sharp peaks that formed a natural barrier on either side. Cyara recognized the vines creeping over the ground as she approached. Small, slender tendrils coaxed from the sparse

385

plants of the desert, they stretched across the ground, alerting him instantly to any intruders. She tried to avoid them, but it was futile. Still, he did not turn as she quickened her pace to catch him up. He knew it was her.

Osheen did not protest as she fell into step beside him. Cyara knew him well enough to recognize the hunch of his shoulders. Silence was not always a good sign.

"You convinced the Faeries of the Fen to come," she said. The little vines moved as they walked, widening the path that they'd made for Osheen to leave room for her as well.

"They were already preparing for a fight. We only had to convince them to join in ours rather than wait for the succubus to come for them in the caves. We came to Eldermist because Taliya was more willing to aid the humans than the fae." He paused. "Maisri did most of the work, as you predicted."

Cyara tucked her wings in tight to prevent one from accidentally touching him. She doubted the caress would be welcome. "Where is she?"

"Safe."

Her shoulder blades contracted nearly to touching.

"You do not trust me." It was to be expected after what she'd done. She had fully understood the consequences of betraying Osheen's confidence and sneaking away. She would not use the excuse that it had been under Arran's orders. Her actions were her own. "I... I understand."

And she did. She truly did. Maisri was the most precious thing in Osheen's world. Cyara loved the child, too. If Osheen said that Maisri was safe, then she believed him without question. She did not begrudge him keeping that information from her if that was truly what he believed the best course of action. Maisri came first, and that was precisely as it should be.

They reached the end of the opening between the two mountains, and Osheen spun. Cyara did not, letting him face her. She was not ashamed of her actions. She would not hide.

Osheen's eyes flared, but he did not try to avoid her.

"She is hidden away in the mountains with the faeries that came but decided not to fight. They've made their own camp, away from the others. Trust is earned."

Cyara's wings drooped. From the flick of Osheen's eyes, she knew he marked the movement.

"I am glad she is safe," she said.

"You found the chalice."

"Yes. It was not what I thought."

She waited for his admonishment. His anger. She knew he could get angry. Even-tempered as Osheen was—as he had to be, with a ward as spirited as the daisy fae—even he was not immune to the emotion.

Ancestors forgive her, but Cyara wanted some of it for herself. She stupidly, recklessly, wanted to know that what she'd done mattered to him. That he cared as much as she did.

"I cannot apologize for my actions." She lifted her brows, daring him to argue with her.

The slithering of vines around them intensified. "Because you do not believe you were wrong."

"I am sorry that I hurt you and Maisri. But not for trying to save Veyka." There. That was the best she could do. The ire that stole over Osheen's features told her that it was not enough.

But the anger did not stay. It was gone in a flash, replaced by something much more dangerous to Cyara's resolve, something she recognized immediately. Longing.

Vines caressed her legs, wrapping around her calves. But it was his hands the reached up to cradle her face. His fingertips that brushed along her jaw as he tilted her chin upward and kissed her.

There was no anger in that kiss. Only months of repressed longing and wondering. He was soft and warm against her, his taste of peppermint and basil and possibility. So gentle... so impossibly gentle. He flicked his tongue across her bottom lip and she opened for him, ready. She'd take everything he offered. Osheen gave and gave and gave, his kiss sweeter than she'd dreamed, even as it lit a fire low in her belly.

Then he pulled away. He ended it. The vines at her legs released her, and his hands did as well. Cool night air rushed in to fill the space, the first hints of spring a promise of tomorrow. A tomorrow they did not have.

There was only one reason for him to kiss her after all this time they'd both spent denying the attraction between them. It was not an offering of hope. It was a goodbye. Osheen believed that one or both of them would die on the morrow.

Cyara held back the tears. She'd shed too many these past few months. That kiss had only confirmed what she'd known from the start. There was no future for them.

77

GUINEVERE

The human leaders were far from happy, but Gwen had given up on that. They were pacified. They'd agreed to Arran's plans for which valley each force would defend, and then eventually to Gwen's for how to deploy those forces on their battlefield at Camlann. She would leave the rest to Sylva. Her house was close enough to the rift to Annwyn that the human leadership retired there. She'd been plying them with wine and biscuits when Gwen left.

Elora was in conference with Agravayn and General Ache, the commander of the Aquarians. Aquarian Fae. Gwen shook her head as she climbed, digging her toes deep into the sand of the dune with each step to keep from backsliding.

Humans in alliance with fae. Terrestrials and elementals working together. Storybook legends come to life.

A few more steps and she crested the dune. Only to find her retreat occupied.

Lyrena glanced over her shoulder long enough to identify her and to flash a grin. She held up a flagon of wine in welcome. "This was meant to be a private party, but I suppose it is bad form not to share with a fellow Knight."

Whatever other expressions she wore on that lovely golden

face, they were lost to the dark as Lyrena swung back around. The valley below was completely bathed in darkness. The succubus needed no light. But Gwen knew they were there. Lyrena did as well. Only the winged faeries patrolling the edge of the valley held them at bay.

Despite her better judgment, Gwen dropped down into the sand. She even accepted the wine. She took a few gulps and tried not to draw any comparisons to the last time she'd shared wine with a friend.

"This was not the future I imagined when I became a Goldstone," Lyrena said after her next sip.

"You thought you'd serve Arthur." They'd never discussed it, but Gwen knew Lyrena's history. The gossiping elementals had been only too happy to share once she'd arrived in Baylaur. And once Gwen became a Goldstone Guard? The late king's betrothed and his mistress serving together? The elementals thrived on that sort of nonsense.

But that was exactly what it was. Nonsense.

"Of course," Lyrena nodded. "And you thought you'd marry him."

"Of course," Gwen echoed.

Lyrena turned to look at her, squinting in the darkness. Then she gave up and drank more wine. Gwen rolled her eyes, an indulgence she only allowed herself because the dark prevented anyone else from seeing.

A single scream echoed from the valley below. One of the faeries had gotten too close. Gwen held her breath, waiting for more screams. More carnage. The lioness sniffed the air, scenting the succubus and trying to estimate their proximity. But the night remained quiet. The battle delayed a few more hours.

"Do you think we'll ever really move on?"

Gwen was not sure if the question was to her or the night. But she answered anyway. "I have moved on."

Lyrena snorted. "I loved the male. You loved the promise of him. Which do you think is harder to let go of?"

Gwen had let go. Arthur was not the one that haunted her. She'd realized months ago that Veyka was the better queen. For all her anger and ruthlessness, her capacity for passion and love far exceeded Gwen's own. Veyka was the queen that Annwyn needed.

"Letting go is not just saying goodbye to the past," Lyrena said, her voice soft. Private. Just for the two of them. "It also means looking to the future."

Gwen followed Lyrena's gaze out into the darkness. A slight smile played across the female's face. Whatever Lyrena saw, it wasn't the succubus that waited in the valley below.

She was so... golden. Full of hope. Gwen had never felt that, not even with promise of an entire kingdom bowing at her feet. Maybe it was the amount of wine that the female consumed on a daily basis. That, at least, she could try.

Lyrena moved at the same time as Gwen, handing her the wine while she reached. Their hands collided first, then their elbows tangled and then—then their faces.

Her golden skin was impossibly soft.

Gwen jerked back. No more wine. She was responsible for thousands of lives. Her mind could not afford to be addled by alcohol... or anything else.

Gwen clambered to her feet, her usual grace stolen by the thick sand. Lyrena watched from beneath raised golden brows. Her gaze roamed—over Gwen's face, to where her woolen tunic stretched taut across her breasts. When she lifted her eyes again, there was no ignoring the ring of glowing light around the pupils.

But Lyrena made no move. She took another drink of wine and smiled. "Someday, I'll convince you to see the light."

Gwen had nothing to say to that, so she retreated, back down the dune into the village. The tiniest, most fragile and secret part of her hoped that Lyrena was right.

78

ARRAN

It was nearly impossible to sneak up on someone with Veyka's honed awareness. Being held against her will for twenty years had left scars deeper than any physical wound. Maybe she was more equipped than anyone to deal with the darkness of the succubus. She'd already survived torture. She'd grown up in darkness.

But as she shifted around on our bed platform, trying to find a comfortable position with both her arms and legs bound, it was hard to imagine her as a creature of darkness. She was so damned beautiful. Her long, pale limbs glowed in the torchlight, the muscles beneath her soft skin bunching and stretching as she turned and rolled. Her white hair was unbound, loose around her shoulders, brushing the tips of her breasts. Naked as she was, I could almost forget that the shackles were a matter of necessity rather than erotic play.

Ancestors. The female could be entirely taken by a monster, and I would still want her. My cock hardened in agreement.

She rolled to her side, back toward the front of the tent, and spotted me instantly. Her abdominals tensed beneath her soft stomach as she pulled herself up to sit, attempting to cross her legs under her and flashing that beautiful cunt of hers in the process before finally tucking her legs underneath her.

"They are ready?" she asked.

I nodded. "As ready as they can be." This was not what I wanted to discuss.

I unsnapped my belt, tossing aside my battle axe and the swirled amorite weapons attached there. "How'd you manage to get undressed?" Leather vest. Then wool tunic. "Did Lyrena have to cut you out of your garments?"

Veyka licked her lips. "Jealous?"

"Maybe."

"She unbound my hands so I could take off the dress. Then once those shackles were back on, she helped with my leggings." She lifted her arms as she spoke, miming removing her dress, but really just showing off her breasts.

Boots. Trousers. I was as bare as she—except for the fucking shackles. Those would be coming off, too. Damn the succubus. Damn prophecies. I needed my wife, and I knew she needed me. This verbal sparring, this blatant avoidance of the real and the terrifying—we both needed it. We needed each other.

She rose up onto her knees to meet me. There was nothing of the succubus in her eyes. That lift of her brows—Veyka. The quirk of her mouth—Veyka. The ring of desire in her irises—it was black.

My hand froze just short of cupping her face.

Veyka rocked back onto her heels.

Veyka's face. Veyka's eyes. Veyka's pain. And I'd caused it.

She turned away, maneuvering her arms and legs around those Ancestors'-damned shackles with the same grace that she moved in battle. She presented me with her perfect, unmarred back—miles of pale smooth, pale skin that gave way to soft rolls around her waist and hips that I needed to get my hands on.

But her shoulder blades moved up and down her back. A breath shuddered through her.

"You are scared of me."

She might as well have shoved one of her daggers through my heart. And I deserved it. She'd put as much space between us as she could, climbing all the way to the other side of the bed. But that was not nearly far enough to escape me. I slid behind her, one knee on each side of her hips. My cock pressed urgently into the small of her back, but I ignored that for the moment. I couldn't stop the groan that escaped my mouth as I fitted myself against her, pressing my chest to her back.

"You've hardly touched me," she whispered. But I was touching her now. Even my argumentative mate could not argue with that. I skimmed my hands up her arms, tucked my mouth into the curve of her neck and let my breath warm her skin.

"I was afraid, but not of you. Never of you. I was afraid for you. I was afraid I would break you. That you wouldn't be able to maintain control." *It was a mistake,* I growled down the bond. There she was at the end of it. I could sense the darkness, the succubus. It never fully receded. Maybe it never would.

I didn't care.

I pressed a kiss to the soft skin beneath her ear, sparkling with amorite. "I am so sorry, Princess."

She didn't turn into my caress. But she didn't pull away. I firmed my hold on her arms, massaging the tired muscles from her shoulders to the crease of her elbows. I cupped the curve of her stomach with one hand, the sharper angle of her chin with the other. Just enough so that I could look into her eyes.

"I could never be scared of you, Veyka," I said. "And this is you. I understand that, even if you don't want to. This darkness has always been inside of you. And I want all of it. I always have."

Her chin trembled in my hand. I stopped it with a kiss. There was no part of Veyka that I did not want. Maybe that made me a monster, as well. Good—I'd lived three hundred years trying to cage my beast. I'd learned only recently that it was impossible; he was me, and I him. And we both loved Veyka more than this world and any other in creation.

"Let me unbind you," I said gently, easing her back into the center of the bed.

She let me guide her down to her back, but she shook her head against the pillow. "No. Arran—if it was just the two of us, then yes. Always yes." She closed her eyes. Not to stymie the succubus, but the pain in her heart. Her eyes glistened with unshed tears when she opened them again. "But there is an entire camp out there. Thousands of our subjects. Allies. You cannot risk unleashing me on them."

"I can make love to you just like this," I promised. I would happily spend the whole night doing it.

"Good. I was counting on it," she said through the tears that leaked down her cheeks. I kissed them away, one by one.

I lifted her hands above her head, pinning them between the pillows. The view of her breasts was magnificent—lifted, heavy, panting. "Perhaps I should have restrained you earlier."

She laughed. Ancestors, that sound. What it did to my cock, already pressing eagerly at her entrance. And her breasts, bouncing like a fucking invitation. But that was nothing to what she did to my heart. I'd feed all the humans in Eldermist to the succubus horde in exchange for one of those honest, glorious laughs.

I was unable to resist the temptation any longer. I leaned forward, licking down from the center of her clavicle all the way to her belly button and beyond, to the tangle of curls at the apex of her thighs. She writhed beneath me, moaning in pleasure and twisting away from the sensation at the same time. But she couldn't get away. She was bound. And bastard though it might make me, I was going to take full advantage and worship her exactly as I pleased.

My tongue traced the sensitive soft flesh above her cunt, but didn't dip inside of it. No, not with those long legs stretching out beneath me. I tasted the seam of her hip, slightly salty from a day of exertion and struggle. Then the inside of her thigh, the scent of her pussy flooding my senses. Still, I continued on. I kissed her ankles—soft, featherlight touches where the metal of the shackles pressed against her skin.

You do not scare me, I told her with the swirl of my tongue.

I adore every part of you, my kisses said as they brushed against her restraints.

By the time I worked my way back up her body, her eyes were glassy with need. She trembled from the force of it. My entire existence narrowed to giving her exactly what she needed.

I settled between her legs, bracing my weight on my forearms, tucked into the curve of space by her shoulders created by lifting her arms overhead.

In the next breath, I sank into her fully. She couldn't open as wide for me, couldn't wrap her legs around my waist, not with the ankle restraints. But that only made her tighter, the sensation pitching even higher for both of us.

I watched her eyes shift and change as I took her, savoring the little sounds she made as she squirmed against me, working to get every fraction of an inch. I kept my movements slow, savoring all the places our bodies touched. My cock sheathed within her, the hard buds of her nipples against mine, scraping over each other.

Our coupling was almost always hard and fast. But not tonight. I savored the way the walls of her pussy clung to me, the delicious sucking sound her wet cunt made as I pulled out. She reached for me, but her hands were bound. I gave her my mouth instead, nibbling at her lower lip, sweeping my tongue inside in slow, languid perusal.

"You are torturing me," she whimpered against my lips.

"I am worshipping you," I corrected her.

I had to stop myself twice, holding my body taut above her to keep from spilling myself too soon. Only once I'd stoked the fire within her, erased all of her fears and replaced them with nothing but burning need, only then did I increase the speed and friction. Not fast, but just enough to push her over the edge. She cried out, demanding I take her faster, harder. But I was in control. I drove her to one orgasm. Then I slid my hand between us and fingered her to another. Only then did I sink my cock inside of her again and let go. One stroke, two. That was all it took. I belonged to her, utterly. I always had. Soul or no, she owned mine.

We were both drenched in sweat, but there was no discussion of washing. I tugged her against me, kissing her softly. I wanted to kiss her all night.

"Promise me you'll come back," I said between those kisses.

Her mouth remained open in invitation, but silent.

"Veyka." I cupped her face, drawing back so I could see her clearly. "No hedging like you did before the Tower of Myda. Look at me and promise."

She looked at me. My beautiful, courageous queen. "What if I can't?"

I pressed my forehead to hers. "You can. The succubus will make you choose. This darkness inside of you—"

"This darkness inside *is* me. It always has been there." Honesty. I'd given it to her, when I told her that I was not afraid. Now she gave it back.

I would give her everything. For Veyka, for my mate, I would beg. "And it belongs to me. With me. You belong with me. Even the dark parts. The succubus will make you choose. Choose life. Choose us."

The words were soft. But she said them. "I promise."

I buried my face in her neck, breathing in the scent of her. We would be apart on the battlefield tomorrow. But I refused to accept an after that did not include both of us.

"Sleep now. I'll watch over you." The succubus came in the night, when the mind was most vulnerable. But I would protect her. Always.

79

VEYKA

I pretended to sleep a few hours. One midnight argument later, and Arran finally agreed to take his own turn. I sat over him while he slept. The fact that he *could* sleep reiterated what his mouth and body had said earlier—he was not afraid of me.

Fool.

No. He loves me. He knows that I would never hurt him.

Or maybe he thinks that he is a match for us.

Us. The succubus inside my head was getting stronger. It was impossible to see with the torches doused, but I knew that if I could look, the bandage wrapped around my hand would be completely soaked. Black.

I cocked my head to the side, my mouth filling with saliva. Black bile surged up my throat, but I swallowed it back down, sputtering.

I pulled my legs tight against my chest and looped my bound arms around them, wrapping myself into a tight ball. *Think of three or four words to describe yourself,* Mya had advised. *Repeat them again and again, whenever you feel the darkness closing in.*

Strong. Friend. Mate. Wicked.

Maybe that last one was a mistake. I'd thought of Arran and

how his whole face lit up when he complimented my wicked smile. But now it seemed to speak to that part of myself where the succubus had taken up residence. Arran was right about that—this darkness had always been inside of me. But it had never threatened to overpower the light. Even in the depths of my depression of Arthur's death, it was not darkness that beckoned but nothingness. Sure, I'd wanted revenge. But this... I wanted to burn the world, then sink down into the ashes and feast on the charred remains.

Strong. Friend. Mate.

I am strong enough to fight this. My friends need me. My mate loves me.

Strong. Friend. Mate.

The succubus inside of me hissed but did not retreat. It fed on the darkness that was me, each bite breaking down the wall that protected what was left of my soul.

Strong. Friend. Mate.

There would be no sleep for me.

80

ARRAN

I was made for battlefields. The most powerful terrestrial fae born in millennia. Blessed not just with one of the terrestrial fae gifts, but both. Fauna-gifted with a beast that stirred nightmares across this realm and others. Flora-gifted with the ability to bend nature itself to my will. Kidnapped in my youth. Separated from my family for most of my adulthood. Honed as a weapon with a singular purpose—to kill in service of my kingdom.

The battle axe that had cleaved flesh from bone for three centuries rested heavy in my hand. A single amorite dagger, the only way to bring down the succubus, gripped in my other. Around me, my lieutenants moved their battalions into position, the entirety of the Terrestrial Army moving with decades of honed purpose. The Faeries of the Fen remained in the human realm, along with the human forces Gwen had gathered from Eldermist, the reunited remnants of the Elemental Army, and the Aquarians under General Ache.

Two battles. Two valleys. One foe.

The fighting in Camlann might already be underway. Communication between our two armies was slow without Veyka to jump between realms at will. The succubus in the Effren Valley were trapped here, in the fae bodies they'd invaded. At least once they took a body, they appeared to be anchored to it.

That was our only advantage.

We had superior numbers, but the succubus felt no pain. It would take a dozen fae soldiers to take down one of the creatures. More of the humans. Many soldiers would die today. Thousands. Maybe tens of thousands. That number was dependent on how long it took Veyka to make her way across the valley.

I could not see her, but the thread of our bond was intact. Somewhere below, she and Mya weaved through the foothills, trying to skirt the horde and avoid notice for as long as possible. My role was to keep the succubus engaged from all sides, to give my mate the best chance of reaching the Tower of Myda.

Isolde and the healers had divided themselves between the human realm and Annwyn. In the Effren Valley, they waited behind the strip of sand that belonged to the Gremog. Even the Gremog would not be able to eat every succubus that stumbled into its domain if there were enough of them; but it would protect the healers and the injured for as long as possible, allowing the bulk of our army to focus on the horde itself.

I reached deep inside of myself, to where those golden threads wrapped around my heart and reached out across time and space and realms. *I love you. I will see you at nightfall.*

By nightfall, this war would be over, one way or another.

Veyka did not respond. The darkness on the other end of the mating bond banked, still simmering but not a fully-formed black mass.

I did not pray. But if there were a time to start, this seemed the moment.

Ancestors, keep her safe.

Accolon... give me your strength on this final battlefield. Nimue, guard my wife, your heir, that she might live to reclaim her soul.

The sun peeked over the eastern peaks of the mountains, bathing the Effren Valley in the first rays of orange-gold daylight. The battle for Annwyn began.

81

CYARA

There was no reason to hold back the harpy. Cyara did not see the signal that Arran gave, but she did not need to. The terrestrial army began to move, and Cyara with it. She had not been assigned to a particular unit or command. There was no controlling the harpy once she broke loose. She was born of pain and fury and she desired only to rain those things down upon anyone and everyone foolish enough to cross her path.

Cyara rose into the air, her wings beating against the cool morning air. Another few seconds and she would not feel the cold. The harpy couldn't feel such mundane things. She rose and rose and rose, high above the valley and the army that had almost reached the black horde. Lines of efficiently organized terrestrials marched in perfect formation. She watched as the wave of black chaos broke against them, undulating back from the force, then slipping through the cracks. The succubus spread like a virus, streams of black that infected.

There were many soldiers in the army below without amorite piercings. Many without amorite weapons. Still, they marched. Cyara had not been able to sleep, the screams too intense to bear. Hundreds of soldiers turned to succubus in the night, unprotected by amorite, too close to the horde. They'd been slaughtered unilaterally. She'd heard their dying gasps.

Now she would decimate those who'd brought that darkness. The succubus who'd come for her friends and her queen.

She scanned the field, letting her eyes see past the mass of fighting to the individuals within. Three fae warriors held off a succubus who'd taken over a male nearly as large as Arran. Another clawed its way up one of their backs. But a wide-winged bird of prey swooped in and plucked the head from its desiccated body.

A female scream sliced through the air, reaching her above all the others. It took too long for her to locate the source—a red-haired female in dark armor, swinging a morning star with one hand and slicing with a dagger in the other. But she was overwhelmed by the succubus bearing down on her, the other soldiers around her occupied with their own attackers. The female was already bleeding from a gash to her clavicle. She was going to die, there was nothing Cyara could do. She should find another target.

The red-headed female screamed again.

The harpy did not care for reason. She burst from the shell she occupied inside of Cyara, clawing her way to the surface. Cyara felt the tingling burn of her skin changing, thickening into an armor that the succubus' teeth could not penetrate. Claws sprang from her fingernails, curving and sharpening into talons meant for ripping apart male flesh.

Males. Males killed her sisters. Males destroyed her father.

Males deserved to be punished. They should die.

Die. Die. Die.

Her leathery wings scissored through the air as the harpy dove for her first victim.

The dead do not scream. But the dying do.

She swept down again and again, saving the females beset by the males of darkness. Weak, feeble males who surrendered their minds. How easily they became prey to those beings from another world. Leaving their females undefended, feasting upon them. She could not allow it. She fell upon them, ripping limbs and hands and heads. Their taste was vile, corrupted. But they died and it did not matter how they tasted.

Down she dove again, to a female with blonde hair so pale it was nearly white, a beautiful female that reminded her of someone that she loved. A terrible shrill cry ripped from her mouth. She did not love. She killed.

A male monster clawed its way across the ground, its legs a mess that could not support it. But it reached the female, sinking the jagged tips of its bony fingers into her legs. Blood flooded her senses. Too much blood. She angled her body, grabbing the monster with her talons and ripping it away. Those deadly talons severed mangled sinew and bone, raining black bile down up on the armies below.

She landed hard in the muck, the red-orange desert long stained black. Another. She needed another. Another male, another to kill. Vengeance. Death. Die—

Pain wrenched up her wing. She screamed as she turned, her talons already reaching. Another male, this one's eyes clear. Scared of her—he should be scared of her. She was the monster he'd made her. All of them, with their bloodlust. Now, she would feast upon theirs. His.

"Cyara! Put him down!"

Her head turned. A male voice—that dared to command her.

She hissed through her teeth, the male who'd thrown the dagger still clutched in her talons, feet dangling uselessly. Useless like the male he was.

"He did not mean to hurt you," the newcomer cried. Another male, dark hair, brown eyes that stared at her with intention. With knowing. He could not know her. It was impossible.

"Put him down."

She dropped the male in her talons, a new quarry in her sights.

"The succubus," he said. He did not back away. Stupid male. "The succubus are the ones you want. Not me."

She grabbed him from the ground like he was nothing. He *was* nothing. Her talons snapped the vines he tried to summon. Puny male. He could not hurt her, could not hold her. He stopped struggling. Good, he realized. Oh, he'd make a tasty meal.

"Hurting me means hurting Maisri."

Her talons stopped from breaking skin.

"You love Maisri. You would never hurt her."

Maisri. She did not know that name. She could not love. Love was a weakness. Love allowed males to hurt her. This male would hurt her, just like all the others had.

An image flashed in her mind. A daisy spreading across a child's palm. Another—dark curls and bubbling laughter. A face, heart-shaped and sweet.

Maisri.

The harpy dropped him and shot into the air.

❧ 82 ❧

EVANDER

They ran and ran and ran. The elemental queen was stronger than Evander had realized, even after watching her spar for months in the training ring of the goldstone palace, defeating her Goldstones and palace guards alike. Lyrena kept pace at her side, always off of her left shoulder, a half-step behind. Her priorities were clear.

He cursed Veyka with one breath, for refusing to use her void power, even as he begged the Ancestors to help her maintain control of her inner darkness long enough to banish the succubus from Annwyn. He'd seen the terrestrial male she'd eviscerated when she lost control of the portal rift. He understood what she'd explained in stuttering words in the command tent. If she took them through the void now, if she allowed the succubus access to that part of her too soon, she might not be able to get back the control she needed to banish them once and for all.

Evander would make sure Mya made it to the tower. She gasped for breath as they cut through the foothills of the mountains, the difference between swimming through the Split Sea and running through the sandy desert more evident with every passing minute. But none of them slowed. They could not. The farther they got around the edge of the valley, the less succubus stood between them and the tower. At least, in theory.

But the horde was bigger than they'd realized.

It had grown during the night. They'd planned to sneak around the back once the horde advanced past the tower that stood in the middle of the valley, beyond the edge of the ruined city of Baylaur. But there was no rear, not anymore. The horde filled the valley nearly to the edges. The only space left free was the strip of land patrolled by the Gremog, and even that would not last forever. Eventually even the sucker-mouthed sand demon would be overwhelmed.

Mya slipped in the sand, but Evander caught her before she slid down the dune into the valley. The others had stopped, finally, and he recognized why. They were parallel to the tower. The shortest length from the mountains to the center of the valley lay before them. And it crawled with black death.

"What do we do?" Mya whispered.

"We fight." Veyka turned to Lyrena. "Give me Excalibur."

The Goldstone reached for the mighty sword, sheathed on her back alongside her own.

"You cannot give her a weapon," Evander protested. He knew better than to reach for Lyrena. The female was as likely as her king to cut off his arm.

Veyka rounded on him. Her arms were still bound, her leg shackles gone to allow for running. But she was terrifying even so, her black eyes shining, lips curling in a sneer that did not belong to the succubus, but to the queen.

"That is a succubus horde. That is an amorite blade. Your wife's best chance of survival is if that blade is in my hands. Leave the shackles on. I can kill them just fine with my hands bound."

If they entered that horde with only Lyrena and him fighting, the succubus would overwhelm them and kill Mya. Veyka would survive. Her soul be lost entirely to the succubus, but her body would live on.

Veyka might lose herself to the succubus. With the sword in her hand, she'd be even more deadly. But at least Mya stood a chance.

"At my back," he ordered Mya. For once, his wife listened. "Use your powers, but don't sacrifice yourself. Do you promise me?" he demanded.

Lyrena handed off the legendary sword. But Veyka watched Evander and his wife, her brow wrinkled as she listened carefully to their words. He did not care what she heard. He needed Mya's promise.

"Yes," Mya agreed, water already spinning from her fingertips. "I promise."

They entered the horde at a run. Five yards, ten, they wove their way through the horde with as much speed as they could, for as long as they could. But they succubus were drawn to Veyka. They clawed for her first, closing in from every side. Veyka beheaded one easily with Excalibur. Lyrena twisted with the grace of a dancer, taking out one that came from the other side. A blast of water sent three of them falling back, and then Evander could not watch Veyka and Lyrena anymore. He had his own queen to defend.

Lyrena took the first injury—a slice down her thigh that would have felled most warriors. She screamed, missing a step, but Veyka was there to cover her, slitting the succubus who'd inflicted the wound open from navel to throat. The amorite did its job. When the monster fell, it did not rise again.

Now it was Veyka guarding Lyrena's back instead of the other way around. Mya sent out spiral after spiral of water. They combined into tidal waves that knocked down rows of approaching succubus. Her water could not kill them. There was no life to choke out of them; they could not drown. She could only hold them at bay. But it was enough. They were closer to the tower now, more than halfway.

They were going to make it.

Until Veyka fell.

She was impressive with her daggers, but in the time he'd been away she'd mastered the massive greatsword as well. But her hands were bound. Graceful and powerful as she was, it hobbled her. She drove the blade straight down through the decayed skull of a succubus, but she couldn't release her hand to swing back and defend herself from the one that attacked her from behind. It sank its fangs into her neck, the features of the male whose body the succubus had taken long since melted away to nothing but black, rotted bones. Veyka ripped the sword loose, but it was too late. She stumbled to her knees.

Lyrena tried to get there. Mya too. But they were too late. Three, four, five succubus fell upon her. She screamed so loud, Evander was sure her mate must have heard it on the other side of the battlefield. He expected the great white beast to break through the horde, demanding justice for his queen. But nothing came. She screamed again, terrible and wrathful and—

The bodies of the succubus flew back, forced away by plumes of shadow. The queen rose from the heap, her fair skin coated in black bile. But it was impossible to tell where it came from. Dozens of scratches marred her skin, and from each of them leaked the darkness of her soul. She lifted her head to the sky and screamed again.

"Veyka," Lyrena skidded to halt, barely keeping her feet under her in the puddles of blood and black spray.

But there was nothing of the queen in the creature's eyes.

She turned to the mass of black around her, the mindless, soulless horde, and smiled.

Shadows shot from her hands toward her golden knight. Evander moved without thinking. If he'd thought at all, it would have been to protect Mya, surely. Not Lyrena.

But there they were, rolling through the blood and bile. The succubus streamed for Veyka now, and she lifted her hands to greet them. Still bound—she was still bound. But those were shadows at her command now. The succubus inside of her had seized control and awakened some new, strange power.

Before Veyka's shadows could greet the succubus streaming toward them, a plume of heat blasted past. A wall of fire rose up, encircling them with golden flames that reached over Evander's head.

Lyrena. The blood flowing from her leg had slowed to a steady stream. At least it wasn't gushing. She was on her feet, hands thrown out on either side of her, wielding fire instead of a blade. A few of the succubus tried it, but they fell back from the pure, cleansing heat.

Evander reached behind him to lower Mya's hands, to tell her to hold back her water. But she wasn't there. A flash of blue cut across his field of vision.

"Stay away from her!"

But Mya didn't stop. She didn't even turn as she ran. "I have to help her!"

She dropped to her knees, grabbing the elemental queen and dragging her down to the ground alongside her. "Veyka, you can do this. You can get back control."

The creature that was Veyka snarled, throwing her body forward, teeth first. Mya dodged, but Evander could not allow it. He dove— "Stay back!" his wife ordered.

Not his wife. His queen.

She did not even look at him. All of her attention was on Veyka, where she resolutely held the female's arm, using her ethereal powers to dig around inside the shell of what had once been a remarkable female.

"You are strong. You have friends who love you. A mate who needs you."

Evander eased in closer, one eye on Lyrena and the horde she held back, the other on Mya and Veyka. Lyrena was bleeding, but her jaw and brow were hard set. The flames did not waiver. It might kill her, would surely drain her, but Evander knew she would hold the line. He let his focus shift entirely to Mya and Veyka. If the succubus Veyka lunged for Mya again, he'd slice off her head.

But Mya ignored him completely. He stepped closer, her words filtering through the death that surrounded them.

"They tortured you. Your mother, the male. They raped you and hurt you. Your father let them. Everyone let them. No one protected you, Veyka. And it was wrong. They were wrong. They were evil," Mya said. She recounted horrors without breaking tone, without letting her own horror show. She'd trained her entire life for this moment, using her ethereal powers to help her people. It had all been in preparation for the moment of direst need, when destiny had placed her here, to help this queen. To save Annwyn and the human realm and the whole damn world. "But you, you are not evil. You are more than what they did to you."

Evander's throat clogged painfully.

He'd never known.

The court believed she'd been sheltered in the water gardens for her protection, a precious, spoiled princess so treasured that the world could not be trusted with her—Ancestors, everyone in Annwyn believed it.

"No," Veyka whimpered. Veyka. Not the succubus.

"You are the monster, Veyka. The succubus is inside you, it *is* you. This is your darkness. Yours. You control it, not the other way around," Mya urged.

Veyka lifted her eyes, and though they were still black, the tears that leaked from their corners were clear.

The heat around them shifted. Evander turned. They all did, watching in awe as Lyrena extended the circle, elongating it, creating a path hemmed in by flame on either side. A path right to the door at the base of the Tower of Myda.

Her arms shook. Blood slid down her face, leaking from her nose and ears, red and bright. She opened her mouth, but the words were too hard to form. She managed just one, and it was for Veyka.

"Go."

This would kill her. This type of power, the cost... the cost would be Lyrena's life. Whether it killed her outright, or she fell to the ground exhausted and unable to defend herself from the succubus.

Evander did not let Veyka second guess her Knight's choice. He hauled Veyka and Mya to their feet and shoved them down the path. They ran, the distance disappearing quickly beneath their feet without the succubus to fight off. The monsters hissed and screeched, clawing at Lyrena's fire, falling into it and burning away to ash.

There was the tower.

Veyka and Mya skidded to a stop, the former wrenching open the nondescript wooden door.

But Mya turned to him. "Release her shackles."

"She could lose control again."

She shook her head, her sapphire blue eyes refusing to consider any course but the one she'd chosen. "There is no other option. I cannot do it once we are up there. You need to stay and block the entrance. She cannot do what she must with her hands bound."

"What if she attacks you?"

Mya lifted a pale blue hand to his face, caressing his cheek. Her touch was cool, soothing, with just a hint of salt. "Then I will fight for my life. And if I die, then it is for a good reason. I will die helping my friends and believing in the light."

"You are too good for this world."

She shook her head. "We are the good in this world. We will protect it."

An immense wave of heat rolled over them. But when it ebbed away, there was no flame left to protect them. Evander shoved them through the door before they could look back and see what was left of Lyrena.

"I love you," Mya said as she turned for the stairs. Evander slammed the door behind them, planting his back against it. There was no lock. He'd have to hold it from the inside with his body and his shortsword. He lifted his head to tell Mya that he loved her, too.

But they'd already disappeared up the tower. "You always need to have the last word," he said to the emptiness.

⚘ 83 ⚘

GUINEVERE

There were just too many of them. The Aquarians and elementals formed a bastion at the center of the army, ramming their way into the succubus horde. Someone had told Gwen that these ones were easier to kill, because they'd taken over human bodies rather than fae. But she noticed no difference. They killed more effectively than any enemy she'd faced as a lieutenant in the terrestrial army, serving under Arran.

They killed the human female named Tally who Elora had grown so fond of during their short alliance.

They killed the ice-wielding female who'd wanted to punish Gwen for slaughtering her brother.

They killed and killed and killed.

At least Sylva was not on this battlefield. The human woman waited in the village to receive wounded soldiers.

Maybe she would die there.

Gwen certainly would.

She shifted from her dark lioness back into her fae from, using the power of her powerful hind legs to leap, transforming in the air and landing with such force that her sword cleaved the succubus beneath her in half.

Her sword was free by the time her knees pushed back up to stand. Three succubus surged for her, she took them all, leaving the male nearest her free to turn and engage in the other direction.

She vaguely recognized the male. She'd been introduced to him once, but he was one human who hadn't seemed important. His place was with Veyka and Arran, with the terrestrials, with their quests. But there he was, fighting alongside the humans.

He was half-witch, she recalled.

But he fought for the humans.

He had a sister. She recalled that as well.

Perhaps it was for her that he fought.

Perhaps it was for her that he died.

A succubus careened into him, thrown off by another human fighting a few feet away. It knocked the man down, falling with him. Gwen would have rolled and come out on top. Slammed her amorite-swirled blade into the creature's chest. But the human was not a warrior. He landed beneath the succubus. The succubus ripped out his throat, then it dug its sharpened bony fingertips into his chest, searching for his soul. Half-witch or not, the man would not heal.

Gwen watched the life leave his eyes.

She felt nothing.

Not even the blade that pierced her leather, nor the sharp pain of her organs being split in two.

She felt nothing as her knees hit the ground. Then her face, straight down into the mud.

She felt nothing.

Then she saw nothing either.

✣ 84 ✣

ARRAN

The perfectly blue sky overhead. The jagged orange peaks. The waves of black that rolled against the terrestrial army, again and again, each time pushing in farther. Closer to the base of the mountains. Gwen had warned—if the succubus pushed us back to the foot of the mountains, there would be no escape. We'd be cornered and crushed. I knew—if it came to that, we'd already lost.

A wall of fire appeared in the distance, burning bright against the black horde. Lyrena. It must be. The flames cut through the succubus, right to the foot of the Tower of Myda. Veyka was still alive. Still fighting. The bond inside of me remained intact, but seeing that proof on the battlefield was more than a comfort. It gave me the strength for the next surge.

I had not asked Isolde to reexamine my magic. What change could a few days bring, after I'd had months to heal? Gaps in my power or not, I had to fight. I reached for his axe, shifting as I ran. The wolf gave way to the male. That power had not deserted me yet. Maybe the next time I tried to shift, it would. But next time was by no means a certainty.

My father's northerners fought at the center, fierce with their assortment of deadly weapons honed against the brutality of the

Spine. They remained fighting, their ranks still strong. Mordred was safe among them. I'd lied to myself when I said that I could not care for him. I could not stop myself from caring.

Veyka had done that to me. She'd opened my heart to love. Not just hers, but those around me. I'd never mourned the losses on a battlefield. It was part of what made me such a brutally efficient commander. But I would not have changed it. Not a single thing she'd given me.

I cleaved apart a succubus with my mighty battle axe. Sank the amorite-swirled blade Veyka had given to into its chest. Then spun to the next. And the next. And the next. The tide was never ending. When I turned again, the wall of fire was gone. There was no time for prayer; but my heart did the work of appealing to the Ancestors for my mate's safety.

If she was alive, I could keep fighting. If she was alive, all hope was not lost.

She would save our realm. I would save her soul.

I swung and swung, destroying one succubus after another. Others fought around me—birds of prey, beasts of the night, flora-wielders who summoned power from the desolate desert ground. But one face caught my attention—its likeness to my own too strong to ignore.

I blinked, nearly losing my arm to a succubus for that pause.

Mordred. *What is he doing here?*

He was supposed to be with the northerners.

I fought my way toward him, unable to stop the pull. It was different than the connection I felt to Veyka, but it was strong. *He should not be here.*

He was a skilled fighter—he'd shown that against Veyka in the Pit. But summoning vines here was nearly impossible. There were no tree roots to call to aid, no grass to hold the succubus down. Just sand and sparse plants he'd never encountered before.

He swung and swung his hatchet, but there were too many of them. Too many between us. He needed an Ancestors-damned battle axe, not that puny hatchet. He needed me—

The succubus dragged him off his feet, down into the miasma of death that coated the ground. I shifted, my beast answering the call with a snarl that drew the eyes of every soldier in the vicinity. I hardly noticed. I surged through the horde, ripping off the heads of the succubus in my way. Shifted again, falling into the mud beside my son.

Blood leaked from a wound on his arm, but it was his leg... his entire left leg below the knee was gone. It would regrow. A fae could heal from nearly anything if given enough time. But too much blood too fast, and he'd lose consciousness. I had to get him behind the line guarded by the Gremog, to the healers. At least he had the amorite piercing. He would not be taken—

"What have you done?" His ear... it was empty. I checked the other, not believing what I saw.

Mordred coughed in my arms, bringing up blood with each heave. Ancestors, he had a chest wound as well. "The others... needed it..."

He'd given it away.

The hatchet still grasped in his hand was swirled with amorite. But he'd given his amorite stud to another soldier.

I fumbled for the piercing in my own ear. He was weakening. If he lost consciousness, the succubus would come for him, surely. They were everywhere, swarming around us. I did not notice which of my soldiers fought around me, giving me these last moments with my son.

The Ancestors'-damned earring wouldn't budge.

The backing—I had to unscrew the backing. But my fingers were slick, a mixture of red and black that stank so strongly it defied description. It felt wrong. Everything about this was wrong.

"Mordred—"

He erupted into coughs again, the force of it nearly spilling him from my arms. But I held him tighter, unwilling to let him go.

"Father."

Thank the Ancestors, he was still talking—but his eyes rolled back in his head, lids fluttering closed. He'd lost too much blood.

He could be healed, but only if the bleeding stopped and he regained consciousness. I tried to push to my feet.

But a low hiss froze my muscles.

His eyes opened. The blood flowing from his wounds was no longer red. He lunged for my throat, and there was only one thing I could do. One last thing for the son I had not known, the son I had not been able to save. I shoved the amorite dagger into his heart.

For the seconds it took for the succubus who'd taken him to die along with my son, I sat there defenseless in the bloody sand. Only when his chest stopped, and every limb hung limp, did I stand.

I shoved the amorite back into my ear. The succubus would not take another person I loved from me today. Not one.

⚜ 85 ⚜

VEYKA

I took the stairs two at a time. If I wasted even a single second, I might lose control again. The control that Mya had helped me wrest back... I was still not sure how she'd managed it. Her ethereal powers gave her access to the darkest parts of me—the parts that had always been there, like she'd said. And Arran before her. They understood me better than I did myself.

But *I* understood that the succubus was getting stronger. And the next time it took over would be the last.

She had not even touched the pain that was seeded in this very tower. I ran past the first level, making the deadly mistake of glancing into that first room.

The portraits still hung, undisturbed. But I could still hear the echoes of my friends' pain.

We bounded up the next set of stairs.

With the witch at the top already vanquished, the magic of the tower did not try to hold us back. Or maybe it recognized me from before, sentient in some way I did not understand. I did not question it—I just kept moving.

I was too much of a coward to look inside the next room, where those terrifying fanged creatures had nearly taken Parys from me the first time. Where Lyrena had made her first sacrifice. Once, those had been the horrors to haunt my nightmares. How small it all seemed, now, with the entire realm hanging in the balance. I would not even know what to say to that female if I met her now.

One more flight of stairs. Mya struggled behind me, not used to the exertion. But I could not stop for her. Not when I was so close to the end.

I braced myself for the remains of the witch—whatever might be left after nearly a year. But when I pushed the door open, the circular tower room was empty. No marks on the ground from her eerie distended nails. No evidence of the fight that had nearly taken my life, nor the succubus that had stolen into the witch's mind.

A large, gaping window overlooked the valley below, its open face drawing a straight line across the sand to where the goldstone palace protruded from the mountains themselves.

I stepped up to the edge and what I saw nearly ripped my heart straight out of my chest.

The horde was *everywhere*. The succubus had taken the entire valley.

The terrestrial army still fought. I could see their greens and browns mixed in with the black of the succubus. But there were no reserves lying in wait. All of our forces were engaged. If it was this bad in the Effren Valley... I should go to Camlann, just for a moment—

Mya's hand gripped my shoulder. "Stay."

It was too fast for her to have used her ethereal powers. She'd understood on some other level. One queen to another.

"What do you need to do?" she asked, her pale blue hand remaining in place on my bare shoulder. Monitoring the darkness.

"I have to let the succubus in." I expected her to jerk back or argue. But she only nodded. And stayed.

The cost of uniting the Sacred Trinity was my soul. But that cost had not been paid when I'd used the grail to drink from the waters of the lake. It would be paid here, now. To save my kingdom, to pull the succubus from this realm and seal them in their own forever, I would have to give up the shreds of myself that remained.

I opened my mouth to say goodbye, to thank Mya for the understanding she'd given me unconditionally. But she shook her head. Those words were not needed between us.

Standing over a battlefield that stretched across two realms, where every being I loved fought for their lives and those of my subjects, I closed my eyes and sank into the darkness.

I let myself feel every terrible thing that had ever happened to me. The years of torture. The male who'd used me again and again for his own power. The mother who'd hated me, feared me and what I might become. The father who'd abandoned me. The brother I'd lost. Charis and Carly, murdered. The betrayals of those I'd thought would protect me. Parys. Excalibur sinking into Arran's chest, his blood coating my hand. The witch I'd slaughtered in the Spine, who'd known all along that this was how it would end.

It hurt in every limb. Every finger and toe, the veins, the sparks of life in my brain. It hurt so fucking much.

I hated them. I hated what they'd done to me. All of that torture, all of that pain, it had given me no choice. The darkness that lived within us all had no choice but to grow inside of me in response to that pain.

The succubus bathed in it, luxuriating in the anger and hate. The blood and vengeance that I craved... it craved. We became one.

Shadows whipped from my freed hands, stretching out across the valley.

The shadows—they were tendrils of the void, pulled from the space between realms and used as a weapon in this one. I'd never dreamed of such a thing. But the succubus inside of me was infinitely creative, and with my powers at hand, it wanted to conquer the world. This realm, and every other.

Agony. Fear. Pain. The taste of them fed my shadows.

Come, the darkness called.

But not to me—to them.

It rose in my throat, leaking from my ears, my eyes, my nose.

Black poured from my body as those shadows expanded, swirling down into the valley, into this realm and through to the next.

Yesssss. I could taste the pain. It was delicious, better than any liquor.

There was a liquor I'd liked once. I'd tasted it in another life-time, one where the light still ruled. I could not recall its name. But that life was gone. I wanted nothing of light. Only sweet, liquid dark.

My shadows whipped around the battlefield—this one, the one beyond it where other beings fought. Less magic, but so much hate those short-lived ones had inside of them. No wonder we were feeding upon them. Their malice for one another was almost as good as the magic the pointy-eared ones had flowing through their veins.

Oh, yes, the feeding here was glorious. But—

But we had to stop. The compulsion was stronger than the desire to feed. The tendrils of shadow curled around my sisters and the feeble bodies they'd taken for their own. They ripped them from their broken legs, their mangled forms, away from the still-living they tore into pieces. Thousands of rifts ripped open in the very fabric of the world. An opportunity—a portal. All of my sisters could come. We'd feed on this realm, then the next and the next, using this powerful body to take us from realm to realm.

But the shadows did not obey. They ripped my sisters from the twin battlefields, forcing them back into our own realm, the origin of darkness and death. And then those rifts closed.

All except for one.

It hung in the air in front of me, in front of the powerful body I'd claimed. I could hear their hisses and cries—my sisters, calling me back. I took a step toward them.

A voice screamed, again and again, reminding me that I was not alone in that tower. Veyka, Veyka, Veyka.

That had been my name, once. But no longer.

❧ 86 ❧

ARRAN

One minute, defeat was upon us. And in the next, the succubus were gone. Ripped from the air, the ground, the bodies where they'd been feeding. Just gone. Banished from our world by shadows that moved with a sentience that sent chills down my spine. The same shadows that had flowed into Veyka in Avalon.

She'd done it. She'd banished the succubus, plucked them from this realm forever.

Around me, soldiers fell to the ground, the toll of exhaustion and the cost of expended magic taking its due.

But I could see it even from where I stood on the other side of the battlefield. In the center of the Effren Valley, at the very top of the Tower of Myda, a portal rift glowed, a spiraling whorl of light. Just like the image Accolon had carved into the standing stones. That part of the prophecy had come true, even without Veyka and Mya's sacrifice.

My selfish heart did not worry about whether or not Mya lived. That portal rift shone, which meant Veyka was still alive.

I reached for her, spinning my consciousness around the golden connection of our mating bond, only to find it... barely there. A single tiny thread was all that remained. And at the end of it... complete darkness.

Veyka. Veyka, listen to me. I know you are still there.

That precious, fragile thread was proof of it. It could not break entirely, because I still lived. The part of her soul that resided inside of me was still safe. She could come back.

Princess, you can hear me. I know you can. The bond is still there, so I know you are still there. Come back to me.

She is gone, a voice too deep to belong to her hissed.

No, my beast growled. *You do not have my permission to go. You belong to me.*

I belong to no one. But she wavered on that last word.

I wrapped every bit of love and emotion around that golden thread. The parts of myself that were broken—the ones she'd healed, and the new wounds that would take years to stitch back together. I gave her everything I had. My soul, because it belonged to her anyway.

You do. You are mine, and I am yours. You are kind and brilliant and loving. Your soul... your soul is beautiful, Veyka. The light and the dark. There can be no light without shadows, no love without loss. But we have already lost enough. Come back, and let me love you for a thousand years, just like we promised.

I can't, Veyka whimpered.

You can, my love. You've been so strong. You have saved us all. You can be strong, just this one last time. Come back to me.

Darkness filled my mind. It flooded the valley, blocking out the sun and the mountains. Shadows so dense I could not see my own limbs, a foot in front of me. Then it disappeared as quickly as it had come. One bright flash, and the portal rift hovering over the tower closed. One breath, and then she was on the ground in front of me.

I grabbed her to me, checking for a pulse, running my hands over every inch of her body I could access.

Angry red welts marred her arms, but they were already healed over. No blood leaked from her. Nothing more dangerous either. The scabbards stopped her from bleeding.

I reached for her face, my hands dark against her stained skin, her matted hair hanging in sheets. But I lifted her face to mine, had to see. I would love her not matter what, for a thousand years and a thousand more after that. But I had to see.

I tipped her head back, my chest filling with light and love and the promise of a forever that finally belonged to us.

Her eyes were blue.

❧ 87 ❧

CYARA

She needed a bath desperately. Even with the harpy gone, the carnage of what she'd done still coated her skin and clothes. But bathing could wait. So could eating, drinking, finding her queen. She knew that Veyka lived; that was enough for now.

Cyara flew above the wreckage of the battlefield, searching. There were so many bodies. So many dead. She always struggled to remember what transpired when the harpy was in control, but this was almost beyond bearing.

Later, she told herself.

Matters of the mind could be settled later. Matters of the heart could not.

But he wasn't there. Not anywhere among the thousands of terrestrials already seeing to the dead. They dragged the bodies into lines that were too long, tried to match up body parts that had gone astray. Her stomach turned. But she flew until her wings trembled.

And found nothing.

He could not be among the dead. Not after everything that had happened... she deserved the Ancestors' punishment, certainly. But not Osheen, and certainly not—

"Maisri!"

Cyara landed hard, her knees buckling. But that did not stop her from running across the compacted dirt in front of the command tent, where the daisy fae had emerged moments earlier. The child flung herself into Cyara's arms, burying her face in the matted copper braid that hung over her shoulder.

Cyara stroked her curls, then her back, counting the child's breaths as she inhaled and exhaled. She did nothing to stem the tears that poured down her cheeks, mingling with stains already there.

Maisri was alive. And so was Osheen.

Too soon, Maisri pulled back. No amount of time would have been enough, Cyara realized. She could have held the child in her arms forever.

Maisri slipped her smaller hand into Cyara's as they both stood. The knight thought her heart might explode right there.

"You weren't in the valley," she said to Osheen. It came out like an accusation, and she didn't try to temper it.

The corner of his mouth lifted. "I went to retrieve her. She needed to know that I was safe."

"So did I." Now that they'd lived through the day, Cyara could admit it freely.

Maisri looked between the two of them, her dark little brows rising. "You both need baths," she declared. Then a second later, "Sylva promised me a snack."

Cyara knew children were resilient, but Ancestors... she was about to fall over from the force of what they'd survived. And this day was far from over. Her mother and the other healers needed help. There were many, many injured soldiers, both human and fae. The fae would heal, eventually. Most of the humans would not be so lucky.

But even as Maisri disappeared back into the command tent, Cyara could not seem to make her feet move. Osheen, on the contrary, was able to shift his weight from one foot to another... though is brown eyes lingered on her.

"You stopped me from killing that terrestrial," Cyara said.

427

His brows knitted together. "You remember."

She shook her head—not in negation, but confusion. "I do not know how. I've always been thankful that I did not have to bear witness in my mind to the actions of the harpy, but... I remember your face. And your words."

She sank her teeth into her lower lip. There had been so many losses today. She did not know Lyrena's fate, nor Gwen's, Mya's, Percival's... but after today, she would have to be strong.

Today, she could face another loss. But tomorrow... she could not be sure. She had to ask now. "Will you ever be able to forgive me?"

Osheen's warm brown eyes widened. He did not try to hide from her, and for once, Cyara did not hide herself either. She let all the hope and longing show on her face. She let the fear through, too.

His eyes searched hers. And they must have found the answer they sought.

"I already have," he said softly.

Cyara nodded. Any more words were beyond her. She nodded again. So many times her head threatened to snap. She forced her chin to still, murmured something about checking in on her mother as she turned away.

He forgave her. The rest could wait.

88

GUINEVERE

"The white hart is supposed to be harbinger of good fortune."

"And she..."

"She ripped it apart. Right there, in the middle of the throne room of the goldstone palace. I have lived there for a hundred years, and I've never heard it so quiet."

Deep, throaty laughter joined in with a lighter, melodious chorus. Two females.

Well, at least the Ancestors had gotten that right about the after realm.

But Gwen suspected that the pain in her side meant she was not actually dead. Though from the way that pain radiated through her abdomen, across her back, and down into her thigh, she could also guess that it had been a near thing.

"She is remarkable," Sylva said. Wood creaked beneath her, as if the woman had shifted in her seat.

"More than," the second voice agreed. So familiar. Tired, very tired. The words rasped out of her throat, changing the tenor of her voice just enough— "And so damned stubborn," Lyrena added.

The elderly woman laughed again.

Sylva was alive. Lyrena too. Gwen supposed the least she could do was crack open her eyes.

"This isn't my bed," Gwen managed, her own voice disturbingly weak.

A hand pressed a cup into her hand. Water—she sipped at it carefully, knowing that if she drank too much, too fast, she'd see it all again in a few minutes.

"We felt a wound this dire deserved an actual bedroom. I moved his Exaltedness from Ferndale down into the pantry," Sylva explained, settling back into her seat.

Gwen did not even try to lift her head. But they'd propped her up on a few pillows, and that was enough to allow her to look around the room. They'd dragged the wingback chair and its wooden counterpart over from the window. She opened her mouth to scold Lyrena for lettering the elderly human sit in the latter, until she actually saw Lyrena.

She looked as terrible as Gwen felt.

The entire left side of her body was burned, an angry, raw red that turned Gwen's stomach. Even her perfect golden hair had been seared away on that side, leaving behind a lopsided braid. What parts of her body weren't covered in burns were coated in blood and black bile from the succubus she'd battled.

Gwen's voice shook. "You need a healer."

Lyrena tilted her head to the side. Deep purple bruises marred the skin beneath her eyes, but those were the least terrible of her injuries. "Isolde is focusing on healing humans. Once she healed us to the point where she no longer feared we'd drop dead on the spot, she ran off."

"Good," Gwen managed. Good for her, at least. Good that the humans were getting treatment. The fae might be in pain, but barring the loss of a head or too much blood, most of them would heal eventually. But Lyrena... Ancestors, she must be in so much pain.

Which reminded Gwen of her own. She needed a poultice, or some tea, or even some of the aural the elementals loved so much.

430

Maybe it would be more manageable in her dark lioness—

"I can't shift." She shot upright—couldn't, fell back down. Sylva was at her side in a second, the speed of her movements belying the gray in her hair and crinkles around her eyes.

"Only you would try such a thing," Lyrena groused. "We just stopped that knife wound in your back from bleeding."

From the state of Lyrena, Gwen knew she hadn't been doing anything other than sitting in that chair. But she understood the implication. She didn't try again.

"Give it time," Sylva advised. "Time is the only medicine that remains the same, no matter what realm you're in."

Lyrena snorted. "Yes, because Lady Guinevere is known for her patience."

She *was* known for her patience. And composure. And she was going to argue with Lyrena about it—when she was less tired, and in less pain.

Sleep, that was how she'd escape both the pain and the two females determined to drive her to distraction.

Gwen closed her eyes—but not in time to miss Lyrena's wink or the flash of her golden smile.

89

EVANDER

"And this is where the High King of Annwyn cut off my arm," Evander said. He curled that arm around his wife, kneading his knuckles into the soft flesh of her hip.

"Ah, yes, the storied Brutal Prince," Mya laughed. "It is hard for me to connect the picture you paint with the male I've met."

Evander blinked. "He led a combined army of fae, humans, and faeries against the most terrifying evil to ever plague our world."

Mya shrugged. "The part I notice is how he drools after Veyka."

Evander scoffed in disgust, though he knew that he was little better. He would never forget that terrifying moment of silence on the battlefield, his back pressed to the door inside the tower, Mya high above him. The succubus clawed to get in, their rasps rattling with death. Then it had all stopped, and the silence of the unknown was worse. But the sounds of battle stayed dead. Mya barreled down the stairs into his arms. The succubus were gone, his wife safe. He would hold tight to her for the remainder of his days, and any onlookers be damned.

He'd shown her the throne room, the terraces, the enormous library, and now the narrow crossing where the Gremog guarded the goldstone palace.

"I'm surprised you've made it this long without asking me which direction to the sea."

She closed her eyes and took a deep breath. For several heartbeats, he thought she was playing some sort of trick on him. But when her eyes opened again, the sapphire was brighter than it had been in weeks.

Mya stepped around him, her eyes searching past the floor of the valley and the still-wrecked city below. Over the ring of mountains, their deep orange tips standing in sharp contrast to the pure blue sky.

"That way." She breathed in again. Evander did not doubt that if there was even a hint of sea salt on the air, she would find it. "How long until we can go?"

Evander huffed a laugh. "That is for my queen to decide."

"A few more days," she sighed, her eyes still on the horizon. "The last of our injured are healed. The palace is cleared. But I want to ensure the city has clean water before we leave."

All of the systems had been destroyed by the succubus. Wells polluted, caches of food destroyed. It would take months to sort out, maybe even years. It was not a task that Evander envied, and one he was more than ready to leave to Veyka and her Knights.

"We must also speak with General Ache about the transport of our new priestess," Mya added.

"Prisoner," Evander corrected. If it had been up to him, they would have said no. Merlin was too dangerous to be kept alive. But in a strange and uncharacteristic act of mercy, Veyka and Arran had sentenced the priestess to banishment rather than beheading.

"I shall be the judge of that," Mya reminded him, though her voice was too gentle for even a reproach. He did not really need either.

She let him bluster, but she knew as well as he did that her edict was the one that would rule. Mya would lay her hands on Merlin and then decide her fate—whether she would be welcomed as a water wielder into their Aquarian home, or have that same magic turned against her, a cage more powerful than any made of fire or ice or wind.

Mya let him turn her back into the goldstone palace. She dropped a hand to his arm. He paused, letting her have the time she needed to anchor herself. She'd done what she could to help the refugees returning to Baylaur using her ethereal powers, but this was not her place, and she could not be responsible for all of their emotional healing. It weighed on her. So Evander stood, an anchor in a swirling sea, for as long as needed.

Finally she exhaled and started back through the towering gold-stone arches. "Will you miss your home?" she asked.

Evander didn't have to look up or look around to know his answer. "This place was never my home," he said, squeezing her hand tightly in his own. "You are the only home I will ever need."

90

ARRAN

The histories of wars did not recount the hours after the battle. Nor the next day or the next week. If it were not for Isolde, more humans would have died from their wounds the day after the Battle of Camlann than had been slaughtered by the succubus in the valley. So named to distinguish it from the last battle of the Great War, fought in the Effren Valley seven thousand years before, and in honor of the humans, who'd lost more than any of us. The fae losses were dire as well. Tens of thousands had walked onto the twin battlefields. Less than half their number walked or flew or ran off.

Veyka had carried many of them herself. She'd used her void power to bring the wounded to the healers, and eventually to help arrange the dead for burial. She moved between Annwyn and the human realm so often, I struggled to keep track of her.

But whenever I reached across the golden thread of our mating bond, I found it stronger than the day before. The darkness was not gone completely. It had been there before and would always linger. But the succubus was gone. We were far from whole; I could not even say that we were healing. It was too soon for that. But we were alive and we were together.

The last of the evening light was ebbing when Veyka took my hand.

We waited for the supper we'd shared with our Knights and other leaders in the command tent, still standing up on the hill, to be cleared away. But we did not wait for the others to leave before slipping out ourselves.

I did not ask after our destination. It didn't matter. Wherever she led, I'd follow.

We walked in silence for a long time. Past the ravine with the rift to the human realm waiting at the bottom. It had been used so frequently over the last week that a path had worn away.

The goldstone palace stood in the distance, silhouetted against the gray sky. It had been cleared out and cleaned, refugee courtiers and servants alike working together to scrub away the stains left by the succubus' occupation. Tomorrow, or the next day, we'd be able to take up residence again. Many of the courtiers already had, as well the survivors from the city below. Those that wanted to return to their homes were offered help rebuilding; those that were undecided given quarters in the palace.

The moon had just crested the tall, fronded trees when Veyka stopped in the middle of a clearing. The clearing where we'd first met, and she'd pretended not to be the queen of the whole Ancestors'-damned elemental kingdom. Where my beast had chased her down and then pleasured her with his tongue.

Would you like me to shift? I offered. I'd be happy to renew that happy occasion with a repeat performance.

Veyka elbowed me. *I want to look up at the stars.*

She settled down into the sand and wispy grass, lying flat onto her back. My cock hardened instantly. *While I fuck you?*

Veyka rolled her eyes and patted the ground beside her.

I laid down beside her, already planning how I would take her this time. She might deny it, but the ring of blue glowing around her pupils told the truth. We both knew how this evening was going to end.

She reached for my hand, lacing our fingers together as she stared up at the sky. *"Born under a double moon..."*

She was looking at the stars, but I was looking at her. I waited for her to recite the rest of the prophecy, but she let it trail off without finishing, harassing her lower lip with her teeth instead.

"I need to go to Avalon," she said quietly.

I rolled up onto my side. She had my full attention now. "Why?"

Her teeth paused their assault, allowing the corner of her mouth to twitch. "Do not worry. I don't intend to harm my half-sister."

"You'd be more than justified," I said honestly. The Lady of the Lake may not have meant us harm, but she hadn't offered aid either. She'd kept the magic of the Sacred Isle contained, leaving Annwyn and the human realm to our fates. If Veyka wanted to exact justice, I would be more than happy to watch.

Veyka's fingers tightened around mine. "Cyara told me that it is Diana's wish to remain in Avalon and continue her training as the Lady of the Lake's apprentice."

"She was the Lady of the Lake's apprentice." In some ways, it was the last piece of a puzzle slotting into place. Of course Gorlois had not stolen just any acolyte from Avalon, but one of the most powerful. It explained the depth of Diana's devastation at what she'd lost—and Percival's near-fanatical protection of her. Maybe some part of him had always hoped to return her to that lost path.

I heard the sand slide beneath Veyka's head as she nodded.

"What do you intend to do?" I asked.

"I will tell Diana about Percival's death," Veyka said. I knew the sadness in her voice was not for Percival, a man she'd barely been able to stand in life. The sadness was for Diana—the sister left behind. And for herself. Because even after emerging victorious against the succubus, the inalterable truth remained. Arthur was still gone.

She cleared her throat, pushing down the emotion. There was something more there, I could sense. But I also knew that my mate would tell me when she was ready. There was no rush—not with a thousand years stretching out before us.

"Morgyn will find that I am not content to let her hide in Avalon any longer. She will keep Diana in Avalon and train her to become a priestess. If anyone has earned the right, it is Diana."

The ferocity in her voice left no doubt in my mind. The Lady of the Lake was formidable. But Veyka Pendragon had looked into her own heart of darkness and emerged back into the light. Formidable was not even close to a sufficient description for my mate.

The stars brightened with each minute we lay in the silence of the clearing. The temperature dropped steadily as the minutes ticked by, but Veyka made no move to stand, and I was content to lay with her forever. Eventually I'd shift into my beast form and offer her his warmth.

There was one more place we must go after Avalon.

A single star fell across the sky, leaving a faint glittering tail in its wake.

I will go with you to Cayltay, Veyka whispered into my mind.

I had not spoken of it. As if by refusing to form the words, I could ignore the reality now interred at the base of the mountains. My son. It was selfish to keep him in Baylaur, rather than return him to the terrestrial court where he'd been raised. But Morgause had decades with him. I'd only had weeks.

I still could not bring myself to speak of it aloud. Veyka had known. She did not say more, but I could feel her reaching out for me across the golden threads of our connection.

It might be better if I face Morgause and Orcadion alone. I did not say it to hurt her, only to spare—

Who, me or them? She cut off my thought. *Never again*, she reminded me. *We may have defeated the succubus, but I have not forgotten our vow. Never parted again. Especially not for Morgause's sake.*

She wrinkled her nose at the last thought.

Laced hands weren't enough. I pulled her in against my side, burying my mouth in her hair and breathing her in. I'd found myself doing it again and again throughout the day, reminding myself that we were alive, that we were together.

Orcadion would not soon forget the slight I'd dealt him in the aftermath of the battle at the Crossing. Morgause would blame me for Mordred's death. I already blamed myself. The Dyad would have to be dealt with. But Veyka was right—we would do so together, as High King and Queen of Annwyn. We'd defeated the succubus. Two terrestrials were hardly of consequence.

Veyka shifted beside me, working the sand beneath us so that she could fit her body in tighter against mine. I released our joined hands and caught the one on the other side of her body, settling it against her hip.

My eyes drifted back up toward the stars—

Veyka moved again, dislodging her freed hand from between us and using it to drag down the front of her dress so she could toy with her breast.

A groan of warning was all I gave her before catching her hips and pulling her on top of me.

I thought you wanted to look up at the stars, my beast growled. There was far too much clothing between us. Trousers, leggings, the layers of her skirt.

You can keep looking at the stars. She disentangled her hands entirely, using the newfound freedom to drag her dress up over her shoulders and away, leaving behind acres of pale skin brighter than the moon overhead.

I cupped her breasts, one with each hand, watching the contrast of her glowing skin against the dark outlines of my fingers with unrestrained awe. *You are magnificent.*

Veyka hummed aloud, the sound filling the clearing around us. But she was not content with playful touches, even when they turned worshipful. There had been no time for this in the last few days of healing and organizing and rebuilding. She'd stolen me away to this clearing for the conversations we could not have anywhere else, but also for this. For us.

I let her tear away the fasteners of my trousers, savored the undulating rhythm of her hips as she slid out of her leather leggings. Her knees dug into the sand on either side of my hips, bringing her down on my cock harder and deeper than ever before.

She rode me slowly at first, her hand splayed across my chest as her hips moved up and down. She rose up until only the head of my cock remained inside of her, then slid down in a gloriously slow and controlled motion. I'd taught her too much about torture in the last year. She was too damned good at it.

Veyka. It was a warning and a plea.

"Aren't the stars beautiful?" she asked between ragged pants. Her legs began to shake—not from exertion, but from the pleasure roiling between us.

"*You* are beautiful." I pushed myself up in the sand, grabbing the back of her neck and dragging her mouth to mine. I plunged my tongue inside of her in time with my cock.

Never again. Never parted. Never lost.

My partner, my mate, my love—in this realm, this life, and all of the ones that came after.

Veyka clung to my shoulders as our hips beat out a fantastical rhythm. It was too fast to be real, too intense to exist in this realm of earth and sky. We were going to be swallowed by the inferno burning between us, dark power joining with light, blood and vengeance and love all twined perfectly together.

Her fingernails bit into the skin of my shoulder just as my canines sank into the tender skin above her clavicle. I tasted her blood on my tongue. The tang of my blood filled the cold air. We came together in a cascade of power, lighting up the entire clearing around us with a burst of white brighter than even the day of our Joining. I was powerless to close my eyes against it. I wanted everything, every bit of her. I always had.

Later, I wondered if the explosion of power had been visible from the army camps below or the balconies of the newly repopulated goldstone palace. Much later, when our breathing had finally returned to normal and my mate was tucked in tight against the warmth of my body, I knew I did not care. Let them see. Let them worship my queen as the goddess she'd become.

The night slowly shifted toward dawn. But I did not need the amorite stud still in my ear to know that I would live to see the morning that awaited.

The words stuck in my throat, but I knew now was the time to voice them. Alone, far from the battlefield. "They are truly gone? Forever?"

"Yes," Veyka said without hesitation, understanding immediately what I meant. "Their realm... I sealed it. When I closed that last rift, it felt different. Like it never had before—like it never will again, I hope."

I had nothing to say to that. She would know better than anyone. She'd banished the succubus from Annwyn, from the human realm, and from her mind—along with the strange shadow power.

"They tried to take me with them. She tried," Veyka said softly.

She—the succubus.

Of course I'd known that. I'd felt her slipping away from me, pulled by the darkness in her own soul toward that land of eternal night. We had not spoken of it, not until now. If Veyka wanted to, I would. I would relive every moment of that trauma for her sake. And if she preferred to let it die in memories, I was fine with that, too.

Veyka's breath tickled the inside of my arm where she'd rested her head.

"You saved me," she breathed.

"You saved yourself, Veyka," I said into her hair. *We saved each other.*

She pinched my side. "Take the compliment, Brutal Prince."

I pressed my lips to hers. "Whatever you command, my queen."

91

VEYKA

Cyara insisted on resuming her position as handmaiden in addition to Knight of the Round Table. Ridiculous. The female never got enough sleep. Her wings were always the first giveaway. They twitched more when she was tired, and on that day in particular they'd been in near constant motion.

"I can do this myself," I insisted. "Tonight, I demand you go straight to your own bed. Arran can see to helping me untangle this confection."

Cyara lifted a copper brow in obvious doubt. "You must actually untangle it and also brush it, Veyka."

I frowned at the complex braid she'd fashioned. It still only hung to my breasts. I'd never grow it as long as my waist again. But with the number of pearls and diamonds and amethyst strands she'd braided into it, Arran would have a busy night.

Perhaps I'd grant him a kiss for each strand of jewels he managed to untangle. I shivered at the delicious prospect.

"Your eyes are glowing," Cyara commented as she added the final piece of my ensemble—the crown.

A new crown, forged from the melted down gold of the old, studded with a thousand gems of amorite given by the survivors—

elemental, terrestrial, human, faerie, Aquarian. I tilted my chin from side to side in the mirror, admiring the way the amorite caught the light and gleamed bright with rainbows against the pure white of my hair.

"Yours will be soon enough," I shot back, unraveling to stand and shaking out the folds of the gown I'd chosen.

Cyara looked away, walking to the corner of the room and fidgeting unnecessarily with the tea set to avoid my gaze. She wouldn't be able to hide once she was in the same room with Osheen. Those two could not keep their glowing eyes to themselves. Though, as far as I could tell, they hadn't actually acted on those desires. Fools.

The door to the antechamber opened and my mate stepped in. Clothed in deep green shot with gold, he looked every inch the High King he was. I had not been able to convince him to wear a matching crown. Though I'd certainly keep trying. I had at least a thousand years to win that argument.

His eyes locked on mine. "Cancel the whole thing."

I bit my lip. "That good?"

I twirled slowly, because I knew *precisely* how good I looked in the gown. The silver collar at my neck held in place miles of frothy purple fabric that faded to pink and then pale orange when it reached the floor. My shoulders were bare to just above my elbow, where engraved cuffs held the draping sleeves in place. But the real wonder was the back—or the lack of it. Every inch of skin, from my shoulders down to less than an inch above the curve of my bottom, was exposed to view.

"I said, *cancel it*," Arran growled, stepping into my space. He caught my chin and tipped it up, holding me in place.

"Did you hear that, Cyara?"

"Heard and choosing to ignore it, Your Majesties," she said, sweeping past and pulling the double doors fully open. "It is time to go."

Arran growled again, but this time it was just for me.

I promise you can take it off of me later, I soothed the beast.

Another growl.

I laughed and took his arm, leading him out through the antechamber and the labyrinth of corridors and courtyards. The entire palace gleamed, the goldstone brighter than ever, the gems embedded in the pillars and arches polished. But nowhere shone more brightly than the throne room where we'd been mated.

Elementals and terrestrials alike lined the walls, vying to see over one another's heads. Elayne and Pant stood with them, the pride in their smiles enough to have me gripping Arran harder so my knees did not give out.

A contingent of blue-skinned Aquarians lingered near the fountains, apparently fascinated that they flowed with aural rather than water. I recognized Taliya hovering in the air near the entrance, always ready to make a quick getaway, still not quite trusting of the fae. Nor the humans, for their part, where they stood in the corner of the throne room nearest the empty thrones.

For once, those thrones were not the focal point. I'd wanted to smash them up, but Arran urged me to take things a bit at a time. For a race that lived hundreds of years, change would be slow. But I planned to sit at my table from now on.

Arran led me to my seat, the golden scrollwork proclaiming it as mine. He stood beside me, though neither of us sat. Not yet.

One by one, they appeared. The crowd held their places against the walls, leaving the way clear for the Knights of the Round Table.

Lyrena and Guinevere entered together, attired in all their Goldstone finery. Then Cyara, in her simple white gown, with her neatly braided copper hair and unshakeable calm. Osheen hadn't even dressed for the occasion, wearing his simple woolen tunic buttoned in the terrestrial style across his chest and up to his shoulder.

The crowd sucked in a breath when Isolde appeared. I did not know how many centuries it would take for everyone to truly believe, truly accept. But Isolde had been my first friend among the Faeries of the Fen. She'd saved my life again and again. Guarded my mate in his time of need. She walked through the crowd, tiny and white, absolutely glowing.

Last came Queen Mya of the Aquarian Fae. Her consort was at her side, though he stepped back once he'd delivered her to her seat.

Arran squeezed my hand. It was time.

"Be seated, Knights of the Round Table."

Isolde took the seat left open by Mordred. Osheen the one that had once belonged to Parys. And Mya, the one that had always been destined for her, the Siege Perilous. As they sat, the table glowed bright. When it faded a moment later, the scrollwork before each of them shone anew.

"Today we invoke the beginning of a new era. One of peace and most notably, of alliance." As I spoke, Arran pulled the communication crystals from his pockets and set them on the table. "We are separated by distance, by custom, by blood. But we shall never be alone again."

Arran arranged them in a line. "One crystal for each kingdom— elemental, terrestrial, Aquarian, and for the independent Faeries of the Fen."

We'd talked about it four hours. Over meals, in the bath, while sparring in the training courtyard. We would always be separated by distance and custom and race. We were different peoples, and that should be honored. But our unity could not be forgotten. With my void power, Arran and I could travel between the kingdoms in the space of a heartbeat. But that power resided with me—and I needed to give some of it back. The communication crystals could not level the discrepancies inherent to our races. But they could give us a starting point for a new future.

"And the last?" Guinevere asked. I smiled across the table at her —because I'd known she would be the one to ask.

"For the humans." I lifted my eyebrows in the direction of their delegation. "Though they will have to squabble among themselves to decide who gets it."

Voices erupted. Humans arguing with humans. General Ache

and another Aquarian I did not recognize stepped up to speak with Mya and Evander. I settled back in my chair, Arran's hand claiming my knee.

Pant and Barkke stood between Osheen and Cyara, a lively discussion already in progress. It hurt, to see Parys' seat occupied. To know that Arthur would never sit on the throne behind me.

I would never stop missing them. That was part of truly grieving —the knowing. Knowing I would never have a brother's love again. Knowing I would never hear the rich raucous timber of Parys' laugh.

We will see each other again.

Yes, we would. Not in this life. But in one of those glorious realms to come.

Arran squeezed my knee, stroking a thumb up along the inside of my thigh. "What do you need, Princess?"

I dropped my hand to cover his as I looked out at my Round Table, my friends, my court. "I have everything I need."

EPILOGUE

"I've been looking for you."

The deep timber of his voice caressed my spine, sliding down the nape of my neck and sending my senses tripping over themselves. I rolled my shoulders to dislodge the feeling, to no avail. Not with Arran. There was no getting rid of the feelings he lit in me.

"I know." I'd felt him tugging at the bond, testing it like a leash. *I am not a dog,* I said without turning.

And yet, it is your favorite insult when you disapprove of my wolf.

"Only in my head," I corrected him. "I'd never insult Barkke by making that comparison aloud."

Arran did not roll his eyes—he insisted that childish motion was still reserved for me. But he sighed heavily, tinged with exasperation.

"How did you even get in here?"

"A lot of hacking away at vines," I admitted, a twinge of guilt edging the pain from the blisters I'd earned cutting away all the greenery that had blocked the entrance. "I'm surprised you did not feel it."

"The older the magic, the more tenuous the connection becomes. It has been years," Arran reminded me, climbing down to where I sat at the edge of the still pool. The waterfall had long since halted, its magic drained by time or the death of the ones who'd conjured it in the first place.

A decade, actually. Almost ten years since the Battle of Camlann. In a few weeks, there would be a celebration. Lyrena was planning it, which meant lots of gold and lots of aural. Honestly, I could not fault her taste.

But that was not the anniversary I was marking tonight.

Our feet dangled well above the water. It made me think of that night so many years ago, when Mya and I had sat on the edge of the Split Sea and I'd finally been brave enough to dip my feet in. Imminent death had a way of seeding false courage.

Arran threaded his fingers with mine, stroking his thumb over the back of my hand. He paused on the ring. It was far from the only jewelry I wore—like most days, I practically dripped with gems—but this simple one was the most special. It always would be. It was the only one I never took off. The one he'd slipped onto my finger before we were even mated, back when I'd refused to believe what he'd known all along. That I belonged to him.

"Are you going to make me ask?"

I lifted one brow. Arran scowled. I reached up and pressed the pad of my thumb to the wrinkle between his dark brows. I held it there until his brow smoothed again. Somehow, he was still frowning. Exasperating male.

His beast growled, a low sound that started in our minds but Arran let bleed into the still air around us. My eyes drifted closed as the sound caressed me from the inside out. I knew Arran was watching me carefully. I took the opportunity to stretch my arms overhead, lifting by breasts and exposing the full length of my stomach which had been hiding beneath the elongated sleeves of my gown.

"Veyka," Arran growled.

I cracked open my eyes. "Yes, my Brutal Prince?"

His eyes burned black and bright. That sparkling ring of dark fire that existed solely for me... seeing it was nothing short of intoxicating, even after a decade. I doubted my reaction would change even in a hundred years.

The corner of Arran's mouth twitched.

Bastard. He knew exactly what he was doing, staring at me like that.

"Why are you here, Veyka?"

To remember.

"I promised Lyrena she could try something," I told him instead. It was also the truth.

"Does it involve fire?"

"Yes." I turned to face him so he could see my grin fully. "She's been working on it with Isolde and one of those clever humans who engineers the fireworks."

Arran tipped his head back until he was looking straight up to where the oval of night sky shone overhead. "I don't see any fireworks."

I sighed heavily. "Terrestrials." So literal. "Come, we should stand back."

Unfolding to my feet, I carefully maneuvered my hands to keep the elongated ends of my sleeves from falling down into the water. I was fond of this particular garment. The pale blue gossamer reminded me of Mya and the other Aquarians. The sheer sleeves fell from silver clasps at my shoulders fashioned to look like crescent moons. The motif continued throughout the gown; a single crescent nestled between my breasts, joining the braided fabric together before it ruffled out into a full skirt. Cyara had even braided aquamarines into my hair.

"Stand back," Arran repeated, the corners of his mouth curving downward. He caught the train of my gown and lifted it so it did not trail along the stone walkway.

"Hurry up," I said, retreating toward the far wall. The greenery had run rampant over the past decade with no one to tend it. It was the only place in the entire goldstone palace with enough water to sustain rich, verdant plants. I tucked myself into an alcove covered in thick ivy.

"What are you up to?"

I pulled Arran in tight against me and kissed him. He hadn't shaved since yesterday, the evidence scraping across my skin as my mouth explored his. The whole lower half of my face would be red from the caress. An image of my own inner thighs, red and tingling from his scruff, flashed in my mind. But before I could shove him down to his knees, the walls started shaking.

The side of the goldstone palace exploded behind us.

"What the Ancestors—" Arran caged me in with his body, pinning me to the wall even tighter, using his body to protect me from falling goldstone.

Of course, we were well away from any actual destruction. The shaking only continued for a few more heartbeats. And it was several heartbeats after that before Arran eased his stance enough for me to look.

I peered over his shoulder. Not *quite* as far away as Lyrena had promised.

The pool where we'd sat moments before was gone. So were the carvings that had once hidden behind the waterfall, the first clue we'd had about the succubus and what it meant for Annwyn. Now the pool had become a waterfall itself, spilling not into another but down the side of the goldstone palace.

Arran eased his body away from mine. The wall we stood against was now a ledge, not even as deep as Arran was tall.

"What have you done?" Arran asked, moving to the edge. I took the train of my dress from his hand and moved slowly to join him. This was not the sort of place for taking chances in long gowns. Not when what had once been the inside of the goldstone palace was now the outside, and the drop was at least a thousand feet.

It was completely unrecognizable. The squat stone buildings were gone. The waterfalls that had muffled so many terrors. The vines Arran had used to cage this place off.

"Some memories need to live on." I lifted his hand to my face, turning my tattooed cheek into his palm. "But others deserve to fade away forever."

He used that hand to guide my face forward. He pressed a kiss to my forehead. Then my lips. "A thousand years."

I smiled into his kiss. "And a thousand more."

Then I slid my hand into Arran's and finally left the water gardens behind.

THE END

Thank you for reading the Secrets of the Faerie Crown series! Already craving your next dark romantasy read? Emberly Ash's new series kicks off with The Frost Witch, releasing in March 2025. Pre-order it now!

Can't wait that long? Visit *www.emberlyash.com* to sign-up for my newsletter and receive the first exclusive excerpts, cover reveal, and all the other official release details. Plus, a bonus Arran & Veyka steamy scene!

ACKNOWLEDGMENTS

There are dozens of people I could and probably should thank, but after writing this book and crying endlessly in the process, I am boiling it down to just two.

To my husband. Thank you doesn't seem like enough. You do the dishes and take care of the kid and feed me when I go into gremlin-mode in my office. You build shelves when I decide to procrastinate on writing. You listen to my endless complaints. You hold me while I cry, for myself and for my characters. There is no one else in the world like you. I wish we had a thousand years, but I will continue to be thankful for every single one we do get. I love you.

To my daughter. You are both the biggest hindrance to and my most important reason for writing. I became an author because of you. I wanted a better life for myself and my family, but without you to motivate me, I may never have taken the leap. Thank you from the bottom of my heart for this beautiful world you have given me. Now, as I watch you learn to write and craft your own stories, I am even more humbled and thankful. Helping you edit your writing gives me the motivation to edit my own. Seeing your joy at publishing your work reminds me that this thing I do is so very special. I love you more.

ABOUT THE AUTHOR

Emberly Ash stole her first romance novel off her mom's bookshelf at the age of ten and never looked back. The author of 12 romance books under her first pen name, Emberly craved something darker and steamier--enter the world of fantasy romance. Her books are dark, twisty, and not for the faint of heart. In the real world, she manages a fire-breathing five-year-old and a grumpy mage of a husband. But you'll most often find her in her hot-pink writing cave, dreaming up your next book boyfriend. Spoiler alert: he's fae.

Find Emberly online at:

https://www.emberlyash.com

https://www.amazon.com/stores/author/B0C55YXHS8

https://www.instagram.com/emberlyashauthor/

https://www.tiktok.com/@authoremberlyash

26423702R00282